Praise for Darcy Burke

"A bad girl heroine steals both the show and a highwayman's heart in Darcy Burke's deliciously wicked debut."

—Courtney Milan, *New York Times* Bestselling Author

"Captivating and romantic. Miranda is my favorite kind of heroine— witty, resourceful, and a little bit wicked—and I loved Fox for loving her as I much as I did."

—Jackie Barbosa, Award-Winning Author

"…fast paced, very sexy, with engaging characters."

—Smexybooks

"Sexy and wonderfully romantic. Her Wicked Ways is a debut every fan of historical romance should add to their to-be-read pile!"

—The Season

"FANTASTIC characters…totally recommend this delightful Regency romance…"

—Romancing the Book

"Intense and intriguing. Cinderella meets *Fight Club* in a historical romance packed with passion, action and secrets."

—Anna Campbell, *Seven Nights in a Rogue's Bed*

"A romance that is going to make you smile and sigh…a wonderful read!"

—Rogues Under the Covers

To Seduce a Scoundrel

To Love a Thief

"With refreshing circumstances surrounding both the hero and the heroine, a nice little mystery, and a touch of heat, this novella was a perfect way to pass the day."

—The Romanceaholic

"A quick fun read! Filled with deception, passion, danger, betrayal, passion, and love."

-My Book Addiction

"A refreshing read with a dash of danger and a little heat. For fans of honorable heroes and fun heroines who know what they want and take it."

-The Luv NV

Never Love a Scoundrel

"Highly romantic . . . this book was wonderful."

—Romanceaholic

"I loved the story of these two misfits thumbing their noses at society and finding love." Five stars.

—A Lust for Reading

"A nice mix of intrigue and passion . . . wonderfully complex characters, with flaws and quirks that will draw you in and steal your heart."

—BookTrib

"An excellent commentary on the power of gossip, but also a wonderful story about two people willing to overcome their differences and to trust in their love."

—Bodice Rippers, Femme Fatale, and Fantasy

Scoundrel
Ever After

The de Valery Code

DARCY BURKE

His Wicked Heart

For Mom and Papa, and for my brother, Rich.
I'm blessed to have a family like you.

Chapter One

August, 1817, London

JASPER SINCLAIR, TWELFTH Earl of Saxton, loosened his cravat as he awaited the arrival of his companion for the evening. He'd never visited this particular brothel, situated in a tiny court off the Haymarket, but a glimpse of its employees below stairs had been enough to encourage him to stay. It was difficult to find a bawdy house whose offerings were worth his notice that wasn't frequented by the upper echelon of Society. And Jasper ought to know. He'd made a hobby of locating just such jewels amongst the filth.

He had high hopes for tonight. His body thrummed with pent-up energy he needed to release before facing his family at his mother's bi-weekly tea tomorrow. He shoved away thoughts of that and focused on the matter at hand. Or rather the matter that would soon be in his hands. He stripped his coat off and threw it over the back of a chair.

The room was functional enough, and a quick review of the bed revealed it to be clean, if not sumptuous. But Jasper didn't require silks or velvets. Just a beautiful woman with skill and an unabashed desire to demonstrate it.

The door clicked, and Jasper's blood heated. He was ready.

He turned, and his need evaporated. Christ, but she was the spitting image of Abigail, a woman he'd spent the last ten years striking from his memory. But now she came roaring back as if he'd met her—loved her—yesterday. His body chilled at the sight of this doppelganger, regret and self-loathing overtaking any sense of desire and commanding him to leave. Now.

He went to the chair and plucked up his coat.

"My lord?" the woman asked, her brow creasing gently. She sauntered toward him. "I'm Tilly. Let me take that." She tried to pull the coat from his grip, but he held it fast.

"No. I'm leaving. This isn't adequate."

Tilly's eyes widened briefly and then she gave a quick nod. "I see. I'm sure I can find us a different room. Something a bit richer, perhaps?"

Jasper shoved his arms into his coat. "You misunderstand. It's not the room. It's you. You're all wrong." He pushed past her toward the door.

She grabbed his arm, her grip surprisingly strong for a slender whore. "I'm sure I can be right. Give me a chance, my lord." She rubbed her breasts against his sleeve.

Jasper glanced down at her nearly exposed nipples. Images of Abigail, sweet and virtuous, rose in his mind. The memories were at total odds with the present scenario—a strumpet in a brothel. He threw off Tilly's hold and made for the door.

She followed him into the corridor. "My lord, you mustn't leave." Her tone took on a dark, desperate edge.

Jasper reached into his waistcoat and extracted a few coins. He tossed them back to her. "Here, that should be more than generous for the scant few minutes I took of your time."

He stalked away from her and descended the stairs. The madam watched him as he crossed through the parlor, her eyes narrowing with concern. Jasper didn't pause to speak with her.

Outside, he withdrew his gloves from his coat pocket. He took a deep breath of sweltering night air and shoved the gloves right back into the pocket. *Hang them.*

Eager to put tonight's disappointment behind him, he took long strides toward the mouth of the L-shaped Coventry Court. His eye caught a couple near the corner of the court and the Haymarket. The man—a gigantic brute, really—towered over the woman. He wrapped his hand around her waist and drew her close against his chest. But she didn't like it. She pushed at him, and her hat went tumbling to the ground, revealing glossy auburn curls pinned atop her head.

Jasper despised a bully, and as the son of the Duke of Holborn, he'd had plenty of experience with one. In several swift strides, he closed the gap between him and the woman being manhandled.

"I said I'm not interested," the woman said, trying, ineffectually, to extract herself from the man's grasp.

Jasper suppressed the need to smash the villain into the ground.

He'd spent the past decade stifling his baser impulses, containing them to the appropriate time and place, but seeing that Abigail lookalike had his senses on overload. Still, he'd learned to master his control. He'd had to. Others got hurt when he didn't. He curled his fingers into his palms. "She said no. Release her."

The brute swiveled his block-shaped head toward him. "And who the hell are you?"

"Your better." Jasper was glad he'd forsaken his gloves. He was ready for battle. Eager for it. "Release her now."

"Push off." With a dismissive nod, the man returned his attention to the redhead.

Unhindered rage poured through Jasper with the speed of a racing thoroughbred. Without censoring his actions, he reached out and wrapped his hand around the larger man's neck. "You're not listening to me." He squeezed his fingers into the man's skin, felt tendons straining against his palm. "Let. Her. Go."

"My lord?" March, Jasper's footman, had silently approached. He'd been stationed just outside the court, awaiting his employer's pleasure.

The villain's eyes widened, and he abruptly released the woman. "I beg your pardon, my lord." He bowed his head and looked at the ground, which was a bit difficult given Jasper's grip on his neck.

Jasper didn't loosen his hold. "If you come near her again, I'll know. And you'll pay for it. Have I made myself clear?"

"Aye," he croaked.

Jasper slowly pried his fingers from the man's flesh, disappointed he hadn't put up more of a fight. With a deep, calming inhalation, he stepped back and straightened his coat. The brute stepped around March and exited the court.

"March," Jasper said, inclining his head toward the Haymarket, where his coach was parked. The footman nodded and took himself off.

Jasper turned to the woman. She stared up at him with wide-eyed shock. Captivating green-eyed shock. Or perhaps wonder.

"Thank you, my lord." Her voice quavered, and she bent to retrieve her hat.

Jasper beat her to it. He fingered the thick felt, thinking it would feel terribly heavy on a sultry night like this. Why was she wearing it?

He looked at her face and simply stared. She was exquisite. The street lamp splashed across her fine-boned features, sculpting the patrician nose, full lips, and saucily dimpled chin. She wore a heavy cloak, which had to be stifling in this heat, but he could tell from the slender curve of her neck and the narrow bones of her delicate wrist that she possessed an alluring figure. She was what he'd been hoping for. What he needed tonight.

"Your hat," he offered. "Though I daresay you might not want to put it back on. It's rather hot."

She nodded. "Thank you. I'm nearly home anyway. I only wear it to disguise myself. Not that it worked this evening." Her hand shook as she accepted the hat from him.

"You've had quite a scare. Let me see you home."

"Thank you, but that's not necessary, my lord." She turned and walked into the court.

He wasn't going to let her go that quickly. He caught up to her in a few long strides. "Where do you live?" The court held a half-dozen ramshackle buildings, the nicest of which was the brothel. Was she one of their doves? If so, he'd take her upstairs in a trice. And maybe offer her a long-term arrangement. She was that beautiful.

"Just there." She pointed toward the brothel.

This was too convenient. His night wasn't ruined after all. "May I come upstairs with you?"

She paused just before the brothel and shot him a horrified look. "No."

Ah, perhaps she was overset after her encounter. "Tomorrow night, perhaps."

"No." She quickened her pace. Past the brothel.

What the hell?

Jasper kept up with her, determined to break through her cool exterior. "I thought you said you lived there?" He gestured back toward the brothel.

She said nothing, and continued walking toward the end of the court.

He snagged her elbow. "Stop, please."

She turned abruptly and glanced down at where his hand was wrapped around her arm. "Unhand me. You're no better than that other man. Worse maybe, since you were so quick to choke him."

Her gaze was direct but dark. He couldn't tell if she was afraid. Christ, he didn't want her to be afraid.

Jasper froze. Images of fights at Eton and Oxford flashed in his brain. "I'm not a violent person." *Anymore.* "And I'd certainly never attack a woman." *Ever.* In fact, several of those rows had been in defense of a woman.

He let her go.

She arched a brow, and he wondered if she believed him. "That's relieving. I live here." She pointed to the shabby building they'd stopped in front of, a four-story hovel with missing shutters, crumbling brick, and a dilapidated roof.

He couldn't keep his lip from curling. She lived in this sty? "You can't."

"I can, and I do." She lifted her chin, giving him a glimpse of a woman who deserved far better than her current station. Which was?

He took in the pair of slatterns standing in front of the boarding house. They were of far lower quality than the women in the brothel next door. But it seemed the entire court was rife with prostitution. There was only one way to determine her occupation. "Why won't you let me make an appointment with you? If not tonight or tomorrow, tell me when."

Now her lip curled. "I'm not available. Now, good night."

She turned just as a man emerged from the boarding house.

"Miss West," he greeted, stepping forward. His gaze lifted toward Jasper, but he quickly returned his attention to Miss West. "Are you all right?"

"Fine, Mr. Beatty, thank you. This gentleman," she indicated Jasper with a wave of her hand, "rescued me from a rather forward bloke and insisted on seeing me home."

Mr. Beatty stepped around her and offered his hand in greeting. Jasper shook his hand, more than a little surprised—and impressed— at the man's nerve.

"Thank you for assisting Miss West. It's a shame she has to walk home at this hour from the theatre. I'd offer my escort, but I'm afraid I'm rather busy with my daughter." The lines around his eyes and mouth creased with worry, making him seem older than his probably thirty years. He turned to Miss West. "I'm sure I can find someone trustworthy to see you home while you're filling in on the stage."

She was an actress?

She threw a glance at Jasper before returning her attention to Mr. Beatty. "You're very kind, but that won't be necessary. Mae is returning to her role tomorrow. I was able to finish Molly's dress and your shirt tonight, however." She pulled a bag from her shoulder, reached inside and withdrew two garments.

Mr. Beatty's face lit up the dim and dreary court. Then the creases returned. "I wish I could pay you, but Molly's medicine was too expensive."

Miss West smiled at him and patted his hand. "It's all right, Mr. Beatty. I don't expect payment."

He hugged the clothing to his chest and offered a hapless smile. "You're surely an angel." His gaze dipped to her hem. "I'll make you a new pair of boots for winter."

Miss West quickly pulled the worn toes of her boots beneath her skirt, but not before Jasper noted the deeply scuffed leather. She replaced the bag over her shoulder and smiled at Mr. Beatty. "Thank you. Is Molly doing better with the medicine?"

"It's hard to tell yet, but I've great hope."

"I shall keep her—and you—in my prayers. Do let me know if you need anything else."

"Yes, ma'am. Evening, sir." He inclined his head toward Jasper then turned and went back inside the boarding house.

Miss West made to follow him, but Jasper wasn't ready to let her go. He moved to intercept her. "What's wrong with his daughter?" he asked, thinking of any way to prolong their conversation.

She stopped short and blinked up at him. "A fever. She's been sick a fortnight." She stepped to the side as if to go around him, but Jasper headed her off.

"You knew he couldn't pay you, yet you made the clothes anyway," he said softly.

She paused, nodded. "He lost everything but his daughter in a fire several weeks ago, including his wife." She lifted her gaze to his and Jasper wondered at the compassion of this woman. She was clearly in dire straits, yet gave to someone even needier.

Jasper touched his finger to her upturned cheek. "He was right. You are an angel."

Her eyes widened slightly, but she didn't jerk away. She stared up at him a long moment, then retreated from his touch. "My lord, I thank you again for your help this evening. Good night."

No, not yet. Please. Though he ached to haul her up against him, burned to strip that cloak away and see the treasures hidden underneath, he forced himself to stand still, lest he frighten her off. "Let me make an appointment with you. I'll pay whatever you ask."

She stared up at him another long moment, seemed to consider his offer. Then she blinked. "No. Please go."

He frowned. This night was apparently destined for the privy. But he still wasn't willing to let her go without trying to stake his claim. He withdrew his calling card from an interior pocket of his coat and handed it to her. "Send a note if you change your mind."

Her fingers curled around the card. She held it aloft for a moment. "I won't," she said.

She must already have a protector; many actresses did. He'd kept one himself for a time. He took in the coarse wool of her cloak, glanced at the hovel she called home, and recalled the sorry condition of her boots. The rage he'd overcome toward the man who'd attacked her reformed and directed itself to the prick who kept her in such squalor. She was a diamond among the coal. She deserved far better.

"Keep the card. If your circumstances change," he gave her a pointed stare, silently urging her to make that change, "please call upon me."

Far more disappointed than he'd been a quarter hour earlier, Jasper pivoted and strode from the court. He turned onto the Haymarket. March fell into step just behind him, but didn't say a word.

His coach stood across the thoroughfare, at the mouth of another court. Jasper hurried across the Haymarket, still busy despite the clock nearing or perhaps already passing midnight. He paused when he reached his vehicle. March moved in front of him and let down the step.

Raucous shouts drew Jasper to turn toward the small court, which was maybe thrice as big as an alley. Lanterns illuminated a circle of people, at the center of which two men fought. The rough sounds of violence drew him forward. He gestured for March to stay with the coach.

Jasper sparred several times a week at Jackson's, a necessary exercise that both calmed and focused him. Tonight, the sounds of fighting—of fists striking flesh, of exertion—moved through him like the finest symphony, a balm for his frayed temper.

He moved closer, to the outermost ring of the circle. Two burly men fought in the center. One's nose dripped blood, and the other sported a swelling eye. The spectators were entirely working class folk. Except one. A gentleman stood at one end, his arms crossed, his face fixed on the fight. He looked vaguely familiar. After a few moments, he raised his hand. "Enough," he called. "Come back next time."

The combatants stopped, their chests heaving. Both nodded but hung their heads a bit, as if that wasn't the decision they wanted.

"Who's next? I'll watch one more bout," the gentleman said.

A young, spry-looking fellow with a hooked nose stepped forward. "Enders, my lord."

"Ah yes, Enders. I hoped you'd come back. Who will take him on?" He surveyed the crowd and when his eyes fell on Jasper, his lips curved into a smile. But then he moved on, dismissing him. Jasper's ire surged. For the second time tonight, he'd been discounted. Rejected.

He pushed through the crowd and stepped into the circle, trained his gaze on the gentleman who'd passed him over. "Me."

OLIVIA WEST WATCHED the fair-haired gentleman stride from the court. She could still feel his touch, making her already heated flesh warmer than she wanted it to be.

She looked down at the card in her hand.

Earl of Saxton

An earl had come to her rescue? And a rather dangerously attractive one at that.

Tilly, one of the prostitutes from Portia's Garden and the closest thing Olivia would allow to a friend, sidled up beside her and looked at the card. "What've you got there?"

Olivia tucked it into the pocket of her cloak. "Nothing."

Tilly arched a brow at her. "I'm not the best reader, but I recognize the word 'earl' when I see it. That gent was an earl?"

"He's no one." Olivia could guess what Tilly might say next. She'd been pestering Olivia the past two months she'd resided in Coventry Court to take up occupation as a lightskirt.

Tilly whistled between her teeth. "Gor, Livvie, you couldn't do better than that. Did he make you an offer?"

"That doesn't signify. I am not in your trade." Olivia turned toward her boarding house, an unfortunate establishment, but the best she could afford if she wanted her own room. And she wanted her own room. She'd spent the previous nine months since her mother's death lodging with other women, having her things ruined or stolen, suffering intrusions at all hours, and finding herself in close quarters with unsavory men.

"You could be," Tilly said, surely about to launch into her favorite topic of conversation: the benefits of prostitution.

"No, thank you." Olivia's mother had gleefully sold her body for money, baubles, meager affection, but more often than not, misery.

"Oh, but surely you'd change your mind for one such as him!" Tilly cajoled.

An image of Lord Saxton crowded her mind. Individually, his features were unyieldingly stark—a prominent brow, wide nose, square jaw. Together, however, they formed a visage that bespoke power, dominance, and beauty. His lips had formed a half-pout, half-purse that, with the intensity of his pale blue stare, gave him an air of ruthlessness. He was, without question, the most striking man she'd ever seen. And he'd smelled of pine instead of rotting London. Yes, Olivia supposed he might be able to lure a desperate woman to sell him her body, but not her.

"I would not change my mind for the prince regent," Olivia said.

Tilly shook her head. "You're touched in the head. Can't imagine why you'd rather work your fingers to the bone sewing clothes what won't ever belong to you. Or treading the boards at the Haymarket, or have you warmed up to filling in for Mae?"

"As it happens, Mae is returning to her role tomorrow night, so my temporary run as an actress is at an end." As was her run as one of the company seamstresses. Mr. Colman, the theatre manager, had sacked her just that evening. He'd hired a new costumer, and her services were no longer required. But these were personal troubles she never shared with anyone.

Tilly plucked at her bodice to reveal a bit more flesh. "Well, that must make you happy then."

It was true Olivia didn't care to act, but any extra money earned could be put toward opening her own dress shop. "It's just as well. I'm afraid I wasn't any good at it."

"Pah, you're always too hard on yourself, Livvie. You know you could make twice or three times as much as any of us." She gestured toward Portia's Garden.

Olivia arched a brow. "I thought we were discussing acting."

Tilly patted her upswept hair. "I'd rather talk about that gent." She cocked her head to the side and regarded Olivia with a suspicious gaze. "You'd tell me if you'd made an assignation with him, wouldn't you? I'd be happy to give you a bit of tutoring before you shag him."

"There's nothing going on. He gave me his card, but I've no intention of contacting him."

Tilly's lips curled up into a wide smile. "But you pocketed it just the same. Let me know when you change your mind, dearie. I'll tell you everything you need to know."

"Oh, Tilly, you're incessant. Good night." She turned and entered the boarding house.

The windowless entry, lit by a single guttering candle in a sconce on the wall, was empty. The stairwell was blister-hot as Olivia climbed toward the topmost floor. She stopped short as she approached the second landing.

Mrs. Reddy, her landlady, leaned against the wall, a cup clutched in her left hand. "'Bout time you showed up, Livvie."

Olivia forced a smile, albeit not a very friendly one. It had been an awfully long day, and Mrs. Reddy was a handful at the best of times. This didn't look to be one of them. "Good evening to you, too."

Mrs. Reddy pursed her thin lips, eyeing Olivia's cloak as if it were lined with coin. "I need yer rent."

Olivia refused to be bullied, especially when her feet were throbbing and she was sweating through her gown. "I paid you for the week only three days ago."

Mrs. Reddy's tone escalated to a childish whine. "But I need a spot of blunt now."

Sympathy was not something Olivia would extend to the gin-addled woman. Not when she would just use the money for drink. It reminded Olivia far too much of her mother's penchant for spending nearly everything she earned on clothes and worthless jewels. "I don't have it. I'll pay when it's due."

Mrs. Reddy wobbled forward, coming dangerously close to the top of the stairs. Afraid the woman might tumble over, Olivia moved up to the landing. She was relieved when Mrs. Reddy turned and stepped away from the edge.

"Livvie, I know you have some."

A very little, but it was her hard-earned savings, scrimped from a tight budget that allowed no room for extravagance or error. Money she needed for her future. "I have none to spare."

Mrs. Reddy advanced on her, wheezing gin-saturated breath. "I already have another tenant lined up. Go get the money, or I'll toss you out."

She had no idea if the landlady had another tenant, but she couldn't risk that chance. Shooting Mrs. Reddy a disgruntled stare, she turned and started up the stairs.

"And it just went up another shilling!" she called after her.

Olivia paused and turned. "Again? You only raised the rent week before last." Any higher and she'd have to move. Olivia dreaded the idea of looking for new lodgings. She could barely afford the tiny attic room at Mrs. Reddy's. She'd be hard-pressed to find another in this part of town, and she refused to move east where rent was cheaper but the neighborhoods were much coarser.

Mrs. Reddy jabbed her cup forward, sloshing liquid onto the floor. "Rent's payable when I say and how much I say so."

Olivia turned and gritted her teeth against correcting the woman's speech. Fourteen years in a vicarage had ensured an excellent education, even if it was wasted in a career as a part-time seamstress.

Hopefully, she would be able to turn tomorrow's dress delivery at Mrs. Johnson's shop into a permanent assignment as a seamstress. Olivia had gone above and beyond what Mrs. Johnson had asked by embroidering the sleeves—a risky move, but one Olivia prayed would prove successful.

When she finally reached her room, Olivia unlocked her door and immediately bolted herself inside. Unbearably hot, she pulled off her cloak and tossed it on the bed. Lord Saxton's card drifted to the floor. Olivia bent and picked it up. Even the paper felt rich.

If she accepted his offer, she could stop worrying about her next meal and concentrate on the dress shop. She might even be able to find better lodgings.

No. She couldn't consider it. She couldn't relinquish her dignity and her virtue the way her mother had.

She set the card on top of the dresser next to her bed, next to the small box painted with roses and vines that had belonged to her mother. Olivia opened the painted box and contemplated her woeful savings. She extracted the rent money and closed her fist around the precious coins. With heavy steps, she turned to deliver the funds to Mrs. Reddy, her mind frantically working as to how she would replace the loss. She simply had to find more sewing and embroidery work. She *had to.*

Chapter Two

JASPER STEPPED INTO the ring as the spectators all fell silent. He moved his gaze from the familiar gentleman and looked around the crowd. Not a single recognizable face. Good.

The other man in the ring—what was his name, Enders?—looked Jasper up and down. "Are you joking?"

Now this pup meant to insult him? Jasper's blood boiled. "Not even a little bit."

The gentleman came to the center. "Hold there, Saxton."

Though Jasper couldn't quite place him, he wasn't surprised the man knew him. "Have we met?"

The gentleman's mouth quirked. "Most certainly, though I daresay you wouldn't admit it. I'm Sevrin."

Jasper knew the name and the scandal, if not the man himself. The viscount was notorious for ruining a girl, his brother's fiancée if he recalled correctly, and refusing to marry her. Ironically, he and Sevrin had more in common than the rakehell would ever know.

"Do you realize you're auditioning for a fighting club?" Sevrin asked, his dark brow arched in suspicion.

Jasper possessed no such notion, but that wouldn't stop him. Denied his original plan for the evening, the idea of pummeling someone beyond the rules and respectability of Jackson's held an indefinable, and quite necessary, appeal. "Of course."

Sevrin paused just briefly, reflecting a flash of surprise before he gave a slight nod. "All right then. Take off your hat and your coat. And whatever else you choose." He gave a half-smile and returned to his spot on the perimeter.

Jasper stripped off his coat. He thrust it and his hat at a wrinkled old man. "Hold this."

He turned back to face his opponent, Enders. The younger man had removed his coat and wore only a shirt, open at the neck. He'd rolled up his sleeves, revealing muscular forearms. Jasper discarded his waistcoat as well and then folded over his cuffs.

Wagers on Enders reached Jasper's ears, stoking the fire in his belly. He curled his fists, eager to demonstrate his skill.

"Go," called Sevrin.

Enders launched forward, fists flying. He moved differently than the men Jasper was used to sparring with at Jackson's. He caught Jasper in the face, but Jasper moved quickly and deflected the man's subsequent blows. Pain raced up Jasper's cheekbone, jolting his senses, but with it came a vibrant, jubilant sensation.

Jasper's feet were light, his hands charged with violent intent, his chest thundered with his elevated heart rate. He answered Enders' attack with a vicious cut to his jaw. Jasper's knuckles stung, but he barely noticed over the exhilaration making his heart pound. With distinct clarity, he saw the glow of the street lamp illuminating their fight, the yelling crowd, the flash of respect on Sevrin's face. God, he felt alive.

Enders delivered a two-punch to Jasper's stomach and side. Jasper danced backward a moment and considered his opponent's technique. Detecting what he thought was a weak spot, he jabbed toward Enders' middle, but the man grabbed Jasper's arm and pulled him off balance.

While Jasper struggled to regain his upright position, Enders delivered a blow to his ribs. Then another to the side of his head. Jasper moved to the right, barely evading a third strike. He stumbled close to Sevrin, who was frowning.

Sevrin's chin ticked up in warning, and Jasper threw himself to the street and rolled. Enders had lunged forward, pitching himself off balance to take Jasper down. Without Jasper to break his fall, he tumbled to the ground face-first.

Jasper jumped to his feet, insulted Sevrin had thought he'd needed help. Enders wrapped his hand around Jasper's ankle and pulled.

"Kick him!" someone yelled.

Staggering to keep his footing, Jasper recognized why this was different than Jackson's. It was still sport, but more primal, borne of man's most basic needs: survival and dominance. He shook off the man's hold, thrilling to this new challenge.

Enders got to his knees, but Jasper kicked him in the chest. His opponent fell backward. The spectators cheered. Jasper's blood surged. He circled the downed man. "Get up."

It would have been easy to conquer the man while he was on the ground, but Jasper didn't want to win that way. He wanted the hard-earned victory. He wanted the fight.

Enders struggled to his feet. They contemplated each other, taking a moment to assess and strategize. Jasper lowered his guard a bit, inviting Enders to advance. His opponent didn't immediately take the bait but considered his options. Finally, he surged toward Jasper, but Jasper timed his movements perfectly. He stepped to the side and drove his fist into Enders' gut. Enders doubled over. Using his elbow, Jasper then struck the back of the other man's neck. Enders sank to his knees, but quickly wobbled to his feet. When he came forward, Jasper landed a fist in the man's warped nose.

"Enough," Enders mumbled through the blood streaming over his mouth.

Jasper stepped back, his chest heaving with exhaustion. The crowd yelled its approval, and Jasper's muscles sang with victory.

Sevrin stepped forward. "Enders, you're in. Saxton, come with me." Without waiting for Jasper, he turned and went into the tavern at the back of the court—a slope-roofed establishment bearing a sign with a black horse.

Jasper stared after Sevrin. Why had the man he'd just beaten been invited to join, while Jasper had been beckoned like a child awaiting punishment? He retrieved his coat and hat from the old man and followed Sevrin inside, intent on pummeling him too, if necessary.

The small common room was crowded with more furniture than people. Sevrin led him to a room at the back where candles flickered in sconces along the walls and on a few rough, dirty tables.

Pain began to enter Jasper's consciousness. His cheek, his side. "Why is Enders in? I beat him."

"Because he's a good fighter, and he's tried out three times. Each time he's better. He'll be a good addition to the club." Sevrin dropped into a chair. "You, on the other hand, are something I hadn't considered."

A serving maid entered with two tankards and deposited them on the table next to Sevrin without a word. She left as quickly as she'd appeared.

The viscount slouched in his chair, assuming a position in tandem with his dissolute reputation. "Sit. If you please," he drawled with a bit of a smirk. "You're a surprisingly good fighter. At first I didn't think you were going to fare well. You fight at Jackson's?"

Asinine question. "Of course."

The viscount smiled, but it was of the self-deprecating variety. "I'm not welcome there. Besides, I prefer a more…visceral bout." He pulled his gloves off, revealing scabbed knuckles. "Did you enjoy it? The fight?"

"Yes." Jasper stared at the man's hands. Then he raised his gaze and noticed the faint yellow tint around one eye and along the line of his jaw. A few days ago, he probably looked as bruised as Jasper felt right now.

"Are you going to sit? Tom's ale is quite good."

Why not? He had no plans to partake in polite entertainment, and certainly couldn't now with his damaged face. He took a drink of the ale. It was better than good. He downed half the tankard.

"What are you doing here?" Sevrin asked.

Jasper shrugged. There was no way in hell he'd share his miseries with anyone. "A fight sounded good." Particularly after his original plans for an illicit evening had gone horribly awry.

"No, I mean what are you doing *here*? Fighting in a court off the Haymarket? You're a long way from the staid, estimable gentleman who's the object of every young—and probably old—woman's desire."

Sevrin's description of him was accurate, but suddenly Jasper wondered how he'd become precisely that man. Instead of the hot-blooded youth who'd ruined a girl and scarcely looked back.

He purposely ignored the question and the emotions it stirred. "So what is this then, a pugilism club?"

A corner of Sevrin's mouth curved up. "I wouldn't characterize it that way. It's a fighting club. *My* fighting club."

"Who's in this club of yours?"

Sevrin lifted his tankard. "No one you know."

Nonsense. Jasper's family prided themselves on knowing everyone, even if, like Sevrin, they weren't of the same quality. "You might be surprised."

Sevrin chuckled before taking a drink and setting it back on the pockmarked table. "Truly, you don't know any of these men. You saw them outside. Laborers, watermen, a few professional chaps."

Now it made sense—*Sevrin's* fighting club. "I see, no gentlemen at all."

"I suppose you won't count me in that number?" Sevrin smiled sardonically. "No, of course not. Despite that, I think you'll fit right in."

With a club made up of common men and led by a reprobate? He nearly laughed, even as the offer tempted him. "I don't need another club."

"You may not need it, but you want it. You could've beaten Enders into the ground, but you savored the fight." Sevrin speared him with a knowing stare.

"Why do you want me?" It was obvious other men, lesser men, tried multiple times to get into this club and yet he'd invited Jasper on his first endeavor. "Is it because of who I am? Are you thinking I'll help improve your reputation?"

Sevrin laughed. Loudly. It was a moment before he regained his composure. "You think I somehow lured you here to better my incontrovertible social standing? Good Lord, man, have you no sense of self-worth? You're a natural fighter. I don't give a pig's arse if you're a butcher, a clergyman, or the bloody prince regent, and the other men don't either. Take the membership or leave it. I don't care." He leaned back in his chair and drank his ale.

A place where he could be Jasper Sinclair instead of Holborn's heir. A place where background didn't matter and men could simply be men. Holborn would hate it, and his father made everything Jasper did his business. But with the parson's trap imminent, perhaps it was time again to do what he wanted. Yes, Jasper wanted in the club as much as he'd wanted Miss West, and unlike her, this club wanted him.

"When do you meet?"

"Most nights. Here. Late, but not too late. There are rules. I'll fill you in tomorrow night."

"Until then." Jasper plucked up his hat and coat and left, feeling more invigorated than he had in years.

THE FOLLOWING MORNING, Olivia departed the boarding house dressed in a simple cotton gown of her own design. Her wardrobe wasn't extravagant, but she viewed herself as a walking advertisement for her services and endeavored to wear something fashionable when conducting business.

By the time she reached Mrs. Johnson's shop in Orange Street, moisture had beaded beneath her gown. Gratefully, Olivia entered the cool interior, toting a basket filled with the gowns she'd been hired to stitch. Mrs. Johnson designed the dresses and pieced them together, then paid women like Olivia to complete them. This was Olivia's third commission from Mrs. Johnson, and she desperately prayed it would become a permanent arrangement, particularly after losing not one, but both of her positions at the theatre.

The front room was empty, save the stark rows of fabric lining the right and left walls. Tables marched along the middle of the shop bearing buttons and ribbons. Though Mrs. Johnson's establishment was smaller than most, it was scrupulously neat. In fact, Olivia thought the space could do with swaths of fabric in the corners and displays of Mrs. Johnson's work. Perhaps she'd suggest such improvements if Mrs. Johnson decided to hire her on.

Olivia made her way through a curtain to the back area, which they used as both a consultation and workroom. She stopped short upon seeing Mrs. Johnson seated with two customers.

The shopkeeper looked up. "Olivia, I'd like to introduce you to my new clients." Mrs. Johnson gestured to the pair—a young woman and a man who, by looks, had to be her father. Their clothing was simple, elegant. Not the finest materials, but a cut above most. "This is Mr. Clifton and his daughter, who is to be married. She's quite taken with your handkerchiefs and wishes to commission a gown embroidered with doves. I've assured her you'd be pleased to stitch her gown."

Olivia's insides gushed with excited expectation. She set her basket on the floor and moved closer to their conversation.

A masculine cough filled the small chamber. "You look familiar to me, Miss…"

"West," Olivia supplied cautiously. His questioning tone eroded the edge of her elation.

Mr. Clifton was a large man, too big for the chair Mrs. Johnson had provided. His knees stuck up, and his elbows seemed to engulf the space. He stared at Olivia, his dark eyes protruding from beneath a heavy brow. Men often stared, but she expected a different sort of behavior from a man chaperoning his daughter.

"Olivia, Miss Clifton's nuptials are in mid-September. I assured her that would be plenty of time to construct her gown and complete the embroidery. Don't you agree?" Mrs. Johnson asked.

Olivia focused on the round-faced Miss Clifton in an effort to ignore the father's rude appraisal. "Yes."

Miss Clifton blinked overlarge gray eyes. Then her face split into a wide grin, and she clapped her hands.

Mr. Clifton coughed again, drawing everyone's attention once more. Olivia found it odd he accompanied this girl on her errand. If she didn't have a mother, surely she had some other female guiding her? Olivia wasn't so far gone from her polite upbringing to comprehend that a young, unmarried girl in Miss Clifton's sphere required a feminine influence.

"I've just realized," Mr. Clifton said, nodding appreciatively—too appreciatively. "You look rather like Mrs. Scarlet."

Olivia's gut tightened. Her mother.

Mrs. Johnson looked from Mr. Clifton to Olivia and then back again. "The actress?"

His gaze traveled over Olivia, lingering on her tell-tale red hair. "Yes."

Mrs. Johnson gave him a placating smile. Olivia expected her to remark that this was an inappropriate conversation to conduct in front of Miss Clifton. Instead, she said, "You must be mistaken, Mr. Clifton."

He smiled, the corners of his mouth jutting up in a grotesque fashion. "I'm certain I'm not." He didn't elaborate, but from the subtle widening of Mrs. Johnson's eyes, she well understood his meaning.

Olivia prayed her dead mother wouldn't cost her more work. She didn't know what to say—and judged protestation as pointless in any case—so she simply folded her hands in her lap and awaited the outcome. And hoped they didn't notice the quiver in her frame.

Mr. Clifton slapped his palm against his knee. "Do you know, Mrs. Johnson, I believe we'd like to hire Miss West outright. My daughter requires an entirely new wardrobe, in addition to the wedding clothes, and I can think of no one better suited to the task than your protégé. She can move into our servants' quarters."

Olivia squeezed her fingers together until she lost feeling in the tips. "No, I don't—"

Mrs. Johnson spoke over Olivia. "There will be a commission to me, of course."

A commission? Olivia stared, unable to blink, unable to process what the woman was saying. Did she not understand what Mr. Clifton was asking? Or was she eager to play the role of pimp?

Lest they arrange the entire transaction without bothering to obtain Olivia's consent, she said as sternly as possible, "I'm afraid I'm not available for that sort of employment, Mr. Clifton."

He frowned, his gaze riveted to Olivia's chest. "You must. I'll not be satisfied with any other arrangement."

Mrs. Johnson leaned toward Olivia and said softly, "This is an excellent opportunity."

Olivia's stomach turned. Was the woman daft?

Mr. Clifton smoothed his large hands—with fingers the size of robust sausages—over his thighs. The idea of him pawing her drew a thread of nausea from Olivia's belly.

"Susana, dear, why don't you go and look at the fabric again with Mrs. Johnson?" Mr. Clifton wrestled out of his petite chair, his mouth turning up in a condescending smile.

Miss Clifton nodded and stood up alongside Mrs. Johnson who led her through the curtain to the front of the shop.

Alone with Mr. Clifton, Olivia's skin prickled. His gaze became much more frank, the dark flint of his eyes scraping over her with languid prurience. "You're even lovelier than your mother. I imagine that's because you haven't yet suffered much use. In a few years, perhaps your skin will lose that luscious, youthful glow, but now…" He smacked his lips together as if he were contemplating a plate of succulent cakes.

She edged closer to the curtained doorway.

He moved to block her exit. "Oh, you mustn't go."

A blistering set down came to her lips, but she knew better than to insult Mrs. Johnson's client. If she could just get around him and escape… "Thank you, but no."

He leaned forward and inhaled her scent. "Are you being overly discriminating, or is it that you haven't yet engaged in your mother's trade? I find that inconceivable." His eyes lit. "Ah! You've a protector, perhaps? He can't pay you very well if you're looking for work in a lowly dress shop."

Her heartbeat thundered in her ears. She'd been propositioned before—twice just last night, in fact—but never in so awful a fashion. "I'm not interested in that type of work."

"Now see here, gel." He snagged her wrist in a brutal grip. Olivia tried to wrench free, but he pulled her against his barrel-sized chest. His fingers bit into her flesh, sure to leave a mark. Cruelly, he grasped her chin while he lowered his head. "Open up now." His humid breath washed over her, and she gagged. No, no, no, this couldn't happen! She brought her knee up and delivered the blow her mother had assured her would wound any man.

Sure enough, Clifton howled with pain and fell to the side onto one of the chairs. The wood splintered beneath his weight and he crashed to the floor in an ungainly mess. Olivia didn't wait to see if he got up. She turned on her heel, plucked up her basket, and raced through the curtain, running into Mrs. Johnson in her dash to safety.

The shopkeeper held her steady for a moment then dropped her arms, glaring at Olivia. "What did you do?"

Miss Clifton, ribbons cascading from her fingertips, gaped at Olivia.

"I protected myself. Mr. Clifton was…too familiar."

Mrs. Johnson sucked in a breath. "Did you hurt him? I heard a noise." She peered around Olivia.

Fright and anxiety suffused Olivia in sweat. She had to get out of the shop. "He's fine. I think."

The shopkeeper returned her narrowed gaze to Olivia. "If you've done him harm, pray he doesn't notify the watch."

Olivia's fear crested into panic. She tried to push past Mrs. Johnson, but the older woman grabbed her arm. "You're a fool to refuse his offer."

"I'm not for sale, Mrs. Johnson." Olivia's voice shook with anger and revulsion. "I was raised as a gentlewoman."

Mrs. Johnson sneered, revealing yellowed teeth. "You're no gentlewoman now. From what I've seen, you can't afford to refuse

Clifton, and *I* refuse to lose his business! If you leave now, you'll never work for me again."

"I know. Here." She pulled the dresses from the basket and thrust them at Mrs. Johnson so the shopkeeper had to let go of her arm. The loss of income, especially for the dresses she'd just brought, was something she'd contemplate—and bitterly regret—later, but now she just had to get out of the shop.

The curtain behind her rustled. Olivia turned her head just as Mr. Clifton's beet-colored face appeared. Sweat ran down his cheek as he limped into the shop, retribution etched into his angry features.

Olivia sprinted for the door and freedom beyond.

"I'm not finished with you!" Clifton's furious promise chased her from the shop.

Olivia ran until perspiration trailed down her back in rivulets. When her lungs felt close to bursting, she slowed. A quick glance over her shoulder confirmed she hadn't been followed. At least not that she could see.

She walked quickly, her breathing coming in fast, hard pants. Mr. Clifton may not be on her heels, but his declaration still rang in her ears.

Twice in as many days she'd suffered attacks on her person. The protective cocoon she'd carefully built in the months since her mother's death was crumbling around her. She supposed it was bound to happen. How safe could a young, unmarried woman with no family hope to be in London?

Olivia forced her panic into a cold knot of determination. Though she'd lived with her mother the past seven years, she'd spent the entirety ensuring her own well-being.

If she could manage to find employment—honest, decent employment—she could continue as she'd done. She'd survived nearly a year on her own, and she refused to let these two lamentable occurrences beat her down. She simply had to find more sewing work immediately. Several embroidered handkerchiefs sat at the bottom of her basket. She made her way toward the Strand where there were several shops that might be interested in purchasing her work.

Her options, like her meager savings and her food stores, were dwindling. She could almost see how her mother had fallen into the position of courtesan. How easy it must have been to accept a protector and enjoy all of the luxuries that accompanied such an arrangement. But Olivia couldn't countenance suffering the unsavory proclivities of the man who all but owned her.

Unless the man wasn't unsavory at all. Like Lord Saxton. Little flutters danced in her belly as she recalled his fair hair and pale blue eyes.

She cringed at the direction of her mind. She wasn't yet willing to take on her mother's trade. And there was the key: *yet.* Which meant she was already beginning to consider it.

Chapter Three

THAT AFTERNOON, JASPER strode into his parents' drawing room. As the space was not yet filled to the brim with Important Persons, he was able to make his way quickly to his aunt, the only person he really cared to see. In truth, he'd rather be anywhere else, but duty dictated he suffer his mother's bi-weekly tea, which was a means to another dutiful end—selecting a wife.

Aunt Louisa, perched upon a settee newly covered with rich olive-green damask, grinned at him. "Sit with me."

Gratefully, he took the empty space beside her. Aunt Louisa's presence might keep the marriage-hunting debs at bay—Jasper preferred to conduct his wife hunt on his own terms—as well as his mother, who coldly tolerated Louisa's presence because one simply didn't ignore one's sister-in-law.

She stared at his face. "However did you get that nasty bruise and that cut on your cheek?"

He'd expected the question given last evening's spontaneous activities. "Promise you won't laugh?"

"When have I ever laughed at you, dear boy?"

"I tripped into the doorframe of my office."

She set her teacup on the table and chuckled.

"You promised you wouldn't laugh."

Her robin's egg blue eyes crackled with mirth. "Sorry, dear. You mustn't tell anyone else that story. Though it will go against your image, say you got into a fight."

Jasper smiled in spite of himself. "If you say so."

"I do. I suppose that explains why you weren't at de Longley's rout last night, but it was unkind of you to make me go alone."

After the devastating loss of her husband three years ago, Jasper had taken special care of her and almost always escorted her to events when he was in Town. "My apologies, Aunt. I confess I needed a respite from Holborn."

She gave him a knowing look. Of anyone, she knew her brother's cruelties best. "Still harassing you about marriage, I suppose."

"Among other things." The duke never suffered a dearth of complaints where Jasper was concerned.

"Have you any say in your future countess?"

Holborn preferred to dictate his choice of bride—had in fact prevented Jasper from marrying once—but Jasper would be damned if he'd allow such interference again. It was precisely that interference that had prevented Jasper from seeking a wife during the past decade. However, now he *had* to marry or suffer his father's meddling. He'd made a deal nearly one year ago to wed, a deal that had allowed his sister to choose her spouse. At least one of them would be happy.

The duke had demanded Jasper marry a woman bearing his approval within one year. And the year was almost up. Jasper needed to declare his intentions soon, before the duke organized a marital situation on his own. He wouldn't put it past his father to concoct some sort of compromise to ensure Jasper married someone 'appropriate.'

"The choice is mine." *For now.*

She pursed her lips while her eyes found the broad shoulders of the duke across the room. His back to them, he stood before the windows facing Grosvenor Square talking with the prime minister and the Earl of Witton.

"I hope he isn't being difficult." Her gaze flashed toward Jasper's cheek for the barest moment, but he caught it—and the unspoken question.

His father hadn't lifted a hand to him in years. Not since Jasper had fought back. "No, not that. I'm quite capable, Aunt."

She patted his knee. "Of course you are, dear. Now then, let me help you." She perused the room. "Berwick's daughter?"

"Fuzzy blonde hair and a sing-song voice? No."

"Miss Donnel? She's lovely at the pianoforte."

Jasper had no intention of selecting a wife based on musical skill. This talk was making him claustrophobic. "She's clearly interested in Foley."

"Ah yes, you might be right. Very astute, my dear. You pay more attention than you let on." She continued her search. "Miss Stone?"

"God, no. The duke keeps suggesting her."

Louisa wrinkled her nose. "Never her, then." She tapped her finger against her knee. "You need someone with above average intelligence. Not too young or silly-mannered. I suppose you'd prefer a beauty."

Surprisingly, he thought of Miss West. She certainly looked the part, but was of course utterly lacking birth. And, whether he liked it or not, his future wife's pedigree was the most important thing of all. Begrudgingly, he knew his father had been right about Abigail at least in one respect—Society may have accepted her as Jasper's countess, but she would never have fit in, nor would she have been happy. She'd been a country miss through and through. Jasper needed a wife who was both capable of mastering Society and eager to do so.

A jab to his side drew him from his thoughts. Louisa peered up at him. "You're thinking of a specific girl. Do tell."

He had to be careful. Louisa always saw what others never bothered to look for. "No one."

The corners of her mouth pulled down, and Jasper knew she meant to call him on his fib. Instead, he got to his feet. "Pardon me, but I need to speak with someone."

"Coward."

He leaned down and took her hand, quickly pressing a kiss to her knuckles. They both knew he'd immediately make his exit.

Except the duke stepped into his path just as he made the door. "Leaving so soon? After last night's pointed absence?" He didn't wait for Jasper's response before launching his next volley. "What the hell happened to your face? You look as though you've been run down by a coach and four. Good God, did you lose at Jackson's?"

Jasper curled his fingers into his palms, a typical response to the duke's presence. Jasper didn't want him to know about the club, but his attempts at hiding things from Holborn always ended badly— from the figurine he'd broken at five, to the bottle of brandy he'd downed at twelve, to the girl he'd fallen in love with at eighteen. As punishment the duke had ensured the consequences of each transgression hurt: the destruction of all of his toys, a diet of bread, cheese, and water for a month, and, most excruciating of all, the complete excision of Abigail from his life.

"No. Not that it's any of your concern."

"It bloody well is. Everything you do is my concern until you provide an heir. Then everything he does will be my concern."

A well-worn conversation. "The poor child's doomed, and he hasn't even been conceived yet."

Holborn unclasped his hands. "What are you doing to secure a wife?"

He wasn't going to question Jasper about the fighting? Jasper, rarely surprised by the duke, blinked. But then Holborn was so fixated on Jasper's bride, he likely didn't care about anything else. At least for now.

Jasper kept a firm grasp on his temper. "I'll meet your silly deadline. Stop pestering me."

"I'll do more than pester. I still like Stone's chit." His gaze strayed to where the young lady in question stood talking with her mother and another pair of women. "Her dowry's nice, and her tits are even nicer."

Jasper stifled a twitch of revulsion. He refused to discuss a female's physical attributes with his father as if she were a piece of horseflesh. "You needn't concern yourself with my selection."

Holborn made a sound that was half snort and half grunt, though soft enough so no one could possibly overhear. A sound he never, ever made in polite company, but then he'd subjected Jasper to many things he'd never do in public. "Of course I do. Your taste tends to run to the gutter, if memory serves." He paused to let the insult—and reminder—hang in the air.

Jasper stepped around Holborn, eager to be on his way.

The duke grabbed him just above the elbow. He spoke low, but the fury in his voice was evident. "Tell me your prospects."

Jasper's temper buckled and snapped, something he never let happen in public. Until last night...twice in two days? He turned his head with an angry intake of breath. "I find it ironic that if you hadn't intervened, I'd have been married these past ten years with an heir and plenty of spares. Don't you?"

"Wed that lowly country sow?" The duke struggled to keep his voice low. "You should thank me for rectifying that abominable situation."

"I'd thank you more for staying the hell out of my life." Jasper neatly shook off Holborn's grip and then took the older man's narrow wrist between his fingers and squeezed. "Are you going to let me pass or cause an even greater scene? If you laugh just now, we might play this off as something bordering genial. If not…"

The duke scowled then chuckled. A dark, tinny sound that might delude the fools of the *ton*, but never Jasper. He let go of his father's wrist and quit the townhouse.

AFTER COMBING WHAT felt like Greater London in search of work, Olivia made her way to her lodgings, her feet aching and her spirit crumpled. The evening was exceedingly warm, and her clothing weighed heavy on her tired frame. At the end of her long day, she had nothing to show for her efforts, save the deposit of ten handkerchiefs on commission with a kindly shopkeeper in the Strand.

Her stomach growled, but she knew she'd go to bed without fully satisfying her hunger. The heel of bread and small wedge of cheese left from breakfast would make a poor excuse for dinner.

At least two of the shopkeepers she'd approached had already heard from Mrs. Johnson, who'd been only too eager to share her negative opinion of Olivia. It didn't matter that she possessed exceptional skill. Tomorrow she would redouble her efforts.

Tilly loitered outside the boarding house. "Livvie," she called, "where's yer lordship this even?"

"He's not 'my' lordship." Olivia wondered if her answer to his proposition might have been different if it had been posed tonight.

Tilly clicked her tongue. "Such a shame. Girls like us wait our whole lives for just one night with someone like him."

Olivia shook her head. "I'm not like you, Tilly."

"Because you don't lift your skirts for coin? Bah, you're no better. Scraping away at some half existence."

Tilly didn't know about her past, and Olivia would never tell her. "I don't want to submit to a man. I can't." Not after everything she'd seen happen to her mother, one man after another taking from her until she had nothing left. Until she was dead.

Tilly propped a hand on her waist, accentuating her undernourished form. "What if you didn't have to submit to him?"

Olivia's ears perked up. "What do you mean?"

Tilly's lips spread into a wicked grin. "I've an idea that'll get you your money without even touching him. You'll invite him over, get him in the mood—it won't take much—then we'll switch places. We'll get his money, I'll be taking a share of course, and I'll get me a spot of fun." Her eyes narrowed deviously.

Olivia shivered. This sounded too dangerous. What if they were caught? "You want to trick him? I'm not sure that's a good—"

Tilly held up her hand. "We'll blindfold him. He'll be so worked up, he'll never know he's shagging me instead of you."

"I couldn't. Tilly, it's too risky."

"Does he scare you?"

Olivia recalled the violent way he'd come to her rescue. She'd been shocked by his quick defense but not really frightened. "No."

Tilly patted her arm. "It'll be fine. From the looks of him, he's got coin to spare. No harm'll come of it."

He *was* a rich nobleman, without any of the cares that crowded her life with pending disaster. He didn't have to wonder about his next meal or whether his choices would be stolen by a violent man seeking his pleasure. However, justifying the act in her mind didn't ease all of her fears.

"I refused him. Won't he be surprised I invited him?"

"Men don't fret about such things. The minute he gets your invitation, all of his thinking will head south between his legs."

That Olivia could believe.

Could this scheme really work? Olivia wasn't sure she could pull off an almost-seduction. If she could, she'd have the money she needed without sacrificing her virtue. What of her honor? She winced, but reasoned it was something she could learn to reconcile, especially after the misery her mother had endured at the hands of men like him. Furthermore, how many times had she heard those same men— her mother's legion of lovers—say that one willing female was as good as the next?

She firmed her shoulders and clenched her fists. "You'll have to tell me what to do."

"Of course, dearie. You'll send him a note inviting him to come the night after next. In the meantime, we've got some work to do." She put her arm around Olivia's shoulders and guided her toward their building. "I don't suppose you have any gowns that show a bit more flesh?"

Olivia glanced down at her chest and touched the demure lace edging her bodice. "I study the current fashion, not the street corner."

Tilly chortled. "Good thing you're handy with a needle, then. Because you need to show more of your bubbies. A lot more."

JASPER ALIGHTED FROM his coach at the mouth of Coventry Court and directed March to return for him at midnight. He then made his way to Miss West's boarding house, his steps eager and his pulse quickening. He was surprised she'd invited him. Her note had been simple, direct:

I've reconsidered your offer. The price is ten pounds. You may come tonight at nine o'clock. I am on the topmost floor.

It was still five minutes until the hour, but Jasper could scarcely wait. He passed the brothel he'd visited the other night, grateful that his disappointment there had turned into something far more exciting. He entered the ramshackle boarding house and took the stairs two at a time.

On the fourth floor, he rapped on the single door. Barely a moment passed before it swung open. She stood in the gap between the frame and the door, candlelight bathing her face and form in its warm glow.

"Good evening, my lord." She gestured for him to enter.

Had her voice been that provocative the other night? He couldn't recall, but he knew for certain she hadn't looked as she did now. Draped in a dark green gown that made her skin shimmer like a pearl, she was achingly beautiful, but it was her eyes that beckoned him. The color of jade, they were luminous, with just a hint of seduction. He was already lost.

She opened the door wider, and he realized he was gaping. He stepped inside as she closed the door behind him. Without her to enslave his vision, he took stock of her room. Just four candles lit the space, but they lent a welcoming quality to the paucity of the tiny chamber. A solitary window offered little relief to the heat. There was a small table to the left of the center of the room with a single chair, then a cupboard, a few rickety shelves, and a small armoire missing one of its doors. Against the right wall sat her narrow bed with turned wood posters at the head and covered with a threadbare quilt. She lived even worse than he'd suspected.

He turned toward her. "We could have done this somewhere else."

She cocked her head. "Is there something wrong with my room, my lord?"

"It's just..." he didn't wish to insult her, "small."

"I doubt we'll need much space."

On the contrary, his mind was already devising lurid pictures of the various ways in which he could take Miss West all over her inadequate apartment. Though he doubted the table would support their weight.

Jasper reined in his thoughts. It wouldn't do to get ahead of himself. "I was surprised to receive your invitation." *After you so coldly stated you would never contact me.*

She moved closer to the window. The flimsy drape fluttered in the faint breeze. She closed her eyes briefly, welcoming the cool night air. Her profile was elegant, proud.

She turned toward him, her gaze direct and warm. "I'm particular about my clients. I don't accept offers from strangers, but given your assistance and...tenacity regarding my safety, I changed my mind. You may call me Olivia."

Olivia. Lovely.

"Do you have the fee?" she asked, sauntering toward him.

Yes, he'd brought it. An expensive sum, but presented with the sway of her hips and the seductive invitation in her eyes he'd gladly pay it and perhaps more. Seeing where she lived, he wanted to contribute to improving her surroundings. He extracted the notes from his coat and handed them to her.

She pivoted and went to the dresser, on top of which sat a pretty box painted with roses and vines. She placed the money inside. The coldness of the transaction ate at him. Why? He'd been the one to approach her. Was it because he felt like he knew her, at least a little bit? Had acted as her champion and witnessed her generosity to those less fortunate when she herself was clearly in need?

Further thought was interrupted as she came back to him, her lips curved in a sensuous smile. Was this the same prickly female who'd refused his escort?

She grasped his lapels and pushed his coat open. He shrugged out of it and laid it over the back of the chair. Deftly, she removed his cravat, her fingers brushing his chin and neck. Lust roared in his veins, as if he'd gone years without a woman. Once, long ago, he'd felt exactly like this—expectant, driven. However, he was no longer a fumbling lad of eighteen. Tonight, there would be no regrets.

Her hand dipped lower, to the buttons of his waistcoat. All moisture evaporated in his mouth as she pushed the garment over his shoulders. It dropped to the floor next to the cravat.

Desire pulsed through him, so strong his vision clouded for a moment. His fingers itched to pull the pins from her dark red hair and stroke the soft flesh of her neck, her back, every inch of her. She smelled of fresh-cut lavender, utterly feminine. He reached for her, but she danced away, her eyes tilting at the corners in a sultry manner.

"Is there something you wish for this evening? Something...specific?" she asked.

He hardened at her invitation. There were a myriad of things he wished for, but the only thing he really wanted was her. "Only you."

She nodded once, moving toward the bed. She crooked her finger, beckoning him forward. "Sit. I'll take off your boots."

Jasper's body thrummed with need. She kneeled before him. The sight sent a surge of blood pounding to his groin. His fingers curled into the threadbare coverlet. He despised this room, this poverty. He would surround her in satin and lace, if she'd let him.

She removed both boots and set them aside. Now she rolled his stockings down, first the right then the left. Her fingers massaged his calves, ankles, and the balls of his feet as she worked.

Around and over, her hands moved. Kneading. Stroking. Arousing. "Do you like that?"

He barely kept himself from groaning aloud. "Yes."

When his muscles tingled from her ministrations, she moved her hands up his legs. He sucked in a breath, anticipating the touch of her fingers against his prick.

She blinked up at him, her dark lashes sweeping over the vibrant green of her eyes. "Do you trust me?"

The question surprised him, dulling the edge of his lust. He trusted no one save his aunt and his sister. But surely Olivia only meant that he should trust her with his care this evening. And that he thought he could manage. "I will, yes."

Her lips curved into a smile and she gestured to the bed. "Lie back."

He did as she commanded, swinging his feet onto the pallet and reclining back against her pillows.

She sat beside him, her hip pressed against his. The intimacy tested Jasper's self-control. She leaned over his chest, her breasts brushing against him. His breathing grew shallower.

Giving in to impulse, he clasped her sides. The smooth fabric of her gown caressed his flesh. Her heat bled through the satin, and he longed to touch her bare skin. He closed his eyes briefly, relishing both the feel of her and the spike of lust arcing through him.

Cotton settled against his eyes. He opened them but saw only blackness. He grabbed her hand, pulling the blindfold away. "What are you doing?"

Her lips tickled his ear. "You said you would trust me."

Yes, he'd said that, but that didn't mean it was easy. "Why the blindfold?"

She pulled her head back and gazed at him intently. Her eyes took on a sparkling, animated quality he'd never seen on her before. Gone, finally, was the wariness, the unease. "Our eyes can inhibit sensation. For now, I'm asking you to just feel."

He nodded, aroused enough to do whatever she asked. She finished tying the fabric behind her head. Her breath gusted over him in a hot little pant. His hips twitched with need.

The blindfold was tight enough that he couldn't see anything. Immersed in blackness, his other senses amplified, honing in on her lavender scent, the sound of her breathing, the beat of her heart against his chest. All of it combined to drive him to an erotic edge.

He curved one hand behind her neck and pulled her face to his. He leaned up, meaning to kiss her…

Her fingers pushed against his lips. "Not yet."

Jasper drew one digit into his mouth, lightly sucking on the tip. He smiled at her sharp intake of breath.

She ran her hands down his chest and it was his turn to gasp. Slowly, she tugged the hem of his shirt from his breeches. Her knuckles grazed his belly, forcing his muscles to clench. He twisted toward her hips, aching for the touch of something—anything— against his swollen cock.

Inch by inch, she pushed the shirt up his torso, exposing each new piece of flesh to the heat collecting between them. Her fingers danced along his skin, driving him farther, deeper into his haze of lust. The anticipation was near agony. It was, in fact, more acute than any pain he'd ever suffered.

He arched off the bed so she could sweep the garment over his head. He felt the breeze as the fabric left him. It stirred her delicious scent and he couldn't stop himself another moment. He slid his tongue along her neck, knowing exactly where she was positioned because he hadn't let her go. She shivered. He pressed his lips to the underside of her chin.

She hovered there, allowing his attention, but didn't tilt her face down. Why wouldn't she kiss him?

But then he felt the slide of fabric against his right wrist and he snatched it from her grip. "Now what are you doing?"

"Trust me." She moved her head and ran her tongue along the outer edge of his ear. With soft lips, she tugged at his lobe and then sucked it into her mouth.

He quivered with need. It took her a moment to secure him, but he was too focused on the ministrations of her mouth and tongue.

Then she moved to his left wrist. This put the swell of her breast close enough to kiss. Jasper didn't hesitate. He pressed his mouth to her skin, praying she'd remove his blindfold at some point so he could watch her undress. He opened his mouth and suckled at her flesh, drawing another gasp from her.

A moment later, she finished her work and drew away. Again, she ran her hands down his chest. It seemed she was in no hurry, and he couldn't fault her. He wanted to extend their pleasure as long as physically possible. Her hands reached the waistband of his breeches and stilled.

Silence reigned, broken only by their rapid breathing filling the space. Need pulsed within him, between them. Unable to stand another torturous second, Jasper pressed his hips up, urging her to continue whatever she meant to do next.

She unfastened his fall. As each button came free, his blood heated and his pulse increased. The absence of sight and the inability to touch her with his hands sensitized the nerves in his flesh. Every time she brushed his small clothes or the surface of his belly, he moved his hips.

At last she stroked him. Lightly, perhaps inadvertently, but he groaned nonetheless. Then she pulled his breeches from his legs and except for his small clothes, he was completely exposed to her. He spread his thighs, inviting her to do as she wished.

"I'll be right back."

He frowned. "I'd like to watch you undress."

"You said you trusted me, Saxton," she said with a light, scolding tone. "I promise you will not be disappointed this evening."

She had no idea what she asked of him, but he forced himself to relax. There would be other times for him to peel her chemise from her breasts.

The swish of her skirts, so alluringly clear to his hungry senses, faded for a moment. A bead of doubt infiltrated his sexual haze—had he been wrong to trust her? More silence. The doubt grew into a dark, fear-laden cloud. His desire began to fade.

Her footsteps, so light and soft, reached his desperate ears. The bed sagged as she straddled him, her bare knees pressing down on each side of his hips. She inserted her hand into the slit of his small clothes and palmed him. Lust jolted his slackening shaft, casting his disappointment aside as if it had never been. So good, except for the calluses…

She didn't have calluses. Her palms had been soft when she'd tied his hands.

He pulled back from the hand stroking him, retreating as far as he could into the mattress.

Unfortunately, it wasn't far enough. "Who the hell are you?"

Her fingers found him. "It's me, Livvie." The voice was too deep, too rough.

His desire fled completely and was replaced with cold rage. Everything about this woman from her touch to her voice to her name was all wrong. "You may think I'm helpless, but I assure you

I'm not. Tell me where Olivia is."

A heavy, gin-soaked breath gusted over him. "I guarantee you'd rather do this with me. Livvie doesn't have my...skill."

Jasper doubted that. Pointlessly, she stroked him again.

He pulled at his bindings, desperate to shove her hand away and remove her from his body. "Stop!" he hissed. If Olivia was nearby, he didn't want her to know she was on to his scheme.

Her hand closed more firmly around his prick. "Who's in control now?"

Her voice now penetrated his confused brain. The whore from the brothel the other night. What the hell was she doing here?

Jasper struggled against his bindings, but they were well tied. "Take off my blindfold and untie me. If you do it quickly—and quietly—I'll give you five pounds."

She tore the blindfold off him. Her gray eyes spat venom. "You cost me a lot more than that the other night. The madam was right furious with me. Threatened to kick me out on the street after you left. She's given me the lowliest, cheapest customers since. I deserve a bloody sight more than five pounds."

Working to take the edge from his voice, he modulated his tone. He needed her to let him go, not squeeze his prick to death—or worse. "Ten pounds, then. Do remember I'm an earl as you deliberate."

Another gust of gin-soaked breath settled over him. "That's more like it." She set to work on his bindings.

When both wrists were free, he pushed her off him. "Cover yourself." He held his finger to his lips, urging her to do so quietly.

Hastily, he drew on his breeches, his hands shaking with rage. "What was your plan?" he asked softly. "And keep your voice down."

She refastened her dress. "After I shagged you, I'd get up to wash and then we'd switch back."

Fury pooled in his belly and spread, filling him with vitriol. Olivia had duped him. Purposefully. Anguish mingled with his anger. *Do you trust me?* She'd lied with every word, every touch.

He pushed his anger out, toward the hapless slut. "This is fraud. I could drag you to the magistrate."

She blanched. "Have mercy, my lord. I was only trying to make back the coin you lost me."

"Go out and tell her you're done." He pulled two pounds from his discarded waistcoat and gave it to her, not because he wanted to, but because he felt bad for the plight he'd caused her. It wasn't her fault she reminded him of lost love. He gave her a dark look. "Don't warn her."

She nodded jerkily. He moved to stand behind the door.

Tilly went into the hallway. Jasper leaned close to the wall. Their voices drifted through the crack near the hinges.

"Did he suspect anything?" *The duplicitous bitch.*

"No."

"Thank you, Tilly. I'll bring your share down later." There was a pause, then, "Was he, that is…"

"Worth it? 'Course. I told you you'd regret not doing him yourself."

There was a loud exhalation then feet scraping across the floorboards. Olivia stepped through the doorway.

Jasper slammed the portal and flattened his back against it. He glared at her with the weight of his wrath. "If you don't yet regret deceiving me, I promise you will."

Chapter Four

SAXTON'S EYES GLEAMED like frost, the flesh around his lips was tight and drawn. Olivia moved farther inside and stepped around the table, putting the barrier between them. "Are you going to hurt me?"

He prowled toward her. "You attempted fraud. More disturbingly, you arranged for a stranger to assault me. Don't you think you deserve some sort of punishment?"

God, she hadn't thought of it that way. Her belly squeezed with nausea, her limbs shook with shame. She probably deserved something, but couldn't bring herself to admit it and put herself at his mercy. "No."

"The law would disagree. I could send for the magistrate." His body was rigidly calm, without visible sign of agitation, save the savage expression on his face.

Fear wouldn't help her. She gathered her courage and squared her shoulders. "You could, but we don't have a contract of any kind, especially if I return your payment." She strode to the dresser and retrieved her mother's box. With trembling hands, she withdrew his money and thrust it toward him. "Here."

He accepted the bills and, without taking his gaze from her, set them on the table. "I don't want a refund. I want you."

Olivia moved back behind the table. "I thought a man like you would find one woman as acceptable as the next."

Heat leapt into the ice of his eyes and his hands fisted. He stood silent a long moment during which Olivia's heart tried to beat itself right out of her chest. "You couldn't be more mistaken." His tone was soft, but razor-sharp. "I'm disappointed you aren't the least bit contrite, particularly after I helped you the other night. Not to mention your insistence that I *trust* you."

Olivia cringed. He'd actually taken her words to heart. If she were in his shoes, she'd demand punishment too. "I'm…sorry." It sounded pitiful even to her ears.

He shoved the table to the side, eliminating the barrier and stopping just before her. Though he didn't touch her, he effectively pinned her to the wall. "Regardless, I *did* trust you. We struck a bargain, and now you are reneging. If you were a man, I would call you out."

She knew enough of men and their honor to recognize that he wouldn't hurt her, especially after what he'd just said. He felt betrayed, but she didn't think he'd resort to violence to seek retribution.

His gaze bored into hers with savage intensity. He was terribly handsome, even in his fury. The already hot room sweltered with the heat coming off his bare chest. Facing him at dawn seemed a palatable notion. She was far more afraid of his ability to seduce her.

Olivia swallowed. "What are you going to do?"

"That depends." Their impassioned breathing filled the apartment as she waited for his response, every one of her muscles tensely coiled. He speared her with a fierce stare. "Tell me why."

Though she knew he'd be insulted, she gave him the truth. "I need money, and your offer is my only hope at present. But I didn't want to lie with you." She hadn't, but now, after pretending to seduce him… She could well imagine lying with him. Probably would imagine it for many nights to come.

A blood-curdling scream from downstairs shattered the tension. Saxton pulled his gaze from her and looked toward the door. Another shriek. He spun about and exited toward the stairwell. Olivia followed fast on his heels.

He ran down the stairs, pausing on the third floor landing. The commotion seemed to be coming from the ground floor so they continued to descend, his bare feet smacking against the wood as he raced. Goodness, he was half naked, she realized. At the base of the stairs, they halted again. Another tenant brushed past them on her way up the stairs, her face white.

Saxton strode toward the open doorway leading to Mrs. Reddy's apartment. The horrid sound of violence bled into the corridor. He disappeared into the apartment. Olivia didn't want to follow him, but she couldn't stop herself from confirming what she heard, the dull thud of flesh hitting flesh. How many times had she suffered the sight of Baron Landringham, her mother's lover, striking her mother before that terrible night when he'd gone too far and Fiona had tumbled down the stairs?

Olivia stepped to the door and froze, paralyzed by awful memories playing out before her in the present. A large man with a round, angry face gripped Mrs. Reddy by her stringy hair. Blood streamed from her nose, and her face bore several wicked marks that were already blooming into bruises.

"This ain't your business," the man said to Saxton, who had moved close to them—too close.

Olivia's heart thudded. Did he mean to intervene? She'd tried that once on her mother's behalf, and had nursed a bloody face and several bruised ribs for her trouble. Still, she hoped he had courage where she didn't.

"It has to be somebody's business." Lord Saxton sounded utterly calm, as if he stepped into such assaults with regularity. "I can't allow you to kill this woman."

"This ain't your affair. Bitch owes me money. She'd rather drink the rent than give it to me. Ain't that right, dearie?" The large man pulled on Mrs. Reddy's hair, causing her to gasp sharply. Tears tracked down her battered face. "Now, take yourselves back upstairs and finish whatever you've got going." He ogled Olivia. "Sorry to 'ave interrupted you."

Saxton spoke quietly, dangerously. "I'm afraid I can't do that until you leave this woman alone."

"She doesn't need your protection. She's taken my beatings before. Knows it's coming when she doesn't have the rent." To punctuate his statement, he slapped her across the face.

Olivia sucked in a breath, waiting for Saxton's reaction. He leapt across the room and hit the heavy-set man several times. After all of the violence against her mother she'd been privy to, she ought to have yelled at Saxton to stop. But this was different. This was necessary. Saxton was saving a woman, not hurting one.

Mrs. Reddy drooped to the floor but didn't crawl out of the way. Olivia rushed to her aid, dragging her to the side of the room.

The landlady shivered while Saxton continued to pummel the large man with vicious intent. Olivia's blood chilled at how quickly he brought the other man to his knees.

Saxton pulled the man's arm back at a nasty angle. "You're going to leave and never return. Is that understood?"

"Goddamn you, I own this building!" the man ground out while trying to suck air into his heaving lungs.

"Is this true?" Saxton asked Mrs. Reddy.

She nodded. "He's me husband's brother."

"Where's your husband?"

"Long dead," Mrs. Reddy croaked.

"How much do you owe this man?"

"Nearly twenty pounds." She shook so violently, her teeth chattered.

Saxton shoved Mr. Reddy's face against the floor then let him go. "How long will you give her to settle the debt?"

The large man turned, but didn't stand. Perhaps he wasn't capable. "Unless you want to pay, it's none of your bloody business."

Saxton glowered down at him. "I'm the Earl of Saxton. Anything I want is my business." With his bare chest and naked feet, Saxton looked less like an earl and more like a warrior of old.

Mr. Reddy struggled to his feet with a nasty grin. "I can call the magistrate, if you prefer. 'E'll just cart her arse to Newgate."

"No," Mrs. Reddy croaked.

"Can you pay him?" Saxton asked, his eyes glacial.

Mrs. Reddy shook her head, defeat dropping her already listless shoulders.

The earl frowned, lines furrowing his wide forehead. "I presume Mrs. Reddy has your direction. I'll send payment in the morning."

Mrs. Reddy straightened and looked up in surprise.

Olivia did the same. "You're going to pay her debt?"

Saxton glanced toward them. "Yes, but now she's in debt to me." He looked back to Mr. Reddy. "Take yourself off. You'll get what you're owed in the morning."

Mr. Reddy massaged his jaw. "You've a mean 'ook, my lord."

Saxton's hands fisted again, and Olivia wondered if he was even aware of it. "Be happy I went easy on you."

Mr. Reddy nodded and left.

The tension coiling Olivia's muscles dissipated. She helped Mrs. Reddy to a nearby chair. Scanning the apartment, Olivia found a bit of toweling and handed it to the battered woman.

Saxton came to stand before the landlady. "How did you come to owe him so much coin?" He sniffed, likely believing the answer was buried in the telltale reek of gin. What else could it be?

Mrs. Reddy put the cloth to her nose and tipped her head back to look up at Saxton. "I gave most of it to me sister. Her husband died, and she's got a son to feed."

He massaged his right hand with his left. "Your brother-in-law seems to think you're buying gin with the money that's owed to him."

Despite her bruised countenance, a flush was discernible on her skin. "Aye, I've a bit of a thirst, but I provide for me sister."

"Why not tell him the truth?" Saxton asked.

"I tried to ask him for money once. Wouldn't even part with a shilling. At first I just told him the tenants were shorting me, but he figured things out a few weeks ago."

This must have been why she'd repeatedly increased the rent. Olivia pitied the poor woman's sister and her fatherless child. She stared at her defeated landlady and suffered a stab of shame for judging Mrs. Reddy as ignorantly as others had judged her.

At length, Saxton folded his arms over his chest. His knuckles were reddened, and a few of them bled. "I'll pay your debt, but I expect you to work it off." He sounded dispassionate, but not judgmental. Olivia couldn't help but respect what he was offering Mrs. Reddy. Which only served to make her attempted swindle all the more distasteful.

Mrs. Reddy blinked with her one good eye; the other had swollen shut. She smiled, revealing blackened gaps in the sides of her mouth. "Won't mind that at all."

Saxton's lip curled. "At one of my estates. In the scullery or wherever your…talents might be best utilized."

Mrs. Reddy sobered. "I don't want to leave me house."

Olivia couldn't believe the landlady's foolishness. "It isn't your house. It's Mr. Reddy's. And if you don't leave he'll return and likely use you as a sparring partner again."

She looked to Olivia, adjusting the cloth over her nose. "Not if I pay him, and Lord Saxton said he'd settle it."

"Not without something in return," he said smoothly, his eyes chilling to ice. "My charity only extends to those willing to work to better themselves." It was a fair expectation from a seemingly benevolent man.

Mrs. Reddy contemplated her lap. When she looked up again, tears leaked from her eyes. "I don't know if I'm equal to the task, my lord."

"You'd prefer to risk Mr. Reddy's violence than do honest work that would help both you and your sister?" Saxton's tone now matched the frigidity of his eyes.

Mrs. Reddy turned her head, perhaps unable to bear the scrutiny of his gaze another moment. Olivia patted the woman's shoulder instead of shaking it, which she longed to do. Tomorrow she would talk her into accepting the earl's offer. Really, Mrs. Reddy had no other choice.

Olivia directed her attention to Saxton. "You should go."

"You'll accompany me upstairs." His mouth was hard. "We aren't finished."

She knew they weren't, but neither did she want to be alone with him. She was afraid of what might happen, what she might allow. "I should stay to comfort—"

He lightly took her arm, steering her toward the door along with him.

Olivia turned her head to look at Mrs. Reddy.

"Go on then. I'll be fine." Mrs. Reddy waved her out.

"I'll check on you in the morning." Olivia trudged from the apartment at Saxton's side, but pulled her arm from his hand.

"You can't stay here." His voice was calm, controlled. In fact, he'd scarcely showed any emotion toward her at all since he'd gone to save Mrs. Reddy.

She climbed the stairs. She didn't like him ordering her about. He didn't own her. No one did. "Of course I can. You have no say in the matter."

He followed close behind her. "Think about what you told Mrs. Reddy. What if Reddy comes back, and she's not here to satisfy his violent urges?"

He made an excellent point, but right now Saxton's presence intimidated her far more than the idea of Mr. Reddy returning. "I don't think he will. And even if he did, he has no quarrel with me."

Olivia preceded him into the apartment and went about gathering his clothes. Saxton closed the door after he entered just as Olivia had piled his garments on the chair. She picked the bills up from the table, meaning to give them to him.

He came to stand next to her. "You can't stay here. Even if it wasn't the dingiest, most horrible place I've ever seen, your safety has been compromised. I insist you come away with me tonight."

Olivia clutched the money, relieved he'd dropped the topic of her failed scheme, at least for the moment. "I appreciate your concern, but I won't feel any safer in your care."

The chill in his eyes made her shiver. "Let us not forget I'm the injured party here. I'm offering you valid assistance that any sane woman in your position would gratefully accept."

"What I did was wrong, but that doesn't change the fact that I don't want to go with you."

His grip on her arm tightened, but not painfully so. "How many times have you and Tilly executed this scheme?"

"Never."

His intense stare curled her toes. "So you screw your other clients. It's just me you defraud?"

She sucked in a breath, wishing he were ugly and cruel instead of devastatingly handsome and justifiably outraged. "No."

His gaze heated and he pushed closer, his bare chest a hair's breadth from hers. It was very difficult to find her voice. "I lied about being a whore. I've never traded my body for money. To anyone."

He pressed even closer, bringing his pelvis against hers. "Should I feel complimented because you considered it with me?" His voice had dropped to a disturbingly seductive tone. The words caressed the side of her neck as he leaned in.

Horrifyingly, her body burned where she came into contact with him. Desire pulsed urgently between her thighs. Air couldn't seem to find its way to her lungs. She wanted…she wasn't sure what she wanted. "I…needed money."

"Then take it." He unfolded her hand, took the money from her palm, and set it on the table. He traced his finger around the edge of her face from brow to chin. She should flee, but could only stand there mute, bound by the promise in his gaze. "The devil," he muttered before kissing her.

His lips were soft and so delicious, like cool water for her parched mouth. He curled his hands around her scalp and slanted his mouth. His tongue licked at her, seeking entry.

She shouldn't do this, shouldn't want this, but God help her she did. It had been so long since anyone had touched her with anything other than passing kindness.

Desperate to lose herself, forget everything that plagued her mind, she opened her mouth to him. With devastating skill, he swept his tongue inside and burned her. Shivers ran to her extremities and collected in her belly in a mass of longing. She lifted her hands and splayed her palms against the smooth heat of his shoulders.

She'd been kissed before, but never like this. He kissed her like he couldn't get enough, as if she were the reason he drew breath. His tenderness and deliberation made her feel precious and beautiful and cherished. The way he stroked her tongue with his, the manner in which his lips played over hers, the tender clasp of his hands holding her close…his touch, his scent, the dark sounds of his body as he worshipped her with this kiss.

She wanted to wrap herself around him. She pulled at his shoulders and he answered by grinding his hips against hers. His erection pulsed against her, making her core unbearably damp.

His hands moved down, sliding to the curve of her lower back. His fingers dug into her, driving her against his arousal.

All the while his mouth continued, stirring her desire until she thought she might burst. His hand skimmed up her side and cradled the underside of her breast. She trembled as pleasure shot through her. His thumb tracked over her nipple. She wanted to weep with the joy of it.

A strong breeze blew the pound notes off the table and one fluttered against her arm before drifting to the floor. *She was not a whore.*

Olivia pulled back. Their mouths broke, and their mingled breath panted hotly between them. She ached for him, but if she accepted his money, she'd lose more than she could bear. "I don't want you. Not like this."

He ran his fingers down her neck and dragged them along her collarbone. "If I lift your skirts right now, your body will tell me otherwise."

The truth of his words only enflamed her more. She had to stop him before it was too late. "You'll force me then."

His features hardened, the desire in his eyes cooling. He released her, and she sagged backward, her thighs quivering.

He turned away. A minute passed, and he didn't move. Olivia waited to see what he would do, too afraid to poke the quiet beast.

Finally, he retrieved his shirt from the chair and drew it over his head. Olivia relaxed, her heartbeat slowing its frenetic pace. He sat on her bed and donned his stockings and boots. She silently watched his movements with a mixture of relief and disappointment. It was for the best. It had to be.

When he was finished, he stood and looked at her, his eyes reflecting none of the heat her body still contained. He picked up his waistcoat and pulled it on, then draped his cravat around his neck. "You should stay somewhere else tonight. Take the money and find a hotel or an inn."

She moved around the table, more comfortable with the obstacle between them. Not because she feared him hurting her, but because if he didn't leave soon, she'd be tempted to finish what she'd started. "I don't want your money." She should have said, *I don't want you* again but couldn't force the lie from her lips a second time.

"Don't allow your pride to overrule common sense. Take the money."

"And what will you expect in return?"

His gaze moved over her with deliberate intent. "Your company. And don't tell me you don't want me. I know a woman's desire, and you *do* want me."

The arrogance with which he delivered his assurances kindled her anger. "You presume too much, my lord."

"I presume nothing except that you will lie, as you're doing right now."

She wanted to dispute what he said, but she couldn't. She merely stood mute while her wanton body warred with her scrupulous mind.

"I'll come back tomorrow after you've had time to reflect on the benefits—both financial and physical—of accepting my offer. If you're still intent to refuse the joy we could both share, we'll find another way for you to earn the money."

She was well aware of the benefits. The money was an obvious need, but the intimacy of sharing a night with him would give her more than food, shelter, or clothing. It would warm her through a hundred—maybe a thousand—lonely nights. But the cost was too dear. She wouldn't change her mind. "Don't come back. I made a mistake."

His features flashed with fury. "Damn it, Olivia. I am *not* a mistake. I am the Earl of Saxton."

And more tempting than the devil himself. She summoned her anger. Needed it if she wanted to keep him at bay. "I'm not interested in a liaison with you. You'll have to satisfy your lust with someone else."

With a few quick steps, he came around the table. She flattened herself against the wall. He didn't touch her, but his lips hovered above hers. "I don't want anyone else. I want you." The barest touch of his mouth against hers, a whisper of a kiss. "Only you."

He pulled back, whisking his coat from the chair. "I'll be back tomorrow."

Olivia sagged against the wall. It was only a matter of time before she surrendered. Because of the money, and because she couldn't deny what he said…and he knew it.

He glanced at the pound notes strewn about by the breeze. "Keep the money. You'll pay the debt—somehow."

Her gaze strayed to the door.

He thrust his arms into his coat sleeves, his face stern and beautiful. "Don't run from me, Olivia. I'll find you."

At last, he left. Her knees wilted, and she slid to the floor. She couldn't be here come tomorrow. Though she knew it would infuriate him, she had to take the ten pounds and run. And pray he never found her.

Chapter Five

JASPER COULDN'T WAIT to hit someone. He strode toward the Black Horse Court and the tavern that bore the same name, his long gait devouring the cobblestones beneath his feet.

He still couldn't believe she'd deceived him. He didn't give his trust lightly, and tonight was a painful reminder why. Nevertheless, he still wanted her. More than he'd ever wanted anyone. More than Abigail.

And not just because of her beauty—Olivia was spirited and intelligent and unafraid to seek her own fortune. God, she'd set him afire. All while lying through her beautiful teeth.

He had great difficulty believing she wasn't a prostitute—the skill she'd displayed before blindfolding him was not that of a virtuous young maiden. Abigail had demonstrated no such prowess.

However, if Olivia were a prostitute, there was no reason for her to have concocted her swindle in the first place. She would've taken his money and provided her services. So why the ruse?

His pace slowed as he turned into the court. He assumed her financial situation was dire, but to blindfold him and leave him to the mercy of some unknown whore was inexcusable. He intended to discover the truth, and maybe, if she could manage to keep from telling more lies, he'd offer to help her in a manner that didn't involve fraud. And if he found her to be as innocent as she claimed, he would argue that trading her honor was never an acceptable solution. Ten years ago he'd allowed his honor to be stripped from him, and he would never, ever let it happen again.

Fisting his hands, he stalked into the crowded common room of the Black Horse Tavern. Sevrin typically sat at a table in the back corner with other members of the club. Jasper's gaze settled on them, and he made his way to the lone empty chair.

"Evening, Saxton. I'd offer you some gin," Sevrin gestured to the bottle on the table, "but I know you prefer whiskey."

Gin sounded just fine after the night he'd had. "Is there a spare cup?"

Sevrin chuckled and motioned for the serving girl, who quickly deposited a chipped mug on the table. Jasper didn't wait for niceties and poured himself a healthy draught. He took a deep, stinging drink, noting the entrance of two women, one with radiant red hair. She wasn't Olivia, but her presence reminded him of her duplicity.

"You ready for conversation yet?" Sevrin asked with a more than a bit of sarcasm. Jasper shot him a warning glance, but Sevrin didn't seem to care. He gestured to the lean young man sitting to his left. "This is Gifford. I don't think you've met."

Jasper contemplated the smoothness of Gifford's jaw, the narrow set of his shoulders. He wasn't terribly young, but neither had he reached full manhood. "Is he old enough to fight?"

Sevrin called for ale. "Don't be an old fart, Saxton."

"Will you fight tonight?" the young man asked.

"Aye." Jasper drained the cup, eager for the gin to take the edge off his emotions. Coupled with a good fight, soon he wouldn't feel a thing.

"Your knuckles have been bleeding, Sax," Sevrin observed. "You already get into it tonight?"

"A necessary interruption."

"I suppose that means you weren't at some Society event. Isn't there a ball or dinner party that needs your attendance?"

A musicale at Lady Ponsonby's, not that Jasper cared. "Probably."

Their ale was delivered—one tankard for each of the three men at the table. Sevrin took a long draught before saying, "I understand you'll be selecting a bride soon."

Jasper swilled the rest of his gin. "How do you know that?"

"My membership at White's is still intact." Sevrin grinned. "There are some things even stiff-necked Society pricks can't take from a viscount. I saw at least a dozen wagers in the betting book as to who she'll be. Care to give me a tip?"

"No."

A crash from the other side of the common room drew their attention. Then came a shriek. Gifford jumped to his feet. Jasper and the others followed.

The commotion grew. Gifford preceded them toward the

altercation. On the floor, a man straddled one of the women who'd entered. "Ye're coming with me."

She struggled, but the man was too big for her. Gifford reached down and threw him to the side. The boy was much stronger than he looked.

The man scrambled to his feet, but Gifford advanced on him. "You shouldn't beat up women." He grabbed the man by the front of his shirt and pushed him against the wall. His head hit the wood with a loud smack. Surprisingly, he didn't lose consciousness.

The tavern keeper rushed to Sevrin. "Not in the common room. We have an arrangement."

Sevrin nodded and moved to Gifford's side. He pulled on the lad's arm. "Go to the back. I'll take care of this." His voice was stern.

Gifford hesitated a moment, then he turned without a word.

"Go with him," Sevrin said to Jasper.

He nodded and followed the youth into the back room they used for fighting. He stepped over the threshold just as he heard a grunt. Gifford stood near the far wall shaking out his hand.

"Did the wall somehow offend?" Jasper crossed the room and studied the lad's hand. "I thought you meant to tear that man's limbs from his body."

"I might've, if not for Sevrin. If not for this club."

Though he'd only just joined, Jasper shared his sentiment. In the midst of Holborn's expectations, he'd needed something he could take inside himself and hold close. Fighting the other night and tonight dulled the sharp edges of his emotions, made the cold requirements of his station palatable. Jasper marveled at the commonality between him and this young man. "I think I understand."

Gifford gave a commiserative nod, his eyes burning bright. "You can do things here, be different here."

Sevrin stalked into the room. "Christ, Giff, you know the rules. No fighting outside this room."

"I know. I'm sorry." He said the words, but he didn't look contrite at all. The fire in his gaze was hot and vivid. "I just couldn't let him bully her."

"You might try words first next time." Sevrin motioned toward the makeshift bar along the wall. "Go on, Giff, have a drink." The young man took himself off, the obstinate jut of his chin suggesting he needed the libation.

A woman pushed open a back door that Jasper hadn't noticed during his previous visits. Several others tried to follow her inside, but Sevrin crossed the room and ushered them out. "Damn prostitutes."

Other members began arriving, each hailing Jasper with a strong handshake or a hearty greeting. Sevrin returned to Jasper's side. "Lightskirts from the neighborhood loitering in the hope of income."

Was Olivia one of them? "Tell me, is there a red-haired beauty among them?"

Sevrin's brows narrowed. "I don't think so. There's a carrot-topped woman, quite buxom, but I wouldn't term her a beauty. Wait, do you mean Olivia West? She lives across the street in Coventry Court with a group of women who do come here."

Jasper turned toward him sharply. "What do you know of her? Is she a prostitute?"

"She doesn't hang about with the others. Come to think of it, I've never seen her hawking her wares."

Just because Sevrin hadn't seen her didn't mean she was innocent. Of anything.

Sevrin clapped him on the shoulder. "You ready?"

"More than." Jasper shrugged out of his coat, eager to banish all thought of Olivia. At least for tonight.

THE FOLLOWING MORNING, Olivia tucked the last of her belongings—her mother's painted box containing Saxton's ten pounds—in her old valise. She'd also stuffed her sewing basket and tattered bag, but she'd still have to leave a few things behind and perhaps come back for them later.

She'd spent the night tossing fitfully. The heat in her tiny, airless room was more than enough to keep sleep away, but coupled with tormenting thoughts of Lord Saxton's kisses and the way she'd deceived him, she'd been helpless to do anything but stare at her ceiling. A ceiling she must now bid farewell. At least she could afford a decent place to stay for the short term.

She lugged her items down the four flights of stairs and set them in the corner of the entry hall. Brushing her hands on her skirt, she turned and went to Mrs. Reddy's door. She rapped twice and waited patiently for the landlady to appear.

The moment stretched, causing a bead of concern to wedge between Olivia's eyebrows as she stared at the door. She raised her hand to knock again, but the portal cracked open to reveal Mrs. Reddy's battered face.

"Livvie," she croaked and opened the door wider. "Come to check on me?"

"Are you all right, Mrs. Reddy?" Olivia tried not to wince as she looked at the damage to the woman's eye and throat. Memories of her mother's countless beatings pounded the recesses of her mind, but she refused to visit them.

Mrs. Reddy waved her hand. "Bah, I've had worse."

Olivia peered around the woman to see if she too had packed her things, but there was no evidence of it. "Are you ready to leave with Lord Saxton?" She kept the tremor from her voice. She could *not* be here when he arrived. Heavens, what if he was on his way even now? Oh, but surely earls didn't rise at this hour.

"I don't think I'm leaving. I'm comfortable here." She stuck her chin out in a thoroughly stubborn fashion.

Olivia wasn't surprised. "You must go. Unless you're content to die at Mr. Reddy's hands." She didn't say that lightly. Olivia firmly believed Mrs. Reddy could very well die from one of his beatings. She'd seen it happen firsthand.

"Doubt it. He likes havin' me to smack around." She exhaled heavily and glanced behind her. A piece of parchment sat atop her small dining table. "His lordship sent a note a little while ago. Threatened to haul me off to debtors' prison if I don't work off what I owe."

Of course he did. Just as he'd threatened Olivia with the magistrate. And then he'd sworn that she'd repay the debt after insisting she take his money. "Lord Saxton is ruthless. I wouldn't take his threats lightly." Not that Olivia was following her own advice. Even now, her feet itched to run.

Mrs. Reddy rubbed her dirty hand across her forehead. "I suppose. He'll be here soon anyway. Guess I have to make up me mind."

Olivia's breath seemed to evaporate right out of her chest. "Soon? When is he coming?"

"Noon."

Relief nearly collapsed Olivia's frame against the door. "He won't give you a choice. If you refuse his demand, he'll take you to prison."

"You think he'd do that?"

"In a trice. Don't you see you can't stay here? He's taken that option away from you entirely." *From both of us.* Anger burned beneath Olivia's already heated skin.

Mrs. Reddy's thin shoulders slumped. "I don't want to work for him."

Olivia didn't blame her, but for Mrs. Reddy it would be far preferable to her current existence. "It won't be bad. I'm sure his lordship is…kind." She reasoned it was acceptable to lie in order to better this poor woman's life.

"I suppose if I don't like it, I can leave."

"And it's not permanent. Once you work off the debt, you'll be truly free. Of his lordship and Mr. Reddy. Maybe you'll be even be able to help your sister."

"Oh, do you think his lordship might give her a job, too? She's far more respectable than me. She's never even had gin. She's a good mum to that sweet boy." Mrs. Reddy sniffed and swiftly pinched her nose, perhaps to stop a flow of tears. An uncharacteristic show of emotion, to be sure.

Olivia had no notion whether Saxton's benevolence would extend to Mrs. Reddy's sister, but if it would encourage the woman to go, why not agree? Especially when Mrs. Reddy clearly cared for her sister and nephew. "I'm sure he would. As I said, he seems kind. He came to your rescue, didn't he?" Ruthless, but kind. She'd never met anyone who could be both. Would it surprise her if he did something for Mrs. Reddy's sister? Olivia didn't want to answer that question. She wanted to get away from the boarding house as soon as possible. But she also didn't want to alert Mrs. Reddy to her departure, which is why she'd left her belongings in the corner.

"So you're decided then?" Olivia asked.

"I suppose I must be. You're a good girl, Livvie." She reached out and patted Olivia's sleeve.

Olivia smiled at the woman, glad this necessary interview was done—and that she'd achieved the desired result. Now she could escape. "I'd offer to help you pack, but I have a few errands I must run. I may be back before you go."

Mrs. Reddy winked at Olivia. "I'm sure his lordship would like that."

Olivia was sure he would, too.

She turned and waited for the door to latch behind her before she went to the corner and picked up her belongings.

Outside, Olivia hurried along the street, the morning sun finding its way into their little court and heating the pavement beneath her feet. Tilly stepped into her path. Her gaze dropped to the valise. "You're leaving?"

Olivia clutched her things tighter, perhaps a reaction to her newfound distrust of Tilly. She'd been a fool to trust her in the first place. She'd hoped to get away from Coventry Court without anyone realizing she'd left. "I'm afraid I must. His lordship was furious. You should've told me he'd discovered the ruse."

Tilly crossed her arms. "He said he'd turn me in to the magistrate. I'm not a good girl like you. I've got debts. I would've gone to Newgate for sure."

So she'd looked out for herself and ignored the consequences to Olivia. "You didn't think about what he might do to me?"

Tilly's eyes widened, and she searched Olivia's face. "He didn't hurt you, did he?"

Olivia pulled back at the vehemence in Tilly's tone. "No. Why would you think that?"

A shiver twitched Tilly's shoulders. "Meg saw him fighting last night at the Black Horse."

This shouldn't have surprised her, given his apparent penchant for violence. Twice she'd met him, and twice he'd fought. Granted, both acts had been for a good cause, but Olivia couldn't ignore the sense of dread curling up her spine. She was aware of the club, run by some viscount, and because of it had stayed as far away from the Black Horse Court as she could. "He's a member of that fighting club?"

"Must be. Lord Sevrin's particular about whom he lets in, and Meg said he was fighting."

A man who enjoyed violence enough to engage himself twice in one evening wasn't a man Olivia wanted to spend time with. It was good she was running. Necessary, even.

"Where will you go?" Tilly asked.

"I'm not sure." She wouldn't tell Tilly even if she knew. Trying to sound as uninterested as she ought to feel, she asked, "Did Saxton purchase anyone's services?"

Tilly giggled, a surprisingly charming sound from such a coarse woman. "Bit jealous?"

"So he did?"

Her giggle escalated to a laugh. "Not that I heard. It's not too late for you. Invite him over again."

Olivia kept her head bent so Tilly couldn't see the flush spreading up her neck. "Why would I willingly seek him out? He's furious with me and likes to hit people for fun."

"He was fairly angry with me and didn't lift a finger. Mayhap his fighting really is just sport. I don't think you need to be afraid of him, Livvie."

But she was. Afraid that she wanted him without care for his money or her position, that he would hurt her in ways that could never be seen on the outside. "Goodbye, Tilly. Do me a favor and don't tell anyone I've gone."

Tilly nodded. "You'll land on your feet. Girls like you always do."

That afternoon, after securing a small room in a clean inn that she could only afford for a short time—unless she wanted to spend the entire ten pounds on temporary lodgings, and she didn't—Olivia made her way along the Strand. Her multiple attempts to sell her wares had so far been fruitless, and with each rejection she found herself thinking of Saxton more and more. She could stretch the ten pounds for quite some time, but she suspected he'd give her more. But if she accepted more, he'd expect something in return—more than he already did.

Would a few nights of pleasure be so awful? It wasn't as if she would be committing to a life of selling her body, as her mother had done. It would be a temporary situation to provide for her long-term needs. Then there was the tiny voice in her head—the one that had kept her up all night. *Don't do it for the money. Do it for yourself.*

The sun burned hot through her bonnet and the lawn of her gown. The basket containing her sewn goods grew heavier with each block. By the time she reached Mrs. Gifford's shop, where she'd left ten handkerchiefs on commission a few days prior, Olivia felt flushed and overheated. The interior was blessedly cooler and she welcomed the relief.

A man emerged from the back as soon as she entered. He was similar in age to Olivia, which immediately put her at ease, as did his warm sherry-colored eyes. They made her feel welcome, comfortable. So different from Saxton's pale blue, which so often imbued a sense of danger or, perhaps more accurately, excitement.

"Good afternoon," he greeted, a smile lighting his face with charm.

"Good afternoon. My name is Olivia West, and I'm here to see the shopkeeper, Mrs. Gifford."

"That would be my mother. Do you have an appointment?"

"I don't, but I'm a seamstress and recently left some embroidered handkerchiefs on commission. I'd hoped she'd had occasion to sell them."

His brow gathered briefly, but in question, not concern. "By chance did these handkerchiefs bear roses and doves?"

Olivia's pulse quickened. "A few of them, yes."

"Allow me." He took her basket and ran his fingers over the topmost item. "Lovely. I think my mother sold all of your handkerchiefs just today. In fact, the woman who bought them wanted to meet you. She was most impressed with your needlework."

The best news! Perhaps she wouldn't need Saxton's money. Olivia barely restrained herself from grinning like a fool. "I'd be delighted to meet with her."

"I'll fetch Mother." He gave her a jaunty wink before depositing her basket on the floor and exiting the way he'd come.

Olivia squeezed her hands together, trying not to succumb to excitement. Just because the woman who'd purchased the handkerchiefs wanted to meet her didn't mean she'd order enough embroidery to solve all of Olivia's problems. Oh, but wouldn't that be grand? It was difficult not to let hope bloom.

Mrs. Gifford, a pleasant woman with a plump frame, emerged from the back room. Her cheerful face broke into a wide grin. "Good morning, Miss West. I'm so glad you've come today."

Mr. Gifford followed. Olivia immediately saw the resemblance in the shape of their eyes and the jut of their chins.

"I understand you've already met my son. Samuel is a dear boy." She looked at him with obvious love, a painful reminder of Olivia's loneliness. "Has he told you about your handkerchiefs? I sold all of them not an hour ago to a lovely woman. She's eager to meet you. In fact, she may still be shopping along the Strand. I'll send my apprentice after her."

Olivia could scarcely believe her luck, just when she needed it most. Fortune must surely be smiling upon her today. It was about time.

"Thank you, Mrs. Gifford. I'm happy to wait."

The shopkeeper nodded her silvery head. "I'll just go and send Becky off then. Samuel, why don't you take Miss West to the sitting room for tea?"

"Of course."

Mrs. Gifford departed to the rear of the store once more.

"The sitting room is just back here." Mr. Gifford retrieved Olivia's basket and led her through a curtained doorway to a small room containing a settee, chair, table, and dressing screen. Presumably this was where Mrs. Gifford conducted fittings.

"I'll just get the tea. Please, sit." Mr. Gifford indicated the striped settee.

Olivia sat and waited for him to return. Her mind continued to spin possibilities regarding the woman who'd purchased her handkerchiefs. Perhaps she would commission enough to allow Olivia to afford new lodgings. Beyond handkerchiefs, Olivia could offer embroidered gowns, furniture covers, and any number of accessories.

Mr. Gifford returned with the tea tray. It had been years since she'd taken proper tea at the vicarage with her foster mother, who was also her aunt. Olivia missed the civilized ritual of it, particularly when teatime with Fiona Scarlet had always included boisterous impropriety.

"Mr. Gifford, do you mind if I pour?"

"Not at all."

He sat in the lone chair while Olivia poured out. "Sugar?"

"Yes, please."

Olivia handed him his cup and then made her own. The first sip was heaven, but it could've tasted like dirt and she wouldn't have cared. Just the simple act of sitting in polite company and enjoying a cup of tea was enough to make this a perfect day. Add to that the potential for substantial income, and she was fairly ecstatic.

He peered at her over his cup. "Your skill with a needle is superior. You must have been embroidering for quite some time."

"Since I was a child. I find it relaxing, as well as profitable."

"My mother called you 'Miss West.'" His face reddened. "I wonder, that is, do you have an address at which I might call on you?"

Call on her? In her youth, she'd imagined gentlemen callers, a courtship, marriage. But in the ensuing years with her mother, she'd given up on such folly. Furthermore, she didn't yet have permanent lodgings. "I, that is, I don't have a residence appropriate for social calls." Goodness, that sounded awful.

"Alone in London… You're a brave young woman, Miss West." Respect shone on his face. "You're an independent seamstress then?"

Olivia nodded, liking that description immensely. She studied Mr. Gifford for a moment. The flesh around his left eye was puffy and red, with just a touch of purple that might be explained away as part of his complexion. However, seated in close proximity as they were now, she had a better vantage point. He definitely looked wounded. "Did something happen to you? Your eye…"

He set his cup down and gave a sheepish nod. "It's terribly embarrassing. I tripped down the stairs."

"Heavens. Are you all right?"

"Yes. I'm afraid I was carrying too many bolts of wool. I apprentice with Mr. Weston."

"Indeed?" He was nice-looking, courteous, and working for the most illustrious tailor in London. Furthermore, he seemed legitimately interested in *her*—not just her person. She allowed herself to feel…flattered.

The bell over the front door of the shop jingled. Olivia's gut clenched. She set her teacup on the table and smoothed her hands over her skirt, glad she'd worn her most respectable gown.

Mr. Gifford leapt to his feet as the curtain moved. An older lady— she was most certainly Quality—stepped through the panels. She was dressed in the height of fashion, but with nary a stitch of embroidery anywhere on her costume. Olivia suffered a moment's concern.

The lady's gaze immediately settled on Olivia. She looked her fill and then smiled, her diminutive features lighting up. She walked to

Olivia and took her hands. "My dear, I am so pleased to meet you. I'm Lady Merriweather."

Mrs. Gifford came in from the back door, which presumably lead to the rearmost room of the ground floor. "My goodness, Becky found you very quickly."

"Yes, and I'm so glad she did," Lady Merriweather said, glancing at the young woman who'd followed her through the curtain.

Olivia stood up and then had to look down at the tiny woman. Lady Merriweather possessed the most vividly blue eyes Olivia had ever seen. At once they made her feel charmed, delighted, and cared for. A peculiar reaction upon meeting someone.

Lady Merriweather turned to Mrs. Gifford, but didn't release Olivia's hands. "I wonder if I might speak with Miss West alone."

"Of course. Come, Becky, Samuel." Mrs. Gifford gestured for them to follow her. Becky departed with alacrity. Mr. Gifford, however, lingered a moment.

He bowed to Olivia. "It was my singular pleasure to take tea with you, Miss West. I look forward to our next meeting."

"Indeed, thank you." Though Olivia had very much enjoyed their tea, she couldn't wait for him to leave. She sensed a barely contained energy in Lady Merriweather, and her curiosity had the better of her.

Once they were alone, Lady Merriweather—still holding Olivia's hands—pulled her down to sit beside her upon the settee. She studied her for a moment, beaming. Olivia couldn't begin to imagine why the woman appeared so happy.

At length, Lady Merriweather relinquished her grip. She pulled one of Olivia's handkerchiefs from her reticule. It was Olivia's favorite with roses and vines decorating the edges.

"Can you tell me how you came to make this design?"

She'd replicated the roses and vines from the painted box that had belonged to her mother. The box in which Saxton's ten pounds currently resided. "I copied it from a memento in my possession."

Lady Merriweather pressed her eyes closed for a moment. When she opened them, there were tears in the corners. "May I ask how you came to have this memento?"

Olivia didn't know what to think of this woman's interest. "It belonged to my mother. She died last year."

Lady Merriweather patted Olivia's knee. "I'm so sorry, dear."

Although she wasn't comfortable with the sentiment, Olivia appreciated the woman's kindness. "We weren't close."

"Oh?" Lady Merriweather asked with a mixture of curiosity and concern.

Olivia wasn't used to this attention. She rather liked what it represented—another person's genuine interest—but she also wasn't terribly keen to reveal too much about herself. "I was fostered."

"I see. And your father?"

That revelation had wrought enough pain and bitterness to last a lifetime. Olivia preferred to lie instead. "He left."

Lady Merriweather reacted in the most unusual way. She took Olivia's hands again and grinned widely. "Miss West. I am here to help you. I believe—no, I know—my husband was your father."

The room swam before Olivia's eyes. *How could that be?* Her hands went slack in Lady Merriweather's grip. She'd been raised not knowing the identity of her father until the day she'd been evicted from the vicarage. Her aunt had furiously revealed that her uncle had sired Olivia with his sister-in-law, Olivia's mother. She couldn't very well share this shameful tale with the gracious and estimable Lady Merriweather. To do so would be to admit her bastardy, her uncle-father's perfidy, and her mother's wickedness. Not only could Olivia not afford to lose a chance for income, she couldn't bring herself to reveal humiliating truths to such an esteemed lady.

Lady Merriweather squeezed Olivia's hands. "Miss West? Are you all right?"

Olivia struggled to maintain a clear head. "Where is he, your husband?"

The shining happiness faded from Lady Merriweather's face, replaced with melancholy. "He died. I'm sorry you didn't get a chance to know him. I should like to remedy that, as best I can since he's no longer with us. I want you to come live with me."

The settee seemed to drop, or maybe that was just Olivia's stomach. She stared at Lady Merriweather's pale blonde hair streaked with white and her face lined with laughter and sadness. She seemed like a good person, someone Olivia could admire. What's more, she believed Olivia was family.

Was there a possibility this could be true? Fiona had never confirmed her paternity, despite Olivia asking. Furthermore, Olivia's uncle had allowed his wife to toss her out when she was but four and ten. Wouldn't a father try to protect his child?

Olivia took a deep breath, cognizant of the hope blooming in her chest. "How can you be so certain I'm Lord Merriweather's daughter?"

Lady Merriweather reached into her reticule and withdrew the handkerchief with the roses that Olivia had embroidered. "The design on the handkerchief, dear. You said you copied it from a painted box. I have an exact replica of that very design in a portrait he painted. There are other reasons, but we'll get to them in time. You need only understand that you *are* Merry's daughter. Without question." Lady Merriweather's blue-blue eyes regarded her with something that might have been pity, but Olivia didn't think it was. No, there was hope in the woman's gaze.

Olivia stared at the handkerchief, scarcely believing this remarkable turn of fortune. "You want me to live with you?"

"Yes. I've a townhouse in Mayfair. Please understand, I never knew you existed until after Merry died. I recently found a letter he'd written about you. I'm certain he would want us to be together. I would be honored if you would give me the chance to welcome you to our family."

Her invitation seemed too good to be true. Olivia simply couldn't comprehend the level of generosity and kindness this woman was demonstrating. Presumably Lord Merriweather—her father—had been unfaithful. Yet here his widow was welcoming his bastard daughter into her home, her life. This was the complete opposite of Aunt Mildred's reaction.

"Why?"

Lady Merriweather lifted one shoulder. "I have no children of my own. Merry's daughter is my daughter."

"You don't...you don't care he had a daughter with someone else?"

There was a twinkle in her eye when she answered. "I might've if he'd done so while we were married, but he knew your mother long before he met me."

Olivia relaxed slightly, allowed her incredulity to melt—just a little—into acceptance. This made a bit more sense. Lady Merriweather had lost her husband, a man she clearly loved and

missed. Olivia represented a link to that loss. Still, this was a great deal
to comprehend. She really ought to share the details of her upbringing
and questionable paternity, but the words wouldn't come, especially
when she longed for the viscountess's tale to be true.

"My lady, I am overwhelmed."

"I insist you call me Louisa." She pursed her lips. Olivia could
almost see the wheels of her mind turning. "We will need to develop
a story of course. You can't be my husband's daughter in Society, but
neither do I want you to be my paid companion. You're family."

Society? Good Lord, what could this woman mean for Olivia to
do? The thought of mingling in London society elicited a wave of
nausea. Because of Saxton. But surely she wouldn't run into him.

"I'm not certain I'm interested in joining Society, my lady. I mean,
Louisa."

"You needn't worry. You obviously possess excellent breeding,
dear." Louisa squeezed Olivia's hands. "We'll go get your things at
once."

Olivia quashed the panic rising in her throat. This was an
extraordinary opportunity. Not only to change her dire financial
circumstances, but to regain what she'd lost seven years ago—the
chance for a real family. A chance that may never come her way again.
If that wasn't enough, and really it was, she had to face the possibility
of accepting money from Saxton in exchange for her virtue and
become the one thing she'd sworn never to be.

In the end, there was no choice at all. She took a leap of faith in
the earnest woman beside her. "Yes, I'll come with you."

Chapter Six

THE COMFORT AND ease of White's encased Jasper like his favorite pair of riding boots. The murmur of conversation punctuated with sonorous exclamations, the sweet scent of brandy and the smoky waft of whiskey, the pomp and arrogance of nearly everyone present—yes, even that was palpable. Jasper reclined in a chair at a table he currently shared with Angus Black and the Earl of Penreith who'd immediately hailed him upon entry and proceeded to bombard him with questions about his absence, both from White's and from the usual Society whirl. If his father's interrogations were annoying, at least his chums had proven amusing.

Black refilled his glass with brandy from the bottle on the table. His brows gathered together, mired in suspicion. "Where did you disappear to the past several nights?"

Jasper pushed his empty glass toward Black for a pour. "I didn't disappear. I just didn't go to the events you attended."

"Ha." Penreith smiled in his typical lopsided fashion. "You weren't seen at *any* events. Save your mother's tea, but if you hadn't shown up there, I'd have thought you were dead."

"Many would prefer that fate."

Black and Penreith laughed. Jasper smiled at how easy it was to deflect his nosy friends.

The door opened, and Sevrin entered the warmly lit interior. He offered his hat and gloves to a footman. A subtle murmur crested about the room as he made his way inside. He paused by the betting book, perusing its contents, before continuing on. No one hailed his arrival or even nodded in greeting. Jasper drummed his fingers atop the table.

He'd never encountered Sevrin at White's. At least, Jasper didn't remember seeing him here. Jasper suffered a twinge of shame, thinking that until recently, he'd never given Sevrin a second thought. He held up his hand in welcome. "Sevrin," he called. Heads turned, a few jaws dropped, the murmur grew to a buzz. Curiously, Jasper found he enjoyed doing the unexpected. There was something freeing about indulging a bit of recklessness.

While Sevrin wove toward their table, Penreith and Black leaned in.

"What the devil are you doing?" Penreith hissed, although why he tried to keep his voice low, Jasper couldn't countenance. As if Sevrin wasn't wholly aware of his reputation and the reaction Jasper's invitation incited.

"Sevrin's a good sort." Jasper stood as Sevrin arrived.

Black and Penreith leaned back in their chairs.

"Saxton," Sevrin drawled.

"Sit with us. Have a brandy." Jasper gestured to one of two empty chairs at the table.

Sevrin and Jasper sat. A footman deposited another glass. As the brandy was still closest to Black, Jasper waited for him to pour. When he didn't, Jasper snatched the bottle up and took care of the service himself. He made a point of leaving the brandy next to Sevrin's glass.

Sevrin held up his libation. "To cordiality."

Jasper answered the toast, raising his brandy. Penreith downed the contents of his glass without pause. Black stared resolutely at the wall behind Jasper's head, refusing to acknowledge a toast had even been made.

Jasper frowned against the rim of his glass. His friends were behaving quite rudely. He drank and then replaced his glass on the table. He wanted to knock their heads together.

"That a new mount I saw you on the other day in the park, Black?" Sevrin asked, his joviality surprising in the face of the other men's contempt.

"Indeed."

Normally, Black would have waxed poetic about his newest horse. Jasper considered kicking him under the table. Instead, he threw him a scathing look.

"Don't see you at White's much, Sevrin," Penreith said.

Sevrin shook his head, his mouth set into an amused half-smile. "Usually too boring."

"For your ilk, I imagine so."

"What does that mean, his 'ilk'?" Jasper asked, purposely

provoking Penreith. He and Black begrudged Sevrin his membership rights because of the rumor that had tainted his reputation. If not for Holborn's interference ten years ago, Jasper would've endured the same ignominy. It hardly seemed just.

"You know, Saxton," said Sevrin. "I typically prefer livelier entertainment." Though he was a noted libertine and rakehell, Jasper had never seen him with a woman. Nor was he aware of Sevrin participating in any orgies or other salacious activities. In fact, outside of the fighting club, Jasper wasn't at all certain what Sevrin did with his time.

Both Penreith and Black sat a bit straighter in their chairs. Black lost his dark expression. Penreith gestured to the brandy bottle with a questioning look. Sevrin answered by pouring into Penreith's glass.

"Er, what sort of entertainment?" Black asked.

Jasper bit back a laugh. Their prurient curiosity had gotten the best of them. Scoundrels. They were no better than him or Sevrin.

Sevrin arched a brow. "Parties and establishments no one in Polite Society would dare frequent."

"Is it true…" Penreith licked his lips. "That is, do you really have your own suite at the Red Door?"

Sevrin lifted his glass, his lips twitching. "I'll never tell."

Suddenly, the air at the table seemed to loosen. Or perhaps it was simply the sticks falling out of Penreith's and Black's arses.

Another hush descended upon the room. A hasty beat of silence that heralded the arrival of a Terribly Important Person. Jasper's neck prickled. The duke.

Holborn's icy gaze surveyed the room quickly. He located Jasper, taking in his tablemates—or rather, just one tablemate in particular— and his mouth pulled down into a severe frown. He made his way toward them with the elegant grace of a cat on the prowl, instead of the aging gait of a man of four and fifty. Though his blond hair was liberally shot with silver and his frame wasn't as powerful as in his youth, women never failed to seek his attention. Furthermore, he rarely failed—surreptitiously, of course—to grant it. Holborn was nothing if not the master of discretion. Jasper wouldn't be surprised if the duchess had little knowledge of Holborn's liaisons, but rather thought the truth was she didn't care. Such a cold marriage.

The duke stopped near the table, but didn't breach the intimate circle surrounding it. His position clearly indicated he expected Jasper to come to him, and Jasper had expected such a summons given his absences the past few days.

"Please excuse me," he said to his companions as he stood.

Holborn led the way to the private chamber he kept for his personal use. The room was small but lavishly appointed. A painting from the duke's collection hung over the fireplace, proclaiming this small space as belonging to him. Even the chairs were the color of the Holborn livery: dark blue with gold-tasseled pillows.

Holborn ground his teeth, a sound that always served to put Jasper's nerves on edge. "You kept me waiting long enough. Unwise, since I'm only more annoyed with you now."

Typically, Jasper found the fortitude to ignore the duke's subtle irritations, but tonight Holborn's very presence had him tight as a new saddle. "Is that truly possible?"

The duke went to the sideboard and poured a glass of aged whiskey. He didn't offer any to Jasper, not that he'd expected such courtesy.

"You were sitting with that blackguard Sevrin. You can't associate with the likes of him."

If only the duke knew Jasper associated with worse at the fighting club. He'd hate Fitch the dockhand or Gifford the tailor's apprentice, which only made Jasper like them more. Jasper crossed to the sideboard and helped himself to some of Holborn's private stock. His whiskey really was superior. "Surely you didn't come here to bother me about who I drink with?"

Holborn ignored the question to fire his own. "What must I do to make you take your duty seriously?"

It wasn't as if Jasper had been a towering failure. He didn't gamble. He didn't drink excessively. He kept his proclivity for visiting tucked-away brothels, well, tucked away.

"With the exception of that incident ten years ago—which you'll never let me forget—I've been the model heir. I realize I'm not James, but seeing he's been gone these past two decades..."

The duke's eyes hardened to near silver. "Don't compare yourself to your brother."

Invoking James' name had been a foolish indulgence spurred by Jasper's irritation. He tried never to mention him because, though

James was long dead, to the duke he would always be the heir. That Jasper had inherited the courtesy title, that it was his *right* to be Saxton and some day Holborn, mattered not. His father's preference for his brother was a wound that never healed.

"If there's nothing else, there are a hundred places I'd prefer to be."

"Tell me whom you plan to court, and you may go."

"Really, and how would you endeavor to keep me here? It's been ages since you tried physical coercion, and I don't recommend you try it now."

The duke's nostrils flared, and his hands fisted. Jasper enjoyed the man's frustration. Holborn knew he couldn't follow through on his threats so easily. But in the end, Jasper was ready to reveal her name. While he hadn't been at the usual Society events the past few nights, he'd been working diligently to ascertain the lady's availability and inclinations. She was beautiful, intelligent, and absolutely above reproach. Also in the marriage hunt, she sought a title and an impeccable reputation—no rogues, no drunkards, no gamblers or spendthrifts. They would suit each other's requirements perfectly.

"Lady Philippa Latham." He quashed a gratifying smirk at the duke's surprise.

Holborn situated himself in one of the massive chairs. "She's amenable to the suit?"

"You needn't sound so shocked. I *am* heir to your dukedom."

"Isn't her father angling for some Flemish lord?"

Jasper had heard that rumor, but until an announcement was made, Lady Philippa was fair game, particularly since she was clearly on the hunt for a husband. "I've given you the name, so I believe we're finished."

Holborn's lip curled, but he said nothing, merely sipped his whiskey. After a long moment during which Jasper contemplated how it might feel to face Holborn in the room at the back of the Black Horse, the duke waved his hand, effectively dismissing Jasper.

Jasper briefly thought of staying, just to be contrary, but such games were for lads with far less experience than him. He turned and left, exhaling in an effort to release the tension roused by the duke.

As he returned to his table, he contemplated visiting Olivia later in the evening. She'd had time to reflect and was now, hopefully, ready to spend the night with him.

OLIVIA STOOD IN the center of her new dressing room at Lady Merriweather's—Louisa's—house on Queen Street in Mayfair. If she were barefoot, she was certain the thick, plush carpet would cushion her toes like the softest bed. Pale yellow paint brightened the walls of the windowless room. A wide oak armoire devoured an entire corner, while a dainty, turned-leg table with a small, slipper chair and a long, cushioned bench with a rose and cream pattern completed the furnishings. Olivia had never seen such fine things, let alone for her to use.

Her meager wardrobe filled a scant fraction of the armoire, but Louisa had promised a plethora of new clothes as soon as they could go shopping, which she'd indicated would be tomorrow.

In a daze, Olivia staggered back into the main bedchamber, a massive room that would easily hold her entire apartment with space to spare. Though she'd slept here last night, she'd wondered this morning if the entire previous day hadn't been a dream.

Her maid—her maid!—finished tidying the bed. Perhaps a decade older than Olivia, Dale seemed capable and intelligent—worldly almost. Her costume was made from finer fabric than most of Olivia's clothes. Olivia crossed her arms over her chest and fidgeted with the sleeve of her gown, feeling as if she didn't belong.

"Oh, I see you're already dressed. I could've provided assistance, miss." Dale offered a warm, friendly smile.

Olivia had never had help dressing. The notion was novel, if not frivolous. But then, much of everything she'd seen since arriving at Queen Street might seem frivolous compared to what she was used to. "That's quite all right. Thank you."

"Very good. Lady Merriweather has requested you meet her in the Rose Room."

The Rose Room? Olivia had seen precisely three rooms last night: the entry, her bedchamber, and the dining room. Four, she supposed, if one counted the dressing room and, really, how could she not count it? Must she also count the grand staircase with its gleaming marble and the gallery leading to her bedchamber with its numerous paintings and sparkling sconces?

Why was she counting rooms at all? Because the townhouse made her feel small. Awkward. Insignificant.

Dale gestured to the doorway. "I'll show you the way." She smiled so pleasantly, so helpfully that Olivia couldn't help but relax just a bit.

Olivia nodded, letting her arms fall to her sides. A moment lapsed before she understood she ought to precede Dale. Goodness, this would take getting used to.

They returned much the way they'd come last night, but upon reaching the entry made their way to the rear of the house to a large room with two bow windows overlooking a manicured garden. Olivia caught sight of roses, herbs, and some sort of climbing vine before Dale indicated she should go through a door to the left.

This had to be the Rose Room. Every bit of its décor was pink or red or cream in color, and the focal point, a large painting hanging between the windows, boasted a profusion of pink and red roses blooming all over the front of a stone manor house. The design of the curling vines was impossible to ignore—it was the same as the vines on Olivia's mother's painted box.

Her heart squeezed. There it was in front of her—proof she belonged somewhere. Proof she belonged *here*. The notion that Lord Merriweather, and not the vicar, was her father became more than mere possibility.

Louisa swept into the room through a different door. "Good morning! I trust you slept well. Dale, please ask Bernard to bring tea and scones." She turned to Olivia. "I wasn't sure how late you might sleep—new surroundings and all. Typically, I breakfast in the breakfast room, but we can enjoy a light repast here if you like."

Olivia warmed to Louisa's consideration. "That would be lovely."

Bernard was the kindly butler Olivia had met upon arriving. She wondered—not for the first time—how many servants Louisa employed. Olivia returned her gaze to the painting, enthralled by how precisely it matched her keepsake box.

Louisa came up beside her. "You see how I unequivocally know you're Merry's daughter. Your handkerchief is exactly the same."

"How is it you knew he had a daughter?" Olivia vaguely recalled Louisa mentioning a letter, but couldn't remember anything else.

Yesterday had been so full of surprise and wonder.

With a gentle touch to Olivia's elbow, Louisa guided her to a rose-patterned, silk-covered settee. Once they were situated, Louisa said, "Merry, bless his soul, passed three years ago. It took me awhile to recover and go through his things." She paused a moment. "I found a letter from your mother—at least I assume she was your mother, but perhaps you'll be able to confirm."

For the first time Olivia noticed a piece of parchment in Louisa's hand.

Louisa continued, "I must admit, I was upset Merry hadn't confided in me, but I can only trust he had his reasons. You see, I always hoped we might have children of our own, but it wasn't meant to be. I was too old when we wed—past forty." Her smile was sad, full of dreams that would never be. Olivia's throat constricted. "I suppose Merry thought it would be painful for me to know he had a child with someone else. He was exceedingly considerate." She handed the letter to Olivia.

Olivia unfolded the missive and recognized the handwriting at once. She'd seen enough of her mother's stage notes to know this letter had indeed been drafted by Fiona Scarlet.

Dearest Merry,
Thank you for the gift. I've taken care of the child—a beautiful daughter.
She will be raised with love and kindness.
Yours,
Fi

Short and quite disputable. She didn't mention *his* child. Nor did she specifically mention receiving a painted box from him. Still, these things were implied and if Louisa was wont to believe them, Olivia wouldn't argue. Especially since she wanted to believe them, too. The chance for this life, to not struggle anymore, to belong... Her throat constricted painfully. Tears welled in her eyes. She blinked furiously, not wanting to cry in front of Louisa.

She refolded the paper and set it on Louisa's lap. "I still can't believe you want me to live here with you."

"Of course I do, dear. You aren't married. You were living alone. Clearly, you needed assistance, and I..." Louisa looked away, but

Olivia saw her blinking. She took the letter and set it on the table in front of the settee before turning to Olivia with an over bright smile. "May I ask who raised you?"

Olivia wanted to hug the other woman, but worried it was too soon for such familiarity. "My aunt and uncle, who's a vicar."

"And what happened to them?"

What could she say? *My aunt expelled me because she believed I was her husband's bastard?* "They had difficulty supporting me. When I was old enough, I came to London to work as a seamstress."

Louisa patted her hand. "I must say I'm shocked you left on your own, and that your foster parents allowed it. Where were you raised?"

"Devon."

She shook her head. "Devon must be full of fools. I can't believe some nice gentleman didn't snatch you up."

One might have done if she hadn't been evicted at four and ten. Olivia said nothing.

Louisa smiled widely, perhaps sensing Olivia's discomfort. "How fortunate that I came upon you as I did."

Bernard chose this opportune moment to enter with the tea service. His timing was so impeccable, in fact, Olivia wondered if he'd eavesdropped. Perhaps that was one of many tools employed by an exceptional servant. He poured out the tea and arranged butter scones on two plates. With a bow, he left as quietly as he'd entered.

"Now, as I said earlier, we need to explain your presence," Louisa said, adopting a business-like tone. Olivia had the sense this woman was used to taking charge. "I can't, of course, present you as Merry's daughter. I want you to move in Society. Enjoy a Season. Find a husband."

Olivia wasn't sure she wanted Society or a Season. A husband? She'd only just begun to consider courtship after her pleasant tea with Mr. Gifford.

Louisa continued, "I've thought this through. I shall introduce you as Merry's distant cousin. As it happens, there is a far-flung branch of his family in Devon, so that works quite nicely. We'll say your parents died—which isn't a fib since they are both deceased—and you've come to live with me. No one will care too much about the particulars, so we needn't be specific. If someone asks where you grew up, just tell them the truth."

Olivia nodded, saying, "Newton Abbott, a tiny village in the middle of Devon." Where everyone knew everyone and though she'd left seven years ago could probably identify Olivia by name if not face. She tried not to think of that.

"That's right, dear. We'll say your mother was related to Merry's branch of the family, but unfortunately any documentation has been lost to fire." Louisa grinned. "I'm quite good at this. Perhaps I should pen a novel."

Olivia wanted to share Louisa's good humor, but the possibility of recognition from her brief stint at the Haymarket lingered, as did her unease. She considered telling Louisa. She owed it to the woman to be forthright, but the words wouldn't come. How likely was the possibility that someone would discern an understudying minor actress was Lady Merriweather's new ward? She settled for a half-truth. "What if someone recognizes me from a shop? I've done work for a fair number of seamstresses."

"I understand your trepidation, dear, but you mustn't be nervous. Even if you look somehow familiar, no one will suggest you're anything other than what I present you to be. At least, no one with proper breeding," she added with a flash of a smile.

Olivia wasn't sure she agreed. Perhaps in a few days she'd feel less like a child about to be knocked down by a runaway horse.

"It's very important this secret stay between just the two of us, Olivia. No one can know the truth. Do you understand?"

Olivia nodded, though the serious tone of Louisa's words did nothing to ease her worry.

"Excellent. The very next thing we shall do is expand your wardrobe." Louisa tapped an elegant finger against her lip. "I hope you don't mind if we don't visit Mrs. Gifford. I'm deeply grateful to her for bringing us together, but she hasn't the variety or quality of Bond Street. I'm partial to Madame Oseary."

Olivia's excitement at visiting Bond Street—a place she couldn't obtain work, let alone purchase anything—was tempered by her anxiety about encountering someone who might recognize her. She'd very rarely worked directly with Quality, so her apprehension was probably unnecessary, but she couldn't completely discount it. "If it's all the same, I'd prefer to make my own clothing. We need only shop for fabric and such." The less time she spent working with seamstresses who might know her or had heard her name—goodness, why hadn't she thought to adopt a different surname?—the better.

Louisa's sympathetic smile was well-meaning. "My dear, you needn't toil in that manner any longer."

It wasn't toiling if she did it for herself. "Truly, I enjoy sewing. I could probably assemble the necessary items before anyone else could. I have some designs…"

"You design gowns?"

Olivia blushed at the other woman's sharp interest. "Yes."

Louisa smiled broadly. "Further proof! As if we needed it. Your artistic skill is surely a gift from your father."

Olivia's gaze drifted again to the painting. Although Louisa was confident in Olivia's paternity, she wasn't as certain. It didn't make sense for two different women to claim she'd been sired by two different fathers. She wanted more proof than the roses and her ability to sketch. "Do you have a portrait of him? My father, I mean?"

Louisa set her cup down with a loud clack. "Certainly! I meant to show it to you straightaway." She went to a table under the painting of the rose-covered manor house and picked up a small portrait.

She brought it back to the settee and handed it to Olivia. "This is your father. There are other portraits I'll show you later, but this is one of my favorites. He painted it himself, and so I keep it there, close to the painting he did of our house in Yorkshire." She settled back down next to Olivia.

Olivia studied the small portrait of the viscount. His eyes looked dark, but it was hard to discern on such a small piece. Perhaps the other portraits Louisa planned to show her would reveal the true color. He wore a powdered wig. "What color was his hair?"

Louisa smiled at the portrait in Olivia's hands. "Quite dark." She glanced at Olivia's head. "But I'd wager your hair came from your mother."

"Yes." A flamboyant stage name—Fiona Scarlet—to match not only her hair, but her spirit. Olivia was grateful Louisa didn't seem to know her mother's identity. How would she feel knowing her husband had sired a child with one of London's most notorious actress-courtesans?

Olivia set the portrait on the table next to the tea service. "Your husband's skill was exceptional."

"I don't suppose you've ever used watercolors?"

Olivia shook her head.

"You shall have lessons," Louisa said. "Merry loved to go to Hampstead Heath and paint. We'll take a picnic there."

Watercolor lessons? Picnicking? This new life swirled before Olivia as tempting as the scones on the table. Olivia put her plate on her lap. It had been ever so long since she'd enjoyed such sumptuous fare. Ever so long since she'd enjoyed anything as much as the past day.

"Certainly, my lord." Bernard's voice came from outside the Rose Room.

"It sounds as if we have a visitor." Louisa grinned. "I imagine it's my favorite person."

"And who is that?" Olivia pulled a bit of scone away and popped it into her mouth.

"My nephew."

A tall, fair-haired devil dominated the doorway. Olivia promptly choked.

Chapter Seven

JASPER STOOD STUNNED, but Olivia's distress galvanized him to rush to her side. Her mouth and neck worked while her face flushed crimson with the effort to dislodge whatever clogged her throat.

What the bloody hell was she doing here?

Louisa looked up at him with panic in her eyes. "Help her!"

He pulled Olivia to her feet. She continued to hack. Instinctively, he patted her back. No improvement. "Bend over."

Olivia looked at him, her eyes full of storms, and did as he bade.

He gave her back a swift thwack and finally heard a deep gasp of air enter her lungs. His hand lingered on her spine. *Was she really here?* After a moment, she straightened then fixed him with a wide-eyed stare. He inched backward, hoping distance might improve his ability to think clearly.

"Goodness, Olivia, are you all right?" Louisa stroked Olivia's back as they both sank to the settee.

Olivia nodded. Was she still trying to get her throat in working order or unable to find her tongue?

Jasper tried to make sense of her presence in his aunt's drawing room. He'd gone to see her last night only to learn she'd left the boarding house with no direction. No one else in the dingy board house seemed to know anything, other than she was gone. He'd considered going to Portia's Garden to interrogate Tilly but had ultimately returned to Saxton House. There, he'd questioned Mrs. Reddy, whom his footman, March, had removed to Saxton House earlier in the day. Unfortunately, she'd claimed to know nothing about Olivia leaving, and Jasper reluctantly believed her.

Frustrated and bitterly disappointed, he'd spent the remainder of the evening in the comforting confines of the back room at the Black Horse.

Today, however, was a new day. He'd planned to search for Olivia after visiting Louisa, yet here she was. If he weren't so stupefied by her presence, he would've been quite satisfied.

He pinned her with a probing stare, which she ignored. In fact, her refusal to look at him would surely draw his aunt's attention. For now, however, Louisa seemed oblivious.

"Olivia, this is Saxton. Jasper, allow me to introduce Miss Olivia West. She's a cousin to Merry, and I've taken her in. Isn't that splendid?"

Cousin to Uncle Merry? A Banbury tale if Jasper had ever heard one. Her scheme to defraud him had failed, and here she was in his aunt's house. *Living here.* He had to assume this ruse had something to do with him. Of the hundred questions that sprang to mind, he started with, "And how did you come to 'take her in', Aunt?"

Louisa's eyes narrowed. "Now, Jasper, don't behave like the duke. Olivia's parents died earlier this year, and she came from Devon looking for her extended family. I'm only sorry it took so long for us to find each other."

He couldn't help looking at Olivia. "Devon?" Then he turned his attention to his aunt. "Odd you never mentioned her."

Louisa arched a brow. Her eyes said, *careful.* "Didn't I? Well, you've been awfully busy of late."

This was embarrassingly true. He hadn't seen her as much as he ought given the fighting club and the charlatan currently gracing Louisa's settee.

Olivia finally looked at him. "I'm pleased to meet you, my lord."

He couldn't let it be that easy, not when he didn't trust her a whit. "You look terribly familiar Miss West. I feel certain we've met."

Olivia's gaze sharpened.

Louisa looked between the two of them. "You can't have met her before, Jasper. Not unless you shop in the Strand." She pierced him with an inquisitive stare. "Do you shop in the Strand?"

The actress had fooled her but good.

"No, of course not." He smiled artificially at Olivia. "I think I know. She looks like an actress I saw the other night at the Haymarket. Yes, that's it."

Olivia's eyes widened an infinitesimal amount, and he allowed himself a smug smile.

Louisa pursed her lips. "Oh, balderdash. Jasper, you're acting like Holborn. Sit down and behave yourself."

Jasper sat, but kept his gaze riveted on Olivia. Oh, she was an excellent actress. She'd watched their exchange with even breaths and nary a spot of color to her complexion. Absolute serenity. As if they discussed luncheon, or whether to ride or walk to the park. But then she'd also completed her seductive trickery with the practiced ease of one born to deception.

Louisa patted Olivia's knee. "Ignore Jasper, dear. He can be a bit of an oaf from time to time, but I love him anyway so do try to overlook his boorishness."

Jasper stared at his aunt's hand feeling a surge of protectiveness. Louisa was *his* aunt. His family. His to keep safe from harm.

Olivia coughed. "I believe I require some water after that incident with the scone."

Jasper got up to go to the sideboard where there was a pitcher of water, but Olivia's gaze found his, arresting his movement.

"Would you mind tapping my back again?" she asked. "I think perhaps a crumb might still be lodged in my throat."

"I'll fetch the water." Louisa hastened to the sideboard.

Jasper sat next to Olivia on the settee and patted her back. Softly, he said. "You're lying to her as you did to me—"

"Don't," she hissed. "Please. Don't tell her about the Haymarket, about…us. You said you wanted to help me."

He steeled himself against the anguish in her tone. "Not at the cost of my aunt's well-being. She deserves your deception even less than I did. I don't believe for a moment you're Merry's cousin."

She clutched at his sleeve, her eyes wide, pleading. "She wants me here. And I have no employment aside from selling handkerchiefs." Her gaze darted to Louisa who had finished pouring.

Of course, this was a far better opportunity than either being his mistress or operating a dress shop. But this wasn't just about her. He had to protect his aunt. He didn't want to see her hurt, not after the depression she'd suffered following Merry's death.

"Please, I can explain everything to you." The anguish in her voice won her a reprieve—for now.

"I'll be watching you. Very, very closely," he said. "And I expect your full and *honest* explanation."

Though he'd fallen prey to Olivia's lies before, he'd have to be as cold as his father not to sympathize with her desperation. Add

Louisa's longing for a child of her own, and he wasn't sure he could bring himself to ruin their sudden connection. Finally, and perhaps most of all, meddling in Louisa's choices felt dangerously like his father's interference in Jasper's life ten years ago. He'd yet to be grateful.

Louisa returned with the water. Olivia peered at Jasper over the rim of the glass as she drank. When she was finished, she handed the empty glass to a concerned Louisa, who placed it on the table.

"Are you feeling better now, dear?" she asked.

Olivia nodded and offered a weak smile. Her gaze kept shifting to Jasper. He read the anxiety—and fear—there and resigned himself to allow this charade for the time being. He turned to his aunt. "What plans do you have for Miss West? May I accompany you somewhere?"

Louisa arched a brow at Jasper. He realized he was still rubbing Olivia's back. Abruptly, he dropped his hand and moved it to his lap. Louisa nodded, thoroughly approving his change in attitude or perhaps the removal of his hand from her charge's person. "That would be lovely. Olivia requires a new wardrobe, so we're going to Bond Street tomorrow. Do you believe she can sew her own gowns? Design them, too!"

He didn't know how to comment on any of that without encouraging a familial connection that he didn't believe existed. So he said nothing but, "I'd be happy to escort you tomorrow. And the day after that. In fact," he gave Olivia a purposeful stare, "consider me at your utter service."

"Lovely." Louisa grinned at him, her eyes crinkling at the corners. "I know you only have my best interests at heart. I assure you, dear, Miss West is exactly who she claims to be. You have my word."

Unfortunately, he didn't have Olivia's. Her fingers flexed and Jasper remembered them caressing his bare chest, disrobing him, brushing against his erection. She'd coerced him into a blindfold, tied him to her bed, and left him to the ministrations of someone else. Miss Olivia West was a master of deception, and he meant to uncover every lie.

THE FOLLOWING MORNING, Jasper—Louisa always referred to and addressed him as Jasper and so Olivia had already taken to first-naming him in her head—arrived sharply at ten of the clock to escort them on their shopping excursion. The rest of their visit yesterday had gone quite well, with no further mention of her origin. Nevertheless, Olivia remained on her guard.

His appearance in the Rose Room had shaken Olivia to her very roots. Louisa hadn't said a word about his insinuations, for which Olivia ought to be grateful, but she couldn't shake a niggling dash of guilt. She should tell Louisa the truth, that she *had* been on stage at the Haymarket, but fear of losing what she'd only just discovered kept her mouth firmly closed.

Their first stop was Deacon and Bothe, one of the largest linen drapers in London. Olivia's steps dwindled to nothing as she entered a seamstress' wonderland. Fabrics of every kind, color, and pattern filled the store. Her fingers longed to stroke every piece. Her feet twitched to dance between each vibrant display. Her eyes couldn't fix on just one thing, instead devouring everything with a child's Twelfth Night-glee.

Jasper and Louisa came abreast of her in the shop.

"Where shall we start, Olivia?" Louisa asked.

Overwhelmed by the need to wrap herself in every square inch of fabric, Olivia tried to focus. "Chronological, I think. Day gowns?"

With a crisp nod, Louisa led the way to a display of muslins and cottons. They spent over quarter of an hour discussing patterns and styles. An employee came to their assistance, noting which fabrics and the quantities they wished to purchase. They moved on to other areas, ultimately finding themselves at a table of rich silks.

Olivia's eye was immediately drawn to a silvery blue shot with dark indigo stripes.

Louisa noted her interest. "You like that? It's rather masculine, but I suppose it would make a nice skirt."

Olivia did like it, but not for herself. The color—minus the stripes of course—reminded her of Jasper's eyes. She snuck a glance at him only to find their full attention upon her. The look he directed, as if they were the only people in the draper's, was dangerous.

She turned back to Louisa. "This would make an excellent

waistcoat for Saxton."

Louisa studied the fabric. "You've such an eye. It certainly would." She motioned to the employee trailing them to mark this down on their list of purchases. "Do you have a design in mind? I didn't realize you fashioned men's clothing as well. How extraordinary."

And probably inappropriate. No, she'd never designed men's clothing before, but the fabric was too perfect for him. A picture of his bare, muscular chest rose, unbidden, in her mind and a design for the waistcoat came along with it. Was it horribly scandalous for her to think of him wearing it without a shirt?

Yes.

She bowed her head to hide her overheated cheeks, hoping Louisa and Jasper wouldn't note her reaction to her thoughts. After a moment in which she composed herself, she said, "I haven't constructed any men's apparel. I'm certain his tailor can manage it."

Jasper removed his glove and stroked the silk. The gesture was more than a bit provocative. He looked at Olivia. "I'd rather you made it."

If she were honest, she'd thank him for the opportunity. The challenge of designing something new was incredibly tempting. Of course, she'd have to measure him and conduct one, perhaps two, fittings. All of that meant time with him. Time *touching* him.

Louisa perhaps sensed Olivia's hesitation. "You should do it if you like. I'll chaperone, of course."

She *did* want to. And if Louisa would chaperone, well then it would be perfectly safe, wouldn't it? "All right, then."

They concluded their business at the linen draper's and exited the shop. Louisa gestured down the right side of the street. "I thought we'd visit the boot maker next. You'll need several pairs, including riding boots."

"That won't be necessary," Olivia said. "I don't ride."

"You don't like riding, dear?"

"No, it's not that. I've never done it." Olivia hated admitting this in front of Jasper. He would likely interpret this information as support of his theory that she was lying about being Merry's cousin. Certainly, the cousin of a viscount would have ridden a horse. Except that Louisa had advised her not to lie, and so she wouldn't. She decided to add, "My parents had but one horse." Which was true—

her aunt and uncle had possessed a rather ancient nag. "We preferred to walk most everywhere. The country is like that, of course."

Louisa nodded. "Well, a riding lesson shan't come amiss then! She's also to have a watercolor lesson in a few days' time, Jasper."

But Jasper didn't seem to be paying attention any longer. He was staring at a boy—perhaps ten years old—struggling to carry far too many packages for his tiny frame. He seemed to be trailing a pair of women who'd no idea he'd fallen behind to pick up a parcel he'd dropped. He bent at the knees, trying to keep the remaining packages balanced in his arms when—*crash*—the lot went tumbling to the sidewalk.

The two women turned with identical faces of shock and dismay. Identical because they appeared to be twins. "Logan! You pathetic whelp! Pick up those packages at once!" one of them ordered, while the other approached him with her umbrella outstretched. She couldn't mean to…

The umbrella landed on the poor child's back as he knelt to pick up the parcels. She lifted the weapon a second time, but it didn't fall. Jasper's hand clutched the end of it and pulled it from the woman's grasp.

She sucked in her breath and raised her head to look at Jasper. "Of all the audacious—" As soon as her gaze connected with Jasper's, the words died on her lips. Lips that suddenly stretched into a grotesque attempt at a smile. "Goodness, my lord. I didn't see you there. I'm sorry, is our boy in your way?"

"Not at all." He still held the woman's umbrella. With his other hand, he helped the lad to his feet. "Are you all right?"

"Yes, my lord." He kept his gaze firmly on the ground.

Jasper seemed to know the boy. "Logan, I should like you to call at Saxton House on Upper Brook Street. I can see this assignment isn't for the best, and I've something else in mind. Here." He removed a card from his pocket and gave it to Logan. "Give this to my butler—Thurber is his name—and tell him I sent you."

Finally, the boy looked up at him, his huge hazel eyes brimming with tears. "But my lord, my mother…"

"This new arrangement requires your mother, too."

The boy swiped his hand over his eyes. "Yes, my lord."

"Very well, then." He turned his gaze, now frost-laden, to the twins. "Please have the Logans' things delivered to Saxton House as soon as possible. Logan, do stop to fetch your mother on the way."

The boy smiled tremulously. "Thank you, my lord." He dashed off.

"But," whined one of the twins, "who shall carry our things?"

Jasper toed one of their packages with his gleaming black Hessian. "That is none of my concern."

Olivia knew how frigid his stare could be, but couldn't feel sorry for the women given how they'd treated young Logan. She could, however, gaze in wonder at Jasper. He really was a decent sort. So different from any other man of her experience. Which made her deception all the more painful.

Olivia looked at him with a burst of respect. "That was most kind of you."

Louisa nodded as she patted Jasper's forearm. "It seemed as though you knew that boy."

"Just someone with a pitiful plight. I recently employed his aunt and had thought to arrange a good situation for him and his mother. Clearly I was unsuccessful with the first try." The grim set of his mouth told Olivia he was not used to failure and it rankled him most fiercely.

Then it hit her—Mrs. Reddy. That was Mrs. Reddy's nephew. Not only had he helped her, he'd also made certain her sister and child didn't suffer.

"Where will they go?" she asked, curious to see how Saxton would ensure their care, but also knowing he absolutely would.

A hint of a smile tugged up one corner of his mouth. "As it happens, I know a boot maker whose family is in need of a new housekeeper." He stared at her in unspoken communication.

Did he mean The Beattys? Had he helped them too? She couldn't help but smile at him. In fact, she had to repress the urge to hug him.

Her smile faltered—she hadn't wanted to hug a man since her uncle, and that had been years and years ago. Her guard was failing, and though Jasper was different from her mother's men, she still couldn't afford to trust him.

Chapter Eight

SEVERAL EVENINGS LATER, Louisa's carriage halted in Berkley Square before a large townhouse at precisely eight o'clock. With its glowing windows and cheerful guests marching up the stone steps, it seemed inviting. However, Olivia was reminded of the Lord's Prayer, which she'd oft repeated in her youth. *Lead us not into temptation…*

"Are you ready, dear?" Louisa patted Olivia's arm while Jasper stepped from the coach.

She summoned a smile but felt as though it might break her face. "As ever."

Louisa nodded and climbed down with Jasper's assistance. Olivia slid to the other end of the cushion, her nerves tightening. Over the past several days, she'd done her best to prepare for this debut into Society, but now, confronted with her imminent presentation, stark fear glued her to the seat. Though Louisa had assured her this was a tiny dinner party, perfect for a first foray, Olivia's stomach knotted with dread.

Jasper held up his hand. Despite her overly tense state, little shivers skittered along the bare flesh above her glove and beneath the puffed sleeve of her silk gown. They'd spent plenty of time together in recent days, but never alone, and his unanswered questions burned between them.

"Are you coming out?" He gave her a half-smile that made her heart miss a beat.

"Yes."

Olivia gathered her skirt between her fingers and stepped down with his aid. The trio ascended the steps to Lord Farringdon's townhouse where they were admitted into an entry chamber glistening with polished marble, and then to the drawing room where the other guests mingled. Olivia clung to Jasper's arm. So many people. Over thirty. More than she'd anticipated. Next time she would ascertain from Louisa what she meant by "tiny."

Jasper leaned down and spoke near her ear. "Don't be nervous. If anyone can maneuver these people, it's you."

Louisa still clutched his other arm and immediately struck up a conversation with the first person they encountered. Introductions were made, and Olivia did her best to remember the gentleman's name, Sir Barnaby Addicock.

Jasper offered to fetch drinks. Olivia watched him complete the task. In the meantime, others joined their circle, which meant more introductions and more names.

"And where is it you hail from, Miss West?" asked Sir Barnaby, wielding a quizzing glass.

"Devon."

"Goodness, that's quite far."

The woman next to him—his wife, Lady Addicock—tapped his elbow with her fan. "My mother grew up near Exeter." She peered at Olivia with interest. "Are you familiar with Exeter?"

"I'm from a very tiny village."

Jasper returned with glasses of sherry for both her and Louisa. Olivia accepted her glass, her fingers brushing his.

Lady Addicock asked, "Do you know Whitestone?"

Olivia shook her head, glad the woman hadn't said Newton Abbott.

"Mother married out of there as soon as she could and never looked back. How are you finding London?"

"Splendid, thank you," Olivia said with more courage. The conversation wasn't going badly at all. Jasper was right, she could manage this.

The woman winked at Louisa as she said, "Lady Merriweather must be treating you to all the sights. Vauxhall yet?"

Olivia shook her head again. She'd been to Vauxhall many times, but never to the boxes these people surely visited.

"The theatre? Of course not, it's summer. Oh, but the Haymarket is running."

A surge of anxiety crested in Olivia's chest, squeezing down on her lungs. She purposely avoided looking at Jasper, instead sipping her sherry. Gulping the amber liquid suddenly held great appeal.

The woman turned to her companion. "Isn't Colman a friend of yours?" The man nodded.

She looked back to Olivia. "Colman manages the Haymarket. Lively fellow."

They knew Colman. Olivia knew Colman. He's the one who'd sacked her. It was too close, too disturbing. She looked about the room, desperate for some sort of escape. A young woman close to Olivia's age stood near their host. She offered Olivia a kind smile.

Lady Addicock continued on. "In fact, why don't we all see a play at the Haymarket tomorrow evening? It would be a dashing good time!"

Olivia snapped her attention back to the conversation around her just as Jasper bumped her elbow, sloshing sherry down her front. "Pardon me, Miss West. I'm not usually so graceless." He regarded her intensely.

She dabbed at her bodice with a handkerchief. That was no clumsy accident. He'd intervened to stop the discussion, but why? To protect her? She looked up at him, but his pale blue eyes revealed nothing.

"Come dear, we'll find the retiring room," Louisa said, taking her elbow.

As they crossed the room, a young woman greeted them. She was slightly taller than Olivia, with a cheery, round face framed with curls the color of the rich chocolate Olivia had enjoyed at Louisa's that morning—such a luxury. "Good evening, Lady Merriweather. Grandfather told me you were bringing your new ward. This must be her."

"Yes, Audrey, dear, this is Miss Olivia West. Olivia, this is Mr. Farringdon's granddaughter, Miss Audrey Cheswick. I wonder, Audrey, if you wouldn't mind showing us to the retiring room. I'm afraid my nephew was a bit clumsy with his drink."

"It's no trouble." She took Olivia's arm. "You're welcome to stay here, Lady Merriweather, I'll have Miss West sorted out in no time."

"Thank you, but I should probably accompany Olivia."

While Olivia was grateful for Louisa's concern, she wanted to show Louisa she was capable. Perhaps she even wanted Louisa to feel proud of her. "Why don't you stay and enjoy yourself? This won't take but a trice."

"You're certain?" Louisa gave her a searching look, underscoring her question. Her awareness and sensitivity to Olivia's nerves was touching.

"Absolutely." She gave Louisa's hand a comforting pat and then allowed Miss Cheswick to lead her from the room.

Miss Cheswick guided her back through the entry hall to a marble staircase. "Grandfather says you're new to Town."

Olivia ascended with her. "Yes."

"Is it overwhelming? I've lived in London my whole life, save summers, of course. Well, except this summer. I stayed with Grandfather instead of retiring to Sussex with my parents." Small swathes of pink colored her upper cheeks. "Sorry, sometimes I ramble. That's why I'm here and not in Sussex. Mother thought I could do with a bit more Town polish."

Olivia's tension eased at Miss Cheswick's familiarity. Perhaps Louisa had been right, and she'd already made a friend.

At the top of the stairs, Miss Cheswick led her to the right and then into a chamber. "This is the retiring room. Actually, it's the upstairs sitting room. And just through there," she gestured to another door, "is a small office my grandmother used to draft correspondence. She was a great letter-writer." Miss Cheswick smiled fondly.

Her casual reminiscences of family reminded Olivia how fortunate she was to have found Louisa. Instead of someone else's happy recollections eliciting a hollow ache, she felt warm contentment spreading through her.

Miss Cheswick frowned down at Olivia's dress. "That's quite a stain. Saxton spilled his drink on you?"

"Yes, but I'm sure I can get it out." Olivia tried to bite back the words, but it was too late. "I mean my maid, of course."

Her hazel eyes sparked with interest. "Did you used to launder your own clothing?"

Olivia wasn't certain how to answer, but once again followed Louisa's advice and offered the truth. "Country life is very different from here." *As was unprivileged London life.*

"Extraordinary. You can get that spot off your dress?"

"Probably." Olivia could and would likely offer her suggestions to Dale. For now, she wanted to get back downstairs to Louisa. "Miss Cheswick, I don't suppose you have something I could use to cover this—a wrap perhaps?"

"Please, call me Audrey." She nodded. "I've just the thing. A beautiful ivory Norwich shawl. I'll go and get it." She left the way they'd entered, closing the door behind her.

Olivia turned to survey the room, which included a smattering of chairs and a settee. There was also a large mirror hung over a table bearing a ewer of water and several small cloths. Presumably this had been arranged for this evening.

She studied her reflection. An amber streak stained her gown from bodice to waist.

The click of the door opening drew her attention. She froze upon seeing not Audrey, but Jasper. He closed the door behind him. "I came to see if you're all right. I apologize for spilling that sherry, but I had to find a way to end that conversation."

"I figured as much. Thank you for your help." She offered a smile, intending to also thank him for helping Mr. Beatty and his children, but the stern look on his face froze her speech.

He moved toward her, his brow furrowed. "I wasn't helping you. I was helping Louisa. I'm rather perturbed with myself for forgetting you are with her under false pretenses. She thinks you some cousin of her beloved husband, but you're nothing more than a common actress."

Olivia understood his protection of Louisa, admired it even. "I won't cause her any harm." Not intentionally anyway. She had to admit the conversation downstairs had come dangerously close to exposing her background, not just to Louisa, but to the cream of London.

"I'm afraid your assurances aren't good enough. I tried trusting you once, and it was a crashing failure." He stopped an arm's length from her. "The time has come for you to tell me what you're doing with Louisa."

Olivia's stomach knotted. She was treading a fine line between truth and deceit. She considered telling him she was actually Merry's daughter, but Louisa had been quite clear about maintaining absolute secrecy. *With everyone.* "Your aunt found me. She's showed you my handkerchiefs and how they match Merry's design. You've seen the box from which I copied it."

His eyes glittered in the candlelight from a sconce next to the mirror. "She also said you came to London seeking your relatives. You mentioned no such search when we became acquainted. I find myself wondering why a young woman with these prospects would try to defraud an earl." He tipped his head to the side. "You can see how easy it was for me to deduce this is merely another of your poorly concocted schemes."

His proximity heightened her distress and, confound it, sparked her desire. She took a step back from him. "It's not, I swear. I *was* hoping to find my relatives, but I had no means." The lie burned her tongue. She planned to speak with Louisa as soon as possible about revealing the truth to Jasper. She didn't know how much longer she could tolerate deceiving him.

"Yet when I offered you my card, your first thought was to swindle me instead of ask for help searching for your family." He shook his head. "Try again."

"I've apologized. I deeply regret my actions." She couldn't keep the pleading tone from her voice and hated that she had to beg this man for anything. "I truly didn't think to ask for your help. You thought me a whore. Men like you don't help women like me."

"'Men like me'?" His eyes narrowed and he stepped toward her. How easy it was for him to look dark and menacing despite his fair hair and fairer eyes. Heat came off him in waves. "You know very little of me, but what you do know, especially what you observed the night we met, should have demonstrated I'm a man who helps people."

"I know that…now." The truth crowded her brain, desperate to be spilled. She couldn't keep up this ruse with him. She didn't even really want to. For whatever reason, his inability to trust her even a tiny amount burned. She glanced at the door behind him. "You have to go. Audrey is coming back."

He didn't react to her warning. "I don't believe you're Merry's cousin, and you obviously lied to my aunt about working at the Haymarket and about our prior acquaintance. Wouldn't Louisa be interested to hear how you tried to swindle me? Furthermore, you took my ten pounds so now I must add theft to your offenses."

Oh God, the ten pounds. How could she have forgotten to return it? "I'll send the money back tomorrow. I meant to. Always. I always meant to pay you back." She was rambling. Her knees were shaking; her stomach was in knots. Perhaps it wasn't too late to ask Louisa if they could leave.

Louisa.

Of course, Olivia hadn't told her about working at the theatre or that she'd tried to trick Jasper. She didn't think Louisa's kindness would extend to an almost-whore. Olivia swallowed. "Please don't tell Louisa."

He didn't answer immediately, but let the silence stretch interminably. "I won't. At least not now, but only because it would upset her. I'd prefer to avoid that." His gaze moved over her with lingering precision. "I've been trying to determine your motive. Is it just the money? Or are you after position and respect as well? Look at you now. Only a week ago you were cooking up ways to defraud gentlemen like me for a mere ten pounds."

How long was he going to torture her with that? "Please stop bringing that up! I've admitted my mistake and will return the money tomorrow. Can that please be the end of it?"

"Not when you've found a way to insinuate yourself into my aunt's life. I'm afraid it's just the beginning."

"I promise I won't hurt her," she said.

"I'll make certain you don't. Just focus on maintaining your scheme and keeping Louisa above it. What happened downstairs can't happen again. If anyone finds out you were an actress and came from God-knows-isn't-Devon, she'd be a laughingstock."

Olivia cringed at the thought of Louisa being vilified. Weakly, she said, "I did, in fact, grow up in Devon."

His lip curled in a thoroughly arrogant fashion. "Perhaps I'll just verify that."

Panic rose in her chest, but Olivia refused to let him see it. It wasn't as if *she* was lying about being Merry's cousin. That much—the one thing he was so furiously disputing—was, ironically, his aunt's invention.

"Go ahead," she said with all the bravado she could muster.

"What's the name of the village?" He didn't move, but she felt cornered all the same.

Despite the mad trembling of her legs, she wouldn't cower. "Newton Abbott."

The door opened suddenly, and Jasper's entire demeanor altered. He moved quickly, putting a chair between them. His face smoothed into a serene expression.

"Pardon me, Miss Cheswick," he said. "I was just checking after Miss West's welfare. So clumsy of me to have ruined her gown. I feel quite terrible about it."

Audrey stood with the shawl clutched in her fingertips. Pink rushed to her cheeks and her mouth hung a bit open. Finally she stammered, "L-l-ord Saxton."

Jasper gave Olivia a slight bow. "I'll see you downstairs. Again, my apologies."

He strode past Audrey and gave her a devastating smile. Audrey's eyes glazed over and her mouth curved up. Olivia could almost see her bones melting under the brilliance of Jasper's attention. Is this how women typically reacted to him? Had Olivia's refusal of him only stoked his anger, already so strong after she'd tricked him?

"No need to mention this to anyone." He took Audrey's hand and stroked her thumb then quit the room.

Astonishing. Olivia could scarcely believe the same gentleman had just pelted her with accusations and threats.

Audrey turned and watched the doorway long after Jasper had gone. Olivia finally approached her and said, "Thank you for the shawl."

She pivoted and handed the lace to Olivia. Still, her eyes were wide and her lips spread in a grin. "He's never spoken to me before. And he...*touched my hand*. Here." Audrey helped arrange the shawl around Olivia's shoulders and adjusted it to cover the stain. "There, that will do for the rest of the evening." She turned and looked in the glass. Seemingly satisfied with what she saw, she turned back to Olivia. "I was hoping to catch Saxton's eye tonight. If he hadn't spilled that sherry on your gown, we wouldn't be up here, and he wouldn't have come to check on you..." Her face drifted into a dreamlike expression.

"Is that why your grandfather is having this party? So you could get to know Saxton?" Olivia asked, grateful for something besides Jasper's interrogation to occupy her mind.

She blushed prettily. "Somewhat. He's rumored to be considering a bride at long last. With so many marriageables away from London for the summer, I thought to bolster my chances." Her eyes brightened. "You're his cousin. Perhaps you could help me?"

Why not? A Jasper occupied with another woman was a Jasper unoccupied with her. And maybe then she could make it through the rest of the party. "I'm glad to help."

But tomorrow would still come, and Jasper wasn't going to accept her lies. She should have known this life was too good to be true.

THE NEXT MORNING Jasper arrived at Louisa's townhouse so that Olivia could take his measurements for the waistcoat she intended to make. He wasn't sure he could maintain his mask of acceptance, not when her lies were completely transparent.

Furthermore, he wasn't sure how his body might react when she touched him.

Despite her deception, he still wanted her. More than ever, in fact. Last night at Farringdon's had been a near thing. Miss Cheswick hadn't caught them in a compromise, but Jasper couldn't be alone with her again. She had become, unfortunately, another Abigail. A woman he desired but couldn't acceptably marry. A woman he could ruin.

Bernard announced him, and he strode into the sitting room. Olivia stood from the settee. She was as beautiful as she'd been last night, her eyes as tempestuous as ever.

"Good morning, Jasper dear." Louisa stood just inside, fairly humming with energy. "Are you ready for your measurements? I've already had mine taken this morning. Olivia has a special dress planned for me. Do excuse me for a moment. I must instruct Bernard to have someone go and purchase a fabric we saw at Deacon and Bothe's." She whooshed from the room like a small bird.

Jasper turned his attention to Olivia. Gowned in a simple yellow frock, she looked fresh and innocent. Too bad he knew better.

She twisted a measuring tape in her hand. "Good morning, my lord."

"We needn't bother with niceties. I've decided it's time for you to tell Louisa the truth."

Her eyes flashed and her head snapped back. "What truth?"

"About your former life. I understand you have this box that Merry painted—and I don't doubt he painted it—but we really can't know where you found it."

She had the skill to look outraged. "It belonged to my mother. That's the truth."

"So you say."

"It is!" She clenched the tape in her fist. "Oh, believe what you will. Louisa and I know the truth."

"Louisa knows the truth you've given her. You were not in London looking for family, and she deserves to know what kind of schemer you are."

"Why? I would argue she deserves the relationship we're building. She wants a daughter, and I want..."

He moved closer. "What do you want?"

Some of the heat left her gaze. "I want to stay here."

He heard the longing in her voice and almost felt sorry for her. But he couldn't sacrifice Louisa for her. "I can't help you lie to my aunt."

Olivia opened her mouth to say more, but Louisa bustled back into the room. "I figured you would have gotten started by now."

Jasper looked at Olivia. "How do you want me?"

Her eyes widened slightly. He hadn't intended an innuendo, but that's clearly how she'd taken it. And he couldn't keep his own blood from heating in response.

Olivia glanced away. "You should remove your coat."

"And your waistcoat, I should think. Maybe even your shirt," Louisa mused. Olivia shot her a worried glance. "It's quite all right, dear. We shan't tell anyone you've seen Jasper bare-chested."

Jasper almost barked with laughter. She'd seen that and more.

Olivia's hands quivered as she fingered the measuring tape. "That won't be necessary. He won't be wearing his waistcoat without a shirt, after all." She shot him a furtive glance and Jasper wondered if she hadn't envisioned him that way. His body tightened. This was dangerous ground.

He shrugged out of his coat and laid it over the back of a chair, just as he'd done at her apartment when she'd seduced him. *Don't think of that.* Quickly, he stripped off his waistcoat and deposited it atop the coat.

Louisa perched on the settee, while Olivia came toward him. "Raise your arms, please. Straight out, yes." She stood before him and measured him from shoulder to waist.

At the first touch of her hand, he sucked in a breath. God, this wouldn't do. He was already hardening. He turned slightly, presenting his back more fully to Louisa.

Olivia looked up at him. "Please stand still."

"I thought you could use the light from the windows." He stared straight ahead and tried to think about the apples ripening on the tree outside.

She stretched the tape across his upper chest, from shoulder to shoulder. With just the lawn of his shirt separating her ministrations from his flesh, he felt each touch with devastating accuracy. His body heated to a nearly unbearable degree. He focused on the damn apples and keeping his arms out. God, she smelled like lavender and honey, so sweet and delicious. *Think of the apples*—also sweet and delicious. *God damn it.*

His aunt's voice interrupted the battle in his head. "We're quite looking forward to the Faversham Ball, Jasper. You'll dance with Olivia, of course."

"Of course." His voice had deepened with desire. Olivia stopped measuring and froze, her gaze fixed below his waistband.

She looked up at him again and the charged look they shared was nearly his undoing. He tore his gaze from hers and damned every single apple on that tree to hell.

She moved behind him and measured from his neck to the base of his spine. The torture was no better there. Then she wrapped the tape around the circumference of his chest and he closed his eyes in sweet agony. Her fingers brushed his nipples and his cock strained against his breeches. If she didn't finish soon he'd make a complete fool of himself.

She lowered the tape to his waist and it slipped. She had to reach around to slide it back into place, and her hands came dangerously close to his erection. He couldn't keep his hips from twitching in response.

"Done!" She snapped the tape in her haste to move away from him.

Jasper didn't dare turn around. He reached back and pulled his waistcoat from the chair, using several long moments to button it. He did the same with his coat.

"Do you have designs for the waistcoat to share, Olivia?" Louisa asked.

"Not yet." She sounded a bit breathless, and the fact that she was as affected as he was did not help cool his ardor.

"Jasper, Olivia is making a very smart day dress for me. Would you like to see her drawing?"

When he'd finally conquered his lust, he turned. Louisa had the design plate on her lap so Jasper had no choice but to go and see it. The sketch was stunning. It would flatter Louisa's diminutive stature perfectly.

He looked at Olivia whose cheeks were still flushed after their encounter. "You're quite gifted." He wanted to know why Olivia would continue to toil as a seamstress now that she'd found a life of ease. "But, Aunt, why don't you hire someone to make the gown? Surely Olivia has better things to do with her time."

Olivia tucked her measuring tapes and Jasper's measurements into a basket full of sewing implements. "I'm pleased to do it. Consider it a hobby, my lord." She kept her gaze averted from his.

"Indeed," Louisa said. "We've promoted a maid to full-time seamstress. Olivia has all the help she needs to foster her creativity." Louisa beamed at her, and Jasper noted her use of the word "we" as if they were a partnership. A family. And he knew right then that he couldn't break his aunt's heart with the truth of Olivia's background. If she wanted Olivia to be Merry's cousin, well, then he would let her. He'd just make damn sure no one else learned the truth, and that Olivia wasn't using Louisa for some nefarious purpose.

"I'm off to my next appointment." He kissed his aunt's hand on his way out, but refrained from offering the same to Olivia. Not because he didn't want to, but because it would be too easy to press his lips to her hand for a moment longer than propriety allowed—and he couldn't do that.

She was no longer a common actress he might pursue in the dark hours of the night far from Mayfair. Now she was the respectable—at least in Society's eyes—cousin of a viscount, newfound ward of the esteemed Viscountess Merriweather. She was untouchable, and unfortunately also unmarriageable since he knew the truth about her.

He had to stay away from her while ensuring she didn't embarrass Louisa in any way. As if those objectives wouldn't keep him busy enough, he also had to prevent the duke from learning about Olivia's background. If he couldn't do that, none of the rest would matter.

Chapter Nine

JASPER KEPT AWAY from Louisa and Olivia over the next few days. He'd dispatched a man to Newton Abbott, just to see what could be discovered. He needed to know if anyone, such as Holborn, would be able to successfully investigate Olivia's origins. More importantly, Jasper wanted to know for himself. He'd accepted her role in Louisa's life, but he still didn't trust her.

He'd taken a drive in the park and made a point of speaking with Lady Philippa, stirring rumors of a possible courtship. She'd been charming and serene, everything a future duchess ought to be. Why then, was Jasper still overcome with thoughts of Olivia?

Because he wanted her more than ever. To circumvent his lust, he spent every night at the Black Horse honing his fighting skills. Tonight, however, he had to go to the Faversham Ball. *Had* to. If one were in Town during August, one simply didn't miss this annual event. Especially when he'd told Lady Philippa he'd be there.

His valet, a tightly-coiled, middle-aged Welshman called Williams whom he'd employed after finding him stranded on the road to York, stared at the powder on the dressing table. "You're going to put *that* on your eye?"

Sevrin had recommended cosmetic powder to lessen the discoloration of the bruised eye he'd received last night. It was that or go out with a purplish tinge that would no doubt invite stares.

"Do you have a better idea?" Jasper asked, looking at Williams in the mirror.

"I'm no lady's maid."

"You're the next best thing."

Williams harrumphed, his very favorite vocalization. "Well then, turn around. Can't very well slap this on with your back to me."

Jasper turned. Williams was not tall, which made his height quite functional for applying the cosmetic. Using a cloth, he dabbed the powder beneath Jasper's eye. Williams frowned. He dabbed a bit more. "Too bad you aren't Welsh. With a darker complexion, all of your bruises would scarcely register." Another frown. Followed by more dabbing. If his lips turned any lower they might just slide off his face. Finally, he harrumphed.

"What?" Jasper turned back to the mirror. A ghastly white circle surrounded his eye. He looked as if someone had doused him in flour.

"I suppose if we made your entire face that color it wouldn't look so…odd."

"Never mind." Jasper took another cloth and wiped at the powder. It streaked, but didn't neatly come off. "Water, please."

Williams dipped his cloth into a basin of water atop the dressing table. "Turn."

Jasper did so, allowing his valet to return him to his normal appearance, even if it was bruised.

Nearly an hour later he strode into the Favershams' ballroom. There was little breeze to stir the hot, late summer air, but the windows were open in the hope of some small relief. Though the crowd wasn't as large as during the regular Season, this was undoubtedly the most attended private event of the summer.

He scanned the throng, seeking the dark brown locks of Lady Philippa. Except his gaze fell upon Olivia's auburn beauty. She stood next to Louisa, cooling herself with a gentle sway of her fan. A handful of male admirers clustered about her like rutting stallions.

Though he ought to avoid her, he made his way toward her anyway. It was as if his feet weren't connected to his brain. Unfortunately, he wasn't the only person seeking her company. His mother and father had chosen the same moment to meet Louisa's protégé. The clinging group of men dissipated in the presence of the duke and duchess.

Jasper's gut clenched. He couldn't imagine what Holborn would make of Olivia. Would he see right through her ruse and call her out?

Louisa inclined her head toward her brother and sister-in-law. "Holborn, Your Grace, this is Merry's cousin, Miss Olivia West. Olivia, my brother, His Grace, and his wife, Her Grace."

Olivia delivered an acceptable curtsey.

Holborn gave her a cursory glance. "You're from Devon, is that right? I once purchased horses from Devon. Never actually went there myself, of course."

Olivia nodded. Her acting skill seemed to hide any anxiety. Or perhaps she simply wasn't nervous. For some people, lies were as easy as breathing.

Jasper's mother turned her blue-gray gaze upon Olivia, giving her a rather pinched look. But then, that was how she regarded everyone. "How fortunate that you found Lady Merriweather." She gave Louisa a bland smile. "I imagine this is quite an improvement over your life in Devon."

Louisa's eyes narrowed, but she possessed too much savvy to draw attention to the duchess's rudely insinuating commentary.

Olivia, for her part, merely blinked and said, "I'm thrilled to be here with Louisa, thank you." *Well done.*

The duchess gave a shake of her impeccably coiffed head. "Still, it must be difficult. A severe change in station, I should think."

And that was quite enough. Jasper offered his arm to Olivia. "Miss West, I believe this is our dance."

Olivia took his arm and inclined her head to the duke and duchess as Jasper led her onto the dance floor. "Actually, you're not on my dance card," she said.

"Would you prefer to remain with my parents? Her Grace was just getting warmed up."

"No, thank you. However did you grow up with them?"

"I had nurses, governesses, tutors. A younger sister to torture. I rarely saw them." Which had been true until James died. Then Jasper had seen Holborn much more than he ever would have preferred.

She nodded as they moved into a square for the dance.

He bent his head next to her and murmured, "I didn't think to ask. Do you even know how to dance?"

She arched a brow and lifted her wrist. "Clearly, since I have a dance card."

He'd noticed the card, of course. "It was a fair question given what I know about you. I didn't mean to insult."

The music began, and for the first few minutes, she focused very intently on the steps. She did, in fact, know the dance, but it seemed to have been awhile since she'd executed it.

They moved apart and then together within the square of dancers. He caught sight of Lady Philippa dancing in another square. He ought to be focusing his attention on her instead of the lovely siren who'd beguiled him, but he still needed to monitor Olivia's actions. The steps came easier to her now, and she moved with grace and precision. She seemed able to comport herself well, and he knew from Farringdon's dinner party that she was more than capable of holding her own in a conversation. He'd been the one who'd panicked and thrown sherry down her dress.

Despite all of that, he couldn't trust that her lies wouldn't be exposed. He had to ensure they weren't or somehow remove the threat. Unfortunately, one didn't "remove" the Duke of Holborn.

When they came together again, she frowned. "You look as if you've engaged in another altercation since I saw you last." She lowered her voice to a discreet level. "I know you fight at the Black Horse."

Never, ever did he allow himself to betray surprise or any other strong emotion in the center of a ballroom, but he faltered and fought to remember the next step. Her hands tightened where they touched him, as if she sought to keep him focused. "I'm sorry. I shouldn't have mentioned that here," she whispered.

She'd rattled him with her curiosity and concern. If they'd met under different circumstances, he was certain he would've liked her. However, given the complications of their acquaintance, he couldn't allow himself to become too familiar. "No, you shouldn't have. But neither should you mention it anywhere else. It's none of your concern."

The dance finally concluded, and Jasper quickly ushered her back to Louisa. Thankfully, his parents had departed the ballroom.

Time to find Lady Philippa. She, too, had just left the dance floor and was now making her way toward the refreshment table in the corner.

Halfway to his mark, an annoying chap called Twickersham stepped in his way. "I say, who's that lovely miss you were just dancing with? I hear she's some distant cousin?"

Jasper looked over the shorter man's shoulder at Lady Philippa. Several men were vying for her attention as one procured her a glass of ratafia. His patience, never in danger of being lost in public, thinned to almost nothing. What was wrong with him this evening? Was he on edge due to Olivia? And if so, was it because of her deception, or because he wanted to take her into a dark sitting room and toss up her skirts? *Do not think of that.*

Or maybe his bad mood had been brought on by Olivia's query about the club. He knew he'd be inviting curiosity with the bruise on his face, but she'd gone one step further. She knew something no one else did. The thought was discomfiting. He preferred people know only what he wanted them to.

"Might I ask for an introduction?" Twickersham continued as if Jasper had answered his initial query.

He curled his fingers into his palms. Twickersham was a sycophantic leech. Jasper would sooner introduce him to a sinking ship. "You'll have to ask my aunt."

Twickersham's tiny brown eyes narrowed. "I suppose I shall. I say, did you get that bruise at Jackson's? Haven't seen you there in some time. Did your opponent eschew hand mufflers? Nasty looking. You oughtn't box without the proper equipment. Quite dangerous."

Surely he wasn't lecturing Jasper about the rules of boxing? Already vexed, Twickersham's nonsense only annoyed him further. Jasper bit back an insult and made to continue on his way.

Twickersham then did something extremely foolish. He grabbed Jasper's arm, halting his progress. "I see you've set your sights on Lady Philippa. Your title may be one of the finest in England, but her father's looking for a foreign husband, perhaps even royalty. I put my wager in at White's—she'll snare a prince."

The final remnants of Jasper's control snapped. He shook off Twickersham's grasp with a harsh jab of his elbow that caught the shorter man in his oversized gut. He pinned Twickersham with a menacing stare. "Don't touch me again. Not if you want to use that hand."

The other man's eyes widened. Already, Jasper could see Twickersham couldn't wait to recount this tale.

In an effort to slow the soon-to-be-gossip, Jasper muttered, "My apologies." He quickly strode away in search of Lady Philippa.

She was no longer near the refreshment table. In fact, he couldn't locate her at all. *God damn it.* The room seemed to tunnel to a pinpoint before his eyes. His hands fisted again and he wanted to pummel Twickersham into the floorboards. He moved closer to one of the open windows, seeking any bit of cool air to soothe his temper.

Eventually his heart rate returned to normal, and the ballroom finally came back into focus. He couldn't quite comprehend his reactions this evening. What had come over him?

"What the devil are you doing sulking in the corner?"

Holborn. This moment only needed his presence.

Jasper struggled to appear calm and controlled. "Seeking a brief respite."

"From what? All you've done is dance with that worthless West chit. I don't care if you were trying to please my sister. You spend far too much time attending Louisa, anyway. You should be courting Lady Philippa."

Jasper's insides ignited, and he strove to keep his anger in check. "I'm looking for her now, actually."

"I saw her going toward the gaming room. It's the second door to the left."

Without a word, Jasper made his way to the gaming room. The door the duke had indicated was closed. Jasper entered. The room did not contain gaming tables or guests.

Save one.

Lady Philippa stood in the center of the room with her hands clasped before her, as if she'd been waiting for him. He fought a surge of panic. If they were caught alone…

"Lord Saxton. I wasn't expecting you."

Which seemed to imply she was expecting *someone*. Christ, he supposed he wanted to marry her, but another compromise even if it was with the "right" woman? His vision tunneled again.

A shock of clarity hit Jasper. He touched her arm as she drew near, but immediately withdrew his hand. "Who were you expecting?"

"My mother. A footman said she needed help with her gown and that I should meet her here."

"Did anyone see you come in here?"

Her amber eyes widened. "I don't think so. I don't know," she said, with an edge of alarm.

"It's all right, but you do understand that we can't be caught here together?" Seeking to soothe the alarm in her gaze, he gave her a benign smile. "I still plan to see you at my mother's picnic day after tomorrow."

She nodded. *Good girl.*

"Go, now. I'll get out another way." He gestured toward the door he entered. Another door presumably led to an adjoining room. A hopefully empty room.

"Thank you," she said, before hurrying from the chamber.

Jasper exited into the actual gaming room and nearly bumped into Holborn's closest friend.

Lord Dalton looked up at Jasper, startled. "I was just going to open that door, try to get a bit of air circulating. Devilish hot tonight, what?"

Holborn's plan was obvious. He no doubt figured it would be easy to set up a compromise, especially for a man as experienced in the art as Jasper.

Before Jasper could say or do anything he'd regret, Black and Penreith hailed him from a nearby table. He quickly made his way to their side.

"Join us, Sax," Penreith invited.

Just then Sevrin stood from a table in the corner. His gaze met Jasper's and he quirked a brow in silent question.

"Thank you, but no."

Penreith followed his gaze and gave a slight frown. "Sevrin?"

Jasper glared down at Penreith. "What of him?"

"It's one thing to chat at White's..."

Sevrin headed toward the door. Jasper followed. He didn't care what Black and Penreith thought. He'd never needed anything the way he needed the club just then. None of the other fighters demanded anything they weren't willing to give in return. It was a shared experience. A brotherhood.

Just now it seemed the only place he truly belonged.

OLIVIA LONGED TO step onto the terrace to escape the suffocating heat of the ballroom. Or perhaps she only wanted to move closer to where Jasper stood conversing with his father. Their relationship seemed complicated and, being without her own father, she wanted to know why.

Instead, she plied her fan and imagined what their intense

discussion might be about. Suddenly Jasper walked away, leaving the duke with a satisfied set to his mouth. He cut back through the ballroom toward his duchess. People nodded as he passed or tried to engage him in conversation. He paused for no one. His gaze, not as pale as Jasper's, though every bit as glacial, traversed the room, but settled nowhere. She imagined it lingered in her direction, but perhaps he was merely noting his sister's location.

"Olivia?" Audrey Cheswick, the girl she'd met at Lord Farringdon's, stood in front of her with another young woman. Olivia was surprised she hadn't noticed their approach. Had she been that intent upon her study of the Duke of Holborn?

"Good evening, Miss Cheswick."

"Really, you ought to call me Audrey. Didn't I tell you to call me Audrey?" She waved a hand as if her address was a triviality. "I've brought my dearest friend to meet you. Lydia, this is Miss Olivia West. Olivia, this is Lady Lydia Prewitt."

Lady Lydia inclined her head. She was exceptionally pretty—everything Olivia imagined a young London miss ought to be: porcelain-perfect skin, warm brown eyes, bright golden hair. "Audrey has told me all about you. London must be quite a change from, where was it? Oh yes, *Devon*." Was that a shudder flickering through Lady Lydia's frame or had Olivia imagined it?

"I'm finding London most diverting, thank you."

Louisa turned from her friend, with whom she had been conversing. She smiled at the two young women. "Hello, dears. Olivia, I'm going to take a short stroll with Lady Montrose." Her gaze held a bit of question. She wanted to be sure Olivia was comfortable. *So thoughtful.*

Olivia smiled to reassure her. "If I'm not here when you get back, I'm scheduled to dance with Mr. Lyle."

With a nod, Louisa linked arms with her friend and departed.

"Mr. Lyle?" Lady Lydia asked, her nasally voice climbing an octave. "Audrey, you didn't tell me Olivia needed our help so drastically."

Olivia closed her fan. "What's wrong with Mr. Lyle?"

Lady Lydia leaned forward, but didn't lower her voice so that it looked like she was imparting a confidence, but in truth was spreading gossip to anyone who chanced by. "Terrible scapegrace. Not a farthing to his name. Charming as he is poor, however. One dance won't hurt, but don't dance with him again."

Olivia began to see the benefit of making friends, although she supposed Louisa would have informed her of Mr. Lyle's reputation later. Likely in the privacy of the Rose Room back at Queen Street. "I won't. I believe more than one dance with a partner signifies a courtship of some kind?"

"Not just tonight. I meant, don't dance with him again *ever.*" Lady Lydia shook her head as if Olivia were a simpleton.

Audrey's friend was rapidly annoying Olivia. Audrey's lack of comment was also troubling. Was her silence due to her inability to squeeze a word into the conversation, or did she agree with Lady Lydia?

An awkward moment passed before Lady Lydia's face lit. "From laundering your own clothes to the premier London event of the Season, my goodness, but you're a lucky girl! Lady Merriweather is most generous, but then she has ample resources. Even luckier, you get to spend time with Saxton in a familial setting. Tell us, what is he like?"

Olivia thought of many answers to that question, most of them inappropriate. A bit of devilish impulse beckoned her to say, *if one can get past his fighting and arrogance, he's wonderfully charitable and kind, and his kisses…* She didn't even dare finish *thinking* that sentence. "I haven't spent all that much time with him. He's most solicitous."

Lady Lydia rolled her eyes. "How boring. He's always so impeccably mannered in public too. Always the stiffest cravat in the room. Such a shame since he's so attractive. Ah well, I'd be willing to put up with his excessive propriety given his title and wealth." She tossed a grin toward Audrey. "Audrey is hoping for a chance with him, but I daresay he's going to choose someone with a flawless bloodline. Lady Philippa Latham perhaps. In fact…" She slid her gaze around the room in a quick survey. "Neither of them are in the ballroom. How…interesting."

"They didn't leave together. Lord Saxton departed by himself," Olivia said, not at all appreciating Lady Lydia's innuendo.

Lady Lydia's laughter tinkled like tiny shards of glass bouncing upon the wood floor. "Audrey, I do believe Olivia might be as cognizant of Saxton's movements as you are."

Olivia hoped her embarrassment didn't reflect in her face. Lady Lydia had her flustered. First she wanted Olivia to share what she knew of Jasper then mocked her for noting his exit.

"Really, you have no idea who Saxton plans to marry?" Lady Lydia asked. "Surely you must know something. At least a tidbit that might encourage or," her lips made an exaggerated frown, "dissuade dear Audrey."

How could Audrey call this harpy her dearest friend? "I'm sorry, I can't help you." She directed this at Audrey, injecting as much sympathy as possible into her tone.

Audrey smiled shyly. "It's all right. The most I was hoping for was perhaps a dance. If Saxton paid me just a bit of interest, it might stir others."

How...sad. And manipulative. And clever. But really, what else did these girls have to do besides find a husband? Clearly the primary objective was to snare the best mate possible, with a title and wealth at the top of the list of requirements. The entire endeavor was incredibly mercenary. Olivia wasn't certain she wanted to participate, but neither was she certain her dream of a dress shop was enough anymore. Life with Louisa had shown her something she'd been missing: the love of a family.

"Well, here comes our answer." Lady Lydia gestured toward the door with her fan.

A beautiful young woman with dark brown hair and the most exquisite ball gown Olivia had yet seen entered. Seed pearls were stitched into the bodice of the dark yellow silk and the skirt hung in a graceful drape to the floor. This was an example of excellent fashion on a splendid form. "Is that Lady Philippa?"

"Yes, and her mother." Lady Lydia sighed rather loudly. "I suppose that means she's not been caught in some scandalous tryst with Saxton."

Olivia nearly choked.

Audrey elbowed her friend. "Saxton would never do that! Haven't we already established his behavior is without reproach?" The speed with which Audrey leapt to Jasper's defense was sweet, if not a tad misguided. Olivia couldn't disagree that he was extremely well-mannered, but 'without reproach?'

A very tall, slender man with graying brown hair approached them.

"Lydia, I'd wondered where you'd gotten off to. It's time to pay your respects to your grandmother."

Lady Lydia rolled her eyes—clearly one of her favorite expressions, Olivia was quickly coming to note. "Grandmother won't know if I've paid my respects or not."

The gentleman smiled placidly. "Nevertheless, it makes me happy." He tilted his head toward Audrey. "Good evening Miss Cheswick, and…" His voice trailed off as he looked at Olivia. His eyes widened briefly. "My goodness, you're the image of…oh, never mind, pardon me." The barest hint of color swathed the high arc of his cheeks.

"Father, this is Lady Merriweather's cousin, Miss Olivia West. Does she remind you of someone?" Lady Lydia asked, the inner tips of her faint blonde brows nearly touching.

Lord Prewitt scrutinized Olivia for a moment. "Miss West, you say? Pleasure to meet you, Miss West."

Something about his intrusive gaze troubled Olivia. She felt certain he'd been about to say she looked like the infamous actress Miss Scarlet. She hadn't considered her resemblance to her mother and she really ought to have done.

"Come along, Lydia," he said. "Time to appease your grandmother."

Lady Lydia tugged at Audrey. "You have to accompany me."

Audrey blinked, looking as if she'd rather do anything but. In the end, however, she offered Olivia a sheepish smile and followed her friend.

Mr. Lyle was making his way toward Olivia. Her stomach sank past her knees. Not only was she about to dance with an absolute reprobate, she might be in danger of becoming tonight's latest *on-dit*.

Mr. Lyle stopped before her. "Shall we take to the floor, Miss West?" He grinned, revealing rather crooked teeth.

Because there was nothing to be done to solve either of her problems, Olivia did the only thing she could, the thing she most recalled from her upbringing at the vicarage: she held her head high.

And prayed.

Chapter Ten

THE FOLLOWING DAY, Olivia and Louisa traveled to Benfield, one of the Duke of Holborn's many estates. Just a short distance outside London bordering Hampstead Heath, Louisa declared it her favorite place aside from Merriweather Hall, which, of course, was no longer hers, having passed to the new viscount.

Apprehension twisted Olivia's nerves in anticipation of her first riding lesson, but more importantly because of her designated instructor: Jasper.

They turned onto the long, oak-lined drive. Olivia surveyed the gorgeous parkland surrounding the manor. She'd never seen an estate so grand, let alone visited one. "Benfield is beautiful."

Louisa tipped her head up to look at the large house at the end of the drive, and blinked her eyes against the brilliant sunlight. "We spent every summer here—Holborn and me. It's hard to imagine now, but we filled many afternoons rolling down that hill there." She gestured to a slope leading away from the manor.

Olivia could see Louisa playing among the manicured lawns, but the duke? She scarcely believed he'd been a child at all.

Louisa laughed softly. "You're thinking Holborn couldn't possibly have frolicked. His instep is much higher now. Our father had little tolerance for frivolity. Much as my brother in his adulthood."

Olivia wondered if Jasper had been a playful child, and like his father, no longer indulged his lighter side. "I imagine the responsibilities of a duke are great."

Louisa waved her hand as if swatting at a fly. "Bah. Greater perhaps in Holborn's mind than in reality. Yes, he has duties. Yes, a vast number of people rely on him, but I don't believe his title is his most important role." Her smile was regretful. "I suppose that's because I don't have children of my own. I should think being Jasper's and Miranda's father would be the most important thing, especially since James died."

Olivia looked at her with sharp curiosity. "James?"

"Oh, of course, you wouldn't know, dear. Jasper's elder brother. He died of fever when he was nine and Jasper just seven." She paused a moment in which her eyes dropped to her lap, and her lips pressed together as if she recalled a somber memory. "Holborn never recovered from losing him. I suppose, in a way, Jasper may not have either."

Olivia had noted the tension between Jasper and his father. Was it because of James? She felt a pang of sorrow for Jasper. To lose a brother, particularly so young, was heartbreaking.

The open carriage drew to a halt before Benfield's warm sandstone façade. A footman helped them down.

"Are you ready for your riding lesson?" Louisa asked.

Not particularly.

They walked around the house to the stable, Olivia's new riding boots crunching in the shell-mixed dirt. A decrepit old man shuffled toward them. "Louisa, dearie."

"Carter!" Louisa hugged the tiny man before turning back to Olivia. "Carter has been working in this stable since I was a child. He put me on my first pony."

"Aye, that I did. Boots was a fine animal." He grinned, revealing nearly toothless gums. "We're saddling Tilda up for ye now."

"Carter could catalogue every horse in the stable over the past sixty-some years." Louisa tossed a wink at Olivia. "Tell us, who do you recommend for Miss West? She's never ridden before."

Olivia, however, did not feel so carefree. Though outfitted in a brand new riding habit—the only garment she'd consented to have made for her—she was harboring second thoughts about getting on a horse.

Carter tugged his chin a moment. "Tulip, I think."

A horse called Tulip? She certainly sounded docile. Carter made his way back into the stable, presumably to notify whomever was readying the horses.

Louisa adjusted her jaunty hat against the glare of the sun. "If you and Tulip get on well, perhaps I'll ask Holborn if we can take her back to Town with us. That way you'll have a mount for the park."

Olivia doubted she'd be ready for a ride across the drive—let alone in the park—any time soon, but didn't voice her concern. More

than that, despite her extremely brief acquaintance with the duke, she
had little faith he'd allow them to take his horse anywhere.

"I'm a bit nervous, Louisa."

"Don't worry, dear. Jasper will be back soon and there's no finer
horseman, including the duke. Though he'd bitterly dispute that." She
chuckled.

Was Jasper a willing participant in today's lesson? Olivia didn't
think he'd refuse his aunt's request, but he still didn't trust her. And,
of course, she'd given him no reason to.

She feared the investigator he'd sent to Newton Abbott would
discover the lie she and Louisa were perpetrating. Lord Prewitt's near-
recognition at the Faversham Ball had set her even more on edge. She
was only waiting for someone to point at her and call out,
"Charlatan!"

She'd put off asking Louisa about sharing their secret with Jasper
because she hadn't wanted to presume too much. Despite the speed
with which they'd formed a close bond, Olivia didn't know Louisa
that well. But the time had come for Olivia to voice her query. "Might
we tell Jasper that I'm Merry's daughter?"

Louisa shook her head. "I'm afraid not. It's best only you and I
know."

Olivia would feel much better if Jasper knew—and accepted—the
truth. She much preferred him as an ally instead of an enemy trying to
thwart her. Perhaps if Louisa understood why Olivia wanted to tell
him, she'd change her mind. "I don't think he trusts me."

"Oh, ignore him dear. Sometimes he's more like his father than he
realizes—look at how he reacted when he first met you. I love my
nephew very much, but he's been schooled to keep himself from
scandal. I'm not at all sure he'd accept you into the family if he knew
you were Merry's bastard." She paused a moment, her brow
furrowing. "He hasn't been cruel to you, has he? I shall speak to him
at once if that's the case."

"No." Olivia didn't want Louisa to talk with him unless she
planned to disclose the truth. Any other encounter might incite him
to reveal Olivia's background, particularly that she'd tried to trick him.
Better if she just continued to weather his distrust.

Louisa gave her fingers a gentle squeeze. Her gaze moved past
Olivia. "Ah, here he is now."

Olivia turned. A lone rider crested the hill behind the stable. He raced down the slope, his thighs hugging the animal. They seemed to move as one.

"Such excellent form," Louisa remarked with pride. "But then his father made certain he is the best."

He reined his horse to a halt in the stable yard and dismounted. The actions were fluid, as if he'd performed them thousands of times. Dressed in buff riding breeches and a forest green coat, he looked every bit the charismatic country gentleman.

Jasper moved forward with a dazzling smile. Olivia couldn't keep her stomach from flipping in response. "Good morning, ladies. You've chosen a fine day to enjoy Benfield."

Carter led a horse from the stable. A dark brown that was nearly black, the animal held its head high, presenting a regal air. Another groom led a second, smaller horse. This one was the color of caramel with a flowing dark mane and sweet brown eyes.

Louisa patted Jasper's arm. "Carter's saddled Tilda for me and recommended Tulip for Olivia. You will, of course, instruct Olivia since she's a novice." Hadn't Louisa notified Jasper of her plan to have him provide the riding lesson?

Jasper arched a brow at Olivia. "I see."

She couldn't tell if he wanted to participate. Suddenly self-conscious, she said, "Unless you're busy…"

"Oh no, dear." Louisa chuckled. "You aren't getting out of it. Jasper's delighted to share his skills. Riding is one of his very favorite things. Perhaps his most favorite, in fact."

He looked at Olivia, his clear blue eyes vibrant in the morning sun. "Indeed. It's no trouble. I look forward to teaching you."

He helped his aunt—currently sporting a cheeky grin—mount Tilda, which she accomplished with absolute grace. In spite of her youthful advantage, Olivia couldn't hope to emulate the elegant movement. She fingered the bulky skirts of her riding habit trying to imagine how to get everything situated while angling her legs just so.

"Don't be frightened," Louisa said. "Jasper will help you up, dear."

He went to stand at Tulip's nose. "Come, Miss West. Tulip's as gentle as the day is warm."

Olivia walked up beside him and looked into her horse's eyes. The animal blinked, but her regard was steady.

"You ought to greet to her."

Olivia started. "Oh." What on earth did one stay to a horse? "Uh, good morning, Tulip?" She looked at Jasper who nodded encouragingly. He didn't seem the sort who would talk to his animals. "Do you converse with your horse?"

"I do. I believe it fosters a close, trusting relationship between man and beast. Or in your case, woman and beast." He said the latter with a sparkle in his eye. Was he flirting?

Olivia was glad to see this side of Jasper again. She turned back to Tulip. "Pleased to meet you. I'm sure we'll get on quite well together. I *hope* we'll get on quite well together." She smiled at the horse, who nodded her head as if she agreed with Olivia's sentiments.

"Jasper, Tilda has missed me," Louisa said. "Do you mind if I go along with one of the grooms?"

And leave her alone with Jasper so he could interrogate her again? No, thank you. "I'm still nervous, Louisa."

"You'll be much better off with Jasper than with me, dear."

Jasper gestured to one of the grooms. "Go ahead, Aunt. I'm certain Miss West will prefer to take things slow." He turned to Olivia. "You don't want to deprive Louisa of an invigorating ride, do you?"

Now she had no choice but to be alone with him. "Of course not."

After a jaunty wave, Louisa and her horse took off up the hill, followed by one of the grooms. Deciding to put all of their arguments and her shameful attempt at trickery out of her mind, at least for today, she asked, "Is that cantering or trotting?"

"Cantering. Would you like to try it?"

Olivia was relieved he seemed to want a pleasant interaction, too. His kind demeanor, however, didn't alleviate her fear of cantering. "No. I mean, not today. I'll be satisfied if I can manage to sit on the horse."

He smiled and it seemed genuine. *Careful, Olivia.*

"Sitting's the easy part. Are you ready to give it a go?"

She nodded, thankful for this easy conversation. He guided her to Tulip's side. "We could use a mounting block, but I'll help you this first time." His hands clasped her waist, the contact jolting her even through the layers of her costume. She made herself focus on the saddle in front of her.

"I'm to sit on this sideways, like Louisa?"

His breath tickled her ear and she startled. "Yes. I'm going to lift you up. Your right leg will go around that pommel." He pointed at a round protrusion at the front of the saddle. "And your left foot will go in this stirrup here." He indicated a loop hanging down the side of the horse.

She looked back at him. A mistake. He was so close. His jaw was freshly shaven and smelled of evergreen. His eyes reflected the sky and his expression hovered near cheerful. The bruise beneath his eye had faded. She wanted to ask him why he was being amenable today. But the morning was so lovely and his concern so divine, she couldn't bring herself to shadow the moment with such talk.

"Ready?"

She nodded. He put his hand under her behind and boosted her. She was not prepared for such an intimate touch, but up she went until she sat on the saddle. Her cheeks were probably scarlet, but she stayed facing forward and hoped he didn't notice.

"Now position your right thigh on the saddle in front of you and bend your knee around the pommel."

She did as he instructed.

"That's right. Don't lean forward even if it feels like you should. Try to position all of your weight on your thigh." He laid his hand there briefly, eliciting another jolt of awareness.

Seemingly unaffected, he picked up the reins and handed them to her. "These are the reins. Don't be afraid to use them to steer. It will be difficult for you to hurt her. I tell you this because every horse is a bit different. Tulip is very responsive, so you won't have to work too hard. Finally, this is the lead rope. I'm going to give it to the groom who will walk with you." He wasn't going to walk with her?

She gripped the reins. "What are you going to do?"

"Ride my horse beside you." His gaze flicked to her hands. "Don't hold them too tightly."

She loosened her grasp. "This is a lot to remember."

"No more than memorizing a script full of lines, I imagine." He winked at her and she was again bewildered. Was he actually joking about her being an actress? As if it wasn't a key point of conflict between them?

He handed the lead rope to a groom, but thankfully not Carter. Olivia doubted the ancient man could walk around the house, let alone control a horse if it decided to run off.

Jasper swung himself up onto his horse, a much larger animal than Tulip. A long scar marred the flank.

"What do you call your horse?" she asked.

"Malheur."

"Isn't that French?" Olivia had learned a little at the vicarage, but had forgotten most of it.

"Yes, it means miserable."

What an odd name. "Is there a reason you call him that?"

He stroked the back of his horse's head. "When I bought him he'd been mistreated."

Her gaze strayed to the mark on the horse. "You rescued him then?"

He shrugged, as if saving a mistreated animal was a regular occurrence. But then maybe for him it was. "I recognized a superior animal and knew I could train him into a good horse."

She refused to let him pretend it wasn't a good deed. "You rescued him."

"What does it matter?"

"It makes you noble." She wondered at his penchant for rescuing things. Had he been mistreated? Suddenly the tension between him and his father took on new meaning.

He gave her one of his patented looks that revealed nothing. He lifted Malheur's reins and said, "Walk." The horse moved.

Olivia took a deep breath. "Walk." She mimicked what he'd done and grinned when Tulip lurched forward.

He returned her smile. Her heart tripped again. She diverted her attention to Tulip. Her pride couldn't afford to be seduced by him.

After several minutes during which they rode in complete silence, Olivia braved conversation once more. "Louisa says you're the finest horseman she knows. How old were you when you rode your first horse?"

"Four. And he was a pony."

"So young?"

"My father insisted on an early start. Dibbles was quite small, perfectly suitable for a child."

She laughed. "Dibbles? That's a far cry from Malheur."

His eyes crinkled at the corners, though he didn't laugh with her. "I've no idea who named the unfortunate creature. He was rather old. I only had him for a year. Then I got a new pony."

"How many ponies did you have?"

He shrugged. "Maybe half a dozen. My father has extensive stables. Here alone he keeps two dozen animals."

"And you ride all of them?"

"No. Some are coaching horses. He doesn't breed here, however. That he does at our family seat in Middlesex."

Scores of horses. His wealth was staggering.

"Dare I ask how many homes your family owns?"

"There are eight entailed, and another two are unentailed, one of them through my mother. Oh, and my sister inherited one from our mother's mother."

Ten—eleven—houses! Until she'd gone to live with Louisa, Olivia had never lived in a house with ten *rooms*.

"Have you changed your mind about cantering?" he asked.

Olivia was just becoming used to the motion of walking. "I don't think so. Maybe next time."

"Do you mind if I ride around the drive?"

"Not at all. I'm sure I could benefit from watching your technique."

He said something to Malheur and shook the reins. They took off quickly, the dirt kicking up beneath the horse's hooves.

After a few moments during which she admired Jasper's skill, Louisa rode up beside her, slowing Tilda to a walk. "You're doing very well, dear! I knew Jasper would set you right."

Olivia watched him ride. She knew next to nothing about horses or riding but it was obvious he was exceptional. "He told me he saved that horse."

"Malheur?" Louisa nodded. "Yes, that was, my goodness, almost ten years ago now. Merry was with Jasper when they went to see the poor thing. Holborn was furious when Jasper bought him. Thought the animal was a waste of time. It took Jasper two years, but he finally rode that horse. Now look at them." Her voice rose with pride.

Olivia barely knew the duke but was predisposed to dislike him intensely. He seemed less like a parent and more of an autocrat, whereas Merry sounded as if he'd been the best sort. Her heart squeezed at the thought.

After a few minutes, Jasper rode back to them. His cheeks were flushed with exertion, his lips parted as he regained his breath. Every line had been wiped from his face. He looked relaxed...free. She'd never seen him like that.

"You were splendid." Louisa beamed at him. "How did Olivia do?"

Jasper flicked Olivia an appreciative glance. "Very well, but she didn't want to go above a walk."

Louisa managed Tilda's reins as the horse danced two steps to the side. "Is that true Olivia? You must take advantage of Jasper's excellent tutelage. After lunch, you should allow Tulip a short jaunt."

After lunch? She hadn't yet dismounted, and they were already planning her next ride.

They walked their horses back to the stable yard. Olivia was more than content to allow the groom to continue to lead Tulip.

"Yes, after lunch, and after you show Jasper the designs you sketched for his waistcoat."

Jasper looked at Olivia in question. "I thought you'd perhaps forgotten."

She slid Louisa an arch glance. "As if Louisa would let me." She grinned so they would know she was jesting. "If it's convenient, you can choose the design you prefer."

"I should be delighted." His gaze lingered on her and seemed to smolder.

Olivia swallowed, hoping to encourage moisture into her suddenly dry mouth.

"Ow!"

Both Olivia and Jasper turned at Louisa's exclamation in time to see her slide off the mounting block. She hobbled a bit before half-sitting/half-falling down on the large square of wood.

Jasper quickly dismounted and rushed to her. "Are you all right?"

"I've turned my ankle." She reached down and wrapped her hand around her boot. "Give me a moment, and I can probably put my weight back on it."

"Nonsense." Jasper was already scooping her into his arms. "I'll carry you inside."

"Oh!" Louisa laughed. "You take such good care of me."

Olivia wasn't sure if Jasper would come back out for her or not. She looked down at the groom who still held the lead rope. "Shall I try the block then?"

"As you wish, miss. I should be pleased to assist you."

Guiding Tulip to the block proved easy enough, but navigating her skirts from the saddle and dismounting required the groom's assistance. Olivia thanked the groom before making her way to the house. Jasper met her at the door.

"Is Louisa all right?" Olivia hoped she hadn't broken her ankle.

"Quite. There's no pain if she doesn't put weight on it. Hence, she's reclining in the library. I've asked the staff to reorganize luncheon in there so we may dine together."

Extremely thoughtful.

"It will take them a few minutes. In the meantime, I thought you might enjoy a tour." He opened the door wide, beckoning her inside.

Olivia hesitated. He'd lulled her into a sense of security, but was it honest? Or did he have ulterior motives now that he had her alone?

"A few of Merry's paintings are hanging in the gallery."

The temptation was too alluring to resist. He knew just how to woo her—at least in this.

"Yes, thank you." She took his proffered arm, hoping she hadn't just agreed to accompany the lion into his den.

Chapter Eleven

Jasper's body tightened with lust. Such a simple touch, but then her proximity was enough to drive him to the edge. He immediately regretted his invitation for a tour.

She shot him a quick glance. It was brief, but contained the same emotions she'd reflected all morning. Anxiety. Uncertainty. Awareness. He didn't trust her—had just dispatched a man to Newton Abbott in Devon yesterday in fact—but he meant to tell her that her secrets would be safe with him. Provided she told him the truth.

A footman held the door for them as they entered the house. Olivia swept the tall black riding hat from her head and gave it to the liveried retainer.

Jasper guided her toward the rear of the entry hall where a marbled staircase climbed to the second-floor gallery. "You did well this morning. You needn't ride after lunch, unless you want to. Aunt Louisa can be a force of nature."

Her lips curved up. "I like that about her. She has such vitality."

"Yes." He liked that about her, too. Loved that about her, actually.

He led Olivia up the stairs and then along the portrait gallery. "These are well-known artists." He gestured to the first painting, a landscape. "Poussin."

Candlelight from the sconces between the portraits washed over her auburn hair. The color was lush and vibrant, like her.

She continued to the next portrait. "Rembrandt?"

Surprising. "Yes."

"I can tell from the glow. His paintings have a kind of light burning within them, do they not?"

An excellent observation. He hadn't expected to be impressed by her, but all morning she'd exhibited courage, intelligence, and wit. "What you describe is called chiaroscuro. This refers to how artists employ lightness and darkness within their paintings. You've an exceptional eye."

She blushed. "My experience is rather limited. Louisa took me to Somerset House. I liked the Rembrandts."

That was one of the days he'd avoided them. A shame, for he would have enjoyed seeing the paintings with her and discussing them. Her passionate interest reminded him of Uncle Merry who'd also particularly liked Rembrandt. Was there perhaps a chance she *was* related to Merry?

They moved to the next painting. He watched her study the portrait of two boys. One sat in a chair beneath a sweeping oak tree reading a book. The other ran across the lawn, two dogs racing behind him.

At length, she said, "Merry painted this."

Incredibly good eye. He held his breath, wondering what else she would notice about the painting. "Yes."

Another moment. Then she tilted her head to look at him. "Is that you?" She pointed to the boy running.

"Yes. The boy reading is my brother." Why had he told her that? He hadn't planned to.

"Louisa said he died." She looked up at him. "I'm sorry."

He should've expected Louisa would share that information. It wasn't, after all, a secret. Just something his family chose to ignore. "I was very young, and we weren't close. As you can see, we didn't share the same interests."

She smiled, easing the tension he felt discussing his long-dead brother. "You seem so carefree there. A different Lord Saxton is teaching me to ride and showing me his favorite paintings."

"I'm not Lord Saxton in that portrait."

"Ah, of course. Your brother was." She was very perceptive, even if she couldn't begin to understand what James' death had done to Jasper, to their entire family.

Moments passed, but Jasper could think of no response that wouldn't lead down a path he didn't wish to traverse. He gestured to the next portrait. "This is another of Merry's. My sister, Miranda."

She walked with him to view the painting of a ten-year-old Miranda petting the nose of her horse beside a lake. "Louisa has told me about her. Is it true she and her husband operate an orphanage in Wiltshire?"

Jasper quirked a smile. "Oddly enough, they do. Well, odd for Miranda. I never would've thought she'd marry a provincial gentleman and live away from London, let alone work at an orphanage."

Olivia looked up at him. "She must be happy."

Blissfully so. "Yes, she's happy." And he'd ensured that by agreeing to marry whomever Holborn decreed by the end of September. The duke had been ready to destroy Miranda's husband to keep them from marrying, so Jasper had traded his freedom for hers. Holborn hadn't cared that Miranda loved Fox beyond all else—a love he returned with a ferocity that made Jasper question whether what he'd felt for Abigail a decade ago had truly been love at all.

Olivia gestured to the painting. "She looks happy there, too. Everything Merry painted is so...alive, or maybe tangible. I can't think of the right word. He captured perfect moments in time."

He was struck by how lovely she was, how poised. Such a shame she wasn't really Merry's cousin. She still wouldn't be acceptable enough in the duke's eyes, but remove that obstacle and she was everything Louisa had said Jasper wanted in a wife...save her inability to be honest.

He turned toward her, so he was facing her instead of the painting. "Why can't you tell me the truth? I wouldn't use it to hurt you. Louisa's happiness is my primary goal."

"I've told you the truth." Her tone was steady. She kept herself positioned toward the portrait.

He frowned. "Do you understand why I don't believe you? You've lied to me from the start."

She blanched, but somehow found the courage to look at him. "I did—in the beginning—and I'm still so ashamed of what I tried to do."

For the first time, he believed her, or at least he wanted to. She clearly demonstrated regret.

He moved closer. "So you maintain that all of this business with Louisa and Merry is the truth?"

"Yes." Her gaze didn't waver. Either her acting ability really was spectacular or she *was* telling the truth. Time would tell. His investigator would be able to confirm her relationship to Merry, and perhaps where she'd gotten Merry's painted box. In the meantime, he could conduct an investigation of his own.

"Do you miss your parents?" he asked, curious to see what she might reveal.

She blinked then pivoted to survey the painting on the opposite wall. "Somewhat."

"Only somewhat?"

"We weren't terribly close. I thought, that is, I wondered if you might understand such a relationship."

Extremely perceptive, but then it didn't take a scholar to see the cavernous divide separating him from the duke and duchess. "I do." They moved to the next painting. "How long ago did they pass?"

"Just last year."

He would've sworn she'd been in London longer than that. She didn't have a country girl's sensibilities. It would be easy enough for him to find out, so he decided to ask her outright. "I've sent someone to Newton Abbott to verify your claims. Tell me, what will he find?"

She turned to look at him, her eyes surprisingly cool and serene. "Louisa insists I'm Merry's family. Why do you want to upset her?"

She'd cut to the very thing that would most wound him—Louisa's well-being. "I've no wish to, but I must protect her from harm." He held up a hand to halt any argument. "I know you claim you won't hurt her, but we've already discussed my understandable lack of faith in you. Now, you didn't answer my question. What will I find?"

He pinned her with the blistering stare the duke had taught him so well. She blinked quickly, but not before he caught the barest flash of something.

"You won't find anything but the truth as Louisa presented it."

"So I'll find records of your birth and that of your parents, tying all of you to the Merriweathers?"

"No, because those records were destroyed in a fire."

"How convenient. Still, I imagine the townspeople will be quite helpful. One year is not such a long time to forget a family's existence."

She lifted a shoulder, seemingly unaffected by the suspicion in his tone. She turned back to the painting. "Does Louisa know you sent someone to Devon?"

"No." He stepped toward her, enjoying their game of cat and mouse despite her lies. "Why, do you think I should tell her?"

She threw him a dark look. "Yes. Or I can."

He begrudgingly gave her credit. Louisa would be furious with him, and Olivia knew it. "Or you could tell me the truth right now, and we'll call a halt to this entire farce."

"There is no farce. There is only you looking for nefarious intent where there is none."

He snaked his hand around her upper arm and pulled her toward him. "You had plenty of 'nefarious intent' when we met. It seems logical you would continue in that vein. Women like you don't wake up with a conscience."

Her eyes were full of storms now. "You were angry when I made an assumption about the kind of man you are, so don't do it to me. You've no idea what sort of woman I am." She gave her arm a shake, and he let her go.

He moved forward, and she pivoted back until she came into contact with the wall between the paintings. "I know you're an actress," he said smoothly, "capable of weaving all manner of deception."

Her lips curved up in a humorless smile. "Misassumption number one. I'm not really an actress. I was only on the stage for a fortnight."

"And why is it you haven't shared that with Louisa if you've nothing to hide? I grant she'd be disappointed, but mostly because you withheld the truth. You should consider telling her. Like me, Louisa prizes honesty."

She arched a brow. "Perhaps I will."

He admired her just then, even if he didn't believe her. "An excellent notion. I'm sure your reasons for working at the Haymarket are sound. How did that come to pass anyway?"

She stood taller and thrust her chin at him. "I came from Devon several months ago and took a position at the theatre as a seamstress. I only filled in onstage for an actress who left temporarily to care for a sick relative. It was then I had the misfortune of encountering—and being bedeviled—by you."

Bedeviled? He'd show her bedeviled. He closed the gap between them until they nearly touched. "And when is it *exactly* that you came from Devon?"

She tipped her head back, but didn't shrink from him. An auburn curl loosened and grazed her ivory cheek. "March."

He took in the graceful sweep of her neck, partially covered from his hungry gaze by the starched collar of her shirt beneath the deep sage green of her riding habit. His lust threatened to destroy any semblance of propriety, which, alone as they were in the gallery, was nonexistent. "So you really are from Devon."

"Yes." Her voice deepened, stirring his desire further.

He tucked the stray lock of hair behind her ear. "And your parents died last year. Were they ill?"

Her breathing hitched as his fingers skimmed the outer shell, and he felt a surge of triumph. "A coaching accident."

"You said you didn't own any horses."

The flash of disquiet in her eyes confirmed the lie. She drew back, and his body regretted that his mind had pursued this course instead of kissing her senseless. "They'd borrowed someone else's carriage." A plausible excuse, but he still didn't believe her.

So disappointing—both her dishonesty and his unquenched lust. "Ah, and therein lies the tragedy."

She turned, quickly, before she showed him any emotion.

Liar.

HE DIDN'T BELIEVE her. And why should he after she'd deceived him, *and* he'd caught her in another lie that afternoon? Keeping the lies separate from the truth was beginning to take a toll on Olivia's brain. She had a monstrous headache. If her hands hadn't been occupied with carrying a tea tray to Louisa's room, she would've massaged her temples.

"Is that you, dear?" called Louisa from the massive four-poster cloaked with pale blue hangings.

"Yes, I've brought your tea." Olivia toted the tray into the large bedchamber and placed it on the table beside the bed. Due to Louisa's swollen ankle, they'd decided to remain at Benfield overnight.

Louisa sat propped against an array of sunshine-yellow and ivory pillows. She smiled while Olivia poured out. "Lovely, thank you."

Olivia pulled a chair near the bed and sat with her teacup. "How is your ankle?"

"It still pains a bit, but it shan't keep me awake tonight. You did splash a bit of brandy in the teapot like I asked?"

"I did." Olivia tasted the brew and decided it was an acquired appreciation.

Louisa sipped her tea and gave a contented sigh. "Wonderful, dear. Are you sorry we weren't able to attend the musicale in Town?"

"Goodness, no. I prefer your company to people I scarcely know." Olivia was grateful for the reprieve from the likes of Lady Lydia Prewitt.

Louisa's forehead creased. "You're not unhappy, are you dear?"

"Of course not. I simply relish our time together." Indeed, today had been nearly idyllic, save Louisa's injury and Jasper's interrogation.

"I do, too." Louisa smiled warmly.

How was it that Olivia could be so fond of Louisa in such a short time? Probably because she knew Louisa felt it, too.

"Oh, we forgot about your sketches for Jasper's waistcoat." Louisa sighed. "This troublesome ankle upset the entire day. I don't suppose you showed him your drawings when he gave you a tour of the house?"

"No, he showed me Merry's paintings, and I'm afraid we quite forgot about the waistcoat." He'd been too busy questioning her, and she'd been too busy trying not to tell him everything.

After the gallery, she and Jasper had returned to the library to dine with Louisa, and he'd left almost immediately thereafter. He hadn't offered a second ride, not that Olivia had minded. Her posterior was a bit sore, and she wasn't sure she trusted herself to be alone with him again—and a groom holding her reins didn't qualify as a chaperone as far as Olivia was concerned.

"Pity. Ah well, I'm sure we'll see him tomorrow."

So soon? His probing questions had further undermined any sense of security she'd managed. He'd sent someone to Newton Abbott, and what he'd find—though of course she couldn't admit it to him— was evidence of her lies. There were no parents who'd died in a carriage accident, or any other way. And she'd left seven years ago, not earlier this year. Her aunt would surely tell Jasper's investigator precisely when, and probably even why, Olivia had left. It was only a matter of time before Jasper knew everything.

"Louisa, would it be terrible if people learned the truth about me?"

Louisa set her cup on the table. "I care for you a great deal, so I shan't lie to you. Bastards, particularly females, are not embraced by Society. Your options would be fewer." She regarded Olivia with a concerned, but empathetic expression. "Please don't fret, dear. No one is going to discover the truth. How could they?"

"Lady Addicock is from a town very near mine. I realize the chances of encountering someone who is familiar with me or my foster family is slight, but it's not completely impossible." Especially if someone went looking. Someone like Jasper. Why didn't she do as she'd threatened and tell Louisa what Jasper had done? Maybe that would put an end to it.

Surprisingly, Louisa's lips curved up into a mischievous grin. This was not the reaction Olivia had been expecting. "I should have told you earlier today, but I'm afraid I quite forgot with the excitement of bringing you to Benfield. I dispatched someone to Newton Abbott to talk with your aunt and uncle, and I'm sorry to tell you that your uncle died."

Although she'd left the vicarage in an abrupt and upsetting manner, Olivia suffered a stab of sorrow. She'd spent fourteen mostly happy years as their daughter. "And my aunt?"

Louisa shook her head. "She went to live with relatives not far from here, actually. A small village called Cheshunt. Do you want me to send someone to ascertain her welfare?"

Olivia had spent many a sleepless night thinking of what she might like to say to her aunt if she could go back to that horrible day seven years ago. Though the pain was still there, Olivia was no longer angry. Indeed, she hoped her aunt might have put the past behind her, especially with both Uncle and Fiona gone. "I think I should like to visit her personally."

"I can accompany you when my ankle's better."

Olivia didn't want Louisa to meet Aunt Mildred, who possessed a cool and rigid demeanor. In fact, Olivia couldn't imagine two more dissimilar women. "Thank you, but I think I should go alone. I do appreciate your kindness."

Olivia smiled but inwardly continued to fret. Though her aunt was no longer in Newton Abbott and couldn't provide Jasper's investigator with the truth, there were plenty of other people in the village who would remember Olivia, even after seven years.

Louisa patted the bed next to her. "You still look worried. Come and sit with me, dear."

Olivia set her teacup on the table and perched next to Louisa.

The older woman took her hand. "I want you to know I will support you no matter what."

These words meant more than anything. Olivia had been thrown out by one mother only to be begrudgingly taken in by another. To be wanted, at last, was beyond wonderful. She couldn't speak past the lump in her throat, so she merely nodded.

Louisa squeezed Olivia's fingers. "I manufactured this ruse to protect you. I don't want you to worry. I want you to enjoy yourself. My goodness, your young life has been far too full of vexation and anguish. You've so many things to experience. I'm very much looking forward to your Season next spring."

"I don't have to find a husband, do I?"

"Goodness no!" Louisa chuckled. She let go of Olivia's hand and picked up her teacup. "There's no rush, dear. You're not even close to being on the shelf. Plenty of girls don't marry during their first Season. "

Like Louisa who hadn't wed Merry until many years later. "You were one of those girls then?"

"Oh, no. I became engaged to someone else my first Season." Her eyes sparkled as she wiggled her eyebrows. "I was quite popular. My father's, now my brother's, dukedom is one of the oldest and wealthiest in the kingdom."

These were facts, not boasts, but they reminded Olivia of the vast differences between them. "I didn't realize Merry wasn't your first husband. Were you happy?"

"Not particularly, but it was my duty. So many chits complain about their status not being high enough, but it can be terribly oppressive." Holding her cup with two hands, Louisa sipped her tea.

She'd no idea someone like Louisa would feel trapped. Did Jasper feel that way? His role as heir to a dukedom had to be rife with obligation. "So you married a man of your father's choosing?"

Louisa nodded as she returned her cup to the table. "That's how it's done." She pulled a face, which was quite humorous on a woman of her distinguished experience. "Wokenham was much older. Nearly fifty." She giggled. "Younger than me now, of course."

Olivia smiled, finding Louisa's mirth infectious.

"But he wasn't nearly as lively. Didn't care to ride. Didn't care to socialize. Didn't care to do much beyond read crop treatises." She inclined her head, with a solemnly respectful expression. "Which served him well, since he owned the finest estate in Staffordshire."

"What happened to him?"

"He died just four years into the marriage. Four long, childless years." Her face fell and she shook her head. "Oh, that's horribly uncharitable of me. He was a kind man, just too far gone for someone of my youth and vivacity."

Olivia knew Louisa yearned for children and could hear it in her voice now. "What did you do after that?"

"Why, I lived the charmed life of a young widow!" She smiled and adopted a far-off look. "The things you can do when you are not beholden to your father or your husband…absolutely glorious."

Olivia didn't precisely know what those things might be, but was fairly certain that as a young, unmarried woman she wasn't allowed to do any of them.

"I missed having a family of my own, but was quite content to make decisions without consulting anyone else. Until I met Merry." Her face softened, revealing the love Olivia had seen so often since coming to live with her. "Suddenly, the ability to play cards all night or jaunt to Bath at a moment's notice didn't matter. Not when I'd found the person with whom I wanted to share not only those amusements, but the simple things, such as sitting together drinking tea." She lifted her cup and offered a mock toast.

Olivia understood. To have a companion to share not only your joys and struggles but also your everyday occurrences seemed a special thing. She didn't think her foster parents had enjoyed such a relationship. And her mother had certainly never sought anything so civilized. Over the last several years, Olivia assumed she wouldn't, either. She'd accepted her lot and made the most of it. But now she had Louisa and could perhaps dare to dream of more.

Provided Jasper didn't expose everything. She wished she could tell him the truth. He loved Louisa enough to accept Olivia, didn't he? Besides, she wanted him to trust her. She owed him that much after trying to trick him. "Jasper was very attentive today with his instruction. I think we could tell him the truth about my relationship to Merry."

Louisa frowned sadly. "I'm afraid not, dear. I know Jasper far better than you, and while he would tolerate your place in my household for my sake, I refuse to burden him with keeping our secret."

Olivia wanted to argue, but couldn't dispute that Louisa knew him better. That still didn't change the fact that disaster was imminent, and she'd have to find a way to circumvent it. She considered telling Jasper anyway, but then she'd be lying to Louisa. *Again.* Furthermore, Olivia could only imagine what Jasper would do if she claimed to be Merry's daughter. His *illegitimate* daughter.

Oh, what a deceitful tangle! All so she could inhabit a society she wasn't even sure she liked. And for what?

She looked at Louisa sipping her tea, the hint of a smile ticking up the corners of her mouth. Olivia couldn't stop the surge of warmth that spread through her chest. For the first time in her life, Olivia truly belonged with someone, and for that, she'd lie to the king himself.

Chapter Twelve

JASPER STROLLED OUT of the Black Horse in the company of Sevrin and Gifford. The club's attendance had been on the low side tonight. Even so, they'd managed four bouts. Rather than participate, Jasper had spent the majority of the evening drinking a bottle of whiskey while thinking of Olivia back at Benfield. This obsession—and it was an obsession—was becoming irksome.

"You've been quiet, Sax," observed Sevrin. He'd been challenged in the last fight of the evening and now nursed a fat lip. Sevrin rarely sustained visible injury, but tonight he'd been a bit slow.

"Is that why you moved like tar?" Jasper teased. "Too focused on me?"

Sevrin gave him a gimlet eye. "No. Though I'm surprised you even noticed, busy as you were studying the intricacies of your whiskey."

Gifford laughed. "You sound like brothers. How long have you been friends?"

Jasper looked at Sevrin, who surveyed him in return. "Not long." But Jasper did feel a certain inexplicable affinity for him. Likely because they were both scoundrels.

Sevrin led them from the court onto the Haymarket. "Where next, lads?"

Jasper usually returned to Saxton House after visiting the club. However, tonight he felt unsettled, hungry. The time he'd spent with Olivia today had left him wanting.

Gifford gestured east. "The Locust?"

The Locust was a gaming hell; that much Jasper knew, though he'd never been there. He was surprised at the suggestion. A young tailor's apprentice didn't seem the type to frequent such places.

Sevrin nodded. "Why not?"

Because he didn't want to return to his cold bed alone, Jasper joined them. Did that mean he'd settle for someone who wasn't Olivia? He recoiled at the notion, but reason told him he ought to consider using another female to eradicate Olivia from his mind. If he could. Doubt nipped his heels as he took long strides to catch up with his friends.

The small, squalid establishment occupied the ground floor of a brick building. Tables littered the main room, which they'd had to enter by squeezing past a drunkard negotiating with an aging whore.

Sevrin towered over a table with four occupants—one snoring loudly—and cleared his throat. "Would you mind?"

"Lookee here." One elbowed another who promptly fell to the floor and didn't get up.

Sevrin took the now vacant chair and sat. "You chaps look about done, am I right?" He smiled, but drummed his fingers expectantly on the pocked tabletop. The two conscious men grabbed the man slumped on the floor and dragged him toward the exit.

Jasper eyed the sleeping fellow. "What about this one?"

"Ah, leave him," Sevrin said.

A wench in an excessively low-cut gown staggered toward them. She looked every bit as soused as the others. "What can I get ye?" She thrust her chest forward suggestively, but the tray in her hand indicated she purveyed beverages in addition to her flesh.

"Gin," ordered Sevrin. Gifford nodded in agreement.

She plucked two cups from her tray and slammed them onto the scarred table. "You?" she asked, directing her bloodshot eyes toward Jasper.

"Whiskey."

"Out, I'm afraid. I'll go get summore. Don' go nowhere. I've got to tell Ada the Vicious Viscount's here!" She smiled widely, revealing a few holes where teeth ought to have been.

Jasper's insides curdled. Any notion he'd possessed to find a bed partner other than Olivia was well and truly dead.

"Lively place you chose, Giff," Sevrin said.

"The Vicious Viscount. Really?" he countered, with an arched brow.

Sevrin grinned. "It's the alliteration I'm sure. Do I seem vicious to you?"

On the surface he was irreverent, irresponsible, and irrepressible. Underneath, however, Jasper suspected there lurked something more. Something dangerous perhaps.

The wench returned with his whiskey. "Somethin' else I can get for ye three?" She moved close to Jasper, but he inched his chair away from her, bumping the knee of the snoring man. He stopped, but just for a second before resuming his loud rumbling.

She pouted at Jasper. "No need to be rude. 'Ere's some girls over there what are interested." She stabbed a finger toward the other corner on their side of the hell.

Jasper turned his head. Three younger, more appealing women stared at them from where they stood gathered in a tiny coven. They looked toward the men's table and then spoke amongst themselves, frequently casting glances back in their direction.

Jasper turned to face the table, determined to keep the unwanted women at bay, and purposefully oblivious as to whether his friends were in agreement. "Ignore them."

The serving wench slunk off.

Sevrin slouched further into his rickety chair, giving no sign he gave a fig about the lightskirts. "You asked me awhile back about an actress, Olivia West. I saw a woman who looked like her at the Faversham's' the other night. I assumed I was mistaken, but then I heard her name mentioned at White's earlier today. Some fellow, Twickenham or something, was going on about her. Is it the same woman?"

Jasper wrapped his fingers around the cup of whiskey and squeezed the pottery. He downed the fiery liquid before answering. "It is."

Gifford sat a bit straighter in his chair. "Olivia West, you say?"

"Do you know her?" Sevrin asked before Jasper could.

"The name sounds familiar." Gifford sipped his gin, regarding them over the rim of his cup.

Sevrin turned to look at Jasper. "Twickenham said she was Lady Merriweather's ward. Lady Merriweather is your aunt, I gather."

"Both statements are correct."

Sevrin leaned forward. "You're being damnably reticent. How is this woman in Society?"

Jasper should have realized someone would recognize her somehow. He was only glad it was Sevrin and not someone with more…influence. Preparing to share the spectacular story of Miss Olivia West, he signaled for more whiskey.

"Miss West claims to be my uncle's distant cousin. There is, conveniently, no evidence of this claim save a painted box that was definitely painted by my uncle and is now in her possession. I've no idea how she came to own this box, but my dear aunt believes she's found a young woman in need of family and care, two things she's desperate to endow."

Sevrin shook his head. "Are you saying Miss West is a charlatan?"

"I suspect as much, yes."

"Why?" Gifford asked, his forehead creasing. "Isn't the story possible?"

"Many things are possible, but Miss West has a habit of lying." He couldn't bring himself to tell them why. That incident was between him and Olivia.

Gifford's eyes narrowed. "How do you know this?"

Jasper gave the young bloke an icy stare. "Suffice it to say that I do."

Gifford said nothing, but gripped his gin before taking another swig.

"Saxton's right not to trust her." Sevrin turned an apologetic gaze on him. "I'm willing to wager she neglected to tell you she's Fiona Scarlet's daughter?"

The haze of alcohol completely evaporated from Jasper's brain. "Fiona Scarlet? Why is that name familiar?"

"She was an infamous actress and courtesan. Bright red hair. Changed her lovers more often than the mail coach to Cornwall changes horses."

God damn it. He knew she'd lied, but this was unconscionable. Any number of people at the Favershams could have made the connection Sevrin did. "Of what class were her paramours? The sort that frequent your club or the sort that frequent White's?"

"Something in between, I think. No one like you would have sought her out."

So perhaps no one at the Favershams recognized her. But he couldn't know for sure. What a disaster. If Holborn learned the truth, he'd get rid of Olivia faster than he had Abigail. Jasper had to prevent that from happening, and he had to ensure his aunt heard the truth from someone who cared. Louisa was going to be devastated.

"Is it possible she can be this woman's daughter and your uncle's cousin?" Gifford asked.

"I intend to find out." Jasper wanted to go to Benfield to demand answers. *Now.* He rose from his chair.

Sevrin looked up at him. "It's past three in the morning. You can't go talk to her now."

Though Jasper wanted to, it would be an hour before he arrived at Benfield. Almost tomorrow. And tomorrow would have to be soon enough. *Except*, his brain reminded him, *tomorrow is your mother's picnic, and you promised Lady Philippa you would be there.*

"Bloody, bloody hell," he muttered and sank back onto his chair. After the damn picnic, then.

At last the slattern returned with another cup of whiskey. Jasper glanced up at her. "Bring the bottle."

OLIVIA'S BORROWED COACH from Benfield reached the vicarage in Cheshunt just after noon. The footman opened the door and helped her descend to the dry, packed dirt. She studied the building, noting it was perhaps twice as large as the vicarage in which she'd lived as a child. Aunt Mildred's relative was apparently more successful in his endeavor than Uncle had been.

She turned to the retainer. "I don't know how long I shall be. Will you wait here?"

"Yes, miss." He hadn't asked why they'd come, and Olivia could only imagine what he speculated. She'd informed Louisa of her specific plans, but told the servants she was only exploring the heath. When they'd gone considerably farther than that, she'd simply told the coachman she was on an errand.

Since Louisa had told her of Aunt Mildred's relocation the previous evening, Olivia could think of little other than visiting the woman who had raised her. She'd barely slept, organizing today's trip in her mind.

A warm, gentle breeze stroked her face, completely at odds with the turmoil inside her as she stared at Mildred's brother's vicarage, about to come face to face with the woman who'd turned her out seven years ago. She walked, haltingly, up the short path leading to the door. The scent of roses filled the air, reminding her of her mother's keepsake box, of Merry, and of Louisa. She'd raised her hand to knock, but didn't strike the wood. With a loud exhalation, she dropped her fist.

What was she doing? She had Louisa, who loved her. Did any of this matter anymore? Perhaps she'd come to show Mildred West she'd not only survived, but also hadn't become the fallen woman Mildred expected her to be. Nor was she the vicar's bastard. How satisfying it would be to inform her she'd tossed Olivia out for nothing.

Or, mayhap she'd come to see if Mildred cared anything for her. The idea that she'd never wanted Olivia, had only suffered her presence out of some harassed sense of duty carved a hollow ache in Olivia's soul.

She straightened her shoulders and rapped on the thick oak. A moment later, the door swung open to reveal a middle-aged housekeeper.

She eyed Olivia with curiosity, taking in the coach behind her. "May I help you?"

"I'm here to see Mrs. West."

"I'm afraid Mrs. West isn't expecting company."

"Would you mind telling her Miss Olivia West is here? I'm certain she'd care to see me."

The housekeeper's eyes widened upon hearing Olivia's surname. "I suppose I can ask."

She couldn't be turned away. Not now. "Is it too much trouble if I wait inside? I'll go if she truly doesn't wish to be disturbed. I've come a bit of a long way…" She offered a pleading, hopeful smile.

With a sweeping look, the housekeeper took pity on her and opened the door wider. She gestured Olivia into the house.

After the opulence of Benfield, the vicarage was dark and small, but well kept. The housekeeper led her to a room directly to the right. The window facing the drive invited much-needed light into the oak-paneled chamber.

She inclined her head toward Olivia. "I'll just speak with Mrs. West."

Olivia studied the interior while she waited. Mildred's sewing basket sat near a chair positioned between the fireplace and the window. How many times had they sat together, stitching in quiet companionship? Or what Olivia had thought was companionship.

"Olivia?"

At the familiar sound of Aunt Mildred's voice, Olivia turned to the door. "Good afternoon, Aunt Mildred."

Dark blonde hair pulled into a severe bun, Mildred stood with her brows knitted and her thin lips pursed until they disappeared. "What an unexpected...surprise."

Olivia's hopes fell at the other woman's lack of affection. She'd so hoped time had soothed Mildred's animosity. "A surprise indeed. I just learned you'd relocated to Cheshunt, so close to London. I was sad to hear about Uncle. I wish you would've sent word."

Mildred brushed her hands over her hips, accentuating her extreme thinness. "To what end? So you and your trollop mother could come to his funeral? I think not."

Stung, Olivia searched for a response. She hadn't expected open arms, but she also hadn't expected the same level of frigidity as seven years ago. It was as if Mildred had just expelled her yesterday. "Do you not know that Fiona passed last year?"

Her expression offered no surprise, no compassion. "No, and I'm not sorry for it."

Olivia knew better than to expect sympathy, especially for the half-sister her aunt had despised. "That's not why I'm here. I came to tell you I've recently learned the true identity of my father, and it's not Mr. West, as you supposed."

Mildred stalked further into the room, her eyes narrowing. "Of course, he was. I don't know what nonsense you're spouting, but you shan't do it here."

"I live with my stepmother now, the dowager Viscountess Merriweather. Her husband was my father."

Her aunt's shrill, mirthless laugh filled the room. "That's quite a tale. And she believes you?"

Olivia struggled to keep her voice even. "She's the one who told me."

Mildred stared at her. "I don't know what you're playing at, and furthermore, I don't care. I want you to leave."

Olivia couldn't keep her emotion in check. She knew she wouldn't get another chance to question her aunt. "Why did you send me away?"

"You know why." She sneered. "Your whore mother lured my husband to infidelity. It's true that men have certain needs…but not with their wife's half-sister."

"That's not my fault. Why do you blame me?"

Hostility radiated from Mildred, her lips curling, her nostrils flaring. "You're the image of her. Looking at you is like looking at her. The sight turns my stomach."

Olivia's nerves stretched. "My mother wasn't a whore. She did what she had to do to survive. It's not as if she sold herself to just anyone." Was she actually defending Fiona?

"A courtesan is still a whore, Olivia, especially one who spreads her legs for her brother-in-law for *free*." She spat the last word with such venom, Olivia shrank back.

"How can you be so certain?"

"Because she bewitched Mr. West! Even years later—fourteen years later to be exact—he was pining for her, writing pathetic love letters. I found one of them, and he couldn't deny it. That very day I sent you to live with the slut. I never should have agreed to take you, but Mr. West was determined to help *family* as he put it. Would that I had known the truth then."

If her uncle had loved her mother, the sentiment had not been reciprocated. She wasn't aware her mother had loved any man. How had he felt when his wife had sent his daughter—at least the girl he thought was his daughter—away?

Olivia thought of the things she had in common with Merry. Did she share any of her uncle's attributes? She tried to think. "I don't look like Uncle."

"No, because you look like your whore of a mother."

"I don't share any of Uncle's interests, but I possess some of the viscount's talents."

"Nonsense. The only talent I recall you demonstrating was embroidery, which *I* taught you."

"I can sketch and paint. The viscount was a gifted artist."

"That proves nothing. This *viscount* isn't your father. You and Mr. West can both read a book faster than anyone I know, and neither one of you can sing in key."

Both of these things were true. Olivia ignored a building unease.

"My hair is both my mother's color and the viscount's."

"What? Your hair is more auburn than your mother's so perhaps you did inherit your father's darker hair. I know it's hard to remember, bald as he was, but Mr. West's hair was once quite dark. Really, Olivia, this is all nonsense." She stepped forward, stopping just in front of Olivia. The pinched look on her face said she'd rather stand in a pigpen. "You've a mark on your head, beneath your hair now, but it was quite visible when you were a baby. Dark pink and shaped like a pear. Mr. West had a similar mark on his head, though it's larger. Surely you recall seeing it, given his lack of hair."

Olivia searched her memory. It had been years since she'd seen him, but yes, she remembered that mark. Her insides shriveled until she wanted to collapse onto the floor and pull a blanket over her head.

Mildred stepped back, a look of triumph lighting her small-featured face. "Now then. I should like you to take your fairy tales and return to wherever you came from. I pity that poor woman who thinks you're some viscount's daughter." She went to the window. "Is that her coach? Is she in there? Perhaps I should tell her the truth."

"No." Olivia was quite glad she hadn't brought Louisa. "She's not there. I'll go." She trudged toward the small entry hall, her shoulders drooping with horrible defeat.

She pivoted to look at her aunt one last time. "I understand why it might be hurtful for you to have me in your house, but have you no good will toward me at all?"

Her thin lips pressed together with a short exhale of frustrated breath. "No. I raised you because it was the Godly thing to do, not from any desire to have my sister's bastard child under my roof."

Olivia finally understood. She'd figured Mildred to simply be an undemonstrative woman. She'd never said she loved Olivia, but she'd cared for her and treated her fairly, if not affectionately. But she'd only done it out of duty, and the moment she'd learned her husband was Olivia's father…well, that had been all she'd needed to eliminate her burden. Pain sliced through Olivia, both because she honestly didn't know who her father was, and because this woman hated her through no fault of her own.

The final moments in the vicarage all those years ago flashed through Olivia's mind, as so many times before. There were countless things she wished she'd said. Olivia stood taller. Despite her defeat, she would find pride. She was not to blame.

"I'm sorry you feel that way. Family is family, and I shall love you in spite of everything. Thank you for taking me in when you did. I've done nothing to be ashamed of, and I actually believe you'd be quite pleased with how I've managed things, owing to your influence."

Mildred blinked. Her mouth opened, but she snapped it shut.

"Good day, then." Shaking, Olivia turned and quit the vicarage. The footman helped her into the carriage, and within a moment they were on their way. She turned to look back at the house, only to see her aunt standing on the front step with her hands on her hips.

She banged her head back against the velvet cushion. Foolish, foolish errand. She'd resolved nothing. In fact, she'd only watered and nurtured a seed of doubt. Doubt that was even now blooming in her mind and sending tendrils of ice to her extremities.

Which man was her father? More importantly, why had none of these people cared enough about her to keep her close?

Chapter Thirteen

JASPER BLINKED AGAINST the bright sunlight as he walked across Hyde Park toward his mother's annual picnic. Blankets were artfully placed about the ground. Little boats bobbed along the sun-sparkled Serpentine. The affair might've looked inviting if last night's excess of whiskey hadn't given him a crashing headache and if Olivia's deception wasn't keeping his mind utterly distracted. Best to get through his obligation so he could be on his way to Benfield.

Lady Philippa sat with her mother, Lady Herrick, on a large blue blanket about five yards distant. Jasper shoved aside his preoccupation with Olivia and made his way toward them.

"Good afternoon, ladies." He smiled at Lady Philippa, a picture of sophisticated beauty with her upswept chestnut hair topped with a splendid wide-brimmed hat tied beneath her chin with yellow gauze.

Jasper deposited himself on the pale blue blanket. The matted grass beneath the cotton offered little cushion to the hard ground, but he didn't plan to sit here long. "Have you taken to the Serpentine yet?" he asked Lady Philippa.

She shook her head. "I'm afraid I'm not too keen on boats."

Jasper gave an inward sigh of relief. One less thing he'd have to do today, which meant he could leave for Benfield even sooner.

"You should walk a bit, Philippa, enjoy the day," her mother urged, with a glance toward Jasper.

"I should be happy to escort you," he offered.

Lady Philippa looked to her mother who answered with a tiny nod. Jasper stood and helped Lady Philippa to her feet. Their gloved hands met, and he felt…nothing, which was a trifle disappointing since he'd be marrying her. He blamed his lack of response on his obsession with Olivia. Soon he would be able to focus on duty again.

He wrapped Lady Philippa's arm around his and led her along the Serpentine. "Do you mind walking by the water?"

"Not at all. I just have no desire to be *on* it." She smiled, her eyes sparkling. She was very pretty, but he still wasn't stirred. She wasn't Olivia.

Jasper searched for a topic of conversation, both to appear a gentleman and to try to keep from thinking of Olivia. "Is your father here today?"

"No, he's in Oxfordshire. You needn't worry he's off scouting husbands for me. Not yet anyway." She smiled. "I jest. The choice will be mine."

He was surprised by her candor. "Choice is a valuable thing."

She peered up at him with intelligent, golden brown eyes. "Yes, we women don't get many of them. You, on the other hand…"

He let out a bark of laughter. "Don't get as many as you think."

Her brows knitted together. "I see." They walked in silence a moment. "Are you here, with me, of your own choice?"

Jasper concentrated on keeping his feet moving. "Of course. There's nowhere else I'd rather be." Now who was the liar?

"I see your parents casting furtive looks in our direction. They have an expectation." She glanced at him with those warm, assessing eyes. "It's all right. Last spring was not my first Season, you know."

He found her wisdom disquieting. But also encouraging. He didn't want a ninnyhammer for a wife. His eye caught his father standing off to the right, chatting with some other gentlemen. The duke wouldn't want a ninnyhammer for a daughter-in-law, either. Well, that wasn't precisely true. She could be a ninnyhammer provided she was a well-placed one.

And that's really all it was, wasn't it? Lady Philippa was plenty good enough, intelligence notwithstanding, because of the "lady" preceding her name. And Olivia wasn't. Even if she were Merry's cousin, her lack of a titled father made her less desirable than Lady Philippa. Just as Jasper's second son status made him less desirable in the duke's eyes.

Lady Philippa paused. "Shall we return?"

Jasper realized he'd continued moving, while she'd stopped. He shook the thoughts of the duke from his mind and turned her back toward her mother's blanket. "May I call on you tomorrow?"

She didn't immediately respond. "No."

He'd bungled this with his inattention. "Oh."

She laughed softly. "I have an appointment already tomorrow.

How about the day after? It would be…nice to see you without your parents lurking about."

Very wise. And understanding. "I should like that." He felt guilty courting her while Olivia was omnipresent in his mind. He owed Lady Philippa more than he was giving her. "We have things to discuss."

She arched a brow. "We do? Are you ready for that?"

"Are you?" he countered, almost wishing she'd say no.

"I suppose I must be."

Now it was his turn to laugh. "Your exuberance overwhelms me."

She blushed, and he wondered if he'd gone too far. "You know how this is, Saxton. A silly dance. But I like you, and I think we may get on well together."

Jasper felt the same but couldn't completely ignore a hollow sensation in the pit of his belly.

Upon returning her to Lady Herrick, he conversed with them for a polite few minutes before excusing himself. Hastily, he strode to where Malheur was tethered with the other horses. The duke arrived as Jasper took Malheur's reins from one of the grooms.

Holborn glared the groom into a hasty retreat. When he turned his attention to Jasper, his eyes were hard chips of ice in his furious face. "Where the bloody hell are you going? This is your mother's annual picnic!"

"Yes, and it's lovely. I've other business to attend."

"Business? What could be more important than courting Lady Philippa?"

Jasper didn't bother concealing his contempt. "I'm going to visit your sister. You're aware, I believe, that Louisa hurt her ankle and is recuperating at Benfield, not that you seem to give a damn. Besides, I've done my duty today. I'm certain you saw me with Lady Philippa."

"A ten minute walk is not courtship!"

"It is for one day. Would you rather I secret her behind a tree and toss up her skirts?"

"Base, foul…" The duke gritted his teeth. "But what should I expect after that country girl? You're an embarrassment."

His constant recollection of that decade-old mistake was beyond tedious. Jasper tried to quell his rising anger. "I'm calling on Lady Philippa day after tomorrow. I may have agreed to marry someone of whom you approve, but never again try to entrap me with her or any other female."

The duke stepped forward, throwing his shoulders back. "I'll do whatever I must to get what I want, Saxton."

Jasper froze as the arrogance of the duke's words sunk in. This was precisely what he was doing to Olivia. He'd do whatever necessary to obtain what he wanted: *the truth from her.* His investigation into her background…was that to protect Louisa or was it ammunition to somehow manipulate Olivia?

He glared in lieu of saying goodbye and swung himself up on Malheur's back. The horse picked up his hooves, as eager to quit the picnic as Jasper. They turned and galloped away through the park.

Nearly an hour later, Jasper arrived at Benfield invigorated. He took the steps two at a time. The footman just barely managed to open the door before Jasper reached the threshold.

The butler, a robust man in his mid-forties called Ruben, greeted him in the entry hall. "Good afternoon, Lord Saxton. Your aunt is resting abovestairs presently."

Excellent. "And where is Miss West?"

"Out, I'm afraid."

Disappointment deflated Jasper's expectant mood. "She's not riding?"

Ruben gave a nearly imperceptible shake of his head. "Exploring the heath via carriage."

Bloody hell. "When is she expected to return?"

"I'm not certain, my lord." Ruben's bushy, dark brows—so at odds with the thinning hair atop his head—drew together. "In fact, she's already been gone several hours. I might have expected her back by now."

A bead of apprehension worked its way down Jasper's spine. "Do you think we ought to search for her?"

Another tiny shake of Ruben's head. "She had a coachman and a footman, my lord. I doubt they've run afoul."

He hated that she wasn't here now. He'd worked himself into a pique on the ride from Town, planning each moment of their encounter.

"I'll be happy to inform you of her arrival," Ruben offered.

He had a better idea. "No, thank you. I'm going to my

bedchamber, and I don't wish to be disturbed."

"Very good, my lord."

Jasper climbed the stairs with considerably less excitement than he had a few moments ago, but with utmost deliberation. He knew which bedchamber Olivia was using, and he would await her there with avid impatience.

IT WAS LATE in the afternoon before Olivia returned to Benfield. She hadn't eaten since breakfast, but she wasn't hungry. More than anything she craved the quiet solitude of her chamber, but doubted she'd get that until later. Louisa had to be wondering where she'd been.

Much to Olivia's relief, Ruben greeted her at the door and informed her Louisa was resting. Olivia took the opportunity to retreat to her room. As she ascended the stairs, she reflected that Benfield seemed even larger and more splendid than usual, punctuating her sense of isolation and disconnection.

There were equally plausible arguments for both men to be her father, but it seemed more likely she was the vicar's spawn. The shared birthmark—which she planned to search for immediately—seemed the most persuasive evidence, because it was visible proof of something she shared with one of the men. The other "evidence" was simply coincidence or could be linked to either of them, which made it useless.

She removed her hat and gloves before opening her door. Once inside the sanctuary of her bedchamber, she secured the lock and sank back against the wood.

She blinked.

Jasper, the fair-haired devil, sat in a chair on the other side of her bed, his long legs stretched in front of him. He'd removed his coat, and his cravat was loosened. His hair was a bit mussed, giving him a careless appearance that only enhanced his good looks.

Instantly, her muscles tightened, ready to flee. "What are you doing in here?"

He rose quickly. "I shall ask the questions, I think. Where have you been?"

Words clogged in her throat as he approached, his pale blue eyes spitting a fire that held no warmth.

He stopped just before her, giving her a thoroughly assessing perusal. "Where. Have. You. Been."

She stepped around him, uncomfortable with the energy pulsing from him, and tossed her hat and gloves on a chair. As angry as he'd been after her failed seduction scheme, he looked even more infuriated now. Her stomach flipped. What lie had he unraveled? For that had to be the reason for his fury.

He grabbed her arm and spun her back around to face him. "You're not avoiding me. Not today."

His eyes bore into hers with singular, steely intent. Her limbs shook with emotion. Fear? She refused to feel that. He wouldn't hurt her, even if she told him the truth about visiting her aunt. Which she couldn't. To share such rejection would be the ultimate humiliation. "I was driving around the heath."

"Liar." His soft tone was at odds with the sentiment. "Try again."

She swallowed, seeking moisture for her parched throat. "I was visiting a friend."

"What friend?" His grip on her arm loosened, but he didn't let go. His touch was almost tender.

How she longed for comfort, yearned for…something and someone. "No one you know. Someone from…before."

"Someone who knew Fiona Scarlet?"

Her insides turned to ice. "How did you know?"

"It wasn't that hard to deduce. I find myself asking *why* I didn't know."

She didn't think it was a question he wanted answered.

"Since Fiona is your mother, it seems highly unlikely you're Merry's cousin. What else have you lied about?"

Olivia swallowed. This was the moment to tell him the truth about Merry, to finally share this burden with someone, but Louisa's admonitions sounded in her head.

There was no use lying about Fiona at least. "Fine, now you know I'm a bastard. Fiona was my mother and my father was a relative of Merry's."

His features flickered with some emotion—pity, understanding?

She couldn't tell because it was gone as quickly as it had come.

"You're still insisting you're related to Merry?" His grip squeezed her arm, but not painfully. He pushed her backward until the backs of her thighs met the bed. "Stop lying. I'm going to find someone in Newton Abbott who will expose you."

He was right. She'd known it was only a matter of time. The time had just come sooner. She closed her eyes, hoping Louisa wouldn't be angry with her.

"I'm not Merry's cousin. I'm his daughter." *Or at least I thought I was until this afternoon, and now I don't know anything.* Tears threatened, but she refused to break down in front of Jasper, just as she refused to share the humiliation of her questionable paternity.

"Bloody rubbish." He let go of her arm and braced his hand on the bedpost on her right side. He towered over her. "Be honest with me. For once."

Suddenly tired of responding to everyone's whim—her aunt's, her mother's, even Louisa's, and most especially Jasper's—she shoved at him so hard he stumbled backward. "Leave me alone!"

She wanted to cry at the contradiction of the moment, demanding he leave her alone when all she wanted was someone to soothe her pain. He couldn't be that person.

Olivia strode into her dressing chamber, intent on shutting the door and locking him out. Except he was too fast. He caught her and they bumped together, hitting the wall. "I will have my answers, by God."

"You'll have nothing from me," she spat. "Why can't you accept me for who I am?"

He stared at her. "You're talking nonsense." He pushed her back against the wall and thrust himself against her, pressing his knee between her legs.

Olivia gasped, both because of his quick movement and because of her body's response. Heat rushed to her limbs, to her core, making her throb with desire.

She didn't want to want him. "Please, let me go."

"I can't." He lowered his mouth to hers and sucked on her lower lip. His teeth snagged at the soft flesh and without thinking, she pulled his head down.

The kiss exploded with fiery need. His mouth slanted over hers, open, wet, hot. He demanded her complete response, and she gave it. Her fingers pulled at the back of his hair. His knee pushed higher until it met her pulsing center.

Abruptly, he pulled back, leaving her aching. His pupils had dilated, obliterating some of the icy blue. She jerked back to awareness and scrambled out of the dressing room. She didn't turn until she'd reached the other side of the room and the bed separated them. "You need to leave."

He'd followed her into the bedroom, nearly around the bed, his chest rising and falling rapidly. "I won't leave without the truth. Why would you be foolish enough to feed me another lie? Merry can't be your father."

"Ask Louisa. She's the one who told me. You know she found me through my handkerchiefs. What you don't know is that she has a letter from my mother to Merry. About me. She's the one who fabricated the story about me being Merry's cousin. She didn't want anyone to know I'm a bastard."

He stared at her. "I can verify all of this just by going to Louisa and asking her."

"I know you can. I invite you to do so, though she'll be angry since she asked me not to tell you."

"What?" He looked befuddled, and she felt a pang of sorrow for him. "Why wouldn't she want me to know the truth?"

"She didn't want to burden you with potential scandal. And she's not certain how like your father you really are."

The anguish lining his face was unmistakable. He hated that his beloved aunt would categorize him with the duke. "She should have trusted me. I can't believe she didn't." He turned away.

Regardless of what had gone on between them or where their relationship was destined, Olivia had to reach out to another person in pain. She went to him and stood beside him. "I'm sorry."

He stared straight ahead. She moved around him to stand in front of him, trying to draw his gaze. She ached to touch him, to wipe the lines from his face.

Finally, he looked at her, and the need in his eyes nearly buckled her knees. She should go back to the dressing room and bolt the door. Instead, she moved closer.

He ran his fingertip down the side of her face. Desire wound through her, quickening her pulse and heating her flesh. His hand cupped the side of her neck and she closed her eyes. His thumb tipped her chin up, forcing her head back. She felt exposed, vulnerable. Her body thrummed with need.

Soft lips dragged along the column of her throat. His mouth opened and his tongue traced hot whorls against her sensitive flesh. God, how she wanted this. Her body, her soul cried out for his attention. Louisa's affection was a balm, but Jasper's desire was like food and water and shelter—everything she needed to survive.

His other hand snaked around her waist and pulled her flush against him. He was hard and hot. She opened her eyes as his mouth continued its downward path. He pulled the fichu from the top of her day dress and his lips worked a feverish trail over the swell of her breast.

He pivoted her about until they were beside the bed. He moved his hand down her neck to cup her breast. She gasped and he froze.

He straightened and looked down into her eyes. "Do you want me to stop?"

She should. This was madness. Men had offered to buy her body since she was fifteen, but her mother—thank God—had never allowed it. A few men had wooed her, but none with the precision and care of this man. He was a generous, solicitous gentleman who saved animals, people in need, and loved his aunt as any son would love a mother. She wanted a piece of him, however she could get it.

Olivia reached up and smoothed her fingers over the lines at the corner of his eye. Then she caressed his cheek. Then she ran her fingertip along the corner of his mouth and finally dragged it across his lower lip. So soft. "No, I don't want you to stop."

They stared at each other a moment. Then his mouth found hers, and she melted against him.

Urgently, his fingers worked the fastenings of her gown. He was quick, expert. Her dress gaped in the front and he pushed it down to her waist. She squirmed out of it until it pooled at her feet. His fingers loosened her stays, and the garment joined her dress.

All while he'd removed her outer clothing, he'd kissed her. His tongue invading and conquering. She met his thrusts and licks with her own, trying madly to keep up with his pace. She clutched at the back of his neck, pressing him to her, keeping him close lest he change his mind and abandon her.

He lifted her and set her on the edge of the bed. He stood between her thighs, drawing her forward until his shaft pressed against her core. She pulled him closer, wrapping her legs around his hips. He groaned.

Desperate to admire and stroke his bare chest, she unbuttoned his waistcoat. In her haste, she fumbled. He pushed her hands away and completed the task, his knuckles brushing against her tender breasts.

She thrust toward him, begging for more. His hands closed over her breasts, heat enveloping each mound. She pushed his waistcoat off and dragged the hem of his shirt from his breeches.

With a grunt, he pulled the garment over his head. While he discarded his shirt, she tried to do the same with her shift, but it tangled at her waist. He reached for the neck of the garment and ripped it down the middle.

He leaned forward, and she thought he meant to kiss her, but his mouth closed over an exposed nipple. Heat and moisture surrounded the straining tip. Olivia moaned, clasping his head to her.

His hips drove forward, pressing his erection into her cleft. She met his thrust, desire spiraling outward from that blissful connection.

With his mouth, he tugged at her flesh, softly, and then with more force. He cupped the forgotten breast then closed his fingers over the sensitive nipple, rolling it. Gently at first, followed by a pinch. She gasped. He moved his mouth to suck at the tortured flesh. Olivia opened her legs wider, needing to feel him closer, harder. She didn't know what she sought, but it was coming closer with every lick and stroke.

He stood up, and she nearly cried out with want. His hands massaged her breasts, cupping, covering, coaxing. Lust pulsed between her legs. It wasn't enough. She needed more.

He stroked down to her navel and lower. His fingers grazed the hair at the apex of her thighs, and she jerked upward. If only he would touch her there. He skimmed the flesh on either side of her pulsing cleft.

Down he traced, until he reached her garters. He dragged one finger around the top of her left stocking. With deliberation, he rolled the cotton down her leg. His mouth followed the stocking, forging an erotic path of lush kisses and sensual licks as he bared each inch of flesh.

She panted with anticipation when he started on her right leg. He pushed her thighs farther apart, leaving her uncomfortably open. It was one thing to have him standing there, but to have him looking at her *there*...she tried to bring her legs together.

With a quick flick, he stroked his finger over her sex. She drew in a sharp breath, but he went back to removing her right stocking. His hand remained poised on her upper thigh, and she didn't try to press her thighs together again.

Down, down the stocking went. Up, up her desire climbed. When she was at last bare, and her entire body quivered with a need she didn't fully understand, he looked his fill.

Slowly, he smiled. That simple act proved just as arousing as what he'd just done to her.

She needed to feel him. "Kiss me again."

He leaned over her, cupped her face, brought his hands down to the curve of her neck. With his thumbs, he stroked over her throat. "I could kiss you here."

His hands moved lower, the palms grazing over her nipples. "Or here."

She arched up, her breasts straining against him.

He circled each nipple with the tip of his forefingers. He continued his path downward, dragging his fingertips over her belly. "Or here."

She quivered in anticipation, hoping his hands would delve lower. He towered over her supine position. He drew a finger over her mound. Her hips bucked.

"Or, I could kiss you here." He stroked her thighs.

Put his mouth there? *He couldn't.*

Every nerve in her body sparked to full awareness. She hovered between uncertainty and desire, unsure of what to do but needing something so desperately she could only pray it would come.

His fingers moved softly over her flesh. It felt wonderful, but she knew there had to be more. He flirted with her, coming closer and closer to the opening. Finally, he slipped his middle finger inside. She gasped, and he withdrew. He returned to massaging the exterior, his thumb rotating over an unbelievably sensitive spot. She lifted her pelvis, wanting his finger inside of her again. She needed more, couldn't bear it if he didn't give her what she craved.

"Do you want that?"

Shame threatened her pleasure, but if she desired something, she should claim it for herself. For all the lonely nights that stretched ahead.

"Yes. Please," she added, lest he continue to taunt her.

He slid his middle finger inside her again. She was slick and his entry was easy. Shivers of ecstasy radiated from her core. She tipped up into him. He moved, slipping the finger out once more. She pushed forward, pleading for its return. He responded with a quick thrust. Olivia cast her head back.

He moved his finger in and out, slowly, gently at first. Then faster, pumping until her hips rose to meet him.

She gripped the coverlet with her fists and forced her eyes open so she could watch him. Watch him watch her. He stared intently at her face while his finger worked inside of her. The connection between them went beyond the visual and the tactile. And then he broke the moment, pulling his finger away. Olivia cried out. She reached for his hand.

He coaxed her back along the bed, leaning down between her legs. And put his mouth where his fingers had been. Just as when he'd kissed her, he didn't seek to coddle her or gently arouse her senses. He demanded total response, sucking hard on the sensitive bead at the top of her opening. Olivia closed her eyes, could barely withstand the pressure down there. Then he licked. The wetness of his mouth combined with her dew until she didn't know where she ended and he began.

Olivia's breath came in sharp pants. So close now. If he didn't release her from this torment soon, she would die.

Then his fingers pressed that delicious part of her that most craved his attention. He worked her flesh to a frenzy. She bucked off the bed, reaching out…*yes*.

She'd been alone so long. His touch, his care, his devotion, even if it was only to her body, filled her with joy. The world opened, and anything seemed possible.

He backed away from her and removed his boots. The setting sun basked the chamber in a warm, golden glow. She stared at his bare chest, riveted while he removed his stockings. He was magnificently built. Darkened nipples crowned perfectly formed muscles. Her fingers itched to touch him. And after what he'd just given her...she couldn't simply lie there.

She kneeled up and ran her hands over his chest. He was hot. She found a small patch of fine hair in the center, but the rest of him was as smooth and hard as carved stone. He tensed, but she thought it was from pleasure.

"My breeches." His voice was dark, rough, dangerous.

Olivia dipped her fingers down to the top of his breeches. Here she encountered another trail of hair disappearing into his waistband. She unbuttoned the fall and traced the blond path, savoring the labored sounds of his breathing.

"Take them off." There was desperation in his tone.

She understood how he felt and smiled to herself. Her knuckles brushed against the part of him he'd pressed between her legs. The part he would soon put inside of her. A new wave of moisture rushed to her center.

His hips thrust forward. She touched him again, this time with purpose. She grazed her fingers along the tip straining against his drawers. He pushed his garments down, but in his haste, the drawers and breeches tangled together. Olivia put her hands over his and pulled the breeches down first. Once they reached his thighs, he tore them from his body. Then she tugged his drawers over his hips. His sex sprang from the linen. She swallowed.

While he stripped the undergarment away, she continued to stare at him. Hair surrounded his erection. And two tight sacs of flesh hung beneath. Curious as to their texture, she touched one. They tensed. Emboldened, she ran her finger up the length of his shaft. The flesh was surprisingly silky, but hard, like his chest. Puzzling how he could feel so soft and so hard at once. Men, it would seem, were made of two distinct opposites.

She reached the tip. Moisture gathered there as it did between her thighs. Could she taste him as he'd tasted her? His hand closed over hers. He circled her fingers around him, guided her palm down to the base and back again. He repeated the motion but with greater urgency. He wanted her to pump him with the same tempo he'd used on her.

Happily, she obliged, and his hand fell away. His eyes were closed, his head tipped back. The dimming light allowed her a dusky view of his masculine features. The rough planes were broken only by the curl of his golden lashes against his cheeks. She pressed her lips to his, wanting to steal the anguish hiding in the lines of his face. He opened his mouth, kissing her with savage intensity.

She worked her hand harder. He stabbed forward with tongue and shaft, sliding into her mouth and fist. With her other hand, she pulled at his hip, guiding him toward her.

With a loud groan, he wrapped his arms around her and pressed her back onto the bed. He followed her, dipping the mattress with his powerful frame, and settled between her legs. He positioned the tip of his shaft at her opening. She rocked her hips up, and he surged forward. She stretched to accommodate his invasion, but there was a burning discomfort as her muscles pulled in a new way. She gasped and tried to retreat. He set his hands on her hips and pushed inside of her.

He froze over her. "I didn't know... You wanted to continue... God, what have I done?" He hadn't expected her to be a virgin.

Olivia cringed at the regret in his voice. She touched his face. "Don't. I did want you. I still do."

He bent down and whispered in her ear. "I'm sorry." He didn't move, just rested within her. Slowly, the discomfort receded. He sat up and put his finger between them, stroked her flesh until pleasure began to build once more.

She pulsed around him, rotated her pelvis up. Then he pulled out. *No, come back.*

He stroked forward then backward. The friction—*God*—was exquisite. His finger continued to work her while he plunged in and out. She wanted more, had to have him deep inside of her. She wrapped her legs around him. He clasped her hips with both hands and drove into her with blistering force. *Yes.* This was what she needed. His breathing grew ragged, his grip more harsh, his fingers biting into her flesh. Then he moved them up to her breasts and squeezed.

Olivia reached up and pulled his head down for a ravenous, penetrating kiss.

He groaned into her mouth. "Olivia. I have to—" Whatever he meant to say next was cut off by a rasp as he pulled out of her. Her pleasure had been intense, but his abrupt departure prevented her reaching the same peak. He cried out, arching his neck back and then fell beside her.

She was cold without his weight pressing her into the bed. She became aware of moisture on her cheek. She wasn't crying. Had he? No, she couldn't imagine a man like him—any man really—shedding tears. His skin was heated, slick with perspiration. That had to be the cause.

He shifted, pulling her back against him. Their breathing regulated. She relaxed in his embrace. Later she would get up and put herself to rights. For now, she allowed herself to feel protected. Cherished.

A knock on the door jolted both of them up.

"Olivia, are you awake, dear?"

Ruined.

Chapter Fourteen

JASPER SCRAMBLED OFF the bed. Had he really just ruined his second virgin? *Bloody hell.*

Olivia also left the bed, her tattered shift still hanging from her shoulders. She picked up her discarded garments as she hurried toward her dressing chamber. "Yes, just give me a moment, Louisa," she called.

He grabbed his clothing and trailed her into the dressing chamber.

Her eyes widened. "What are you going to do?" She pulled on a dressing robe, covering her lush curves.

"I'm going to get dressed."

Her gaze raked his nude body. Lust poured through him.

She turned her head but not before he saw her cheeks redden. "You're not going to tell Louisa?"

"God, no." He pulled on his breeches.

She nodded and left, closing the door behind her.

He drew his shirt over his head. She'd been a virgin. He never would have done it if he'd known. But then, he hadn't asked. His hands fisted.

After a moment during which he couldn't form coherent thought, Jasper pressed his ear to the wood. Olivia had admitted Louisa. Their conversation was too muffled. He eased open the door to reveal a thin strip of the bedchamber. He didn't want to see, just to hear.

"How was your outing, dear?"

"Pleasant. I'll tell you about it at dinner. Your ankle must be feeling better."

"Indeed, I think we can return to London tomorrow. I understand Jasper arrived. Perhaps he'll dine with us."

He couldn't have dinner with them. Not after what he'd just done.

He sank onto a cushioned bench. Slowly he pulled on a stocking. Christ above! His boots were still out there.

Jasper sprang to his feet and began an apprehensive circuit around the small room. He was a defiler of virgins. Again. Yes, they'd both been as eager as he, but damn it, he was no better than his father alleged.

At last he knew the truth about her bait and switch scheme. Her virginity wasn't the proof, but her vulnerability. He knew her regret was real, recognized it in himself. And if she hadn't lied about that... Could he trust her? Could she be Merry's daughter? Louisa evidently thought so. And if she wanted to trust Olivia, perhaps he should too.

But there were still so many lies. Louisa needed to know Olivia was Fiona's daughter. She was bound to find out, and it would be best if she heard it from Olivia. It made no sense, however, to ever let her know about his and Olivia's prior acquaintance, and certainly not their current relationship.

Which was what? She couldn't be his mistress. That would devastate Louisa. But neither could she be his wife. What the hell was he thinking? She was the bastard daughter of a notorious actress. The duke would get rid of her, just as he'd done with Abigail. That would also devastate Louisa. What a goddamned mess.

The dressing room door creaked open. He opened his eyes and tipped his head up. Olivia stood in the doorway with his boots in her hand.

Jasper cringed. "Did my aunt see them?"

She dropped them at his feet. "No, thank goodness."

Quietly, he pulled on his other stocking and then his boots. "I didn't know you were a virgin."

She'd assumed a position on the opposite side of the room, near her dressing table. "I know. I should have told you." She crossed her arms. "Would you have stopped?"

"Yes."

"Then I'm glad I didn't tell you." She straightened and gave him a defiant look. She would have been imposing if she wasn't wearing a dressing robe and her hair didn't appear as if she'd been totally and blissfully fucked.

"From now on, I want total honesty from you." He stood. "About everything."

She nodded. "What are you going to do now that you know the truth?"

"We have a problem. I'm afraid it's going to be very easy for someone to link you to Fiona Scarlet. Your bastardy—sorry—can't be discovered. Louisa would be a laughingstock, and my father would make your life miserable. If you think you were in dire straits before..." He could only imagine what the duke would do. He'd exported Abigail and her parents on a ship to America as if they'd been goods destined for market.

She sat down on the chair at the dressing table. "I should leave."

He wanted to go to her, but knew it would be a mistake. He couldn't touch her again. Ever. "Louisa wouldn't want that. I'll figure something out."

"Are you going to stay for dinner?"

He allowed a wry smile. "I don't think that would be wise." He should see Louisa before he left, but her lack of faith in him hurt. He had to talk to her about it, but not now.

Jasper was already outside Olivia's bedchamber before he realized she'd never told him about her errand. He'd ask her another day. He'd meant it when he'd said no more lies—because he'd wanted to protect Louisa. But now he had to protect Olivia too.

IF OLIVIA'S BED at Benfield hadn't reminded her totally and painfully of Jasper, she'd have hidden in it all day. Instead, she spent the morning closeted in the library while her maid prepared for their return to London.

The words in the book she was vainly trying to read blurred together. Since she hadn't turned a page in over a quarter hour, she dropped the novel onto a table beside her wing-backed chair. She picked up her sewing basket and removed the pieces of Jasper's waistcoat. Last night when she couldn't sleep, she'd gone ahead and selected a design and cut the fabric. Normally, stitching would soothe her anxiety, but even that sounded too difficult to accomplish at present.

In a fit of nervous energy, she set the waistcoat aside, jumped to her feet, and paced before the fireplace. She'd relived the events of the previous day over and over in her mind, and couldn't stop herself from doing so again. Her encounter with Aunt Mildred had left her raw and vulnerable.

After such despair, Jasper had given her unimaginable joy. For a brief while, she'd forgotten that Merry probably wasn't her father and that she ought to leave Louisa immediately.

Louisa. Not only might Olivia be perpetrating a lie by accepting her care, she'd behaved scandalously under Louisa's very nose, and with her nephew, no less.

Olivia had also spent a good portion of her sleepless night trying in vain to find the pear-shaped birthmark on her head. Instead of a small pink mark, she'd only found one brownish discoloration at the back of her scalp. Her hair had made its shape impossible to discern. She could neither confirm nor deny Aunt Mildred's matching birthmark theory, which meant she still couldn't know which man was her father.

The library door opened, arresting Olivia's pacing. The footman admitted Jasper's parents. Dear heaven, this abysmal day only wanted this. Olivia summoned as complacent an expression as she could manage. "Your Graces."

Jasper's mother was coolly beautiful, with blue-gray eyes and blond hair. Her only detracting feature was the lines around her mouth indicating she likely frowned more often than not. Even now, her lips were pressed together in an expression of distaste or disapproval. Or likely both.

The duke handed his wife into a chair away from the fireplace where Olivia had been pacing. "We've come to join Louisa for luncheon. We understand she had a bit of an accident."

Olivia couldn't help but note it took them two days to come when Benfield was only a short ride from Town. He'd also pointedly said they'd come to join *Louisa*, not Louisa and Olivia. "How kind of you. Yes, she turned her ankle but is feeling much better. In fact, we're to return to London shortly."

The duke's mouth pulled into a thin specter of a smile. "After luncheon, I presume. I daresay I'd be disappointed to have come all this way for nothing."

Her Grace studied Olivia as if she were a curious object. No, that was too benign. Perhaps an old pair of shoes she'd forgotten she possessed—and didn't particularly care for. "What are your plans, Miss West, now that you've Louisa's…assistance?"

Like their son, they doubted the veracity of her relationship to Louisa. Why did none of these people accept the word of Louisa, a member of their own family? As much as Olivia loved Louisa, she was glad she needn't claim these people as relations.

"Yes," the duke said, "do tell us what you plan."

Olivia glanced at the door, willing Louisa to arrive. "It's enough for me to enjoy Louisa's company."

The duchess peered down her long, thin nose. "Surely you have grander designs than that."

Was Olivia so different because she didn't possess their brand of ambition? She could never explain to these people that until a fortnight ago, she would've been quite content to someday own a tiny embroidery shop. "No, not really."

The duchess' eyes narrowed almost imperceptibly. "You are doing well in the role of companion. We've been suggesting such an arrangement to Louisa for years, lonely as she is."

The duke continued to stand behind his wife's chair, his gloved fingers intermittently drumming against the top, just above the duchess's head. "And where is it you hail from again?"

"Devon."

He nodded once. "Presumably you've been decently educated." He glanced at the book Olivia had discarded. "You were just reading?"

Olivia bit back a sarcastic retort in which she said she'd tried but had stopped upon reaching the word *insufferable*. "Yes, Your Grace. I was raised in a vicarage."

The duchess turned and looked up at her husband. "A vicarage? I don't recall Merriweather being related to a vicar."

Olivia inwardly cringed. Jasper was right. She couldn't keep the truth from being discovered.

The duke returned his wife's gaze. "To my knowledge, Merriweather didn't have an impoverished branch to his family, vicar or otherwise." Slowly, he turned his attention back to Olivia. "We assume you were without financial support since you journeyed all this way to search for family. How fortuitous you found my sister."

Olivia didn't know how to respond, so she didn't.

The duchess settled back against the chair and pinned Olivia with another withering stare. "No doubt you could take on work as a governess should you decide you don't like being a companion, or after Louisa passes on."

They speculated about Louisa's death? Olivia gritted her teeth. "I like living with Louisa as *family*. I truly have no other aspirations."

"Not even marriage?" Her Grace lifted a shoulder. "It's not impossible you might draw the interest of a decent young man. You are rather pretty, despite the red in your hair."

Olivia prayed Louisa would arrive soon and that she was ready to leave for London immediately. Dash the duke and duchess and their plans for luncheon.

"Mmm, you're quite right, my dear," he said. "Still, I don't think Louisa need expend effort husband-hunting, especially if Miss West isn't particularly interested. She may, however, change her mind." He gave Olivia a pointed look that clearly said he didn't believe her lack of ambition, and that he would be watching.

Devastating as it was not to know her father's identity, she was only glad he wasn't someone like the duke. She felt a pang of pity for Jasper.

No, she felt more than a pang of pity. She felt a surge of longing that warmed her chest and spread out to her extremities. Also, a wave of protectiveness. He'd given her solace yesterday when she'd needed it most. As evidenced by her encounter with Aunt Mildred, there were so few people who truly cared.

Could Jasper be one of them?

"What's that on the chair?" the duchess asked.

Oh, dear. The pieces of Jasper's waistcoat. Olivia quickly stashed it back into her sewing basket. "Just some embroidery I'm working on."

The duchess looked as if she would say something else, but Louisa limped into the library with her cane.

"Oh, here you are, Olivia dear." Louisa inclined her head toward her brother and his wife. "Holborn, Your Grace."

Olivia looked at the duke, surprised and perturbed he wasn't helping his sister. Yes, she was exceedingly glad *he* wasn't her father. She rushed to offer her arm to Louisa.

"We've come to ascertain your health," Holborn said. "And to take luncheon with you."

Louisa pursed her lips. "Mmm. Well, I'm feeling quite splendid enough to return to Town, thank you. Pity you came for luncheon, and we're just leaving." Her brittle smile and oversweet tone said it was anything but. Olivia tried very hard not to grin and only just managed to succeed.

"Oh, come, come. You simply must stay." It sounded like an order instead of a polite request.

"Why, because you deigned to visit?" Louisa *tsked*. "Cook will serve an excellent luncheon. One I daresay you'll enjoy as much without my presence as with. Besides, Olivia has a watercolor lesson later this afternoon."

Olivia perked. With everything else crowding her head, she'd quite forgotten the appointment. She retrieved her sewing basket, anxious to leave.

"She's every bit the gifted artist Merry was."

Olivia wasn't sure she evidenced as much skill as Lord Merriweather, which only added to her doubt. If he wasn't her father, she had no right to be here with Louisa.

Yet hadn't the duke said Louisa needed a companion? Furthermore, she clearly held strong affection for Olivia. Was pleasing an old woman enough reason to continue a lie? If it was a lie. Could Olivia find the truth?

Suddenly, she was eager to return to London—and not just to escape the nauseating company of the duke and duchess. Perhaps there she could seek answers regarding her paternity. Surely someone who knew her mother could help her determine which man had fathered Olivia.

"Olivia, dear? Are you all right?" Louisa asked.

Too late, Olivia realized the conversation had continued without her. She managed a sheepish smile. "I was just wondering what Mr. Landsdowne might want me to sketch today. We painted fruit the last time."

The duke and duchess narrowed their eyes.

Olivia began to understand. It mattered little if she were intelligent or well-spoken. With a dubious past and inferior ambition, her traits and skills were without consequence in this world. Of much more value were her background and her potential for future success—as defined by Society. Lord, how could she ever hope to fit into Louisa's life?

Louisa steered Olivia toward the door. "Come dear, our coach is ready. Enjoy your luncheon, Holborn."

The duke watched their departure with heavy-lidded disdain.

JASPER GUIDED HIS phaeton along Piccadilly, the mid-afternoon traffic thicker than usual. Beside him, Sevrin perused the people strolling the sidewalk below.

"I appreciate your invitation this afternoon. Spectacular vehicle, Saxton," he remarked. "I feel as if I've perhaps arrived. Surely to be seen in the coveted seat beside you will elevate me from wretched degenerate to rakish libertine."

Jasper's mouth ticked up in a half smile, despite the regrets and concerns oppressing his brain. "You're both of those and more."

Two ladies peered up at them from beneath the wide brims of their bonnets. Sevrin tipped the edge of his hat. "True enough. But why me? This illustrious space is usually reserved for your...*acceptable* friends. Penreith. Or Black."

"Does it matter why?" Jasper didn't want the company of his "acceptable" friends. Being with Sevrin made his reclaimed, albeit secret, status of "ruiner" slightly more palatable. At least with Sevrin he was amongst his own kind—wretched degenerates and rakish libertines they were.

"No," Sevrin said, peering at him sideways. "It's just unlike you. And last night at the club, you barely strung a sentence together, which is also unlike you. If the club has devolved you to some form of grunting wild man who prefers the company of scoundrels, perhaps I'll disassociate you."

Jasper threw him a sour look. As he did so, his eye caught a figure moving amongst the pedestrians on the sidewalk. *Olivia.* It had to be. If she tilted her head up just a bit...there!

He drew the horses to a halt. What was she doing here on Piccadilly?

"Why're we stopped?" Sevrin asked.

Jasper turned in his seat, uncaring that he held up traffic.

"What the devil are you doing, Saxton? You can't stop in the middle of the street." Sevrin craned his neck. "What are you looking at? Wait, is that Miss West?"

Jasper handed him the reins. "Here."

"What?" Sevrin stared at him as if he'd grown another nose. "No."

"I need to talk to her." Find out why she was out walking alone. Her background was troublesome enough, but need she draw even more attention to herself?

"You don't."

"I *do*."

"Move along!" someone called behind them.

With an oath, Jasper ripped the reins from Sevrin's slack grip. "Worthless. I *should've* brought Penreith or Black. They don't talk back."

"If you prefer the company of sycophants, I'm definitely disassociating you from the club."

"Fine." Jasper watched Olivia disappear into the crowd. "Maybe I'll start my own society."

"I'm having a bit of fun, Sax." Sevrin studied him intently, his ever-present veneer of joviality gone. "You're clearly not. What the hell is going on with Miss West?"

Jasper clutched the reins and turned his head. "We'll follow her."

"No." Sevrin put a firm hand on Jasper's arm. "You can't go trailing her. She's not some nobody actress anymore. You run after her, it'll be the meatiest gossip on everyone's plate tonight—and not in a good way. Trust me, I know what it's like to be the butt of scandal. You don't."

"Only because I'm Holborn's son."

"Are you saying without that name to hide behind, you're no better than me? I don't believe it."

Suddenly Jasper knew why he'd invited Sevrin today: to unburden himself. His insides twisted. "Believe it. I'm...like you."

Sevrin stared at him. "Like me?"

Jasper didn't look away. He deserved whatever Sevrin would say, and more.

After another long moment, Sevrin's nostrils flared. "You ruined her—Miss West."

The feel of the reins lightened in Jasper's hand, as if he lost his grip with everything around him. "Yes."

"Don't think that makes you like me." Sevrin's dark eyes narrowed slightly. "Everyone knows about my past. No one has a clue you got carried away with your aunt's new charge."

Here was his chance to…what? Seek absolution? Understanding? Commiseration? He blew out a pent-up breath. "And a girl ten years ago."

Sevrin turned toward him in the seat. "*What?*"

Jasper stared ahead at the vehicles crawling in front of them. "She lived near Edgewater—my estate in Yorkshire."

"You ruined another girl?" The incredulousness in his tone was almost amusing.

"You see, I'm no better than you." He tossed Sevrin a cynical smile. "Worse actually. I've got one up on you."

"What happened? Why didn't you marry her?"

She thought of Abigail, but oddly, the features of the trollop from Coventry Court entered his brain first. He searched for the memory of Abigail's face, but it seemed blurred. What he did recall, however, was his consuming need to possess her. And the feeling had been reciprocated. Neither one of them could wait to bed the other, and so they had—propriety be damned.

He gave Sevrin the truth. "The duke wouldn't allow it."

Sevrin gaped at him. "You let him make your decisions for you? If you wanted to marry her, you should have done."

"I would have, but she left." She and her family had disappeared. The duke had "consoled" him by saying she wouldn't have made a very good duchess, and that as a country-bred girl she would've been miserable in Town. "It was several months before I learned Holborn had sent her away." He rasped the words out, emotion hardening his voice.

Sevrin shook his head. "What happened to her is terrible, but you have to let it go."

The traffic began to loosen. Jasper urged the horses to a steady walk. "Is that what you did?"

He looked away. "You have a new situation now, one you can do something about."

Sevrin was right. Olivia needed his help. He had to keep her safe from Holborn's machinations. Somehow, he had to bury the secret of her parentage.

"I need you to help me," he said.

"Don't ask me to drive your phaeton again while you chase after Miss West."

"Actually, I do need you to do that, but not so I can chase after Olivia. You'll drop me on Queen Street so I may speak to my aunt." Jasper needed to tell her he knew the truth, and that he planned to ensure Olivia stayed with her. "I also need you to talk to those women who come to the Black Horse. Ascertain what they know of her background. If any of them know she's Fiona Scarlet's daughter, they can't reveal the relationship to anyone. Offer them any sum."

"Any sum? Saxton, you can't pursue this woman. Even I know from my comfortable seat in the gutter that you can't marry her."

Why had Sevrin jumped to that conclusion? "I never said anything about marrying her. I have to keep her secrets safe for my aunt's sake. If Holborn learns of her parentage, he'll cast her out as quickly and definitively as he did the last inappropriate girl who tried to infiltrate his family."

"So you buy off anyone who can reveal she's Fiona Scarlet's daughter. Then what? Aren't you supposed to be courting Lady Philippa?"

He was due at her townhouse in little more than an hour. "I am, and I will." Right after he went to Queen Street.

Chapter Fifteen

OLIVIA WALKED QUICKLY along Piccadilly, anxious to get home before Louisa returned from her afternoon calls. Her trip to the Haymarket hadn't been as successful as she'd hoped. No one at the theatre had known Fiona Scarlet more than twenty years ago. Olivia did, however, learn the name of an old woman who'd dressed many of London's actors, both at the Haymarket and the royal theatres. She'd obtained the woman's address and planned to visit her as soon as possible.

"Why, good afternoon, Olivia." The overly sweet voice of Lady Lydia Prewitt halted Olivia mid-stride. "Goodness, you aren't *alone*, are you?"

Engrossed in her thoughts, Olivia hadn't been paying attention to her surroundings. Consequently, she'd failed to notice Lady Lydia and Audrey Cheswick strolling toward her. With their *chaperones*. Olivia briefly considered ignoring them and hurrying by, but ultimately rejected this idea, figuring it might be more detrimental than if she offered a rational excuse for being out alone. Now if she could just think of that reason…

"Good afternoon, Lady Lydia, Audrey." Olivia offered her sunniest smile. It wouldn't do to appear guilty. "I was just out for a quick walk."

Audrey's brows drew together. "Don't you live on Queen Street? That's rather, er, invigorating."

"I wanted to see the reservoir in Green Park," Olivia improvised. Green Park was just on the other side of Piccadilly. Hopefully they didn't notice she hadn't come from that direction.

Lady Lydia shook her head. "My dear Olivia, you must realize this isn't Devon! You can't simply go for a stroll in Town by yourself. If you crave solitude, have your chaperone walk ten paces behind you. I do."

Indeed, two maids lingered several yards behind the two young women. "I shall keep that in mind, thank you." Olivia made to continue on her way, but Lady Lydia spoke again.

"I've been thinking of you, actually." Lady Lydia regarded her with narrowed eyes.

Olivia stopped, her body suffering a chill despite the afternoon heat. She hoped Lady Lydia's interest didn't have anything to do with Lord Prewitt almost recognizing her. Had he later informed his daughter of just who he suspected Olivia to be?

"Oh?" was all Olivia could manage to say.

"Yes, I was thinking about the costume you wore to the Faversham Ball. It was quite stunning. And today, your walking dress...that coral hue does wonders for your complexion. You must tell me the name of your modiste."

Louisa and Olivia had discussed how to address this very question, but it hadn't yet been raised. They'd agreed on a very simple, and honest, answer. "I designed the dresses."

Both Audrey and Lady Lydia's eyes widened. Audrey smiled, her expression softening to one of...admiration? "How extraordinary."

Ever the interrogator, Lady Lydia asked, "Who assembled them?"

"We employ some very talented maids." Olivia gave a purposefully enigmatic smile.

Lady Lydia's mouth formed a practiced pout. "How disappointing." She toyed with the ribbon of her bonnet for a moment. Then her eyes lit. "Unless you have a spare design you wouldn't mind parting with. I'm certain my dressmaker could do the garment justice."

Olivia had no intention of allowing someone else to make her designs. She tried to think of how to politely decline.

Audrey gently elbowed her friend. "Surely this is a hobby for Olivia. If she gave one to you, only think how people might harass her for their own design." She turned to Olivia. "You're very talented."

"Thank you." Olivia warmed at Audrey's defense and her genuine praise.

Lady Lydia's features hardened. The reaction was not of her typically rehearsed variety. "You're right, Audrey. How gauche of me to have even asked." She flicked Olivia a look tinged with some emotion. Jealousy perhaps?

Olivia didn't want Lydia to take her refusal personally. She didn't want to share her designs with anyone, except family, like Louisa. And Jasper. Dear Lord, when had he become 'family?'

Gathering herself from her wayward thoughts, she smiled at Lydia and said, "Perhaps you can come to Queen Street one day, and I'll show you my drawings."

Audrey nodded. "That would be lovely."

"Yes, we shall," Lady Lydia said, recovering her usual busybody mien. "Father is always telling me to welcome new friends into Society."

The reference to Lady Lydia's father only served to remind Olivia of the dangerous game she played. Even now, Lady Lydia could be aware of Olivia's relationship to the notorious Fiona Scarlet. But since she hadn't said anything, perhaps she didn't know. Or, more likely, she was waiting for a prime moment during which to share this juicy morsel. Either way, Olivia's patience with the interlude had expired.

"I'm afraid I must be going. You're quite right that I ought to have a chaperone."

"Would you like to take my maid?" Audrey offered.

"No," Olivia said. "Thank you, but I haven't all that far to go. Being from the *country*, I'm an excellent walker so I'll be home in a trice."

"Good afternoon, then!" Audrey called after her as she continued along Piccadilly.

Determined to get to Queen Street as quickly as possible, Olivia took long strides at double time, and was therefore out of breath when she reached her destination. Exhaustion slowed her ascent of the front steps. She smiled at Bernard as he opened the door and admitted her inside.

"Good afternoon, Bernard."

"I trust you're feeling improved?" he asked.

Olivia had pleaded a headache in order to avoid joining Louisa on her calls this afternoon. Then she'd told Dale and Bernard she thought a walk might help. "Yes, thank you. Has Louisa returned?"

"No, but Lord Saxton is waiting in the Rose Room."

Olivia's pulse—already hammering from her walk—sped faster. What could he be doing here? With Louisa gone... She refused to consider the possibilities. What had happened between them couldn't happen again.

With a nod, Olivia walked to the drawing room.

Jasper stood in front of Merry's painting with his back to the door. He turned, and Olivia couldn't stop herself from gasping. His lower lip was swollen at the left corner where an abrasion marked his flesh.

She walked right over to him. "You've been fighting again."

His lips pursed. "I didn't come to discuss that."

His firm tone chased away her concern. "All right. Why are you here then?"

"I saw you on Piccadilly today. Where were you going by yourself?"

She didn't want to tell him about her search for her father. It was bad enough he knew she was a bastard. If he or Louisa knew Merry may not be her father, why they might just toss her out as Aunt Mildred had done.

"I took a walk," she said. He opened his mouth, but she held up her hand. "Yes, I realize I should've taken a chaperone, and I shan't make the same mistake again."

"Very well. I'm glad you realize you're Somebody now. If you want to embrace this life with Louisa, you must leave all that you were behind."

He was right, but that didn't mean she appreciated his dictatorial attitude. Why was he acting so cold?

"Are you angry with me because I went out alone?" Or was he angry about what had happened at Benfield? She hadn't seen him since then, and while her insides quivered like a Christmas jelly, he seemed cool as frost.

He shook his head and moved to the mantelpiece, keeping his face averted from her. "I'm not angry." He turned, and his frigid expression had disappeared. "We need to keep the identity of your mother secret. Who knows about her?"

Goodness, the list could be endless. "The employees at the theatre."

"Excellent, I can take care of them. It's really too bad you didn't use an alternate surname, however."

She smiled wryly. How many times had she thought that same thing? "I might've done if I hadn't already introduced myself to you as Miss West."

He arched a brow. "Yes, and keeping me from the truth was very important." His tone reeked of sarcasm.

"To Louisa," she gently reminded him. While she hated that Louisa hadn't trusted him, she wanted him to know it hadn't been her preference.

He nodded almost imperceptibly. "Who else?"

She searched her memory. "My mother died not quite a year ago, and I lived with her most of the time during the past seven years."

"That long?" he asked. "How did you manage to stay—"

"Innocent? It was difficult at times, but the one thing my mother was good at was protecting me." On more than one occasion she'd provided special favors to keep Olivia out of harm's way. Olivia couldn't quash a shiver of revulsion.

Jasper came toward her. "What is it?"

"Nothing. Living with Fiona was…problematic."

He paused before her, a bare arm's length away. "Tell me."

She could at least be honest with him about this. "I asked about your fighting because it frightens me. Several of her lovers hit her. They liked to inflict pain." She gave him a piercing stare, wishing she could see all the way into his heart. "You don't like that, do you?"

His pale eyes widened almost imperceptibly. "No. Did any of these men hurt you?" His hands fisted.

Just the one when she'd tried to intervene on Fiona's behalf, but she couldn't tell Jasper that. Not when he already looked so furious. She couldn't encourage him to have violent thoughts. "No. They hurt Fiona. The last one pushed her down the stairs, and she died."

He exhaled. "I'm sorry. That's not why I fight," he said, the ire dissipating from his gaze. "You saw what I did for Mrs. Reddy. I would never hurt a woman."

She knew that, in her heart. Still, a man who enjoyed violence unsettled her. Not that anything Jasper did should matter—what he did had no bearing on her. Their relationship existed for Louisa. If not for her, they would part and never speak again.

"What do you plan to do about the theatre employees?" she asked.

"Aren't there more than just them? What about your mother's lovers?"

Olivia recalled Mr. Clifton and Lord Prewitt. The former had been quite certain—and accurate—in his recognition, while the latter had only supposed. Or had he? For all she knew, he'd made the connection and was even now spreading the *on-dit* about London.

"There were so many. I don't know if any of them would recognize me." Clifton didn't circulate in the same set, and so Olivia didn't see the point in mentioning him, but she had to tell Jasper about Lord Prewitt. She swallowed. "There was one instance…"

His eyes flashed and he moved forward a half step. "What? Tell me."

"At the Faversham Ball, Lord Prewitt said I looked familiar. He didn't mention Fiona's name, so for all I know he could've thought I looked like his childhood governess."

Jasper pressed his lips into a thin line. He looked a bit like his father just then. "Doubtful. But you say he didn't seem certain?"

"It was a passing comment, and that was days ago now. Surely we would know if he'd started a rumor?"

He nodded. "Probably. Still, I'll need to do a bit of investigating."

"What are you going to do?"

"Ensure none of these people mistakenly say you're Fiona Scarlet's daughter." He turned and walked to the windows, presenting his back to her.

"Louisa said people would believe what we tell them, that no one would be boorish enough to contest what she said."

"Perhaps." He turned. "I also wanted to ask about your trip on the heath the other day. You never told me where you went."

She wanted to block that horrid visit from her mind. "I went to see my aunt. She was my foster mother."

His eyes narrowed. "So you lied about living in Devon?"

"No, no," she rushed to say. "My uncle died, and she moved to Cheshunt to live with relatives. Since she was close, I decided to pay a visit."

He nodded, accepting what she said, but then he moved forward with an intent look. "You said you lived with your mother seven years. Why did you move from Devon?"

Though she wanted to be honest with him, some things were too painful to reveal. She couldn't tell him Mildred had thrown her out after learning her husband was Olivia's father, even if that proved to be false. Olivia offered a half-truth instead. "My aunt never particularly cared for me. Raising her half-sister's—her half-whore-sister's—child was a burden she never accepted. I left."

His lips formed a grim line. "I don't think that's everything. By now, you should realize I'm quite aware of when you withhold information."

"Like you refusing to tell me about why you fight?" She stepped toward him, afraid of the answer to her next question, but determined to ask it anyway. "Did the duke…beat you?"

He stared at a spot over her head, saying nothing.

Her frustration mounted. "Tell me *why*. I can't reconcile this violent nature of yours with your other attributes, which include a vast generosity for those less fortunate. " She knew from her experience with Fiona that some men just needed violence. The way others needed love. The question tripped from her lips. "Do you need to fight to feel…whole?"

His gaze turned frigid. "I had wanted to speak with my aunt as well, but as she has not yet returned, I shall call tomorrow instead." He stepped around her, careful to make a wide swath, and left.

She turned and watched him go, disappointed that despite what they'd shared at Benfield, neither one of them was ready to trust.

JASPER rushed from Louisa's townhouse, nearly stumbling down the front stairs. He wished he hadn't allowed Sevrin the use of his phaeton. Without it, he couldn't very well make a rapid escape.

Why had Olivia kept on him about the fighting? He understood she didn't like it, given what she'd endured with her mother, but what he did had nothing to do with her. Wouldn't ever have anything to do with her after he quashed any gossip about her and married Lady Philippa.

What really bothered him, however, was that he couldn't answer her question. Why *did* he fight? He'd long enjoyed the sport, but at the Black Horse it had become something more. Upon reflection, he realized he'd visited the back room of the tavern *every day* since joining, whether to fight or merely to watch. And the thought of not going speared his insides, though he knew that day would come. How would he explain this hobby, the various bruises and cuts, to his new wife?

His aunt's coach pulled to a halt in the street. *Bollocks*. Though he'd initially come to speak with her, he now preferred to avoid her. His interview with Olivia had been unexpected, and her interrogation as well as her evocative presence had quite upset his equanimity. He needed to maintain some semblance of composure for his appointment with Philippa. Talking with his aunt about her lack of faith in him would only further threaten his ability to remain in control.

The coachman leapt down to open the door. Jasper had no choice but to paste a smile upon his taut face. A smile that promptly vanished as the duke stepped from the carriage. What was left of his poise slipped another notch.

"Saxton." Derision marked his tone. "You're just leaving?"

Jasper's temple began to throb. "Yes, I've an appointment with Lady Philippa." Though the thought of it at this moment only contributed to his oncoming headache.

"I presume you've come to see your aunt, but here she is." He helped Louisa down and scanned the street. "Where is your vehicle? You can't have been here long enough to send it to the mews, unless you've been awaiting Louisa for some time."

Louisa gave her brother a derisive glance. "Perhaps he's been visiting with Olivia. How is she? She had a bit of the headache earlier." Louisa stared at Jasper's mouth. "Oh my, what happened to your lip, dear?"

"Er, nothing."

The duke directed him a pointed, assessing look, but didn't address the injury. His lack of comment was suspicious. "Hmm, something must be in the air. Your mother left tea with an aching head."

"That's why you're with Louisa, then?" Jasper was surprised the duke hadn't demanded the coachman drop him at Holborn House first.

"And to see her home. Her ankle is paining her a bit." He cast a dark glance at Jasper. "I do have a care for my sister. As you seem to for Miss West. I trust she's feeling better?"

Jasper had to admit to seeing her, though he knew his father was ferreting for just this information. "Yes, she is well."

The duke's eyes narrowed. Definitely processing, and by the look of it, judging this knowledge. "Since you're on your way out, I'll drop you at Herrick House for your appointment. Unless you're waiting for your horse or phaeton?"

Normally Jasper would've preferred to walk—all the way to York—than ride with his father, but he couldn't ignore the warnings sounding in his head. The duke was dangerous when inquisitorial, and Jasper didn't like that he'd set his sights on Olivia—it was the very thing they needed to avoid.

Louisa frowned slightly. She hadn't missed the tension between father and son. "I'm sorry I missed your visit, Jasper."

"It's quite all right. I'll call on you tomorrow." He bussed her cheek before following his father into the dim interior of Louisa's coach.

The duke wasted no time in launching an attack. Of course he couldn't let Jasper's battered lip go unremarked upon. "I know you're not fighting at Jackson's, yet nearly every time I see you of late you're displaying some sort of injury. Either you've become the clumsiest man in England, or you're fighting somewhere else. And poorly I might add, given the way you look most of the time."

"Not clumsy."

"Where?"

"Nowhere you'd know. Why did you really escort Louisa home?" Jasper hadn't believed the duke's declaration that he *cared*. No, he likely had far more nefarious motives. Motives that perhaps involved Olivia.

"Your mother and I are suspicious of Miss West. Her sudden appearance and immediate acceptance by Louisa are troubling. We don't recall a vicar in Merriweather's extended family."

"You could be mistaken." Jasper worried it was already too late to keep Olivia's background secret.

The duke barked a hollow laugh. "Not bloody likely. She's got to be an imposter."

Perhaps there was a way to circumvent Holborn's suspicions. "I had the same thought. I dispatched an investigator as soon as she arrived. I expect information any day."

Holborn's eyes widened. He grunted with…approval? "I'm surprised you thought of it. Pleased, but surprised."

It was as much of a compliment as Jasper had ever received from the man. "I wouldn't worry about Miss West. She's of little consequence. I don't believe she has any particular ambition, nor does she seem to covet Louisa's fortune."

"So she says. Oh yes, she gave your mother and me the same pretty speech. I still don't trust her. Probably that God awful ginger hair."

Jasper sought to keep his temper in check. "I will share the report when I receive it from my investigator."

The duke leaned back against the squab. Sunlight filtered through the window and glinted in his sapphire eyes. "You've a particular interest in this girl, but you know she's not good enough."

"Of course not." Though in his mind he knew what the duke said was true, admitting it aloud scraped at his insides. "I plan to marry Lady Philippa. We are, in fact, on our way to her house," he added with more than a touch of irony.

Holborn snorted. "Very well. When do you plan to announce? Her Grace and I will host a dinner of course."

"I plan to speak plainly with Lady Philippa today. Her father is currently in Oxfordshire attending to estate matters, but I believe she plans to write to him to request his return."

"Indeed? This day is full of revelation about my wayward son. Perhaps you'll manage to come up to snuff after all."

The coach halted in front of Herrick House. Before Jasper could escape, the duke said, "I'll be waiting on that report. If it's lacking, I'll send my own man to discern the chit's true identity. I won't put up with some gutter-born pretender riding the Holborn coattails. And you'd do best to stay away from her. Visiting her without Louisa's chaperonage will land you in precisely the same predicament as ten years ago. If it hasn't already." He delivered a probing stare that churned Jasper's simmering ire into full-blown rage.

Without a word, he exited and stood on the sidewalk until the duke had pulled away. Jasper was in no condition to see Lady Philippa, but she was expecting him. He had to get his emotions under control. God, he hated that the duke was right about him. He hadn't been able to keep his hands off Olivia and, questionable background or not, she hadn't deserved to be ruined.

Olivia's questions echoed in his mind. Did he need this violence to be whole? He'd always believed his father had needed to exert physical superiority in order to maintain control—their relationship had worsened after the duke realized he couldn't literally force Jasper to his will anymore. Was Jasper no better?

Suddenly, his long-held doubt of Olivia sickened him. Who cared if she was a Nobody from some backwater village? Hadn't his sister found happiness with just such a person? A gentleman with no title, no fortune, and no approval from Holborn. Furthermore, Louisa needed a companion and by all accounts, Olivia fit the bill. Perfectly. Jasper believed what he'd just said about her character. She was without guile and seemed to genuinely care for Louisa. Whereas he was a blackguard cut in the image of his father.

Reluctantly he made his way up the steps to Herrick House. With spectacular effort, he quashed his emotions and summoned his most charming smile. His objectives were simple: ensure Olivia and Louisa were undisturbed and happy, marry Lady Philippa, and keep his hands off Olivia.

Chapter Sixteen

JASPER ARRIVED AT Louisa's townhouse rather early the next morning. The conversation with his aunt couldn't wait another moment. Her lack of faith was slowly eating away at him, and coupled with yesterday's encounter with Holborn, he'd completely bungled his call on Lady Philippa. He hadn't discussed the engagement at all. He'd reasoned that he needed to solve the problems surrounding Olivia first. Then he could focus on Lady Philippa.

Bernard admitted him to the Rose Room where Louisa would join him momentarily. Jasper stood before the painting of Merriweather Hall. Remarkable how the roses and vines perfectly matched the box Olivia had in her possession. A gift from Merry to his lover.

Jasper tried to imagine his kindly uncle chasing after an actress of Fiona Scarlet's infamy. Merry had been handsome, Jasper supposed, but without the bearing or stature of someone who would command attention. He'd been intellectual and witty, as well as artistic, of course. Perhaps that was the part of his nature that had appealed to the actress—and what had driven him to pursue her.

Later he'd met and fallen in love with Louisa, and Jasper could truly think of no two people more meant for each other. He knew Louisa missed him terribly and understood why she would want to find his daughter—and never let her go.

"Why, Jasper, this is an early call!" Louisa hummed into the room with a bright smile.

Jasper met her in front of the settee and kissed her cheek. "Good morning, Aunt. I'm afraid I have a few things to discuss with you, and they couldn't wait."

Her forehead creased. "This sounds serious, dear. Shall I ring for tea?"

"No, thank you. Let's just sit." He gestured to the settee and then joined her there.

Now that the moment was here, he couldn't seem to find the

words. *Why did you lie to me?* seemed harsh. *Why don't you trust me?* sounded needy. He settled for, "I know the truth about Olivia."

She scarcely reacted to what he said, merely tipped her head to the side. "And what is that?"

She couldn't mean to continue lying to him? Jasper suppressed his frustration. "I know she isn't Merry's cousin. She's his daughter."

Louisa pursed her lips. "Olivia told you this?" She didn't look upset at all. Perhaps just a touch disappointed.

Jasper's temper pricked. "Yes, but only because I learned some telling facts about her and she had to confess. Louisa, I don't think you contemplated this ruse very thoroughly."

Now she frowned. "There is no 'ruse'. I know Society will not accept her as Merry's bastard. I did what I had to in order for her to be a member of my family."

"Do you include me in 'Society' instead of as a member of your family? Is that why you kept the truth from me?"

At last, Louisa revealed a shock of surprise, but then Jasper hadn't bothered to keep the hurt from his tone. "Jasper, my dear boy, I only wanted to protect you from knowing the truth. I know how hard you've worked to keep yourself from scandal."

"Yes, but I would think of all people, you would trust me. *Me.*"

She took his hand between her small, soft palms. "I can see I made a terrible mistake. It's been far too easy for me to believe you're like your father, if only because you try so hard to fit into the image he's cast for you."

Jasper shrugged. "That is my duty."

"Yes, but you needn't fill the role he's created. His way is not the only way."

Jasper knew that, but he'd grown up following the path of least resistance as a means of self-preservation. "You can't assume that what you see on the outside is who I am on the inside. I thought you knew me better than that."

"Oh, dear, I do." She squeezed his hand. "But perhaps you need to let that person on the inside out a little more often."

Jasper wasn't sure he could do that. He'd let Olivia see more of him than anyone since Abigail. But to the world at large, he was Saxton. Heir to one of the oldest dukedoms in the realm and utterly above reproach. He had to maintain that façade lest anyone see straight through to the violence-loving ruiner of women beneath.

"I will try."

Her bright blue eyes were wide with regret. "I'm so sorry. Will you forgive me, please?"

Jasper hugged her. "Of course."

She patted his back and held him in a tight embrace for a long minute. When he sat back, she brushed at her eyes. "You've turned me into a watering pot."

Jasper waited for her to regain her composure before continuing. "I'm afraid Olivia wasn't completely honest with you. Do you have any idea who her mother was?"

Louisa shook her head. "All I have is a note from a woman named Fi. Olivia said she died last year."

"And you didn't think to ask anything else?"

Alarm began to register in Louisa's gaze. "Olivia said they weren't close. Most of her upbringing was by her foster mother in Devon."

"Her mother was Fiona Scarlet. You're familiar with that name, aren't you?"

Jasper had learned that before Olivia was born, her mother had been one of the most celebrated actresses at Drury Lane. However, some disagreement between her and another actress had caused her to be sacked. After that, she'd fallen somewhat out of the public eye, except that she'd began to be known for her liaisons with titled gentleman such as Merry. Soon it became known that Mrs. Scarlet didn't maintain monogamous relations with her lovers, and the rank of her clientele fell drastically. After a few years, her name had become a memory amongst most of the Upper Ten Thousand.

Louisa clasped her hands tightly together in her lap. "Yes. Is that…was she Olivia's mother?"

"Yes."

"Merry…" Louisa looked away. After a moment, she said in a strained voice, "I had no idea."

"You can see why this is a problem. If I was able to discover this secret, only think of who else might know."

Louisa returned her gaze to his. Unshed tears glistened in her eyes. "How did you find out?"

Jasper couldn't tell her the entire truth. While he wanted there to be no lies between him and his aunt, he couldn't bring himself to tell her he'd met Olivia before, that Olivia had tried to swindle him. That would remain a secret he would never share.

"She looked familiar to someone at the Faversham Ball."

Louisa raised a hand to her gaping mouth. "Oh no, who?"

"It doesn't matter. I'm taking care of everything." He still needed to talk with Prewitt, but planned to very soon.

She dropped her hand to her lap and blinked against her tears. "Jasper, I don't want to lose her."

Jasper took her hand and vowed not to let her fall into the crippling sadness that had claimed her after Merry died. "You won't."

"You're such a dear, dear boy. I never should have kept the truth from you. Of course you would help me." She shook her head as a tear fell down her cheek. She pulled a handkerchief from her sleeve and dabbed at her eyes. "See, an utter watering pot."

Jasper rested his palms on his lap, suddenly restless to fix this problem as soon as possible. He'd run Prewitt to ground today and would then visit the Haymarket to ensure no one there breathed a word about Olivia West.

Once Louisa regained her composure, she shook her head. "I've been terribly selfish." Her tone had recovered its strength and her gaze had turned determined. "I wanted so badly to have Merry's daughter in my life, I didn't think about the consequences to anyone, including Olivia. I'm not even sure she likes her new situation."

"I'm confident she loves being here with you." Not only did Jasper seek to soothe Louisa's concerns, he knew it to be true.

"That may be. But I'm not certain she's comfortable in Society."

"It's an adjustment for her."

"Perhaps I'll take her to York, to the dowager house at Merriweather Hall." Louisa looked at the painting. "Yes, we'll do that immediately."

Jasper hated that idea, but recognized it was probably for the best—for everyone, not least of all him since he couldn't keep from thinking of Olivia and wanting to touch her and kiss her and do all manner of inappropriate things to her. Yes, better for everyone if they went to York. "An excellent notion."

Louisa's eyes widened. "Oh! But then I shall miss your engagement, and I don't want to do that. When will you be announcing?"

Jasper wished he knew. He supposed today's tasks would take him closer to ensuring Louisa's and Olivia's well-being, but he still wasn't ready to put a definitive timeframe on his betrothal. "Soon. But don't let my engagement dictate your plans," he added, somewhat half-heartedly.

"We'll wait. You're taking care of things with Olivia—and I trust you completely to do that." She gave him a pointed look filled with warmth and love.

He couldn't help but smile in return. "Thank you."

Jasper left a few minutes later, glad the discussion with Louisa had gone so well. He only hoped the rest of his day followed suit.

THAT AFTERNOON OLIVIA was spared having to lie to Louisa for the second day in a row. She'd planned to claim another headache in lieu of going to Lady Montrose's for tea, but Louisa had been the one to beg off in order to take a restorative nap. Which had left Olivia free to visit Mrs. Pitt—her mother's one-time dresser—to continue her investigation into her paternity.

The Strand was busy this afternoon as she made her way to Villiers Street where Mrs. Pitt supposedly resided. The woman was quite old. Olivia only hoped she still drew breath, because without her, she may never learn the truth. Of course, it was also possible Mrs. Pitt would be no help at all, but Olivia chose not to ponder that.

Mrs. Gifford's shop was just ahead, but Olivia would turn from the Strand before she reached it. If she weren't so intent on her purpose, she'd stop in to visit.

"Miss West?"

Olivia paused and raised her head. Mr. Gifford approached, a welcoming smile warming his thin face.

"Good afternoon, Mr. Gifford."

"I've been hoping you'd come to see us. Mother and I have wondered after your welfare."

"How thoughtful of you both." Olivia itched to continue her journey, but also didn't wish to be rude. "I'm on a rather quick errand here in the neighborhood. I should like to stop in and see your mother—and you, of course—for tea. Perhaps another day?"

"We'd be delighted. I'd be honored to walk with you, if that's acceptable."

She didn't really want company, but perhaps his presence would soothe her nerves about the upcoming interview. "Certainly. I'm going to Villiers Street, there." She pointed just ahead.

Mr. Gifford offered his arm. Olivia placed her hand on his sleeve and walked alongside him.

"How is it? Living with Lady Merriweather, I mean? Do you attend balls and routs and such?"

"Mmm, yes. It's a bit overwhelming, to tell the truth. I adore Louisa, however, and so I'm willing to partake in the activities she enjoys."

"I understand. I humor my mother in much the same way."

Olivia wasn't necessarily *humoring* Louisa. She didn't dislike these events. No, she felt as if she didn't really belong. Perhaps her visit with Mrs. Pitt would change her perspective. Olivia dearly hoped it would.

They turned into Villiers Street. Olivia looked for the address—it would be on the same side of the street on which they walked. She scanned the buildings as they strolled.

"Do you mind my asking about your appointment?" he asked.

"Merely visiting an old friend."

"Commendable of you to remember those of us from your former life."

She didn't know him well enough to predict whether he was being genuine, but couldn't completely discount the odd lilt to his tone. "I have many dear friends who I shan't forget regardless of my address."

"It's good to hear you say that. Can Mother and I expect you to call soon, then?"

"Of course. Thank you, Mr. Gifford." Olivia withdrew her hand. He bowed to her, but didn't immediately continue on his way. After an awkward moment, Olivia said, "Well, good day, then."

"Oh." He smiled crookedly. "Good day." At last he ambled back toward The Strand.

Olivia exhaled before walking up the steps to the house and rapping on the door. She was answered by a portly woman of middle age with a kind, round face. "Yes?"

"I'm here to visit Mrs. Pitt." Olivia offered a pleasant smile. "I understand she boards with you?"

She scanned Olivia, perhaps to determine her purpose. "You here to buy some scarves?"

"Scarves?"

"I suppose not, then. Does she know you?" A trace of skepticism crept into her tone.

Olivia thrilled to the fact that Mrs. Pitt was indeed still living at this address. "Not exactly. She knew my mother, and I was hoping to speak with her. My mother died last year, you see."

The woman's face softened. "My condolences. Of course, come inside. I'll show you upstairs."

The interior of the house was dim and smelled of fresh-baked pastry. Olivia's mouth watered as she followed the landlady to the first floor. Yellowed paper with a leaf pattern peeled back from the wall where the stairs opened to a landing. The landlady led her across the small space to an open doorway. Inside, a small woman sat hunched over her knitting beside a window open to Villiers Street below.

"Mrs. Pitt, I've brought a visitor." She looked inquiringly at Olivia. "Miss Olivia West."

The old woman's head perked up, but she didn't look in their direction. In fact, she looked at nothing. Her eyes were the dark cloudy gray of someone whose vision had succumbed to cataracts. "Who?" She spoke loudly as if her hearing were also impaired.

"Miss West. I believe you knew my mother, Fiona Scarlet." Olivia blushed as she said this and sneaked a glance at the landlady to gauge her reaction. She was so used to people passing judgment based on her mother. However, the landlady's face reflected nothing, giving Olivia to believe—thankfully—that she'd never heard of Fiona Scarlet.

Mrs. Pitt set her knitting in her lap. "Dear Fi. How is she, love?"

Olivia was careful to speak loudly and clearly. "I'm sorry to say she passed last year."

"I'll just leave you to visit." The landlady retreated from the small chamber.

Mrs. Pitt's mouth drooped. "'Tis a shame. Sit, love. I'd often wondered what happened to Fi's child. Sent you off to live with her sister, isn't that right?"

"Yes." Olivia perched on a straight-backed chair, anticipation rushing through her at Mrs. Pitt's obvious knowledge, at least of Olivia's childhood. "I was hoping you could tell me about my mother, back when you dressed her, say twenty years ago or so."

Mrs. Pitt chuckled as she picked up her knitting once more. Her fingers worked rapidly, weaving the yarn at a remarkable pace given her blindness. "Your mother was a popular actress. Well-liked by men, the object of jealousy for most women, particularly the other actresses."

Olivia could think of no way to ease into her question and so she simply said, "I've come to ask about my father. I'm hoping you can help me determine his identity."

"Your mother never told you?"

"No. I'd been given to believe he was my uncle, a vicar married to Fiona's half-sister. However, I've recently learned another man, a viscount, may have been my father."

The stitches mounted until Mrs. Pitt started another row. "Mmm. I take it neither one can confirm your paternity?"

Her insides clenched. "No."

Mrs. Pitt's needles clacked against one another. "Why do you think this viscount is your father?"

Olivia had come for information, but had the distinct impression she was now the one being interrogated. "His widow is quite certain. The viscount and I share specific traits. And my mother was in possession of a hand-painted gift from him."

The ancient lifted a bony shoulder in a half-shrug. "It sounds as if you have your answer, then."

"The vicar and I also share specific traits. My aunt is equally convinced *he* is my father. Did you meet either of those men?"

"I'm sure I know which viscount you refer to. Merriweather, isn't it?"

Olivia sucked in a breath, hope surging in her chest. "Yes."

"Aye, he skulked around the theatre quite a bit back then." She chuckled. "Hopelessly besotted with Fi. Most men were. How'd she pass?"

"One of those men, actually. Her protector pushed her down the stairs."

Mrs. Pitt shook her head sadly. "I worried she'd go that way. Fi didn't always choose the best lovers. Sometimes you need to listen to your mind instead of..."

Your heart? Did Mrs. Pitt mean Fiona had loved some of these men? Or did she refer to something...baser? "Did my mother fall in love? I didn't think she loved anyone but herself."

"Oh, you poor child. Fi was as selfish as they come. No, Fi didn't fall in love easily. Her heart wasn't the body part leading her." Mrs. Pitt's paper-thin lips stretched into a smile. "Ah well, there are some things a girl doesn't need to hear about her mother."

Though Olivia never approved of her mother's behavior, she found this woman's insight irresistible. "I'd like to know."

"All right, then. Fi liked men. She'd lust after one, establish whatever situation she could, and when she tired of him, she moved on. Over the years, there were a few who didn't grow bored as quickly as she did. They didn't fancy being thrown over for the next gent. I always worried one of them would take their anger out on her. Such a shame." Her voice trailed off, and her knitting slowed. "I'm truly sorry for your loss, love."

"And the vicar?" Olivia asked.

"Aye, he was a persistent fellow. Another of her madcap followers. He came all the way from Devon to visit her after she'd spent the holidays with them.

"But none could hold a candle to Oliver St. Jermyn." Mrs. Pitt's voice gained in strength and vigor, as if she warmed to this subject. "He was an actor. I do believe he was the one man your mother truly loved. They looked as if they were made for each other—her with that bright red hair, him with dark auburn locks—like a matched set."

Olivia's gut clenched at the description of St. Jermyn. And his name. *Oliver*. Instead of definitive answers, she'd found more doubt, more uncertainty. "What happened to him?"

"Killed by a footpad before she delivered you. Fi was devastated. I think St. Jermyn even meant to marry her."

Olivia felt a pang of sorrow for her mother, but also for herself. Another closed door. She fisted her hands in her lap, the kid of her gloves stretching taut over her knuckles. "You really don't know who my father is?"

"I suspect the only one who did was Fi. However, it's possible even she couldn't be certain." Mrs. Pitt set her knitting down once more. "Does it really matter?"

For as long as Olivia could remember, she'd longed for the love of a parent. Her aunt and uncle had provided for her most basic needs, but care and consideration had not been included. Now, with Louisa—someone with whom she shared no blood connection— Olivia knew the love of a true family. "I thought it did."

"People will always believe what they wish. If you're worried people do not accept you as this viscount's daughter, they are not worth knowing."

Tears burned the backs of Olivia's eyes. Mrs. Pitt was right, but acceptance in Society was paramount if she meant to continue to live with Louisa.

"Love, you'd do best to look forward, not back. I know this seems terribly important to you now, but some day—maybe soon—it won't. Be honest and true to yourself, and things will turn out right." She smiled again as she plucked up her knitting once more.

Olivia could think of nothing else to say, no other question to ask. Slowly, she rose from her chair, hating that she hadn't got what she'd come for, that she'd probably never find an answer. "Thank you for your time, Mrs. Pitt."

"You're welcome, love. You seem a charming, intelligent gel, and I'd wager you're every bit as pretty as Fi. Do whatever you must to live with your head held high. The only good opinion worth having is your own."

The sound of clacking needles filled the small space as Olivia made her way toward the stairs. On the ground floor, the landlady met her with a nod. Olivia thanked her and stepped out onto Villiers Street.

Though she hadn't found the answers she sought, she felt a sense of peace. She'd been wrong not to tell Louisa the truth about her background and planned to rectify that mistake immediately. She knew with certainty that Louisa wouldn't judge her, that she'd embrace her as warmly as ever. Because they were family.

Chapter Seventeen

"Is Louisa still napping?" Olivia asked as the butler admitted her into the townhouse.

Bernard closed the door. "No, but she is taking tea in her room. I believe her ankle is giving her a touch of trouble today."

"Thank you." Olivia nodded and went upstairs, eager to see Louisa at once. At Louisa's door, she rapped softly.

"Come," Louisa answered.

"Good afternoon, dear. Were you out for a walk again?" She smiled from her chair positioned in front of the garden-facing windows. "Your cheeks are a lovely pink."

"Yes, it's quite beautiful outside." Olivia removed her bonnet. Sunlight streamed into the room, bathing the chamber with warmth and cheer. How quickly Louisa's townhouse had come to feel like home. Which made her objective all the more difficult. But it had to be done. Olivia forced herself to perch on the edge of Louisa's bed, though she would've preferred to pace and fidget her anxiety away. "I've some news to share."

"Oh?" Louisa straightened. "This sounds serious."

Best to just get it out. "I'm afraid I haven't been completely honest with you." If Olivia's cheeks had been pink before, they positively burned now. How she wished she'd been forthright from the start. When had she become so deceptive? First she'd tried to swindle Jasper, then she'd withheld information—pertinent information—from the person who'd treated her more kindly and generously than she'd ever dreamed possible. Louisa deserved better.

Louisa immediately stood and came to sit next to her on the edge of the bed. "I know dear. Jasper told me everything."

Jasper? What had he told her? He didn't know anything about her paternity. As far as he knew, she was Merry's bastard. Her gut tightened. Had he somehow learned this truth as well? He'd be furious with her for lying again. "He did?"

"Yes, he came to see me this morning. I was going to speak with you earlier, but I just didn't know how to start. I'm so sorry about everything."

She was sorry? Olivia frowned in confusion. "I don't understand."

"Jasper told me about your mother. About Fiona Scarlet."

Olivia was momentarily speechless. She'd planned to reveal this truth today as well as the question of her paternity, but hadn't conceived of Jasper telling Louisa. Not after he'd sought to help her. "You're not angry?"

"Not at all, dear. I can see why you wouldn't want to tell me, and I don't blame you. Though I never would've judged you for it."

Olivia didn't have trouble believing that, which was why she'd felt so guilty about keeping the secret. "I know, and I'm sorry. I should've trusted you."

Louisa smiled. "Yes, well, it seems trust is something we should all work on. I made a grave error in not trusting Jasper. You were right all along. I should have told him immediately that you're Merry's daughter. He is, in fact, helping to ensure no one learns the truth of your background."

The truth. Olivia didn't even know the truth and probably never would. The mystery of her paternity would remain that: a mystery.

"Olivia?" Louisa touched her arm.

"Sorry, I was woolgathering. I'm glad that you and Jasper talked." It was beyond time to be completely honest—or as honest as she could be. She'd never reveal her liaison with Jasper. Best to let that molder in the past. "However, Jasper doesn't know the rest."

Louisa's brow wrinkled. "There's more?"

"Yes, about my father."

"Merry?"

Olivia's chest burned. She wished, more than anything, that she'd been able to prove Merry had been her father. Aside from pleasing Louisa, there was nothing Olivia wanted more. "Yes, Merry and, ah, others." There was nothing for it but to just get the words out. "I didn't have a headache yesterday, and I didn't have a pleasant visit with my aunt in Cheshunt. You see, she evicted me from her house upon learning her husband had sired me. Or so she believes."

Louisa's color deepened. "But that's absurd. Merry is your father."

Olivia smiled sadly, yearning for Louisa's assertion to be true. "I only wish he or my mother were here to confirm it. My aunt raised evidence—quite as sound as yours unfortunately—that the vicar could be my father."

Louisa's brows gathered over her troubled eyes. "What sort of evidence?"

"Shared traits such as you describe with Merry. Also, similar marks on our scalps." Olivia couldn't help but notice Louisa's shoulders slumping ever so slightly, but she didn't want to stop until she'd finished. "I'd hoped to find someone who knew my mother. Someone who could confirm my paternity. I found a woman." Louisa's head perked up. "I'm sorry to say she added further confusion. A third man, named Oliver St. Jermyn, loved my mother and unlike the others, she loved him in return. We share the same hair color and it's possible my mother chose my name for a reason. For my father." Olivia tensed as she shared her theory and her anguish.

Louisa turned her head. Her fingers played with the lace edge of her coverlet. Olivia's body trembled in the enveloping silence. Finally, after several minutes, Louisa faced Olivia once more. "Your mother could have named you after the man she loved regardless of who sired you. Perhaps *she* didn't even know the truth."

Olivia had also considered this, but hadn't wanted to dwell on her mother's perfidy. "It doesn't really matter now. The truth shall never be known." She steeled herself to say what she must. "I should leave."

"No!" Louisa's blue eyes sharpened as she grabbed Olivia's hand. "You're right about one thing—it doesn't matter. I don't care if Merry was your father or not. You're a daughter he would be proud of, a daughter I'm proud of. Perhaps I'm a foolish, lonely old woman, but I enjoy your company. You don't truly wish to leave, do you?" Her gaze was searching, expectant.

A daughter she was proud of. A daughter who'd tried to use Jasper for financial gain and who could never be the virtuous, marriageable debutante Louisa wanted. She really should go, but the thought of returning to her loneliness was more than she could bear. She struggled to speak around the ache in her throat. "No."

"I want to be clear. I want you with me, wherever that may be. We don't need to stay in London, in Society. You said you didn't want to find a husband, at least not right now. I was thinking we might adjourn to York, to the dowager house at Merriweather Hall."

Olivia felt a burst of love for this woman who understood her so much better than either of her two supposed mothers. "I should like that very much." Though if she were honest, she would miss just one thing about Society. The very thing she'd dreaded from the start and had now grown quite fond of: Jasper.

"Excellent. We shall leave as soon as Jasper announces his engagement."

Olivia's mood deflated again. She knew Jasper would marry, and she knew it wouldn't—couldn't—ever be her. Still, the knowledge that it was imminent was a bitter reminder of what she could never have. She supposed she ought to regret their liaison, but she couldn't. Not when she would cherish the memory always.

"Olivia, dear, would you care to join me in the Rose Room for tea? Do you have a project you can work on? What about Jasper's waistcoat? I haven't seen it at all. Are you making progress?"

She was, in fact. Working on it was a constant and usually pleasing reminder of the afternoon they'd spent at Benfield. Now, however, the thought of stitching the pieces together as she recalled every line and plane of his form made her sad.

Pasting a smile on her face, she rose from the bed to fetch it. "It's coming along quite nicely."

Louisa's face lit up. "Perhaps he can wear it for his engagement dinner."

"That would be lovely," Olivia said. Lying, it seemed, was a necessary evil. Especially to one's self.

THE DARK, TIGHT air of the Black Horse welcomed Jasper like an old friend. The club had already convened. He heard the unmistakable sounds of flesh hitting flesh just before he opened the door to the back room.

Jasper scanned the low-ceilinged chamber and found Sevrin standing near the makeshift bar with Gifford. Sevrin raised a hand and Jasper cut through the spectators, eager for a glass of whiskey.

"You're late," Sevrin said.

Gifford filled and handed him a glass.

Jasper accepted the brew. "I was at the Haymarket talking with the manager, Colman."

"Ah, what news?" Sevrin asked.

"After I explained myself, he was most eager to keep Miss West's employment secret. He also understood the benefits of handling any inquiries about her mother with the utmost discretion."

Sevrin arched a brow. "You 'explained yourself'? Why do I think that's a euphemism for bribery?"

Jasper threw back his shoulders in mock affront. "I don't need to stoop to such tricks. I merely explained the advantages of having the support of the Earl of Saxton."

Gifford snorted. "Sounds like bribery to me."

Sevrin laughed, and Jasper couldn't help but smile with him. It *had* cost him a hundred pounds, plus he'd offered his support if Colman ever needed it. Colman—eager for any sort of patronage—had been more than amenable. He wouldn't say a word about anyone named Olivia West and would ensure his staff didn't, either. The latter would be difficult to guarantee, but it was the best Jasper could do. He doubted anyone would go to the trouble to question theatre employees. Anyone that wasn't Holborn, that was. He had to consider outright telling his father about Olivia and asking him to leave the matter alone.

Jasper wasn't sure he wanted to lead that untamed horse out of its paddock.

"Why are you bribing the theatre manager?" Gifford asked.

"He's trying to make sure his aunt's ward isn't revealed as Fiona Scarlet's daughter." Sevrin looked at Jasper. "I spoke to some of the women who come around. One or two knew Olivia was Fiona's daughter, but didn't think much of it. I imagine to them, a mother like her is the same as any other."

Jasper was pleased with this news, though he wished Sevrin hadn't mentioned Olivia's mother in front of Gifford. The less people who knew—regardless of their station—the better.

Gifford set his glass on the bar. "It's coincidental you're talking about her. Miss West, I mean. I saw her just this afternoon."

Surprised, Jasper moved closer to Gifford in order to hear him better. "You know her?" He suddenly recalled Gifford saying her name had sounded familiar that night they'd gone to The Locust.

Gifford gave a light shrug. "I couldn't place the name before, but later realized she'd sold some things in my mother's shop—before she went to live with your aunt."

Jasper feared he was about to catch Olivia in another lie, and he didn't like it. "Where did you see her?"

"She came back to the neighborhood to visit."

Olivia had explained the same to Jasper, but was there more to it than that? Gifford wasn't a bad looking chap, and Jasper liked him well enough. Did Olivia have some connection to him? Jasper felt a stab of jealousy. "She came to see you?"

"Not exactly, though she's promised to do so. She visited some old woman who worked in the theatre. I knew you wanted the truth from her, and so I stood below the window and listened to their conversation." Shamefully, Jasper didn't admonish him for eavesdropping. He was too interested in what Gifford would reveal. He tensed as Gifford continued, "You said she'd claimed to be Lord Merriweather's cousin, but from what I heard, she's told your aunt she's more than his cousin. She says she's his bastard daughter."

Jasper actually sighed with relief. No new lies. "I already knew that, but thank you for sharing what you overheard." Because the information wasn't helpful, Jasper felt slightly less charitable toward Gifford for eavesdropping.

"Do you also know she really has no idea who fathered her? She was interviewing this woman in the hope of discovering her paternity. Your uncle is only one of several potential men."

Sevrin leaned forward. "The devil you say."

Jasper had lifted his glass to take a drink, but now dropped his arm, causing whiskey to slosh from the glass onto his hand. *She'd lied after all.* All this nonsense about a painted box pointing to Merry as her father.

Jasper had thought they were past the lies, that she'd been honest with him the day they'd made love. But he'd known she was hiding something with her unchaperoned walk. He should have demanded the truth.

Gifford coughed, drawing Jasper's attention. "As long as I'm telling you this, I should also mention that she seems to be her mother's daughter in every sense of the word."

"What do you mean by that?" Jasper's throat constricted, forcing the words out in an angry rasp.

Now Gifford turned slightly to face him. "She's looking for the wealthiest title she can find. A girl from her station with the *ton* at her feet... She's taking full advantage of her new position."

No, no, that couldn't be true. Surely she would've tried to snare *him* by now. His blood ran cold. He'd lain with her. Was she hoping he might compromise her and force a marriage? No, she couldn't be that calculating. But he recalled her plan to swindle him. She'd been precisely that calculating.

Sevrin laid a hand on his shoulder. "Sax, do you really believe that about her?"

"I heard her say it, Sev." Gifford took a draught of his ale. "She made some comment about being smarter than her mother and doing better for herself."

Jasper's fingers encircled the glass like a vise. "She's the daughter of a whore. The night we met, she concocted a scheme to defraud me using her body. Then, just the other day, she gave herself to me, probably in the hope of garnering a marriage proposal. Yes, I have to believe it of her."

Gifford set his tankard on the bar with a thud. "I'm fighting next. Saxton, join me in the ring. You could use a good bout."

The lure of violence beckoned most fiercely, but the siren's call was even stronger. Jasper knew he shouldn't, but he was going to see Olivia. Right now.

He set his glass down. "Next time." He turned to go.

Gifford grabbed his arm, surprising Jasper. "Why not now?"

"Another time." Jasper shook the younger man's grip away and strode toward the back door.

"Wait." Sevrin caught up to him and followed him outside. "Where are you going?"

"None of your concern."

"Right." Sevrin ran a hand through his dark hair. "Still, remember who you are. If you're caught with her, she wins. That is, if you really do believe she's out to trap you."

Jasper couldn't believe anything else, no matter how much he wanted to. His chest ached.

"I won't get caught. I want her away from my aunt. Tonight."

Sevrin nodded. "Godspeed, then."

Jasper turned and left. His carriage waited at the mouth of the court. His feet were leaden with betrayal and despair. He had only himself to blame. He knew he couldn't trust her and yet he had. He'd taken her lies like a child gathers sweetmeats. And, as with too much sugar-laden food, he now felt sick.

OLIVIA SAT UPRIGHT at the sound of her door opening. It was quite late, but she hadn't been asleep. She'd stayed up working on Jasper's waistcoat until her eyes were beyond tired, but she was nearly finished.

"Who's there?" she called, her heart racing. The lantern next to her bed didn't cast enough light to see the door.

The door clicked shut, and a shadow fell across her bed. "Get up."

Jasper. Olivia cringed at the fury in his tone. "Jasper? Why are you here?"

"Get up. Now."

Fear pulled at her insides. She threw off the covers and stood beside him. "What's the matter? Is there an emergency of some kind? Louisa—"

He grabbed her arm and plucked up the lantern then dragged her toward her dressing chamber. "Just stop. You don't give a damn about Louisa."

What had happened? Why was he treating her like this? Olivia dug her heels into the carpet just outside her dressing chamber. "Let go of me, and explain yourself." She tried to pull her arm free, but he tightened his grip.

"You don't get to issue orders. I've had more than enough of your lies, and you will leave. Now."

Tears stung her eyes. "Tell me what's happened. Why are you acting like this?"

He pulled her into the dressing chamber and set the lantern on a table. "Get dressed."

"I'm not doing anything until you tell me what's going on." She shook her head. "No, even then I'm not doing anything. I'm not leaving Louisa."

He wrapped his fingers around her other arm and held her in front of him. "You'll do exactly as I say. I'm through with your lies and your machinations. It all ends now. I know you've tried to pass yourself off as Merry's daughter, taking advantage of Louisa's kindness and vulnerability. You've no idea how Merry's death devastated her and for you to purport to be his daughter, to give her hope for some kind of happiness with someone of his blood..." He thrust her away. "You make me sick."

Oh, God. He knew Merry might not be her father. She closed her eyes, hating herself for not telling him. Like Louisa, she should have trusted him. "I'm sorry. I should have told you." She opened her eyes, but the fury in his gaze made her look away from him. "Everything I told you before at Benfield was true. I just didn't tell you there was a chance Merry wasn't my father." She flicked her gaze back to his. "It was too humiliating." And painful. Her heart ached to claim him as her father.

His eyes were colder than every long winter's night. "It doesn't matter. Your lies are finished. You can't stay with Louisa another day. Get dressed."

"No! She doesn't want me to. She knows all of this."

He froze. "What?"

"Louisa knows. She doesn't care. She still wants me to stay."

"Tell me everything. And don't lie." He stepped toward her, his features dark with angry menace.

Olivia stood her ground. She deserved his ire. "I told you I visited my aunt." He gave one very stiff nod. "She'd thrown me out when I was four and ten upon learning her husband had sired me. Since then, I believed my uncle was actually my father. Until Louisa found me in that shop and connected my handkerchiefs to Merry's paintings."

Jasper's hands were fisted, but he listened in stoic silence.

"Louisa sent someone to Devon to speak to my foster parents, but my uncle had died, and my aunt had relocated to Cheshunt. I went to visit her to tell her Merry was my father. She'd been so furious upon learning of her husband's infidelity and that he'd sired a child with my mother. I wanted to alleviate her pain, but she insisted Louisa was mistaken, that her husband was my father, not Merry. Neither my aunt nor Louisa could verify my paternity beyond a doubt, so when we got back to Town I talked to people who knew my mother before I was born. I was hoping one of them would know the definitive truth."

"But none of them did." His voice was flat, emotionless. At least he didn't sound angry anymore.

Olivia's shoulders slumped in defeat. Retelling this only underscored the fact that she'd never know the truth. She looked down at her hands. "There's a third man, an actor. And who knows how many more." Tears threatened, but she refused to break down in front of him. He likely hated her after discovering yet another lie and wanted her as far away from the only person who'd probably ever truly loved her.

She regarded him with a pleading look. She may not want to cry in front of him, but she had no problem begging. This was too important. "Please don't ask me to leave Louisa. She wants me to stay, and I want to, too."

He said nothing and the silence grew until it filled the room as if it were another being.

His brows were drawn, and his hands were still fisted. He didn't look as angry as before, but lines of anguish bracketed his mouth. "Why did you give yourself to me?"

She hadn't expected that question, wasn't sure how to answer it. At length she said, "I needed you." It was the most honest thing she'd ever told him.

"You have no ulterior motive? No scheme to somehow trick me?"

Of course he would go back to that. He still hadn't forgiven her for trying to swindle him. She shook her head. "No, nothing." She still wanted him. Boldly, she stepped toward him. "There are no tricks, no plots, just me wanting you."

He flinched. "How can I trust you?"

"I swear there are no more secrets between us. I've told you everything, more than I've ever shared with anyone. No one knows about my mother, about my aunt, about my...shame."

She watched the emotions play across his face as he hesitated—compassion, wariness, determination. Finally, desire. He took two steps and touched the side of her face. "That is not your shame, but theirs."

He tipped her head back and kissed her. His lips were gentle yet demanding. She needed no persuasion to open her mouth and meet his tongue with eager licks. One of his hands cupped the back of her head while the other pressed her lower back taut against his hardened frame. Her hands encircled his neck and held onto him as if her life depended on it. And maybe it did.

Suddenly, he broke away from her and stepped back. "I can't." He turned and went back to the bedroom.

Olivia followed fast on his heels. "Please don't go."

"I have to. I can't do this with you again. I have more honor than that."

"Your honor isn't at stake—I'm no Society miss. You've been more honorable with me than I've probably deserved. I want you to stay."

Moonlight spilled through a gap in the curtains and arced across his face, highlighting the rough planes. "Don't say that. You deserve far better than you've gotten. Your life has been at the mercy of others, including mine."

That was true. He could easily expose her as a bastard daughter of a whore. But she knew he wouldn't. "You won't hurt me."

"Perhaps I already have. I had no right to take advantage of your vulnerability at Benfield."

"You didn't. Why can't you accept that it wasn't your fault?"

"Because I've done it before." The words came out on a whisper that Olivia could barely hear. But she didn't dare ask him to repeat himself. She could see what saying it had cost him. He turned away from her, his hands fisted again, his mouth compressed tight. "I ruined another girl, long ago."

"What happened to her?" Olivia asked because she thought he wanted to tell her. She supposed she wanted to know, but it wasn't the most important thing to her right now. Soothing him, giving him comfort when he'd given it to her—that was paramount.

"The duke got rid of her. She wouldn't have been an acceptable countess—or duchess—in his eyes, and so she simply disappeared."

Olivia's gut twisted. "You loved her."

He nodded, and Olivia's heart broke for his loss. She went to him and touched his face, turning him back toward the glow of the moonlight. "I won't leave you. Not tonight."

Chapter Eighteen

WITH A BURNING stare, Olivia kissed him. Jasper knew he should go, tried to make his feet move, but in the end, he wrapped his arms around her and clasped her close. The kiss became two, then three, their lips touching, sucking. He shouldn't allow her to seduce him, but he needed her. Just like she'd said she needed him.

She slanted her head and opened her mouth over his. Her tongue thrust inside. His fingers bit into her back, holding her against him with a ferocity borne of desperation. She didn't seem to notice or mind, for she kissed him with an intensity that spun his mind from his body until he couldn't think, only feel her hands stroking through his hair, sliding over his collar.

Jasper shrugged his coat to the floor while her fingers worked at his cravat, tugging the knot loose and tossing the fabric aside. He plucked at the buttons of his waistcoat, pulling one completely off the silk in his haste. Before he could rid himself of the garment, she was pulling his shirt from the waistband of his breeches. Her fingers grazed his bare flesh. Desire catapulted through him.

His waistcoat joined his coat and was quickly followed by his shirt. His arms still raised, she stroked down his chest. She studied his nipples, her fingertips circling them. Slowly, he lowered his arms, trying to keep hold of his restraint when he wanted nothing more than to lay her back on the bed and sink deep inside of her.

But she was controlling this. She had wanted it, asked for it. Never had he acquiesced command. Never before had it seemed important, vital.

She lifted her gaze to his in silent question. He gave a slight nod, and she smiled. The effect was devastating. Jasper groaned, eager for whatever she might offer. She turned and climbed onto the bed and beckoned him to follow.

She kneeled atop the coverlet and he sat beside her until she pushed him back against the pillows. Once he was fully reclined, she pulled his boots and stockings from his feet.

Jasper schooled himself to lie still and not help her. Her fingers moved to his waistband then paused. His pelvis thrummed with the need to arch up toward her. Instead, he waited, his breath drawn.

She lowered her mouth to his chest and lightly kissed his aching flesh. He cast his head back against the pillow as she opened his fall and tugged his breeches down his thighs. His breathing came heavier while her lips burned a trail toward his hips. She couldn't mean to…

Cool air rushed over his loins as she stripped away his small clothes, leaving him naked to her desire. Moments passed in which her mouth moved down with agonizing languor. Jasper tensed, his hips suspended in a tight arc.

He closed his eyes as her hand encircled his shaft. With exquisite care her palm rose up to the tip, employing the same method he'd instructed those many days ago—was it a week or a month or even a year?

She licked at his hipbone, eliciting a gasp from his lips and a jerk from his thighs. In giving her control, he'd weakened his. He didn't know how long he could last. Her hand worked another blissful moment and then her breath fell across his swollen flesh and his entire body went taut. She paused.

His eyes flew open. He angled his neck so he could look down at her. The silken length of her auburn hair flowed over his thigh. Her fist was wrapped around his cock, her mouth poised… Heat rushed through him at this provocative vision. "May I?" She didn't finish the question, but her meaning was clear.

Jasper nodded, unable to form words.

Then her lips were upon him and he lost all ability to think of anything beyond her touch. Gingerly, she kissed his flesh at first, her lips exploring, her hand continuing to grip him at the base. She opened her mouth wider, allowing her tongue to graze the tip. He knew moisture leaked, felt her draw back in surprise. He resisted the urge to hold her head to him, force her back to quench his need.

He didn't have to. She renewed her assault, this time with more surety. Her mouth closed over him and somehow, God somehow, she knew to slide her hand up until it nearly met her lips. Then down again as her tongue worked in delicious circles. Pleasure built within him. He thrust his hand into her hair, unable to keep himself from her another moment. She sucked, her mouth tightening around him, drawing his seed forth. No, he didn't want this to end. Not yet.

He hadn't really abandoned his control, merely allowed it to subside. For her. Careful not to steal what he'd so gladly given, he tugged at her hair. "You have to stop."

She lifted her head. Her cheeks were flushed, her eyes bright. "Why?"

"Because I don't want to come like that."

Her eyes widened. "Oh. I thought you liked it."

"God, yes. But I want to be inside of you. I want us to share tonight." He knew it was true, just as he knew there shouldn't even be a tonight. He thrust the reality of their incompatible stations—an heir to a dukedom and the bastard daughter of a whore—from his mind, refusing to let it intrude. "Come up here."

He held out his hand, and she placed hers in his palm. Reluctantly, she let go of his cock and slid up his body. He ground his teeth, working to keep himself together. Because she'd started this and because she'd seemed so eager to drive the encounter, he guided her to straddle him. The heat of her core pressed against his lower abdomen.

She still wore her voluminous nightgown, much to his chagrin. In silent question, he ran his hand up her thigh beneath the linen. To answer, she pulled the garment over her head and threw it to join his clothing.

Jasper inhaled at her naked beauty. Her flesh gleamed palest ivory in the moonlight. The tips of her breasts lured him like rose-colored velvet. He leaned up and took one into his mouth, sucking the nipple into a tight pebble.

She gasped and threaded her fingers in his hair. He massaged her hips, settling her lower against him, seeking her warmth against his aching shaft. He ran his left hand up her side to cup her other breast. The soft weight of her filled his palm. She felt so good. He lifted his other hand and wrapped it around the breast he suckled. Raising his mouth, he tweaked both nipples. Then he returned with greater fervor, drawing on her flesh, nipping and sucking at it until she moaned. Moisture seeped from her as she ground her hips down against him. Jasper arched up, his cock rubbing her clitoris.

He moved to her other breast with savage precision. He licked around the nipple, squeezing her flesh. She pushed down on him again. Pleasure pulsed through his belly. It had to be soon.

He kept his mouth on her, but widened her legs. He stroked down her body, his fingers seeking her wet cleft, the flesh satiny soft and so, so hot. She cried out and her muscles clenched. She was so close and he'd barely touched her there. The level of her desire humbled him.

Parting her flesh, he guided himself inside. He wanted to thrust deep, claim her body with a vicious stroke, but this was her night and so he waited for her direction.

She sat forward slightly, her body angled perfectly to receive him and then she pushed herself down until she'd taken him completely inside. He fell back with her movement, releasing her breast with a groan. She followed him, moving over his chest until her nipples brushed against him. Her knees came up on either side of him.

Her eyes had been closed, but now they opened and studied him with wonder. He returned her stare. Slowly, she rose up, her hands pushing against his chest. He burned with need, praying for her to establish a rhythm that was quick and hard. She came back down again, her cleft swallowing him whole, her eyes widening the smallest bit. He gripped her hips, and the movement loosened something within her. She moaned and pitched herself forward, her mouth taking his in a lustful, impassioned kiss that sent him to the very edge of sanity.

Her hips moved up and down, establishing the rhythm he craved. She rotated wildly against him, seeking release. He moved his hand to stroke her clitoris. Almost immediately she cried out against his mouth. She pulled up, giving him greater access. He pressed his thumb against her in swirling circles to create a throbbing friction. Moisture coated his shaft while her muscles clenched around him.

Her body jerked; she lost control of the rhythm. God, no, he couldn't let it go yet. In one fluid, desperate arc, he turned her to her back and drove into her, continuing the ebb and stroke. She wrapped her legs around him, her hips rising to meet each thrust. His seed pulsed forth. He had to get out. *Now.*

But he couldn't. He buried himself deep and took her mouth in a ferocious kiss. She was his. If not forever, then for now. God yes, for right now. The moment stretched into blissful eternity, his body pumping his insecurity, his desperation, his craving into her, the only comfort he could recall. Perhaps the only comfort he had ever known.

THE NEXT AFTERNOON, Olivia sat in the Rose Room stitching the buttons on Jasper's waistcoat. Last night had been a revelation in so many ways. She didn't think she'd ever opened herself to anyone the way she had to Jasper. He'd demanded her absolute honesty, and she'd given it. Not out of fear, but out of the desire to have someone with her. Someone who wouldn't judge her. Somehow—impossibly given the way their relationship had begun—Jasper had become that person.

He'd left her early, before it was even light. He'd kissed her brow. There had been no talk of another encounter or of the future. But neither had there been talk of regret. Olivia had no expectations where he was concerned, especially after hearing about his past. He'd already made the mistake of falling in love with someone he couldn't marry. She didn't think he'd do it again.

And she was definitely someone he couldn't marry. Though her background might be secret, he knew the truth—and she believed his duty wouldn't allow him to choose her.

Bernard came into the drawing room. "Lady Lydia Prewitt and Miss Cheswick are here to see you, Miss West."

Olivia stabbed herself in the finger, and then rubbed her thumb over the stinging flesh. They'd wasted no time in visiting as they'd promised. "Please have tea sent in. Thank you, Bernard."

So kind of him to announce the guests instead of bringing them directly. Olivia would stitch him a new handkerchief as soon as she finished the waistcoat.

She jerked her head up. The waistcoat! She couldn't let them see her sewing a garment that Jasper would presumably wear in public. Quickly, she stuffed the garment into the basket at her feet and shoved it under the settee.

Lady Lydia entered, her sharp brown eyes assessing the room. Audrey followed, offering a cheerful smile. "Good afternoon, Olivia." Her gaze went to Merry's painting. "Lord Merriweather's, I presume?"

Of course, Audrey was well-acquainted with his work. Her grandfather had several of his paintings in his townhouse, which Olivia had viewed at Lord Farringdon's dinner party. "Yes, that's Merriweather Hall in Yorkshire."

Audrey joined Olivia on the pink brocaded settee. "It's beautiful. He possessed such skill."

"Yes, but could he sketch gowns? Don't think I've forgotten your promise to show us your drawings." Lady Lydia untied her bonnet as she inspected the room. She ran her fingers over tables and knick-knacks, and paused to study the garden through the windows.

Olivia ignored Lady Lydia's odd behavior. "How are you, Audrey?"

"Oh, she's a bit excited, I daresay." Lady Lydia finally landed on a cream and rose-striped chair adjacent to the settee where Olivia and Audrey sat. "Mr. Evensrude called on her yesterday."

Audrey blushed. Olivia had no idea who Mr. Evensrude was, but if Audrey was pleased by his attendance, then Olivia would be too.

"Oh, he's no Saxton, of course, but he's no Lyle, either." Lady Lydia cast Olivia a superior glance, perhaps meant to remind Olivia that she'd been silly enough to dance with Lyle. "Still, I hope you don't encourage Evensrude too much, Audrey. You can do so much better. After all, Saxton isn't betrothed yet, and there may be a way you can attract him."

Surprisingly, Audrey glared at Lady Lydia. "I highly doubt that. You're cruel to even suggest it."

"Nonsense. You're a lovely girl from an impeccable family. I know the wagers say he'll marry Lady Philippa, but I can't imagine her agreeing. As staid as Saxton might be, she's even moreso."

Bernard entered with the tea tray just then, interrupting further conversation—at least for the moment. As soon as he'd settled the service on the table and departed, Lady Lydia started back up. "No, I don't think that way is closed. Leave it to me to come up with something." She smiled as she leaned forward. "Do you mind if I pour out?"

Olivia shook her head, and Lady Lydia proceeded to serve the tea.

"What would you do to encourage Saxton's attentions, Lady Lydia?"

Lady Lydia glanced up as she poured the third cup. "Oh, listen to me. I'm afraid I was a trifle overzealous. He's your cousin, of course. I mean him no harm. I'm sure he'll marry whomever he wishes."

Audrey leaned close to Olivia. "She really does mean well. It's just that sometimes her mouth moves faster than her mind."

Olivia would have to trust Audrey's judgment. After all, she seemed to enjoy Lady Lydia's company, else why would she spend so much time with her? "Audrey, do you possess a fondness for Mr. Evensrude?" Olivia asked.

"Well, that's not really a pertinent question, now is it?" Lady Lydia asked as she poured milk into all three cups and added liberal dollops of sugar. It seemed Olivia's preferences for her beverage were not to be taken into account. Lady Lydia continued on, "It's quite natural to develop a *fondness* for an inappropriate male. Surely you've harbored a tendre for someone for whom you shouldn't?" The corner of her mouth quirked up.

Olivia kept her face impassive, but of course she was harboring just such feelings at present. Was there a chance Lady Lydia knew that? But how could she? No one was aware of what had transpired between her and Jasper, not even Louisa. And they'd conducted their liaisons right under her nose, much to Olivia's shame.

Lady Lydia leaned forward conspiratorially. "I have." Her eyes sparkled with suppressed glee. "Do either of you know who Lord Sevrin is?"

Olivia shook her head.

Audrey's eyes widened. "You can't mean…"

Lady Lydia nodded, her lips curving into an almost seductive smile. "Tell me you don't think he's handsome."

Audrey plucked up her cup. "Of course, he's handsome, but he's also a scoundrel. Why, you know the rumors about him."

"They make him all the more delicious, don't you think?" Lady Lydia picked up her cup for a brief sip.

"What rumors?" Olivia felt compelled to ask, though she didn't really care to hear gossip, especially about someone she didn't even know.

Lady Lydia peered at them over the rim of her cup. "He *ruined* his brother's fiancée a few years ago."

Olivia was glad she hadn't yet picked up her tea for the shaking of the fine china might have revealed the faint tremor now coursing through her—*ruined*—body. Good heavens, what would they say about Jasper and the secret buried deep in his past?

"And can you believe, he's been seen with Saxton of all people!" Lady Lydia remarked with exuberance.

Audrey's mouth gaped. "Never say so!"

"Yes, but it's yet to be decided if the pairing will harm Saxton or help Sevrin. I, for one, believe it will do the latter."

"Which is why Sevrin's captured your interest." Audrey shook her head, a half smile curving her lips. "There's no such thing as a reformed ruiner of young women, Lydia."

Olivia wanted to know what Jasper had to do with any of this. Could Lady Lydia somehow be hoping to use his connection with Sevrin against him? Say, to encourage him toward Audrey? Surely a young woman like her couldn't be so diabolical.

"Yes, well, perhaps Saxton's infallibility will rub off on Sevrin. Saxton's untouchable." Lady Lydia set down her cup and her fingers hovered over the assortment of cakes. "I daresay *he* could ruin a girl and get away with it."

He *had*. With two separate women apparently, not that anyone knew it. Olivia busied herself with her teacup, stirring the brew and then bringing it to her lips. She took the smallest of sips in deference to her churning stomach.

Audrey arranged a napkin on her lap. "No one is infallible, Lydia. Not even Lord Saxton could escape Society's censure if he behaved poorly. More likely, his impropriety would generate an enormous scandal." She blushed. "I'm sorry, Olivia. How rude of us to discuss Lord Saxton in this manner. He's your cousin, after all."

Olivia's mind was spinning. "It's all right." She began to truly understand why Louisa had wished to protect him from the shameful truth of Olivia's parentage. Although, her mere presence threatened him as well as Louisa.

Bernard stepped into the room once more. "Miss West, there is a Mr. Gifford here. Shall I show him in?"

Goodness no! Mr. Gifford mingling with the likes of Lady Lydia may not be scandalous, but it would be awful nonetheless. "I'll just speak with him briefly. Please excuse me for a moment, ladies." She got up and hurried after the butler before Lady Lydia could say something obnoxious.

Bernard took her to the entry hall, where Mr. Gifford stood in the center of the pale marble floor. "Good afternoon, Miss West. I hope I'm not disturbing you."

After the butler retreated, Olivia said, "Good afternoon, Mr. Gifford. I have guests at present." Olivia wished he'd arrived first so she could've sent Lady Lydia and Audrey away.

His cheeks flushed slightly. "Oh, then I'll be brief. It was so pleasant to see you yesterday. I wondered if you're content here?"

The question startled Olivia. "Yes, quite."

He smiled a bit sheepishly. "Of course. It's just, well, an old friend of my mother's has taken ill, and she's looking for someone to manage her millinery shop. She sells gloves, hats, and the like. I immediately thought of you."

Olivia's pulse quickened. How she would've thrilled to such an offer just a few weeks ago. Indeed, if it wasn't for Louisa, she would not only consider the arrangement, she would leap at the opportunity. "If I wasn't so happy here, I would be tempted. Thank you for giving me a chance, however."

He glanced away, his mouth turning down. "I see. Since you'll be remaining here, would it be acceptable if I called on you?"

Oh dear. Would it? He was a friend, but not anyone she would see socially in her new life. How did one navigate multiple social classes? "I presume so." That wasn't really an answer, but it was the best she could offer at present.

Mr. Gifford smiled, but his eyes didn't reflect the sentiment. There was something darker there, disappointment perhaps? "I'll let you get back to your guests. Hopefully, our paths will cross again soon."

She nodded. "I should like that. In the meantime, please give my best to your mother."

"I shall. Good afternoon, Miss West." He took her hand and bent low, brushing his lips over her bare knuckles. "Until next time."

"Good afternoon, Mr. Gifford."

He took his leave while Olivia stared after him. His touch had offered none of the thrill a mere look from Jasper elicited, but she couldn't expect that. Not when Jasper commanded so much of her mind and spirit. Perhaps in time she would be able to welcome another man's attention. The thought made her sad. She didn't want another man's attention. She wanted Jasper.

Olivia made her way back to the Rose Room. Audrey and Lady Lydia had stood. "Oh, there you are. We thought perhaps you'd been detained. Who is Mr. Gifford anyway?"

Under the direct scrutiny of Lady Lydia's azure gaze, Olivia panicked. "He delivered something from a shop."

Lady Lydia's nose wrinkled. "You spent that much time with a tradesman? Your servants can accept your deliveries, Olivia." She sighed. "We'll get you turned around sooner or later, won't we, Audrey?"

They left before Olivia realized she'd avoided showing them her sketches—happily. The more time she spent with Lady Lydia, the less she wanted to share anything personal, especially her unfinished designs. They represented the dreams she'd nourished through all of the lonely years she'd endured with Fiona. Dreams someone like Lady Lydia could never understand.

She went to the large rosewood desk in the corner of the room. She retrieved her sketches from the top drawer and fingered through them.

As she looked at each drawing—some barely started, others nearly finished—she contemplated Mr. Gifford's visit. How ironic that a perfect employment situation should arise now that she'd finally found a home. She couldn't deny the notion of independence and the opportunity to design were exciting, but the love of a real family with Louisa was even more appealing. She only wished she didn't feel as if she were straddling both lives. She could never leave her mother's infamy behind, no matter how entrenched she ever managed to become in Louisa's Society.

"Miss West," Bernard called from the doorway.

Olivia set her drawings on the desk and turned.

"Lord Saxton to see you."

Even his name sent a thrill up her spine. "Thank you, Bernard."

The butler departed as Jasper entered. Olivia's heart tripped over itself, and she couldn't keep from smiling. He walked in, but merely nodded.

He'd made no promises. Last night was in the past, and they would continue forward as if it had never been. For the first time, Olivia was glad she was used to being disappointed and alone.

Chapter Nineteen

JASPER QUELLED THE urge to take Olivia in his arms and kiss her senseless. Last night had been a beautiful refuge from reality, but it was done. Once he ensured Olivia's background remained secret, he could focus on his own life—and he was nearly there.

He still hadn't been able to get Prewitt alone, but expected to see him that night at Vauxhall. A friend of Louisa's was hosting a party and she was close with Prewitt's mother, whom he escorted everywhere.

He walked to the fireplace, at the opposite end of the room from where Olivia stood near the desk. He needed to keep his distance, both physically and mentally. To aid his purpose, he summoned his frostiest demeanor. "I came to tell you my investigator returned from Devon today."

She remained near the desk, apparently content to keep as much space between them as he was. "Oh? What did he have to say?"

"He confirmed what Louisa's man already learned—that your uncle died and your aunt left Newton Abbott. Some villagers remember a girl who lived with the vicar and his wife, and that she left many years ago, but they've no idea why. Your secret is safe, at least in Newton Abbott." Her posture relaxed, and he continued. "I also spoke with Mr. Colman. No one at the theatre will recall an employee named Olivia West."

Her brow furrowed. He tried very hard not to think about kissing those delicate wrinkles away. He didn't want her to worry anymore. But it wasn't his place to want that. She could no longer be his concern.

"How can that be?" she asked. "I was a seamstress there for several years when my mother was an actress."

"I made sure Mr. Colman realized I was a better ally than enemy."

"You did that?" She didn't say 'for me,' but he heard it in her question anyway.

"I told you I would ensure you and Louisa would be happy. Just as you've ensured me there are no more secrets to unearth." Even after last night, after he'd told her about Abigail, he didn't know if he could really trust her. And in the end, it didn't matter. He'd done all he could to keep her past hidden, and now it was up to her to be forthright.

"Thank you," she said

They looked at each other a moment, and Jasper realized he ought to leave. But she interrupted his intention.

"I have your waistcoat." She crossed to the settee and pulled her sewing basket from beneath it. She extracted the garment, and the blue and silver fabric shimmered in the sunlight streaming through the windows. "Would you like to try it on?"

That meant partially disrobing in front of her again. He couldn't trust himself to do that.

She must've sensed his hesitation. She handed him the waistcoat. "Here, I'm sure the fit is excellent. My measurements were sound, and I'm, ah, familiar with your frame." She blushed and looked away. "My apologies. I shouldn't have brought that up."

"It's fine." His voice sounded strained, likely because he was trying very hard not to relive last night's bliss. "But I shouldn't have taken advantage of you again."

Her gaze flew back to his. "You didn't. I completely initiated last night. If anything, I should apologize to you."

"Let's just put the entire thing behind us." And because he had to make absolutely certain their liaison stayed that way—in the past—he added, "I'll be announcing my engagement soon."

Her eyes flickered the faintest amount of surprise, but not enough to indicate she was completely unaware. "Congratulations."

Jasper's mouth tasted bitter. What kind of blackguard was he to have lain with Olivia while he was planning to marry Philippa? The worst kind, of course.

"Jasper, I didn't know you were here!" Louisa breezed into the drawing room with a grin. "Oh, and Olivia's finished your waistcoat! How splendid. You must wear it to Vauxhall tonight."

"Nothing would give me greater pleasure." *Unless Olivia takes it off of me later. Stop it, man.* He'd consider avoiding tonight's endeavor altogether, but he needed to talk with Prewitt. Then he'd be done with Olivia. For good.

OLIVIA MADE A show of tidying her drawings and replacing them in the desk drawer as Jasper kissed Louisa's cheek and left. He'd been quite clear in his dismissal of her, but what had she expected? She'd known even last night as she'd drawn him into her bed that making love to him would be a solitary thing. Well, a second solitary thing.

She blinked back a tear. She would not cry over this. She'd survived much worse than…than…what? A broken heart?

Foolish, foolish girl! He was heir to a dukedom. She could never have a future with one such as him. What she'd shared with him was more than she could hope for. And now she had to do as he'd said and put it behind her.

"Bernard said you had guests for tea?" Louisa asked.

Olivia turned to see Louisa helping herself to a cake from the tray. Then she perched on the settee.

"Yes, Lady Lydia and Miss Cheswick."

"Delightful. I'm so pleased you're making friends, dear."

Olivia wasn't sure she'd call them *friends*, at least not Lady Lydia. "Audrey is quite nice."

Louisa chuckled. "I gather you've figured out Lady Lydia? She's a bit of a wolf. I knew you were a smart girl. No need to steer you away from bad decisions."

If Olivia had joined her in eating a cake, she would've suffered her second choking fit in the Rose Room. She was currently the queen of bad decisions.

Olivia sat down next to Louisa. "When you say Lady Lydia is a wolf, what do you mean?"

Louisa swallowed the remnants of her cake. "She's been molded by her great-aunt, the *ton's* most notorious gossip. They use information to sculpt their feared positions in Society. And Lady Lydia is quite adept. Surely you've noticed how Miss Cheswick trails after her?"

"Yes, and I don't understand it."

"Because, as I said, you're too smart for such nonsense. It's good to be friendly with someone like Lady Lydia, however, because you never know when she might sink her wolf-like fangs into you. She's a terrible busybody."

Whose father could very well have the most interesting *on-dit* of the summer: Lady Merriweather's new ward was nothing more than a bastard whose mother was a notorious whore. Olivia had to believe that if Lady Lydia possessed this information she'd use it. But to what end? Perhaps to force Jasper into marriage with Audrey? What a spectacular notion—and a baseless one at that. Audrey would never agree to such mischief.

"I can see that. She was quite interested in speculating about Jasper's betrothal."

"Well, that actually makes her quite normal," Louisa said. "Everyone is speculating about his betrothal."

"Do you think it will be Lady Philippa?" Olivia recalled the beautiful young woman's perfect poise and elegance. She would make Jasper a stunning and more than appropriate wife.

"I expect so, yes." She frowned. "Though, the longer he takes, the more I question an engagement at all. It's not like him to dawdle. Once he makes up his mind, he usually follows through quite quickly and definitively. Like with that horse of his."

Olivia didn't agree, but only because Jasper had just assured her that his betrothal was imminent. She wouldn't reveal that to Louisa, however. She didn't want her suspecting their relationship went anything beyond that of "cousins."

Louisa stood and went to the desk, on top of which sat a stack of unopened mail. "I suppose we'd best field these invitations. You don't mind helping do you, dear? I don't want to go to anything that doesn't sound appealing to you." She returned with the missives and sat back down, placing them in her lap.

She looked through them first and plucked one from the middle. "This is addressed to you, dear."

Olivia accepted the sealed parchment. She didn't recognize the handwriting. Her heart lurched as she unfolded the paper. The neatly penned words screamed from the page.

Leave Lady Merriweather's house or your true parentage and background will be made public. The bastard daughter of Fiona Scarlet has no place in Polite Society.

She angled herself so that Louisa couldn't read the note over her shoulder, and tried to keep her hands from shaking. Who would have sent this?

Louisa looked up from the invitation she was reading. "Who's that from, dear?"

"Just a note from…Mrs. Gifford," she fabricated. "She sends her best wishes."

"How kind of her." Louisa went back to reading.

Olivia should probably tell her the truth, and might yet still, but for now her mind was whirling. Jasper would want to know. She'd tell him tonight. Tonight! He planned to speak with Lord Prewitt. Was it possible he was too late? Had Prewitt already acted? But why send a note like this instead of spreading the gossip? Only someone who wanted her gone would have written such a thing.

Who wanted her gone?

Once, not too long ago, she might've said Jasper, but now she knew he wouldn't do that. It wouldn't be like him to send a note anyway. Last night he'd come to evict her, regardless of the hour, but had changed his mind once she'd convinced him she wasn't a threat. Had he now changed his mind back? But no, he'd just been here and was still committed to helping her. He wasn't behind the note.

Any number of people may not approve of her if they knew the truth, but only one would want to get rid of her. Just as he'd gotten rid of Jasper's first love. The Duke of Holborn.

She folded the letter and set it in her lap. Though she wanted to tell Jasper, she couldn't bring herself to make an already tense relationship between father and son worse. Not when she would give anything to have a father of her own.

JUST PAST TWILIGHT Jasper strolled through the Grove at Vauxhall. He nodded at people promenading and sitting at the tables surrounding the orchestra. Music filled the warm night air as he made his way to Lady Badby's supper box.

His gaze immediately fell on Olivia. Her auburn hair was artfully styled with pearl-encrusted combs. Though she sat, her upper body was visible, revealing a blue gown also decorated with pearls along the bodice. She sat next to Louisa and laughed at something his aunt said. He'd never seen Olivia look lovelier.

He forced himself to look around the table for Lord Prewitt. He easily found the man's mother, a small, ancient creature seated next to Lady Badby, their host. At last, he caught sight of Prewitt just returning from walking with…Sevrin? What the devil was he doing here?

Jasper strode to meet them. "Good evening Prewitt, Sevrin," he said as he joined them.

"Evening, Saxton." Prewitt nodded his head, covered in a wealth of dark gray hair.

Jasper sent Sevrin a questioning glance. "Saxton, I was just accompanying Lord Prewitt to Lady Badby's box. I understood you would be here this evening and thought I'd stop by."

Jasper wanted to ask, *but why did Prewitt allow you to speak with him?* Had Sevrin's reputation improved that much since Jasper had befriended him?

"I'm glad you did. Capital evening." Jasper searched for a way to broach the subject of Prewitt's recognition of Olivia.

"Say, Saxton. There's something a bit familiar about your aunt's ward," Sevrin said, casting a long look in Olivia's direction. Jasper wasn't sure what Sevrin had in mind, but he seemed to have a strategy so he followed along.

"Is there?" Jasper subtly directed the question at Prewitt, slightly turning his body toward the older man.

"I thought so, too," Prewitt agreed then shook his head. "But I have to be mistaken. I thought she looked like an actress. That was before you lads were out in Society."

"An actress?" Sevrin tapped his chin as if he were contemplating this notion. Suddenly he held up his finger and grinned. "I've figured it out. Lady Dalrymple."

Prewitt frowned. "His aunt's ward doesn't look a bit like her. Lady Dalrymple has a wide…shoulders and very dark hair."

Jasper held his breath. What tangle was Sevrin creating? Was Prewitt about to insist Olivia looked like Fiona Scarlet?

Sevrin chuckled. "You're quite right, she doesn't resemble Lady Dalrymple at all, but Lady Dalrymple has a portrait in her drawing room—I believe it's her husband's great-grandmother—and the subject is the exact replica of Miss West, I swear."

Jasper nodded slowly. He knew the painting Sevrin spoke of—though he briefly wondered how Sevrin did—and while the woman did possess the same color hair, he wouldn't go so far as to say Olivia was an 'exact replica'. Nevertheless, he went along with Sevrin. "I do believe you're right. It's a striking portrait, quite large. Surely you've seen it, Prewitt?" He waited anxiously for Prewitt's response.

"I have. Indeed, I think you're right, Sevrin. I knew she looked familiar."

Sevrin smiled. "Ah well, mystery solved."

"Incidentally, what actress did you mean?" Jasper wanted to know Prewitt's relationship—if there was one—with Olivia's mother.

"Oh, I can't even recall her name. Scarlet maybe? Ruby?" He waved a hand. "I saw her at Drury Lane once. Remarkable talent."

Jasper tried not to let his relief show.

Lord Prewitt gave a slight bow. "Now, please excuse me while I check on Mother." He turned and joined Lady Badby's party.

"I wasn't sure where you were going with that," Jasper said softly.

"That was rather fun." Sevrin looked about. "Is there anyone else we can bam?"

Jasper gave him an exasperated look. "Thank you for your help."

"Any time. I don't really plan on crashing Lady Badby's party. Will I see you at the Black Horse later?"

"Probably." His gaze strayed to Olivia. "I'm going to take Olivia for a promenade and tell her she has nothing to fear from Prewitt."

"Now?" Sevrin elbowed him in the arm, drawing his attention from Olivia. "Do you think that's wise?"

Jasper gave him an acerbic look. "What, are you the duke now?"

Sevrin snorted. "I know how difficult it is for you to keep your hands off of her. I'd inquire as to whether your affections have waned, but I can see from the way you look at her they haven't."

Christ, was Jasper that transparent? That wouldn't do. Perhaps walking with her wasn't the best idea. He could just as well visit her tomorrow.

He elbowed Sevrin back. "Mind your own business. I'll see you later."

"Good evening, my dear boy," Louisa called as Jasper neared the box.

"Good evening, Aunt, Miss West." He bowed to each of them before turning to his hostess. "Lady Badby, thank you for your invitation."

A tall, slender woman with jet-black hair shot through with silver, Lady Badby had been a friend of Louisa's as long as Jasper could remember. Though given to gossip, Lady Badby had always treated him with fondness and care. Tonight her eyes sparkled with ill-suppressed glee. "Thank you for gracing us with your presence. Is there any chance Lady Philippa will be joining us?" She fixed him with an inquisitive stare, her lips pulling up in an expectant smile.

So she hoped her little party might garner the summer's most coveted *on-dit*? Was that why she'd included him?

Beyond Lady Badby, Louisa rolled her eyes. "Augusta, don't be gauche."

Lady Badby laughed, seemingly unbothered by Louisa's admonition. "Oh, my dear Louisa, you know I had to ask."

"You had to do no such thing. Now, Jasper, take Olivia for a promenade."

Her command made Jasper's decision regarding whether to talk with Olivia tonight or tomorrow. Tonight was just as well. Better to get this over with so he could focus on Lady Philippa. His insides felt hollow.

"It would be my pleasure." He waited for Olivia to get up and move around the table. He offered his arm as soon as she joined him. Louisa beamed at them as he escorted Olivia away from the box and down the Grand Walk.

They were several yards removed when she said, "You're wearing the waistcoat."

He passed his hand over his chest. "It's my favorite. Fits divinely. My valet thinks I should sack my tailor."

She laughed, and his insides turned to jelly. He had to find a way to prevent such reactions to her.

"Have you been to Vauxhall before?" he asked.

"Yes, many times. My mother loved to come here." There was a wistful quality to her voice that led him to believe Olivia loved the gardens too. "Do you mind if we go to the Hermit's Walk? I often escaped there."

"Certainly." Jasper turned her onto the Grand Cross Walk. "What was your relationship with Fiona like?"

She was quiet a moment. "She didn't treat me like a daughter, more like a friend who came to stay with her. And she wasn't overly happy about it, especially when I wasn't as free-spirited as her."

Jasper knew what it felt like to disappoint a parent, and was frustrated on Olivia's behalf even years later. "You'd been raised in a vicarage. What did she expect?"

Olivia smiled sadly. "That's precisely what I wondered, but then she never wanted me."

Jasper's chest pulled. He'd been second choice, but to never have been wanted at all? He didn't know what to say, so he simply laid his hand over hers.

She shrugged, the muscles of her neck and shoulder rippling elegantly with the soft gesture. "Fiona soon realized a fourteen year old girl wasn't a hindrance like a baby or small child would have been." Her gaze flicked up to his. "Not that she would have allowed such interruption. She simply carried on with her life while I kept out of her way."

Her life, as Olivia put it. The life of a courtesan. "And were you privy to her activities?"

As they turned onto the Hermit's Walk, she glanced up at him. "If you're asking if I was aware of her profession, of course. She usually had a protector who paid for our lodgings, so we moved as often as she changed lovers. A few times, her protector didn't want me in the same house and so he paid for me to lodge elsewhere. I preferred that, actually."

It sounded lonely. He never wanted her to experience the hollowness of solitude or the sting of rejection again. "I spoke with Lord Prewitt this evening. Though you looked familiar to him, he couldn't place you as Fiona's daughter. And I made sure he never would."

She paused near the end of the Hermit's Walk and turned to look at him. "Goodness, what did you do?"

"Only steered him in another direction. He thinks you look like Lord Dalrymple's ancestor." She looked at him quizzically and he laughed softly. "Just trust me. He won't bother you."

"I do trust you." She smiled. "Thank you."

She trusted him. It sounded a simple thing, but he knew it had to be difficult for her, given her past. She'd never been able to rely on anyone until Louisa. He was only glad he'd ensured Olivia never had to leave her.

A whistle sounded and all of the lanterns in the gardens flamed with light. She jumped. "Oh!" Then she laughed.

Jasper smiled with her. "Have you never seen the lamps lit?"

"Yes, once or twice, but I wasn't expecting it." She looked around them at the glowing lanterns as the footmen who'd lit them disappeared into the foliage. "It's so beautiful."

Suddenly Jasper was grabbed from behind and thrown to the ground with brutal force. Olivia shrieked. Jasper turned over to see his attacker. Gifford? The young man stood over him with a look of fury. Dressed in breeches and a loose shirt with the sleeves rolled up, he looked ready to fight.

"Get up," he growled.

Jasper leapt to his feet. "Olivia, go back to the Grove."

She stepped forward. "Mr. Gifford, what are you doing here?"

"Protecting your honor. I know Saxton ruined you. The bastard thinks he can violate you without repercussion because of your station. His kind always takes advantage of people like us, Miss West." He launched himself at Jasper, fists flying.

Jasper wasn't ready for the speed and precision of the younger man's attack. He'd watched Gifford fight and knew he was quite skilled. But now, on the receiving end of the man's anger, and dressed in entirely too many close-fitting clothes, he wasn't able to adequately deflect the blows.

"Mr. Gifford, stop!" Olivia cried.

"Stay back!" Jasper called. He danced backward to buy time to pull off his coat, but Gifford followed him and landed a punch to his cheek before Jasper got his arms free.

He charged forward, catching Gifford around the middle. They tumbled to the ground. Jasper quickly rolled and jumped back to his feet. He was ready for the man now.

They circled each other a moment, trying to gauge the other's weakness. Gifford was well protected. Tall and lithe, he moved quickly, his hands perfectly poised to attack and defend.

Jasper needed to get Olivia out of here. "Olivia, go back to the Grove."

"I won't leave until he stops. Please, Mr. Gifford, I'm not angry with Saxton."

"You should be! Why are you with him?"

Jasper took advantage of the younger man's momentary focus on Olivia. He jabbed forward and hit Gifford in the face and gut. He retreated quickly before Gifford could answer.

Gifford grunted then turned his furious gaze on Jasper. "Olivia, you're a fool if you think you'll ever be accepted by Society." He kept his attention on the fight. "Your true background will come out."

"What the hell are you talking about?" Jasper asked. "You're not threatening her, are you? That would be a grave mistake."

"I'm threatening *you*!" Gifford struck out and caught him under the chin and again in the side of the head.

Pain radiated through Jasper's temple. Gifford kicked at Jasper's middle, catching him in the side as Jasper moved to avoid him. He spun, facing off with the younger man once more. But Gifford didn't hesitate. He dashed forward and sent several blows, which Jasper barely deflected. Gifford may not have been the biggest man at the club, but he was easily one of the strongest.

Jasper needed to finish this. He flew at Gifford, his fists pummeling at his chest and head. Gifford stumbled backward. Off-balance, he couldn't get his hands up. Jasper landed several punishing blows.

"Jasper, please, stop!" Olivia's anguished plea broke through his focus. He paused, allowing Gifford to regain his footing. Then he glanced at Olivia. It was a terrible mistake.

From the corner of his eye, he saw Gifford's arm move down to his boot. Steel flashed in the lantern-light. Jasper dodged to the right, but it wasn't enough. Gifford sank a blade into Jasper's left shoulder.

White-hot pain stabbed through his arm and down into his chest. Jasper's vision darkened for a moment as he wobbled. Gifford raised his hand again, but the blow didn't fall. He was pulled to the side and thrown to the ground. Sevrin stood over him, his boot crushing Gifford's wrist into the dirt until he dropped the knife.

"Saxton, are you all right?"

Jasper nodded even though the agony in his shoulder was like fire. He looked at Olivia, pale and frightened in the lamplight, but unharmed.

"Miss West, take Jasper home. I'll take care of Gifford." Sevrin stared down at the young man in cold fury.

Olivia came and looked at Jasper's shoulder. Her mouth tightened with worry.

"Get my coat. I don't want to draw attention to this." It was astounding no one had come at the sound of the fight, but then the Hermit's Walk was small and rarely sported much traffic.

While Olivia fetched his coat, Jasper tipped his shoulder forward to see the wound. He was rewarded with an agonizing streak of pain up his neck and down his arm. Blood seeped through a hole in his waistcoat. His *favorite* waistcoat, damn it.

She tried to help him into his coat, but it hurt too goddamned much. "Are you all right?" she asked, her voice full of concern.

"Fine," he gritted through his teeth. "Just drape it over my shoulders."

"Saxton, you can't go back through the Grand Walk. Cut through the garden here." Sevrin pointed at the end of the walk. "There's no path, but you'll find your way out, I imagine. Go, quickly. I'll come by later after I deal with this."

Gifford hadn't moved since Sevrin had pressed his foot into his wrist. He stared up at the sky in mute anger, his face taut.

Jasper nodded. "We'll be at Queen Street." He took Olivia's hand and led her into the foliage. One of the lamplighters had disappeared this way. Sure enough, there was a slight path. It was dark, but enough light from the walks streamed through the trees and shrubbery to illuminate their way.

A branch hit him in the arm and he grunted. Olivia tightened her grip and took the lead. At long last, they emerged from the gardens and onto a path near the entrance.

Olivia paused. "We came by carriage. Did you also, or did you come by boat?"

"Carriage."

She pulled him through the entrance. They found his coach first. The footman opened the door automatically, but then his gaze arrested on Jasper's shoulder.

"March, I need you to fetch the doctor." Jasper grimaced as a sharp wave of pain spiked his shoulder. "Have him meet us at my aunt's townhouse on Queen Street."

"Yes, my lord." He darted away faster than Jasper had ever seen the man move.

The coachman climbed down and assisted Jasper inside. Olivia followed, sitting beside him. The coachman lit the lanterns, and asked, "Queen Street, then?"

Jasper nodded.

The door shut. Olivia eased his coat away and tossed it on the opposite seat. Carefully, she probed at his shoulder. Her face was drawn, and she was paler than he'd ever seen her. "I'm sorry about your waistcoat. I'll make you another." She unbuttoned the garment and pulled it off. It followed the coat to the other seat.

She unknotted his cravat and slid it from his neck. Gently, she pushed his shirt away from the wound and then dabbed it with the cravat. The neck opening wasn't large enough and so the shirt tried to creep back over his torn flesh.

"Pardon me." She grasped both sides of the open neck and rent the fabric to his waist.

Lust flooded him. He would not have thought it possible to become aroused with the agony in his shoulder, but at this moment the pain faded until he was only aware of her leaning over him in the sensual lamplight of the swaying coach.

She bent one leg under herself and turned toward him while pressing the cravat against the wound. "The bleeding seems to be slowing."

He forced himself to listen to her words, instead of mentally undressing her. "Does it require stitching?"

"I don't know." She turned her attention to his face. "I don't understand why Gifford would attack you."

Gifford's actions made sense given he'd been the one who'd told Jasper about Olivia's search for her father and her purported quest for a titled husband. "I think he possessed a tendre for you. He's the one who told me Merry might not be your father. He listened to a conversation you had with some woman."

Olivia drew back with a gasp. "He didn't."

Jasper nodded. "He also tried to make me think you'd infiltrated

Louisa's home with the sole purpose of snaring a wealthy, titled husband. He clearly didn't want me thinking very highly of you." They were the actions of a jealous man, something Jasper realized he could relate to. When he thought of Olivia with Gifford or anyone else, his gut churned.

She refolded the cravat to use a fresh length of the fabric as a compress. "He visited me at Queen Street this afternoon. I think he hoped to court me, but I wasn't encouraging." She looked at Jasper with regret.

He lifted his good arm to stroke her face. "It's not your fault he stabbed me."

"Nevertheless, I wish I could stab him back."

Chapter Twenty

OLIVIA HAD NEVER experienced a true need to hurt someone, however that was precisely how she felt about Gifford right now. All the times she'd seen her mother beaten, she'd hated it, but because it was violence against another—innocent—person. The same with Mrs. Reddy. But this feeling, this fury, was different. It filled her up and gave her warmth, even as it cast her into darkness. Is this how Jasper felt when he fought?

"You don't mean that, but I appreciate your anger on my behalf." He gave her a half-smile.

"I do mean it. I have this power, and I want to wield it to hurt Gifford. Is that what you feel like when you fight?"

His thumb traced her cheekbone, and she had to battle to keep herself from succumbing to his caress. "Somewhat, but my goal isn't to inflict pain. I want to exert myself in a strategic manner. Fighting takes thought and skill. Too much emotion clouds your judgment. I'm afraid that's why I didn't fare too well tonight."

Olivia thrilled to his words. "What do you mean?"

"Isn't it obvious?"

Uncomfortable with his blistering stare, she directed her attention to his wound. She kneeled up and peeled the cravat away to check the bleeding. Slower now, but still flowing. She rotated the fabric to a fresh spot and pressed anew. He flinched and dropped his hand to his lap. She regretted the loss of his touch, but it was for the best.

There was no help for it—she was falling in love with him. And while he might feel something for her—had hinted at it just a moment before—they had no future together.

"Earlier, you said you trusted me." His voice was low and rough.

She had. *She did.* When had that happened? She'd even told him about living with her mother. She'd never told anyone how isolated she'd felt. But she couldn't hope for something she could never have. "I don't trust anyone. Not really." The words hurt her more to say than they could possibly have hurt him.

His lips hardened, giving him that cold, arrogant look she hadn't seen of late. He gripped the side of her head, tangling his fingers in her hair. "I want you to trust me. I *need* you to trust me." He pulled at her head, his fingers twisting her hair. "Tell me you do."

How could she ignore the anguish in his voice? They'd both been alone for so long, without anyone to trust...or to love. She couldn't deny him. "I do," she whispered.

They hit a bumpy patch of road and her hand pressed into his shoulder. He sucked in a breath.

"Tell me again." He pulled her head down.

She stared at him.

"Tell me." His voice was ragged with desire.

"I trust y—"

He swallowed the rest of the word with a searing kiss, his lips drawing on hers in desperate need. She shouldn't allow this. She should move away, but she needed to keep pressure on his shoulder...

"Your shoulder," she said against his mouth.

"Can burn in hell." He palmed the back of her head and licked at her mouth. Passionate, burning kisses meant to ignite and excite.

The coach hit another large bump, and she nearly fell from the seat. Against her better judgment—a judgment that was really quite absent at the moment—she straddled his lap. She stroked his chest, running her left hand up across the heated expanse of flesh.

He opened his mouth and deepened the kiss, seeking to own every part of her. She slanted her head and met him lick for lick and thrust for thrust. She ground down against him, relishing his hardness between her legs. The undulating movement of the carriage created friction between them, sending delicious sparks of pleasure through her thighs and belly.

He broke the kiss, but only for a moment. "Olivia," another breathless kiss, "I need," he tugged at her lips with his teeth, "you." He moved his hand to her waist and pulled her down while he arched up. She gasped into his mouth, straining against him, using every muscle to appease the hunger growing at her core.

Frantically, his hands searched beneath her skirts, draping the silk around them like a curtain. He found her slick flesh and stroked her opening, never releasing her mouth from his. She rotated her hips against his hand, her knees pressing into the sides of his thighs, all the while never loosening her pressure on his shoulder. She gripped his uninjured shoulder as well, giving her balance as she rode his touch.

He moved his wounded arm, but she didn't release the compress. With difficulty, he opened his breeches. She would've helped, but adding her hands to the tumble of skirts and his fingers—God, his fingers. He slid one deep inside of her and she cried out, her teeth grazing his.

"Yes," he coaxed, his finger pumping in time with her hips.

"I need—" The wave crested higher, driving her onward. She felt him at her opening, the damp head of his shaft pressing into her. "Oh, yes." She pushed down, sheathing herself on him until she was stretched and full and lights danced behind her eyelids.

His hands gripped her waist. She savored the pleasure of having him inside of her, but only for a moment. His fingers dug into her backside, urging her upward. She slid herself up and then he brought her down again. Up, down, while he drew on her tongue and suckled.

Nothing mattered but this act between them. This giving and taking, this primitive need to both vanquish and surrender. Her pleasure built to a white-hot frenzy. She gripped his shoulders, heedless of his wound. The cravat slipped, but she was too close to euphoria to care.

He drove their movements, sensing the loss of her control. Faster, with rapid precision, his hips rose to meet her as she began to dissolve. He thrust deeper, grinding her down against him, the sound of their bodies filling the small, hot coach. She felt him stiffen and allowed herself to let go. Her limbs quivered in ecstasy. She cast her head back, emitting a series of ragged breaths and a low groan she was sure couldn't belong to her.

He buried his face in her neck, his lips moving against her skin in crazed utterances of half-words and cries of joy.

Moments, or perhaps hours, later she slumped against him. He twitched, and she straightened. "Your shoulder!" She plucked up the cravat and quickly found a non-saturated stretch of fabric to press on the seeping wound. "That was, perhaps, ill-advised."

He arched a brow at her. "I disagree."

She pulled her leg back, releasing him from her body. The wetness on his sex rubbed against her thigh, and she dabbed at it with her skirts. "We should be arriving shortly."

He nodded, refastening his breeches while she situated her skirts. They rode in silence, the musky scent of the coach and still-rapid beat of their hearts leaving no doubt as to what they had just done. Olivia ought to be shocked, at least by her own behavior. However, the truth was she'd wanted this, even if she hadn't expected it.

The coach slowed. Olivia ran a hand over her hair.

"You barely look ravished. Not at all like that first time."

She recalled the mess of her hair that afternoon and blushed.

The coach halted. She pulled the cravat away when the door opened and gathered up Jasper's discarded clothing. She couldn't look at the coachman as he helped her down. Next, he aided Jasper, saying nothing of his torn shirt or giving any inclination of what had occurred. Olivia led them into the house, hoping the doctor would arrive shortly.

She informed the butler of Jasper's injury. The staff bustled to prepare his room and provide the implements necessary to treating his wound.

Jasper sat propped up in bed, his shirt gone from his torso. The wound had finally stopped bleeding.

Olivia stared at his bare chest and arms, dusted with pale blond hair. He was muscular and fit, his broad chest tapering to lean hips. She would have looked farther, but the coverlet obscured her inspection.

She raised her eyes to his. His mouth quirked, then his lids drooped in silent invitation. Her body quickened, answering his seductive call.

A maid arranged a basin and bandages on the table next to the bed. A footman brought steaming water while another positioned lamps around the room to provide ample illumination for the doctor.

Olivia inspected the wound under proper lighting. It was a neat slice. He ought not suffer any ill effects, provided it didn't fester.

He turned to the footman arranging lamps. "Whiskey, if you please."

"Of course, my lord." He left the room.

The maid also departed and the second footman had gone to get more water.

Alone with him, the air in the room thickened. How could she desire him again with even more ferocity than half an hour ago?

Bernard entered, as unflappable as ever. One would think he was announcing tea instead of caring for a wounded gentleman. "Your footman sent word that Dr. Marsden is not available. He will call upon you as soon as possible."

Jasper pinned her with a hard stare. "You'll have to do it. Fetch your needle."

Olivia's pulse raced as anxiety tripped along her nerve endings. "I can't do that."

"You can. Your skill is unparalleled. Pretend I'm just another piece of embroidery."

She flushed and her hands shook. "I can't."

He grabbed her hand and looked into her eyes. "You *can*. I trust you."

Her heart squeezed. If he was willing to trust her, she couldn't turn him down. She forced herself to relax and nodded.

The other footman arrived with a tray bearing a glass and a bottle of whiskey. He placed it next to the basin, now full of steaming water.

Olivia turned to him. "Will you please fetch my sewing basket? It's in the Rose Room."

"Yes, miss." The footman hurried to complete the errand.

To busy her quaking hands, she poured Jasper a glass of whiskey. The decanter clanked against the glass, and she shot him a sheepish look.

"You'll do fine," he assured her as he accepted the whiskey. He promptly drained it and handed the glass back for a refill. Olivia obliged, filling it a second time. She would not begrudge him spirits. In fact, she wondered if a swallow might do her some good.

The footman entered bearing her sewing basket and handed it to Olivia. She set it on a chair set aside from the bed and extracted a needle and thread. Her fingers quivered, which made the simple task of threading the needle quite difficult. Relax, she told herself, and took a deep breath.

At last, she pushed the thread through the tiny hole. When she turned to face her patient, a chill washed over her. She must've reflected her anxiety because Jasper reached out and touched her hand.

"Don't doubt your skill, Olivia. You'll stitch me as well or better than Marsden."

That wasn't likely, but she didn't say so. The bed's height was perfect so that she could stand at his shoulder and sew the wound together. Blood had welled again. She dipped a cloth into the hot water and cleaned the torn flesh as well as she could. Jasper didn't make a sound.

She took a deep breath and set the needle in place. Jasper's suggestion sounded in her brain: *pretend this is your finest piece of embroidery.*

She pushed the needle through his flesh.

Louisa bustled into the room. "Good heavens, Jasper!"

Olivia jerked, pulling the needle with less care than she would've liked. Jasper flinched.

Louisa rushed to stand beside Olivia. "What happened? Lord Sevrin said you'd been stabbed."

"And so I was, Aunt." He looked at Olivia. "Please continue. I'd prefer you finished quickly."

"Yes, of course." Olivia set another stitch, thinking eight or ten ought to do the trick.

"Louisa, pour me another whiskey if you would." He gritted his teeth as Olivia pulled another stitch tight.

Louisa handed him a rather full glass, which he gripped so tightly, Olivia feared he might break it. "Why is Olivia suturing your wound? Where's the doctor?"

"Unavailable," Olivia said. "Jasper insisted I could do just as well."

"An excellent notion." Louisa peered over her shoulder.

Olivia pierced his flesh again. She had to admit it wasn't as bad as she thought. If things didn't work out with Louisa, perhaps she could reinvent herself as a surgeon. What nonsense, *of course* things would work out. Jasper had ensured that all of her secrets would remain buried.

Louisa shook her head. "I can scarcely credit you being stabbed at Vauxhall."

Jasper drank half the whiskey. "Footpads are everywhere, I'm afraid." He gave Olivia a look that clearly stated it was best if they didn't tell Louisa the truth. He was probably right, but oh, how she hated lying.

Olivia set the last stitch and tied off the thread. "Done."

Louisa handed Olivia a small pot of lumpy paste from the tray. "It's good you came here. Cook's remedy will keep the infection away. Noxious stuff, but Bernard swears it works wonders. He employed it for some blisters a while back."

Olivia dolloped the poultice on his shoulder and spread it atop the sutures. The tray also bore small pieces of fabric, one of which Olivia draped over the wound. Then she took a length of linen and wound it around his shoulder and under his arm several times. She bound it tightly, but not so much that he couldn't move his arm.

Louisa studied Olivia's handiwork. "Well done, dear. Now we must add healing to your repertoire of talents. You will make some lucky gentleman a splendid wife."

Olivia glanced at Jasper. His blue eyes were vivid in the brightness cast by the numerous lamps. Vivid, but inscrutable.

Jasper finished his whiskey and handed the empty glass to Louisa. He twitched his shoulder, testing the bandage. "Louisa's right. You could have a future as a healer."

"No, I said she'd be a brilliant *wife*." She smiled and took Olivia's arm. "Come, let us allow Jasper his rest. The servants can tend to his needs."

Olivia reluctantly left, but not without a backward glance. His gaze was intense, but he said nothing. Three times now they'd surrendered to temptation, but what did it mean? He had no intentions toward her and neither did she expect any. As far as she knew, he still planned to marry…and soon.

Then she and Louisa would journey to York while Jasper lived the life he was meant to, without her.

OLIVIA STOLE ALONG the softly lit corridor, two flickering sconces at either end providing just enough illumination to find her way. It was half-two in the morning and the house was dead quiet, which was a good thing. She didn't need anyone asking why she was visiting Jasper's bedchamber in the middle of the night. She paused outside his door, her ears straining for the slightest sound within. Hearing nothing, she turned the handle and stepped across the threshold.

A male hand clamped over her mouth. The man pulled her inside and pushed her back against the wall while he closed the door. He brought his finger to his lips. He tipped his head in silent question. She nodded in response.

Slowly, he lowered his hand. "Sorry."

Olivia straightened her wrapper, her heart thudding wildly. She'd never been introduced to him, but of course she recognized Lord Sevrin after his rescue tonight. "Who were you expecting?"

"No one, which is why I reacted that way. I was asleep. I suppose I forgot where I was." He gave her a sardonic smile.

"Goodness, where do you normally sleep?"

His smile deepened. "Nowhere as nice as this." Before she could question that enigmatic comment, he continued. "You're here to visit him?" He gestured toward the bed.

Ruby-colored hangings were pulled closed around the four-poster, obscuring Jasper from her sight. So much for checking on her patient.

"Is he asleep?"

Lord Sevrin rubbed the back of his neck, drawing her attention to his open collar and the general disarray of his appearance. He was quite handsome, but Olivia wasn't tempted by him, as she knew many other women to be, including Lady Lydia. "Something like that. More like unconscious. He overimbibed with the whiskey, I'm afraid."

She nodded, quashing her disappointment. What had she hoped for—another bout of lovemaking? She was a fool for expecting anything.

Lord Sevrin stepped back and offered a slight bow. "I regret we haven't been properly introduced. I'm Sevrin."

"Of course, I know who you are."

He inclined his head. "Dare I hope you recognized me because Saxton pointed me out, or are you aware of my more, ah, notorious nature?"

"I'm afraid it's the latter."

"Please don't hold it against me. Would you care to sit for a moment? I'd hate for you to have come for nothing."

Was he propositioning her? A man of his reputation...

He chuckled softly. "Please, Miss West, my interest doesn't go beyond our shared concern for Saxton. You're quite safe with me."

Despite everything she'd heard, she relaxed. She'd met plenty of scandalous men when she'd lived with her mother, and she didn't sense any danger from the viscount.

She took one of the two chairs set near the fireplace. Glowing coals cast a scant bit of light, which was fortified by twin lamps burning on the mantelpiece.

Lord Sevrin sat beneath one of the lamps. A faint tinge of yellow ringing his left eye became visible. She scanned his features for another injury.

He gave a discreet cough. Olivia had been caught staring.

Quickly, she said, "I'm surprised to find you here at this hour."

Sevrin stretched his legs out and leaned back in the chair, assuming a position a gentleman never would in the company of a lady. She considered being affronted, but didn't think Sevrin meant any offense. "I imagine so," he drawled. "Although my presence is far more acceptable than yours. I came to speak with Saxton about Gifford."

She felt like an ingrate for not thanking Sevrin immediately. "Thank you for coming to Jasper's, er, Saxton's rescue. What happened with Mr. Gifford?"

"I dragged him to the magistrate. I believe he's the newest inhabitant of Newgate."

Olivia couldn't find the charity to be sorry for his imprisonment. He'd *stabbed* Jasper. "I still can't believe he attacked Saxton like that."

Sevrin frowned. "I was quite shocked."

The dark expression on Sevrin's face reminded Olivia of the anger she now felt about Gifford. She leaned forward. "Do you know him?"

"I do."

Olivia waited for him to say something more, and when he didn't, she opened her mouth, but he finally spoke.

"You didn't say what you were doing here."

He was questioning her behavior? Perhaps rightly so, but coming from him the query seemed ludicrous. Nevertheless, her aunt and uncle had drilled propriety into her head from the nursery, even if her actions of late was sorely lacking. She felt compelled to justify her unchaperoned, middle-of-the-night visit.

"I am naturally concerned for Saxton's welfare. He is...Louisa's nephew." And since Sevrin had employed a deflective tactic to steer the conversation, she would do the same. She wanted answers from this enigmatic man. "You've a bruise around your eye. Tell me about the club at the Black Horse."

The corner of his mouth ticked up. "A collection of miscreants—I include Saxton in that description though he's definitely the most well-bred of the lot."

Olivia bristled. "Jasper isn't a miscreant. He's kind and generous."

"Indeed?" He didn't sound doubtful, merely curious.

"Yes, he helps people in need. Animals, too. He doesn't like others to suffer."

Sevrin was silent a moment. He seemed to ponder her words. "I understand," he said softly. "We sometimes seek to protect others from that which afflicts us most."

Olivia thought of the duke. Beyond the strained and perhaps even hostile relationship she saw with her own eyes, what had Jasper endured? Did he seek violence because he knew nothing else? She ached to go to him, to give him what he couldn't seem to give himself—understanding, solace. Love.

Jasper had told her he fought for the strategic exercise, but she knew it was more than that.

"Why do you support this club? What is its purpose?"

His gaze was probing, but different from the intensity of Jasper's crystal stare. His mouth turned down. "Before tonight, I would have said it's a brotherhood, but Gifford's attack on his 'brother' would dispute that."

Olivia recalled the bruises on Gifford's face the day she'd met him. "Gifford was a member of the club?"

"Unfortunately, yes. I've never seen a member behave like that. But then, I've never tried to mix classes before."

"But you're not in the same class as those men."

He winked at her. "In name, but in deed, I'm far worse."

She didn't think he was going to elaborate, and anyway, she wanted to know about Jasper. "Why did you accept Jasper into the club?"

"He's an excellent fighter. He seemed to need it. Each man participates for reasons of his own. Reasons I'm not always privy to. Some fight to build confidence. Others work out their aggression. For

Saxton, I think, it fills a void."

Olivia's body stilled as she considered this. The room seemed especially quiet, save the deep breathing coming from the curtained bed. What was Jasper missing in his life that he filled with fighting?

Sevrin shrugged. "Perhaps I'm mistaken. Truly, I haven't known Saxton very long. But he seems a man of deep emotion who is looking for something. I wonder if that something might be you."

Her pulse tripped. "Jasper has spoken of me?"

"As much as men do. But yes, I know how important you are to him. It's a good thing. I think you might actually save him."

From what? From the duke? "He needs saving?"

"Everyone does, Miss West. Most of us just aren't lucky enough to find someone like you."

But Olivia couldn't be Jasper's savior. The threatening letter she'd received meant her time with Louisa—and with Jasper—was nearly at an end.

JASPER CRACKED AN eyelid. The room was blissfully dim, though morning sunlight burned the backs of the damask drapes covering the windows. He tried to sit up, but pain exploded in his shoulder and he lolled back against the pillow.

"Awake at last?" Louisa stood from the chair near the bed, her face creased with concern. "How are you feeling?"

"Ah, fine," he lied.

She poured him a glass of water from the pitcher on the bedside table. Though she was in a fresh gown, her skin was pale and dark bags barely supported her drooping eyes. "Louisa, have you slept?"

She handed him the water. "Not much, I'm afraid. I've been too worried about you. You're not allowed to leave me."

His wound was scarcely as dire as that, but he understood her concern. She'd lost a husband she dearly loved, and he was now the closest member of her family—until Olivia had arrived.

"Where's Olivia?" He took a long draught, easing his thirst.

"It's early. Just half-eight. I'm not sure she's gone down to breakfast yet."

Jasper ignored a stab of disappointment that she hadn't visited him in the night.

Louisa perched on the edge of the bed. "Jasper, why haven't you asked me for my betrothal ring? You remember my offering it to you last spring?"

"I do." He just hadn't wanted it yet. For then he'd have to actually propose. And with each day, the notion of marrying Lady Philippa grew less and less palatable. Because of Olivia. How could he consider marrying someone else while he was either making love to Olivia or thinking about making love to her?

She nodded. "If you'd rather choose something different for your bride, I'll understand."

Suddenly an image of presenting Olivia with Louisa's betrothal ring sprang into his mind. Good Lord, what a notion. He couldn't think of a single person who wouldn't be shocked. But only because she wasn't expected, not because she was the bastard daughter of a courtesan. And if no one knew the truth about her, why *couldn't* he marry her?

"It's not that," he said. "I'm just not yet sure who she's going to be."

Louisa's eyes widened. "But I thought you were settled on Lady Philippa."

He hadn't ever told her so, but Louisa knew he'd paid her specific attention over the past fortnight. "I was. Rather, the duke was."

"You mustn't let him dictate your life." She looked away and frowned. "I should have intervened ten years ago."

Jasper twitched against a jolt of pain in his shoulder. Merry had been the one who'd told Jasper about the duke sending Abigail and her family away. Jasper assumed Merry hadn't told Louisa because she'd never once broached the subject. "You mean with Abigail."

"Yes."

Jasper downed the remainder of the water and replaced the empty glass on the table.

"Do you want to know what I think?" she asked.

Not really. He was humiliated enough that he hadn't done right by Abigail, that she'd disappeared at the duke's hand, and Jasper hadn't been smart enough to stop his interference, let alone be aware of it.

"I think you're punishing yourself for that perceived failure," she said.

"Perceived? I did fail."

"You didn't. That was entirely Holborn's fault. But this isn't about him. It's about your guilt over Abigail. I know how grief and regret can overwhelm one's life. But you have to move on. Maybe then you'll actually be interested in marrying someone."

"I *am* interested in marrying someone." Olivia's face swam before him. *Impossible.*

Louisa regarded him with wide, somewhat mischievous eyes. "Really, who?"

He couldn't tell her. He wasn't even sure he believed it himself. Holborn would be furious. Furthermore, Jasper had no idea if Olivia even wanted to marry. She'd said on more than one occasion that Society made her uncomfortable, and though Prewitt had been easy enough to dissuade, who else might uncover her past?

"I'd rather not say."

"So secretive." She patted his knee through the coverlet. "I'm sure whomever you choose will be perfect—for you. And that's all that matters. You needn't please me or Holborn, or anyone but you."

"What do you think the duke would do if he didn't approve my choice?" Jasper could well guess. He'd be particularly livid since Jasper had agreed to gaining his approval in exchange for not meddling in Miranda's marriage.

Louisa tilted her head to the side. "What is it you're really afraid of? That he won't approve your wife or he won't approve you? He's never gotten over the loss of James, but that's his grief, not yours. If Holborn's approval is that important to you... Well, only you can decide. I only ask that you be happy."

Happy. He thought of teaching Olivia to ride. Watching her navigate Society with charm and grace. Sharing time with her and Louisa, like they were a family.

He squeezed Louisa's hand. He'd always loved her, but never more than that moment. "Thank you."

She stood from the bed. "You're quite welcome, dear. If you're able, the coach is ready to take you to Saxton House. Dr. Marsden will be meeting you there at ten. I assumed you'd be more comfortable in your own bed."

He'd hoped to see Olivia, but it seemed he would be rushed out before he had the opportunity. It was just as well. He needed to think. He couldn't really be contemplating marriage with Olivia?

"Thank you, Louisa. For everything."

She leaned down and bussed his cheek. "It's my privilege to dote."

After she left, Jasper stared at the ceiling. Olivia was so far from the woman he'd imagined marrying. Since Abigail, he'd always assumed his wife would possess lineage, wealth, an impeccable upbringing, and the ability to serve as the consummate hostess to the future Duke of Holborn. How would Olivia possibly fulfill that role? Was it even fair of him to ask her to?

He drummed his fingers against the coverlet, uncertain of what to do. His hand stilled. Last night they'd both shared their trust. If he truly had faith in her, he'd let her decide what she wanted and what she was capable of. Abigail had never been given that choice. Olivia deserved that and more.

Chapter Twenty-one

THE FOLLOWING MORNING was the second Sunday Louisa had taken Olivia to church at St. James. Today's sermon about John the Baptist was both seasonal and familiar to Olivia given her upbringing at the vicarage. She'd had little occasion during the years with Fiona to attend church and appreciated the opportunity to do so again.

As she and Louisa passed through the narthex, Lady Addicock paused, issuing an invitation to tea, which Louisa accepted. Olivia turned at the barest touch on her elbow. The Duke of Holborn peered down at her with sharp interest.

"Miss West, might I have a word?"

Olivia stepped away with him, just far enough away from Louisa and Lady Addicock to have a separate conversation. She dipped a brief curtsey. "Your Grace."

"You will not attend tea with Louisa. Plead a headache. Plead a hatred for tea. Plead whatever you wish, but I will drive you home in my carriage."

Olivia wanted to plead abduction at the top of her voice, but decided that might cause more harm than good. Without responding to him directly, she went to Louisa and made her apologies. Louisa's surprise that Olivia had chosen to accept a ride home from Holborn was detectable in the slight arch of her pale brows. Olivia suspected there would be a discussion later.

The duke led her from the church without offering his arm. "What did you tell her?"

"That I was feeling a bit queasy." Because she was.

"Very good."

His coach was very near the entrance. A footman helped her alight and then closed the door after Holborn took the rear-facing seat opposite her.

"The duchess isn't with you?" she asked, reluctantly admiring the posh interior with its thick velvet squab and crystal clear windows.

"We needn't bother with idle conversation. I've arranged for this meeting in order to have a straightforward discussion about your presence in my sister's house."

She gave him her loftiest stare, which she feared was nothing compared to the visual setdown he could deliver. "'Arranged' is a rather polite word, don't you think?"

"Very shrewd, but then I suspect you're far more devious than either Louisa or Saxton give you credit for." He leaned back against the squab, appearing as comfortable as Olivia was nervous. "You must leave, of course."

"Of course," Olivia mocked, though her stomach was churning. "You sent the note yesterday."

His brow arched. He looked disturbingly like Jasper in that moment. "Note?"

There would be no reason for him to lie. Olivia felt uneasy. "I received a note instructing me to leave Town."

"Which you ignored, I see. No, I didn't send such a note, but I must applaud whoever did. It also gives proof to the primary reason you must leave. You will sully our name—Louisa's name—if you do not."

If he hadn't sent the note, who had? And at what point would the author share his or her knowledge with the world? Olivia had to reluctantly admit the duke was right. She could very well ruin Louisa.

She only wanted to know how the author of the note and the duke had learned the truth, particularly when Jasper had worked so diligently to cover her tracks. "How did you find out?"

"I have the ability to discern whatever information I desire, Miss West." He folded his slender hands in his lap. "And since others also know of your origins, it's safe to assume your secret—if it ever was one—is out.

"Furthermore, your relationship with my son will not be tolerated. If he chooses to employ you as his mistress, that is his prerogative. However, for you to engage with him as you have…" He gave a stiff shake of his head. "You're a whore just like your mother, but then I expected nothing more."

"I'm not like my mother." Perhaps not exactly, but her behavior with Jasper showed they were more alike than Olivia cared to believe. She felt light-headed.

"Why, because you don't take money for your favors? I'm certain you soon will. Blood is everything, and blood always wins out." He delivered this with sinister finality, as if he knew the cage she'd been born into and would personally ensure she never escaped it. Which was precisely what he was doing now. Restricting her to the life he believed she deserved.

She glanced out at Mayfair passing. They would reach Queen Street shortly. She regarded him with sincere dislike, her fingers shaking atop her lap. "You can't know me or my future."

"I've already told you I know anything I wish. As Holborn, I enjoy freedoms and intelligence you can't hope to comprehend." His pomposity would've made her jaw drop if she hadn't been working so hard to maintain an icy façade of her own. "I'm not completely without pity, however. I'm prepared to give you a small purse to get wherever you need to go. Though Coventry Court is a nice walk, especially this time of year."

She refused to betray her anger. Anger that was slowly blunting with the approaching edge of doubt. "It is," she said evenly, her mind working toward what, a defense? "Louisa doesn't want me to leave." Neither did Jasper, but only for Louisa's sake. It didn't bear mentioning since the duke would be less than sympathetic.

His lips spread in an awful, patronizing smile. "My sister is soft-hearted, particularly in this. She's always wanted a child of her own. A clever girl like you knows that and exploits it."

Olivia sucked in her breath. "I care very deeply for Louisa."

"Your feelings do not signify. I expect you to be gone tomorrow."

He'd come to issue demands and ultimatums. She was to have no choice, just as when her aunt had evicted her. Was she never to have a family to call her own? Time stretched as she struggled to keep her voice from cracking. "If I don't?"

"I shall make things very unpleasant for you, Miss West."

His statement evoked a trembling in her limbs. She crossed her ankles and clasped her hands in her lap, trying to occupy her body before it revealed her anxiety. "You can't mean to reveal my past. To do so would only realize your worst fears."

He leaned forward slightly. The confines of the carriage shrunk so that she felt as if she were trapped in a small hole with the most abominable person she'd ever met. "Let me be clear, Miss West." His tone was nauseatingly authoritative, as if he were speaking to a simpleton. "I don't *fear* you, or anyone else for that matter. Arranging to have you removed from Society, whether by unfortunate compromise or some other…circumstance will hardly be a trial."

She stared at the duke with newfound fear. "You're quite serious."

The carriage drew to a halt. "If you truly care for Louisa, you'll leave her alone. I understand she wants to fill some void, but there are plenty of worthy young women for her to coddle. I'm certain you'll make her understand why you have to go." He reached inside his coat and tossed a purse onto her lap. A small amount of coins gave a muffled clink within the velvet pouch. It was a very ugly sound.

Olivia felt the weight on her lap like manacles around her wrists. She knew she had to go, to protect Louisa, but she only wished it hadn't come to this. Perhaps she could do one thing. "I'll go, but I'm going to demand something in addition to this money."

The duke snorted. "You're in no position to negotiate. Be glad I don't rescind my generous offer." He inclined his head toward his *bribe*.

His arrogance was unlike anything Olivia had ever encountered. "From what I can tell, you don't care too much for your son—your living son." The duke's eyes darkened, but Olivia gathered her courage and surged forward. "It's not too late for you to appreciate the son who's here. He's a man you could, and should, be proud of. Will you please do your best to ensure he's happy?"

He sneered. "You foolish chit. Everything I do is to ensure his happiness. You think you would make him happy? You've no notion how to be a mistress to someone like Saxton, let alone his countess. Among a myriad of responsibilities, you'd have to be presented at court. Good God, can you imagine? I cannot." The duke rapped on the door and it immediately swung open. "I trust you begin to understand why you have to go."

Unfortunately she did. But oh, how she wished the duke were wrong!

The footman helped her to the street. Olivia tucked the purse into her pocket as she trudged up the stairs to the house. Behind her, the coach rattled away, but Olivia didn't turn. She thought about his threat, *whether by unfortunate compromise or some other circumstance*. What did he mean by compromise? Did he intend for her to be ruined?

How ironic then, that she already was, and at the hands of his own son.

But no, he wouldn't want that exposed—and neither did Olivia.

Bernard opened the door. She mustered a weak smile before walking directly up to her room. *You're a whore just like your mother.* She wasn't! She hadn't traded her virtue for anything but her own desire. Her affair with Jasper hadn't been based on money and, furthermore, it was quite over.

It wasn't too late to reclaim the life she'd been proud of. She wondered if the position Gifford had mentioned was actually available or if it had been some sort of ruse. Since he'd so brutally attacked Jasper, she'd be a fool to trust anything he said. Still, she could check with his mother. Indeed, she probably ought to visit Mrs. Gifford anyway. She had to be sick over her son's actions and the fact that he was now lodged in Newgate.

She closed her door behind her and went straight to her dressing chamber. She didn't even possess a trunk in which to stow all of the belongings she'd accumulated in the short time she'd been with Louisa.

Tonight she would attend one last event with Louisa—a ball. She would smile and laugh and behave as if her world wasn't about to fall to pieces. Perhaps she'd be fortunate and Jasper wouldn't even be there. Louisa had said he was recovering well from his wound, but surely he would stay home and rest.

She pulled the duke's bribe from her pocket and dropped it onto her dressing table. She shouldn't take his money, but why not? In fact, it was truly a pity she hadn't demanded more.

SINCE ARRIVING AT the Coddington Ball, Jasper had been subjected to the excessive delight of his mother and the satisfied arrogance of the duke. Though unspoken, their expectation that he would announce his betrothal this evening was palpable. Probably because everyone in the ballroom was whispering about it.

Such a shame then that he meant to disappoint them. The only reason he'd dragged himself out of bed was to see Olivia and make it clear his affections lay with her. First, however, he ought to take a moment and speak with Lady Philippa. He had no desire to shock her by paying public attention to another woman.

Though he scanned the room for Lady Philippa, his gaze kept settling on Olivia. Gowned in emerald silk, she was breathtaking. The bare column of her neck screamed for jewels and kisses, and not in that order. That idiot Twickersham approached her, and before Jasper knew what he was doing, he'd joined them.

Jasper gave Twickersham a cursory head-nod and bowed to Olivia. "Miss West." Louisa was turned slightly from them, involved with a group of her friends.

"Lord Saxton, good evening." Olivia directed a pointed look at his shoulder. "I trust you are well."

He warmed at her concern. "Quite, thank you."

Twickersham wrapped Olivia's hand around his arm. "I was just about to lead Miss West onto the dance floor."

Jasper's mind screamed against the toad touching her, but what could he do? Olivia gave him an apologetic glance as she moved onto the dance floor.

Jasper stared after them, his hands fisting. While the bloated idiot positioned himself with Olivia and another pair of dancers, Jasper considered leaving. However, his departure would prevent him scrutinizing the way Twickersham held Olivia's hand a bit too long during the dance. Better to stand here and fume.

"Jasper, dear, you're glowering." Louisa touched his sleeve. "You don't look at all like a man on the verge of providing a month's worth of good gossip."

He tore his gaze from Olivia and her offensive partner to look down at his aunt beside him. Was his fury that transparent? "What?"

"Your betrothal? Is it imminent?"

Jasper returned his attention to the dance floor.

"Aren't you going to answer me?" Louisa asked. "Goodness, your shoulder isn't paining you, is it? Perhaps you should return to Saxton House. I realize this is the last ball of the summer, but there will be other opportunities to announce your engagement."

He kept his gaze focused on Twickersham's hands. "I'm not here to announce my engagement."

Louisa followed his gaze. "Who are you staring at?"

"Olivia. She shouldn't be dancing with that idiot, Twickersham. Aren't you supposed to be chaperoning her?" His question came out much sharper than he'd intended. He glanced at his aunt.

Louisa's eyes widened. "It's just a dance, Jasper." She looked at him shrewdly, and he was unable to turn back to watch Olivia. His aunt *knew*. She always saw what others never bothered to look for.

"Why aren't *you* dancing with her?" she asked.

"I intend to."

She grinned then. A face-splitting, heart-warming, life-affirming grin—the kind that lit up an entire ballroom and caused you to smile in return despite the fact that some nitwit was dancing with the woman you loved.

Oh yes, he loved her.

"Excellent," Louisa said. "Why don't you get some punch? I'm sure Olivia will be parched when she's finished with the set."

Jasper hesitated. He preferred to stay and supervise.

Louisa leaned close and whispered, "You can't stand there and scowl."

She was, unfortunately, correct. And as luck would have it, he caught sight of Philippa near the refreshment table. He took himself off.

When he was nearly to the table, a large, ham-faced gentleman with bushy brows stepped in his path. "You are Lord Saxton?"

Was this man approaching him without an introduction? Jasper made to push past him.

"I'm confident you're Saxton." He kept his voice low. "Your aunt is Lady Merriweather."

Jasper froze and stared at the man. "What do you want?"

"My name is Clifton. I know your aunt's ward." The statement was full of insinuation and arrogance. He moved to the periphery of the ballroom.

Jasper clenched his teeth as he followed the man—he had no other choice. His hands fisted, pulling on the seams of his gloves. He pinned the man with a vicious glare when he reached the edge of the room. "Make your point."

Clifton's dark eyes narrowed, making him look like a snake slithering toward its dinner. "I'm prepared to reveal her true identity if you don't agree to my terms."

"I won't be extorted."

"I don't want money. I want her. Tomorrow. Delivered to my townhouse. I will send the direction."

Jasper nearly punched him then. He closed his eyes briefly and tried to summon the cool-headed man he'd been before he'd started fighting at the Black Horse and before Olivia had come into his life. She'd thrice tempted him to behave in ways he knew he shouldn't, and now he wanted to tear this man's arms off. For her.

"I'm not giving you Olivia."

"I tried convincing her to leave of her own accord, but she didn't. Now it's up to you to give her over to me."

Jasper looked at him sharply. "What do you mean you tried convincing her? You didn't approach her, did you?" He advanced on the man.

Clifton stood his ground, seemingly unaware of Jasper's broiling ire. "I sent a letter, but I doubt she would've shared it with you."

What letter? She'd kept something else from him? His anger mounted.

Clifton stepped closer, adopting an even more hushed tone. "Your family won't want the taint of her background marring your name. I think you'll ensure she's at my house tomorrow. I have a friend at the *Times*. I know they'd be dead interested in this story…"

Jasper drove his fist into Clifton's face. Though he'd used his good arm, the quick movement sent a stab of pain to his left shoulder.

The large man staggered backward with a snarl. The people surrounding the refreshment table—including Lady Philippa—turned to stare.

Clifton came toward him, his hand fisted. Jasper was ready, despite the pain pulsing in his wound. The other man hesitated.

"Aren't you going to try and hit me?" Jasper taunted. A touch on his arm drew his attention. Lady Philippa stood at his side.

"Saxton, come away."

It was all Jasper could do not to launch himself at the bastard. "He offended me."

"You can't do this in a ballroom," she whispered urgently.

Of course, he couldn't. But he could do it on a dueling field. "Clifton, I'll see you at dawn. My second will call on you later this evening."

Clifton's color paled a bit, but he gave a stiff nod. "I'll send for my second at the *Times*."

His meaning was clear. The secret of Olivia's background would be printed in the newspaper for all of London to read and judge.

Jasper watched in mute fury as Clifton left the ballroom. Lady Philippa's touch reminded him of where he was. The entire ballroom hadn't come to a halt, but at least two dozen people stood staring. He glanced at Philippa, whose eyes were calm. "Please excuse me."

She dropped her hand and nodded. "Will you be all right?"

"Fine." He brushed by her and made his way past gaping ball-goers on his way to the nearest exit. He now owed Lady Philippa a Goliath of an apology and would beg her forgiveness tomorrow. But first he needed to find Sevrin to act as his second.

He reached the corridor and was nearly to the stairs when Holborn cut him off. "What the bloody hell was that?"

"The man offended me."

"Then you call him out, you don't strike him in public in the middle of a goddamned ball!"

"I did call him out." Jasper pushed past the duke and moved toward the stairs. "I need to find my second."

"Good Christ, Saxton, what could he have possibly done that would be worth a duel? I didn't even recognize him. Go back inside and smooth the damage with Lady Philippa."

Jasper glared at him then made to step forward again, but the duke grabbed his right—and thankfully unwounded—arm. His fingers bit through Jasper's clothing into his bicep. "You're not going anywhere. Get back in that ballroom and dance with Lady Philippa. I've spoken to Coddington, and he'll announce your betrothal at midnight, if Herrick is amenable."

"*I'm* not amenable. I'm leaving."

"If you do, I'll ensure your little harlot doesn't know a moment's peace."

Jasper stared at him. "How did you know?" His encounters with Olivia should have been nearly impossible to discover.

The duke's grip tightened, and the bruising pain reminded Jasper of his youth. "I know anything I please. Your mother noted that waistcoat you wore to Vauxhall. She saw your whore working on it at Benfield. Her Grace also saw you walk off with her toward the

Hermit's Walk and disappear. Fortunately, Her Grace did an excellent job covering up for your complete lack of discretion."

Jasper's fingers itched to push Holborn down the stairs. How dare he insult Olivia? "She's not a whore." Just a liar who still didn't trust him. Why hadn't she told him about Clifton's letter?

"What is she, then? Your future countess, like that worthless chit ten years ago? I protected you from your foolish heart then, and I'll do it now. Someone like her can never make you happy. She'll embarrass all of us, and you'll grow to resent her. Just as she'll grow to resent you for putting her in an impossible situation. You can't expect her to entertain the peerage?"

Jasper hated that the duke's arguments weren't complete nonsense. He'd had the same thoughts about Olivia himself. And knowing she still lied to him only exacerbated his doubt. Weakly, he disputed Holborn's reasoning. "You make assumptions."

Holborn squeezed his arm painfully. "Why can't you do this one thing? James would've married the right woman years ago, but you've dragged your feet and now put this entire family at risk of unparalleled scandal. Not even your wayward sister stepped this far over the line. Damn it, Saxton."

"Yes, *I'm* Saxton! Me, not James." Jasper swung his arm away, but Holborn wouldn't let go.

The duke's foot slipped on the top stair. His grasp on Jasper loosened as gravity sucked at the lighter man. Jasper leapt in front of him and grabbed the railing for stability. His shoulder screamed in agonized protest. With his free hand, Jasper gathered a fist full of Holborn's coat and set him firmly back on the floor. Jasper's efforts lost him a few stairs, but he stopped himself before he tumbled to the hall below. He lightly rubbed his upper arm, where pain radiated down from his shoulder.

Eyes wide, chest heaving, the duke stared at him. "Don't do this," he croaked. "Please, I'm begging you."

The duke was begging him? All Jasper had ever wanted was this man's approval. He could have it if only he'd marry Philippa. But liar, schemer she may be, he couldn't leave Olivia to the fate of the Cliftons of the world.

"You'll ensure Miss West's background remains secret. That man in the ballroom—his name is Clifton—claims to have a friend at the

Times. Right now he's delivering the tale of her past."

The duke straightened his coat. "I'll see to it immediately."

Jasper couldn't believe he was making this bargain, but it was the best he could do for Olivia. She could have a happy life. "Let her stay with Louisa. Louisa will take her to York. You need never see her."

"Done."

Jasper nodded. He couldn't imagine announcing a betrothal tonight. Not with Olivia watching. "I'll finalize things with Lady Philippa tomorrow. The banns will be read next Sunday."

The duke looked as though he wanted to argue, but he pressed his lips together and nodded. "The duchess and I will plan an engagement dinner for Saturday next."

Jasper's gut churned. He wanted nothing more than to dive into a bottle of gin surrounded by the comforting sounds of violence. It was too bad his wound would prevent him from joining in.

Chapter Twenty-two

OLIVIA HAD WATCHED Jasper hit Clifton from across the dance floor. The people around her were unaware of the spectacle, but she'd been unable to keep her eyes from Jasper all evening. As soon as Clifton had approached him, her heart had seized. Had Clifton sent that note? What was he doing here, and why was he talking to Jasper?

She feared she knew. And then when Jasper had struck the man, it became obvious. Jasper had sworn to keep her secrets safe, and he'd gone to extremes to do so.

Then Lady Philippa had intervened. Even from this distance, her care and concern were evident. As was his reaction. He'd backed down, and Clifton had walked away. It was all Olivia had needed to see.

Olivia turned to Louisa who'd been deep in conversation with Lady Addicock. "Excuse me, Louisa, I've a terrible headache. Would you mind if we went home?"

Louisa's forehead creased. "Of course, dear."

Lady Badby descended upon them in a flurry of bright red ostrich feathers stabbed into her hair. "Did you see Saxton nearly flatten that gentleman?"

Clifton was no gentleman, but Olivia remained silent. Louisa's eyes widened. She shot a questioning glance at Olivia. It was an odd reaction and put Olivia further on edge.

"What happened?" Louisa asked.

"He hit a man over by the refreshment table." Louisa and Lady Addicock turned their attention in that direction. "Oh, they're gone now," Lady Badby said with a wave of her hand. "Lady Philippa seems to have smoothed the situation. Oh, she'll make Saxton a marvelous countess, provided her father doesn't now deny him."

Louisa gave Lady Badby a frigid stare. "No one will deny Saxton. I'm sure his reasons for striking that man were sound." Olivia agreed wholeheartedly.

"Let's hope so, for he plans to meet him at dawn. He's gone to fetch his second."

Olivia fought to maintain her composure, but seemed to let something show. Louisa's gaze narrowed briefly, but then she turned back to Lady Badby. "I'm sure this is nothing but baseless rumor, Augusta. And as a personal favor to me, I'd ask that you refrain from repeating it."

"But, I was standing rather close by. I heard—"

Lady Addicock looped her arm through Lady Badby's. "Come, dear, let us go discuss the weather or something else inane." She steered Lady Badby away from a quite visibly annoyed Louisa.

"Yes, let's go, Olivia," Louisa said, taking her arm.

It took them several minutes until they could navigate their way through the ballroom. From the conversation surrounding them, it was apparent the story of Jasper's altercation and impending duel had spread through the ballroom like a midsummer fire. However, by the time they reached the exit, they heard this: "Holborn has denied the duel will take place. The man—an unfortunate drunkard called Clifton—insulted Lady Philippa. Of course, Saxton wouldn't put up with that."

Louisa's head perked up, but she said nothing. They left the ball in utter silence until they were firmly ensconced in Louisa's coach.

Louisa turned to look at her. "Now, dear, please tell me why you asked to go home. I don't believe for a second it's due to a headache, though I daresay you may actually have one now."

Olivia smoothed her skirt, searching for what she might say.

"Please don't lie, dear. There's no reason to. You know I love you, don't you?"

Olivia's throat constricted. She nodded, and tears filled her eyes. She blinked furiously. "That man that Jasper hit is someone from my mother's past. I met him in a shop not long before you found me. He...propositioned me."

Louisa's mouth pursed. "The blackguard. So that's why Jasper hit him."

"I'd thought so, but perhaps Clifton did insult Lady Philippa."

"That's indeed possible but doubtful. The coincidence of him approaching Jasper, and his connection to you is too great. No, I'm certain he said something to insult *you*."

"But why would Jasper behave like that on my account?"

"Isn't it obvious, dear? My nephew is quite in love with you."

Olivia nearly choked even as a joyous thrill shot through her. "He's not."

"He certainly appears to be to my eyes. I can tell you one thing for certain. I don't think he plans to marry Lady Philippa."

"Why?"

Louisa looked happily smug. "Because he told me."

"What did he say?" She was nearly breathless hoping Louisa was right.

"That he wasn't yet ready to marry."

Olivia noticed Louisa hadn't said anything about Jasper making a verbal commitment to Olivia. For now, this was all Louisa's—perhaps hopeful—speculation. She likely adored the idea of her two favorite people being together. Olivia's heart ached—she adored it too.

"He didn't speak of me, did he?"

Louisa lifted a shoulder in nonchalance. "No, but I know my nephew. And, fool that I've been, I've finally noticed the way he looks you. It's the way Merry looked at me."

Olivia wanted it to be true more than she'd ever wanted anything. But she knew shared affection wouldn't be enough for them—it hadn't been yet, despite the times they'd made love. If Jasper had ever meant to make promises or declarations, the opportunity had come and gone.

She thought of the duke's ultimatum. The time had come to put an end to this entire farce. "I have to leave. Tomorrow."

Louisa's brow furrowed. "Why? I thought we agreed you wanted to stay with me. We'll get things sorted out with Jasper and then you two will go to York for an extended holiday."

Olivia smiled sadly. "There's nothing to sort out, Louisa."

"Don't you want Jasper?"

"I do. I love him, but we can't be together. I will always be who I am, and I'm not a countess or a duchess."

"Nonsense. You can be whatever you like. You're the smartest girl I know, and Jasper loves you. He won't let you go."

"He will," Olivia said firmly.

"I promise you he won't. I know him better than you, dear. He

made a mistake long ago, and he won't make the same mistake twice."
Olivia knew she spoke of Jasper's first love. Was it possible he would
defy his father, his very duty, and marry her instead of Philippa? She
could scarcely countenance such a reversal.

"What about the duke?"

"Oh, piffle. He'll be furious, but he'll have to get over it. You're
not afraid of him, are you, dear?"

Not for herself, no. But for Louisa and Jasper... "He paid me
money to leave. If I don't, he said he would ruin me."

Louisa's features darkened, and her lips drew back in a sneer.
Olivia had never seen her look angry. Or more like the duke. "My
brother is a self-involved ass. He'll do no such thing."

"Louisa, I wouldn't be able to forgive myself if my presence
somehow ruined you."

"Ruined me how? So the Lady Badbys and Lady Lydias of the
world ignored me? That, my dear, would not be a hardship."

Olivia couldn't help smiling.

"And I don't think we care if you have the opportunity to marry
well since you'll be marrying Jasper."

She longed for Louisa to be right. "How can he marry me if
Society knows about my mother and that I'm a bastard?"

"It's all gossip and rumor, dear. There is nothing to substantiate
any of this. You are charming and intelligent, and you will win every
single person over with your grace and poise. Soon people will laugh
about the far-fetched notion that you're the daughter of a courtesan.
Especially when Holborn will refute it."

"But he won't."

"Olivia, dear, please allow me to deal with my brother.
Occasionally, he needs reminding as to who is the elder sibling—duke
or not."

Could this really come to pass? Louisa convincing the duke to
keep quiet? Jasper marrying *her*? Did he really love her? Her heart
flipped over.

The coach slowed, and they pulled onto Queen Street.

"I know it will be difficult, Olivia, but do try to get a good night's
sleep. In the morning we'll get this all sorted out, and before you
know it you'll be the Countess of Saxton."

Olivia wouldn't sleep a moment.

JASPER STEPPED OUT of his coach into the warm, late summer night air, eager for the gin that would dull the ache in his shoulder and the pain in his heart. At last, he'd won the approval of the duke, but at what cost?

Though his mind knew marrying Philippa to be the correct choice, his heart—and regions south of that—ached for Olivia.

It was early for the club, but Jasper went directly to the low-ceilinged back room. He fetched a bottle of gin and a cup from the bar and settled himself at a battered table set with four chairs. A butcher, Hopkins, came in a few moments later and joined him. He set his ale-filled tankard on the table.

"Tom said you were back here. Wasn't expecting you tonight—Sevrin told us what that bastard Gifford did to you. How's your shoulder?"

Jasper poured the gin into a chipped cup. "All right."

Hopkins bared his teeth. "I'm only sorry that son of a bitch is in Newgate. Might have to break him out so the club can show their disapproval."

Saxton raised the cup in appreciation of the man's sentiment and downed a healthy swig. The noxious liquor burned a hole straight to his gut.

"Gin?" Hopkins asked. "I thought ye were a whiskey man."

"Tonight calls for stronger libation."

"I see."

They drank in silence a moment, Jasper filling a second cup, before another man came in. He also sat at their table, and soon he and Hopkins were detailing the manner in which they'd school Gifford if he ever crossed their paths. That these common men would jump so quickly and completely to Jasper's defense was a bit surprising…and touching.

Sevrin strode into the room and made his way directly to their table. "Saxton, what the hell are you doing here?"

Jasper set his half-empty cup on the table. "Seems as though you expected me to be here, since here you are."

The other men chuckled.

Sevrin hauled Jasper to his feet. "You're going home."

Jasper shook him off then grimaced as pain radiated from his shoulder.

Sevrin cringed. "Christ, I forgot about your shoulder. What the hell were you thinking hitting that man at a ball?"

Both Hopkins and the other man gaped at him then broke into laughter. "You hit someone at a *ball?*" Hopkins pounded the table with his fist.

Jasper actually wanted to laugh with them, but perhaps that was due to the effects of the gin. "You were there?"

Sevrin nodded. "According to rumor, you're either fighting a duel at dawn, about to announce your engagement to Lady Philippa, or both. What the devil is going on, and how does Olivia West figure in all of this?"

"I'm not fighting a duel, though I'd considered it. You'll be happy to know I'd selected you as my second."

"I'd have done it if he refused," Hopkins interjected. He and his tablemate were riveted on the conversation.

Jasper continued, "My engagement to Lady Philippa will be announced soon. There's to be a dinner on Saturday. I'll make sure you're invited." He turned to the men at the table. "I regret to inform you I cannot invite either of you, unfortunately. I mean no offense."

Both men laughed again. "None taken!" Hopkins answered.

"You have yet to mention Miss West." Sevrin looked and sounded irritated. In fact, his good humor was glaringly absent.

"There is nothing to say about Miss West." The words were acrid on his tongue.

Sevrin's eyes narrowed. "You great ass, there's plenty to say. Why are you marrying Lady Philippa when you're clearly in love with Miss West?"

What did Sevrin know about any of this? "You of all people should understand the vagaries of marriage and why one would choose one bride over another."

"Actually, I understand why one would choose *no* bride over being leg-shackled, but we're not discussing me. You can choose whomever you like, and you like Miss West."

"It's none of your bloody business, but I can't marry her."

Sevrin arched a brow. "Can't or won't?"

"It hardly signifies."

"Wait." Hopkins held up a hand. "If you love this West girl, why are you marrying someone else? I understand you lords have your own set of rules, but it seems to me that marriage is marriage regardless of your address. Unless, of course, you're just as happy marrying this other gel."

He wasn't, but that didn't signify either. "Yes, we have our own rules, and the rules say I should marry this other 'gel'."

"Nonsense." Sevrin scoffed. "Who did you hit?"

"Someone who can make Olivia's life miserable. But I've rectified all of that. Her secrets are safe—forever."

Sevrin gave him an incredulous look. "What deal did you make with the devil?"

What an apt description of the duke. "Olivia's secrets will remain inviolate, and I'm going to marry Philippa. It's done."

"It's not done, but when it is, you can't undo it. You'll be married to her *forever*."

"I'm willing to do it for her." He'd do anything for Olivia.

Sevrin's eyes narrowed. "You do love her."

"More than anything." Even though she'd lied and continued to lie. But he didn't care. She had to have a reason for keeping that letter from him. He knew she did. They couldn't have shared what they'd shared otherwise. She'd said she trusted him—and he knew in his bones that she did.

Sevrin gave a half smile and shook his head. "You really are a great ass. Whatever deal you've made, unmake it."

"I can't. The duke has given his full support. Olivia will be safe behind his protection."

"Protection he'd have to offer his daughter-in-law, the future goddamned duchess. Saxton, are you really that stupid?"

"It's not that simple," Jasper argued. The warmth of the gin was wearing off.

"I'm with Sevrin," Hopkins said. "You're a right nodcock." The other man nodded his agreement.

Sevrin poked him in the chest. "You seem to forget you're the future Duke of Holborn. Whatever power your father wields, you have at your disposal."

"But what if it's best for everyone if I marry Philippa? What if that's what Olivia prefers?" And perhaps this was the true heart of why he'd made the deal with Holborn. He didn't really know what Olivia wanted. Had no idea if she loved him the way he loved her.

"Concern yourself with what's best for you and Olivia. The rest will fall into place."

OLIVIA HAD TRIED to sleep, but after tossing and turning the past two hours, she'd finally abandoned the enterprise. Despite everything Louisa had said, she couldn't imagine Jasper arriving tomorrow and declaring his eternal love. Even if he did love her, she felt certain he'd do as he ought and marry Lady Philippa. A well-born and estimable woman who would make an excellent countess.

She entered her dressing chamber and went to the armoire. Inside hung the trappings of a lady. A lady Olivia could never hope to be. Whatever she learned, however she managed in Society, she would always be the bastard from the country whose mother had made a name for herself by spreading her legs. Others might not be aware of it, but Olivia was, and the shame at times was overwhelming.

Louisa didn't want her to go, and truthfully Olivia didn't want to leave her. But neither could she remain here. She felt confident Louisa would help settle her in a nice village somewhere. Not Devon. Not Cheshunt. And definitely nowhere near York or anywhere else Jasper would take his bride.

Olivia pulled her old valise from the corner and laid it atop the rose and cream cushioned bench. Methodically, she extracted pairs of stockings from the dresser and folded a half dozen into the valise. Then she moved on to chemises, taking but two. She was so engrossed in her task that she failed to hear the intrusion into her solitude.

"Where are you going?"

Olivia jumped. She turned briskly, clutching a chemise to her chest. Jasper lounged against the doorframe, resplendent in his evening clothes, despite the fact that his cravat had been loosened. He crossed his arms and wore a deep frown.

She purposely ignored his question—and the heady desire coursing through her body. "What are you doing here? It's practically the middle of the night."

"Practically, yes."

He came into the room, his presence engulfing the small space. His familiar scent of pine teased her senses. The need to go to him, to touch his beloved face, kiss his delectable lips was visceral.

"I came to tell you about my engagement. I wanted you to be the first to know that the banns will be read next Sunday."

Olivia's vision tunneled. She knew marrying Philippa was for the best, but having him here in person to deliver the news hurt unbearably. She could find no reason for pleasantries. Not when her heart ached. "You came here at this hour to tell me that?"

"Of course." He smiled, a rather magnanimous affair that revealed nothing of his thoughts. Olivia grew suspicious.

"You still haven't told me where you're going." He moved closer and peered over her shoulder into her valise.

His proximity sent her pulse hammering. "I don't know yet."

He was close enough to kiss. If she wanted to. And how she wanted to. But she kept herself stiff.

"Might I suggest York? It's especially lovely in the fall. By October, the leaves are simply gorgeous." His gaze raked her from head to slipper as he drew out the last word.

Olivia pulled her wrapper more tightly about her body. "I don't think I'd like York."

"Really?" He tucked a curl behind her ear and traced the outline of her jaw. "I love it there and can't imagine anything I'd rather do than spend the autumn there with my bride."

She found difficulty swallowing. "Then you should take her."

He searched her gaze. "But you just said you wouldn't like it. Perhaps I can convince you." He kissed the side of her neck, gently at first, then sucked at her flesh. He pulled back. "Do you think I can convince you?"

Olivia had completely lost track of the conversation. "Convince me to do what?"

"Marry me, of course."

She twined her arms around his neck and kissed him. Heat suffused her limbs as she leaned up and poured all of her heart and all of her soul into their embrace. He returned the kiss, his lips and tongue blistering her mouth with sweet precision. His hands scooped her close, bringing her up against his hardened frame. His erection pulsed against her abdomen, hot and heavy through the thin layers of her wrap and night rail.

She loosened her hold and pulled back, but he wouldn't let her go far. "Jasper, why?"

"I love you."

Her knees turned to jelly, and she sagged against him. "Oh, I love you, too."

"Is that a yes?"

She wanted to hear him say it. "I didn't realize you'd asked me a question."

He looked at her expectantly, his blue gaze piercing all the way to her heart. "Marry me, Olivia. Please?"

She nodded. "Yes."

"Excellent." He bent his head to kiss her again.

She put her finger between their lips. "But how? What about Lady Philippa? What about the duke?"

His tongue darted out and licked the tip of her finger. "Philippa will understand."

Olivia tried to ignore the decadent sensations shooting up her arm and spreading through her body. "You haven't told her yet?"

"I thought it was more important I speak with you first." His tongue continued its work against her flesh.

"And the duke?"

"Will be livid, but I don't care." He sucked her digit into his mouth. Heat flooded Olivia's core.

Jasper pushed open her wrapper and clasped her waist. Her nipples pebbled as his gaze locked on her barely covered body with ravenous hunger. He leaned down and latched his mouth on her breast, his tongue dampening the cotton covering her flesh. His hand came up and cupped her, holding the mound to his lips. Olivia closed her eyes in ecstasy.

He reached behind her, and she heard the valise fall to the floor. He guided her to stand on the bench, and she opened her eyes, curious as to what he was doing. He peeled off his coat and sucked in his breath as it slid from his shoulder.

"Your wound?"

"Is healing."

She helped ease his coat off, and it fell to the floor. He unbuttoned his waistcoat, and she gently pushed it from his torso. Then she tugged his cravat free and dropped it atop his other discarded garments.

He moved closer; the top of his head came to her breasts. He slid the cotton of her night rail up her legs, the soft fabric grazing and sensitizing her skin as it ascended her thighs and then her belly. He pushed it up past her breasts and then pressed his lips between them. His hands released the gown and cupped her. He flicked his thumbs over her nipples and gave each a light pinch. Olivia gasped and pulled the night rail over her head. He moved his hands up and pressed her raised arms back against the wall, keeping them elevated. Standing on his toes, he sucked a breast into his mouth, his lips and tongue working the nipple into a tight frenzy. Olivia clutched the night rail in her fists as her body thrummed with need.

Jasper continued his assault on the other breast, keeping her pinned against the wall with her body open to him. He licked and sucked, driving heat to her belly and moisture to her core. She moaned, and he released her arms.

His mouth descended. Between her breasts, along her belly, past her navel—pausing just to swirl his tongue inside the slight indentation. Belatedly, she realized she could lower her arms. She dropped her night rail and clutched at his head.

He clasped her waist and drew her pelvis forward to his mouth. One long finger traced down her mound and grazed the nub at the top of her most private place. She bucked against him in need. His hand moved between her legs and parted her thighs. Gently, he stroked her heated flesh, coaxing murmurs of delight from her mouth.

He slid one finger into her tight warmth, and she gripped his hair. Then his mouth descended and sucked that nub into a fevered heat. Olivia laid her head back against the wall and let the sensations overwhelm her. His mouth worshipped her while his finger met her thrusts. Then there were two fingers, and that was so much better. He pumped her and licked her, and coherent thought left her brain.

Then he turned her against the wall. Her swollen nipples pressed against the hard surface. She turned her head to the side, gasping as she hovered near the brink. Why had he stopped?

His finger traced down her back, followed by his tongue. Shamelessly, she pushed back against him. His hands cupped her bottom, and he licked the base of her spine.

"Kneel," he said.

She'd no idea what he'd do next, but she trusted him. Yes, by God she trusted him. She kneeled and he pivoted her body so that she was lengthwise on the bench, with the wall to her right. He moved behind her and stroked her bottom again. Then her back. Slow, languorous touches that didn't come close to satisfying her. She pushed backward, seeking something, anything that would bring her release.

One of his hands left her body for a moment. Then he clasped her hips and brought her back. His hot flesh nudged her cleft. God, yes. Olivia pressed back and he sheathed himself inside of her. She wrapped her fingers around the edges of the bench.

He stayed like that a moment. Her flesh accepted him, and very quickly she wanted him to move. Slowly, agonizingly, he withdrew and then just as slowly entered her again. He moved one hand up her side and reached around to her breast. He plucked at her nipple as he continued his slow penetration and withdrawal. In, out, in, out. Sensations built inside of her, and she couldn't keep herself from moving back and forth with his rhythm. But it wasn't fast enough. She wanted more.

She reached back and grabbed his thigh urging him faster. He complied, spearing himself inside of her with delicious force. Faster now, he pumped. He moved his hand from her breast and rubbed it along her upper back until he cupped the back of her neck. He pulled her head back and ran his tongue along the shell of her ear. "Come for me," he whispered.

His other hand wrapped around her hip and flicked her sex. Olivia cried out as sheer bliss ruptured any semblance of calm and sent her over the edge of sanity. She squeezed her eyes shut and still saw light. Blinding, beautiful, soul-shattering light.

He clasped her hips again and drove deep, pummeling her until he cried out.

His rhythm slowed. Olivia rested on her elbows, letting her head fall forward as she came back to earth.

After a few minutes, Jasper stood and helped her to a sitting position. He found a cloth and handed it to her to wipe herself, turning his back to offer a bit of privacy. Then he came back and scooped her into his arms.

She gasped. "Careful! What about your shoulder?"

"It's fine. It barely pains me at present."

She gave him a mock frown. "Still, I worked hard on those stitches and prefer you kept them in place."

He carried her to the bed and laid her atop the coverlet. He stared down at her and exhaled. "I can't believe you're mine."

She smiled up at him. "I can't believe you're mine." She scooted to the side and pulled the covers down. "Now take off your clothes and get in here with me."

He quickly complied and soon they were in the cool softness of the bed, Olivia wrapped tight in his arms, her head against his chest. "Do you have to go?" she asked.

"Not right away. Seems a shame to let a naked female in bed go to waste."

She grinned up at him. "A shame indeed." She kissed his nipple, and he sucked in a breath. "I look forward to when you don't have to leave."

"Very soon, my love." He kissed her forehead and then turned her to her back. He rose over her with a wicked leer. "But first..."

Olivia pushed him over and climbed on top of him. "You mustn't overwork your shoulder."

"I do love a commanding woman." He chuckled. "I'm yours."

"Forever," she said, as she brushed her lips over his.

"Forever."

Chapter Twenty-three

FOREVER, IT TURNED out, was much shorter than Jasper realized. He'd secreted himself out of Olivia's bedroom when the morning sun had just begun to flirt with the horizon. He rode his horse out of Louisa's mews wearing a wide grin and humming a ridiculous tune.

It was so early, he noted, that he could keep his dawn appointment with Clifton if the man was stupid enough to meet him. But presumably the duke had taken care of this. Perhaps he'd even sent word to Saxton House, not that Jasper had been there to receive it.

When Jasper entered his townhouse, he was immediately greeted by his bespectacled butler, Thurber, who appeared as unruffled at daybreak as he did at midnight. The man—another of his rescued retainers—was unnatural.

He inclined his head at Jasper. "May I offer congratulations, my lord?"

Jasper slowed as he entered the hall. "For?"

"Your nuptials."

Ice filled Jasper's veins. "What do you know of my wedding?"

"A note arrived a few hours ago from His Grace. He delivered it personally. He was, ah, rather pleased and shared the news with us directly." Thurber handed him the missive.

Jasper felt like he'd swallowed a jar of lead. He opened the parchment and the marble seemed to fall away beneath him.

I've taken care of Clifton and his newspaper nonsense. I took the opportunity to share the news of your engagement with his friend, who was more than happy to print that story instead of the fabrication Clifton provided.

You've made me very proud.
Holborn.

Bloody, bloody hell. His engagement to Philippa was going to be in the newspaper. *That very morning.* Hours from now all of London would know he was to be married—but to the wrong bride. Jasper crumpled the missive in his fist. There was no way he could stop it.

OLIVIA AND LOUISA stepped out of their coach on Bond Street at ten o'clock for their appointment with the boot maker. Olivia thought of Mr. Beatty and his daughter. Instead of him crafting her a pair of boots with whatever was left from his clients, she'd now have the most fashionable—and likely most expensive—boot available. Although she knew Jasper had helped Mr. Beatty, she wanted to share some of her good fortune with him and his family.

"Louisa, would you mind terribly if I visited a few people I knew from before? I should like to ascertain their welfare and perhaps ensure they have a comfortable winter."

Louisa beamed. "You're every bit as generous as Jasper. Such a benevolent pair you'll make."

They were just about to step into the shop when they heard, "Louisa!" Lady Badby made her way toward them, her overlarge hat swaying atop her head. Olivia and Louisa paused and waited for her to arrive.

"Good morning!" she huffed. "I wanted to be the first to congratulate you on your nephew's betrothal. It's not a surprise, of course, but a sad day for hopeful young ladies all over England."

Louisa glanced at Olivia but revealed not a bit of surprise. "Thank you, Augusta."

"Do you know when the wedding is to take place? I presume they'll wed at St. Paul's. Don't you agree? But then perhaps you don't know. I'm sure his bride is considering her options."

Lady Badby didn't so much as look at Olivia, which gave Olivia to understand that *she* was not the bride, regardless of what Jasper had told her just a few hours before. Her hands began to shake, and so she clamped them together at her waist.

"Ah, well, I must be off. Oh, there's Lady Dalrymple. I wonder if she's heard…" Lady Badby took herself off.

Louisa turned to Olivia and pulled her into the doorway of the boot maker. "I don't know what to say, dear. I've no idea what happened."

Nor did Olivia, but neither would she reveal to Louisa what had transpired last night. Her humiliation over trusting Jasper was more than she could admit to herself.

But it didn't make sense! He hadn't ever lied to her, and she didn't think he'd started last night. Not after what they'd shared. And not when he'd felt so terrible about compromising her virtue in the first place.

"I'm all right, Louisa." She wasn't, but she was trying to be. There had to be an explanation. If there wasn't, she was glad she'd left her valise half packed.

JASPER DRUMMED HIS fingers on the mantle in the drawing room of Herrick House while awaiting the arrival of the earl. This was going to be a very distasteful meeting.

Lord Herrick entered. He was a tall, lean man with thick, dark hair and a stoic demeanor. Where Lady Philippa was charming and witty, her father was colorless and serious.

"Good of you to save me the trouble of calling on you this morning, Saxton. I received your note early this morning and saw the *Times*, but since when are you betrothed to my daughter?"

He opened his mouth, but before he could speak, Lady Philippa swept into the room. "Since never," she said. "Lord Saxton proposed, but I declined. What I should like to know is how the 'news' came to be in the paper."

Jasper wouldn't dispute her story. It was the best way for her to retain her sparkling reputation. He couldn't fault her a bit for coming up with it. "It appears to be a misprint, Lady Philippa. Perhaps a rumor gone amok. I deeply regret its consequences."

Lord Herrick had stood quietly watching their exchange, but now he spoke up quite furiously. "This is a disaster. Philippa's marital prospects will be ruined." He directed his dark gaze on his daughter. "Philippa, you'll marry him anyway."

"Absolutely not. I've no wish to marry him." She elevated her chin, and Jasper couldn't tell if she spoke the truth or not. He deeply regretted disappointing her if she'd hoped for a proposal.

Her father glowered. "Think of your reputation."

"I'd rather think of my future happiness." She speared her father with a rather pointed stare that Jasper found curious. "I've decided we will not suit." She turned her attention to Jasper. "My lord, will the *Times* print a retraction stating the news was false?"

"I'm confident they will. I'll do everything in my power to lessen any impact upon you."

She gave a slight nod, but it was enough for Jasper to conclude she was not unhappy. "Then it's settled. I shall expect you to manage the gossip to your best ability."

"I appreciate your understanding. Again, I apologize for this grave error. I truly have no idea how it could've occurred."

She nodded, and Jasper took that as a conclusion to the interview. He bowed to her and to Lord Herrick and left, relief quickening his step.

That had gone far better than he'd imagined. Now, if only his meeting with the duke would end so well.

OLIVIA FOLLOWED LOUISA up the stairs to Jasper's townhouse. Her nerves were on edge; she wasn't at all certain she wanted to see Jasper. She was too afraid of what he might say. That last night had been a dream, or worse, a lie.

Louisa, however, insisted the columnist who'd reported the engagement had erred, and she intended to question Jasper about it immediately.

Jasper's butler admitted them into the cavernous marble entry. It was easily twice as large as Louisa's. "Good morning, Lady Merriweather, Miss West. Lord Saxton is currently out. Would you care to join His Grace in the drawing room?"

Louisa's brows shot up. "His Grace is here?"

"Indeed," the butler said. "He's been waiting half an hour, though I informed him I didn't know when Lord Saxton would return."

Louisa turned to Olivia. "This is a bit curious. Yes, Thurber, we'll wait with my brother."

They followed the butler straight through the entry to the drawing room. The duke stood upon their arrival. He'd clearly been drinking tea—it looked as though he'd been here awhile.

He smiled at them, or at least Olivia surmised it was supposed to be a smile. His lips pulled back, but his frosty gaze just didn't match the expression. "Louisa, Miss West."

"Holborn, what are you doing here? I can't recall the last time you visited Saxton at this hour of the day, let alone *waited* for him."

"Surely you saw the *Times* this morning?" he asked.

"Actually, no. We had an early appointment, and I planned to read the paper at luncheon."

"And here I assumed you'd come to congratulate Jasper on his betrothal to Lady Philippa."

Olivia's knees weakened, but she managed to stay standing. Louisa touched her arm.

"I'm here to discuss specifics with Saxton," the duke continued.

"I see," Louisa murmured. She cast an apologetic glance at Olivia, but it seemed to mask another emotion—anger perhaps. Her bright blue eyes flashed. "When do you expect this blessed event to take place?"

"By the end of October, I should imagine."

"Pity. Olivia and I had planned to travel to York for the autumn. I suppose we could return for the wedding." She gave Olivia's arm a squeeze.

"I should hope so. You and Saxton are quite close, and of course, you're both more than welcome." He attempted the grotesque semblance of a smile again.

There was something most suspicious about his behavior. He'd never treated Olivia with anything bordering kindness, let alone civility. Most often, he made rude comments and cast her disparaging looks. Why was he attempting to be pleasant now? Was it because his son was marrying the woman he'd selected?

"Well, we needn't stay, dear," Louisa said. "Clearly Saxton has business this morning." They turned to go, but the duke stopped them.

"Is there something I can tell Saxton for you? The reason for your visit, perhaps?"

Louisa turned her head and gave him a cool smile. "No, thank you, Holborn."

They walked toward the door and had to stop short as Jasper stood at the threshold. His gaze softened when he looked at Olivia, and again her knees threatened to give way.

"Pardon us, Saxton." Louisa's tone dripped frost. "We understand you and Holborn are discussing wedding details this morning."

Jasper's brow arched, and he looked past them at the duke. "Indeed? I had no knowledge of such an appointment. If I had, I would have been saved the journey to Holborn House this morning." He glanced at Olivia and gave her a mischievous wink. What was he up to? "I regret to inform you, Holborn, that I will not be marrying Lady Philippa. As it happens, she has no desire to marry me."

Chapter Twenty-four

JASPER WATCHED THE play of emotions over Olivia's face. With her back to the duke, she let everything show—anger, surprise, and now suspicion. He wanted to tell her that the announcement was entirely Holborn's doing—and he would—but he'd already reasoned that it was easiest and best for everyone if he allowed Holborn to believe what Philippa had told her father: that she'd refused Jasper.

There would be time enough for him to accept Jasper's marrying Olivia, which would now have to happen in the quiet of York or somewhere equally distant from London in order to preserve Philippa's reputation. He didn't think Olivia would mind. In fact, he rather thought she'd prefer a wedding outside the spectacle of Society. He knew he would. His pulse raced at the thought. He wanted to leave with her today.

Holborn strode toward him with fury etched in his features. Olivia and Louisa moved to the side. "Did she refuse you because of your behavior last night? I can't believe you hit someone in the middle of a ball. Did I raise an animal?"

Olivia stepped forward. "It was my understanding, Your Grace, that Saxton was protecting Lady Philippa's honor. Surely you can't find fault with that."

Jasper tried not to let his mouth hang open. Given what Olivia knew at this moment—that Jasper had planned to marry Philippa while he was making love to and proposing to *her*—he couldn't believe she was defending him. And defending his violence! He ached to wrap her in his arms and declare his unworthiness.

"I can, and I do find fault." He glowered at her a moment before turning his anger on Jasper. "We had an agreement."

"Yes, and I met my side of the bargain. I can't force Lady Philippa to do anything she doesn't wish." And because he couldn't resist the taunt, he added, "Would you have wanted me to compromise her as publicly as possible?"

Olivia sucked in a breath, and Jasper regretted saying it. He was going to have a job convincing her he wasn't the greatest ass in England.

"I wanted you to honor our agreement. You give me no choice."

Jasper's patience fled. He advanced on Holborn until they stood nearly nose to nose. "You gave *me* no choice, and now, through no fault of my own, I'm going to make my choice. There will be no marriage with Lady Philippa."

The duke stared up at him—Jasper had a solid two inches over the man—in mute fury. The muscles in his jaw worked while his gaze cast a chill that could likely be felt in Sussex.

"Are you going to marry that chit?" He jerked his head toward Olivia.

Jasper's blood sang. "I am."

"You ruin the title."

"No, I enhance it," Jasper spat with glee. "Just as you taught me to do. I don't expect this to soften you toward her, but Merry was her father. She possesses noble blood and will execute the duties of countess—and duchess when the time comes—with poise and grace." He leaned forward slightly, forcing the duke to tip his head back. "You will leave her alone, and that is the end of it."

Jasper stepped away and allowed himself to look at Olivia and his aunt. Louisa brushed a hand beneath her eye, and Olivia stared at him, wide-eyed.

Thurber stepped into the drawing room. "My lord, Lord Sevrin and his…friends are here to see you."

Sevrin didn't wait to be invited. He moved past Thurber followed by Hopkins and a half dozen other men from the club. Sevrin took in the other occupants of the room and arched a brow. "It's a party here this morning."

Jasper arched a brow, bemused as to their presence. "So it would seem."

"We saw the *Times*," Sevrin said. "It was evident you needed help figuring things out." The group of men surged forward, and Jasper schooled himself not to laugh. They were going to beat him into marrying Olivia? How he loved that club. How was he ever going to convince Olivia that he needed it?

"I was just explaining to the duke that Lady Philippa has chosen not to marry me." He gave Sevrin a very slight nod trying to silently communicate that this fact should not be disputed. "I was also explaining that I'll be marrying Miss West."

The men relaxed. A few clapped each other on the back and grinned. Sevrin laughed softly. "Our work here is done then."

"What the hell is all of this?" The duke demanded.

"Just a group of friends."

The duke's lip curled. "'Friends'? This lot?"

"We came to ensure his welfare," Sevrin said. "And that of his bride. We would hate to hear anything scandalous about her, or see anything unfortunate befall her."

"Indeed," Hopkins said while flexing and unflexing his hand. The rest of the men moved slightly forward again, their expressions turning serious—and determined.

Jasper looked at the duke. His expression had slipped, revealing a flash of concern. He quickly veiled it beneath his mask of disapproval. "You think to intimidate me?" he asked Jasper.

Jasper gestured toward his fighting brothers. "Not me, them. I did not invite them this morning, though they are most welcome."

"You really will ruin the title."

"I won't, but if I have to, I'll have no trouble ruining you. Society's approval is far more important to you than it is to me." Or so Jasper had come to realize. Nothing was more important than Olivia's approval, and right now that was the only thing worth fighting for.

The duke wavered another moment, his gaze flicking back and forth between Jasper and the men from the Black Horse. At last he said, "Keep her away from me." Then he stalked from the room.

Sevrin grinned. "Now, I think our work really is done. Congratulations, Saxton."

All of them surrounded Jasper and either shook his hand or clapped his back. One laid a hand on his wounded shoulder and Jasper flinched. "Eh, sorry about that," Hopkins said sheepishly.

"I'm only sorry we can't tar that fellow, Gifford," one man said.

"I think he'll spend plenty of time in Newgate," Sevrin said. "Now, lads, let's leave Saxton and his bride to themselves. I'm sure they have things to discuss." He bowed to Olivia and the other men did the same. Olivia's cheeks pinked while Louisa grinned broadly.

After they departed, his aunt rushed to hug him. "My dear boy.

Well done! Who were those men?"

"I belong to a fighting club. They're my friends."

"Indeed? How extraordinary. I knew there had to be a reason for your various bruises. There was no way you'd suddenly turned into the clumsiest man in England." She glanced back at Olivia who hadn't moved. "I'm going to return to Queen Street. I'm sure you'll deliver Olivia at some point. Olivia, dear, I'll have our things packed for York. We'll leave on the morrow."

She gave Jasper's hand a squeeze before sweeping from the room.

Jasper stood and watched Olivia a moment, unsure of what she was thinking. He took one step forward, but she took one back. "I'm sorry."

"What agreement was Holborn speaking of?" she asked.

Jasper steeled himself for her anger. "I'd agreed to marry Philippa in exchange for him leaving you alone. I wanted you to be happy with Louisa, and he guaranteed it."

"So you did plan to marry her. What were you doing with me last night?" Her voice was so wounded, her face so pale.

Jasper wanted to hold her, but he daren't move for fear that she'd flee. "I did plan to marry her—for about an hour. I went to the Black Horse and my friends—Sevrin and that lot—talked sense into my foolish brain. Then I came to see you. Unfortunately, the duke got ahead of himself and shared the news with a reporter at the *Times*."

"But you said Philippa refused you."

"I had to. Philippa's reputation is at stake. I have to let Society believe she refused me."

"Won't your reputation suffer?"

"I don't give a fig about that."

Her eyes flashed with disappointment. "Why, because by marrying me you'll be ruined anyway?"

He couldn't stand the distance between them another moment. In three large strides he was before her. He took her hands in his. "No, because now that I have you, nothing else matters. I do still have you, don't I?" He sank to his knees, prepared to beg if necessary. "I know you're probably feeling distrustful. I felt the same last night when I heard you'd received a threatening letter and didn't tell me about it." Her eyes widened. "But I decided it didn't matter. I trust you, Olivia. I know you had a reason for not telling me."

She nodded sheepishly. "I assumed the duke sent it. I didn't want to further damage an already horrid relationship."

He smiled at her. "You needn't worry on that count—I'm certain there's nothing else that could further tarnish how I view the duke."

She blinked at him, and he realized there were tears in her eyes.

He squeezed her hands. "Please don't cry, Olivia. See, I'm begging. Trust me, love me, marry me."

"I think I like your fighting club friends. I won't mind if you continue with your membership."

He laughed, joy coursing through him. "They're good sorts."

"The best since they chose you."

"Does this mean you choose me too?" His heart stopped a moment as he waited for her response.

She pulled on his hands. "Oh, stand up and kiss me, Jasper."

Epilogue

London, March 1818

"ARE YOU SURE you want to go?" Jasper asked as Olivia pulled her gloves on. "I'll understand if you'd rather stay home and rest." His gaze flicked to her waistline, which hadn't yet begun to reveal the child growing inside of her.

She smiled in response. "I know you'd rather stay home, but we promised Louisa we'd go to Lady Badby's dinner party." Furthermore, she wanted to show everyone, particularly Jasper's parents who would no doubt be there, that she was more than capable of being Countess of Saxton.

He wrapped an arm around her waist and pulled her against him then nuzzled her neck. "I'd much prefer you here, alone, but I suppose I can share you for one night."

Thirty minutes later they ascended the steps to Lady Badby's townhouse. If the line of carriages were any indication, her dinner party would be far too populated for a sit-down meal.

They'd offered to bring Louisa with them, but she'd declined, saying she wanted to watch their grand entrance. Olivia stifled an urgent stab of anxiety. Everyone's attention would be fixed on her and Jasper. They hadn't been out in Society since they'd quietly wed in York the previous September.

As promised, Louisa was waiting for them in the drawing room, though she was hard to spot at first given the thick crowd. She cut a path to them, beaming. "You look splendid, dears."

"Louisa, I thought you said this was a moderately-sized dinner party?" Olivia said, though she'd long ago learned Louisa's idea of "moderate" was perhaps not what others would define.

Louisa shrugged. "I can't imagine all of these people had legitimate invitations, but Augusta won't turn them away. She's over there preening under her success. You're the toast of London already, and she snagged your first appearance."

Lady Badby was speaking with several people, her befeathered head bobbing and her beringed hands gesticulating. Just behind her stood the Duke of Holborn. Olivia looked about for the duchess, but didn't see her. They hadn't seen or heard from either of Jasper's parents since leaving London in the fall.

They had, however, spent time with Jasper's sister, Miranda, and her husband, Fox, who'd come to their wedding. And now they were here as well. Miranda strode toward them, her husband trailing in her wake.

She beamed at Olivia and took her hands. "Ah, there you are." She lowered her voice. "You're glowing, dear. Is there something I should know?" She arched a brow at Jasper.

"How can you tell?" Olivia asked.

Fox slid his hand around his wife's waist, completely unaware—or perhaps uncaring—that such public affection was frowned upon in London. "You should know by now that Miranda notices everything."

Miranda gave Fox a playful look. "A mother senses these things." Their son was just a few months old.

"Is Alexander here in London with you?" Olivia asked. They'd visited after his birth, but she dearly hoped to see him again.

"Of course." Miranda's eyes sparkled with merriment. "You don't think the duke and duchess would deign to visit their grandson in rural Wiltshire?"

Olivia felt Jasper's arm tense beneath her fingertips. She looked up at him and saw him staring at the duke. "Everything all right?"

"Mmm, yes. I think so." Jasper had visited his father before they'd traveled to York. He'd assured Olivia that despite the duke's behavior up to that point, he wouldn't trouble them. He'd also sworn that he hadn't threatened his father in return, but Olivia still wondered why the duke had so easily agreed to leave them to their happiness. "I'll just go and see."

"I'm coming with you," Olivia said.

"Brave girl," Fox noted. "I'd offer my support, but I don't think my presence will help your cause."

Miranda grinned at him. "Oh, he was practically pleasant when we visited them yesterday with Alexander."

Jasper arched a brow at his sister as if he didn't believe that at all. Miranda laughed and winked at Olivia as Jasper drew her toward the duke. Holborn clasped his hands behind his back as they approached.

"Good evening, Your Grace." Olivia offered a curtsey.

"Good evening." The duke gave a slight bow. Olivia slid a glance at Jasper, whose eyes widened almost imperceptibly. He hadn't expected anything so polite. Neither had Olivia, but she was acutely aware of how closely everyone in the room was watching them so she'd hoped for civility at the least.

"Is Her Grace here?" Jasper asked.

"Yes, somewhere about." The duke attempted a tight smile, but to Olivia he looked as if he were suffering a stab of arthritic pain. "I trust you are both well?"

Jasper covered her hand with his. "We are, thank you. Your solicitude is much appreciated."

"Of course." The duke inclined his head, but his eyes were frigid. He'd publicly accepted them, but not privately. Still, it was precisely what they'd hoped. After all of his threats and thwarted attempts to drive Olivia away, he'd surrendered.

People began to move toward them tentatively. The evening passed in a blur for Olivia until just before midnight when she found herself alone while Jasper fetched her a glass of lemonade. The duke appeared at her side.

"Have you been waiting to pounce?" she asked.

"A bit, yes."

Olivia didn't want to play games. She knew where she stood with this man and accepted it. "Tell me why."

"Why I've allowed you to stay?" He looked out at the drawing room instead of at her. "You're an actress. You can play the part of Jasper's wife at least well enough to fool Society."

She laughed softly. "You don't think much of me or Society."

"He was going to marry you, no matter what I said or did."

Olivia's heart warmed, knowing the duke was right. Jasper would never let her go. "We're going to have a child. Probably late in the summer. Don't tell Jasper I told you."

The duke looked at her now. The faintest sheen glowed in his eyes. Not tears, but there was something inside him keeping his soul from shriveling completely. "Will you send word when he comes?"

He. Holborn expected nothing else. Olivia nodded. "I will."

Later, Olivia sleepily curled against her husband's side in their massive four-poster bed at Saxton House. "I had a nice time. I still prefer York, but I can manage a few months in London each year. Especially with Louisa, and hopefully your sister can come periodically, when the orphanage allows."

His fingers stroked her upper arm. "I will follow wherever you lead."

She looked up at him. "Did you enjoy tonight?"

"You're trying to ask about my parents. I admit I was shocked by their polite behavior."

"You didn't really expect them to cause a scene?"

"Not particularly, but I've given up trying to predict Holborn. I'd like to think he has more sense than to cause the very thing he's so afraid of, but he can sometimes be rash, as he was in my youth." He'd told Olivia plenty of tales of his father's cruelty, but her heart never failed to squeeze when she thought of Jasper's childhood. It actually made her lack of a father preferable.

She'd come to accept that she would never know the identity of her father, but she also accepted that she'd spent fourteen somewhat happy years with foster parents who had given her kindness if not love. And she supposed Fiona had loved her in her own way. But now she had the love of a true parent in Louisa, and that was more than she could have dreamed. Instead of feeling as if her life were missing something, she felt full, complete. Loved.

She snuggled up against Jasper and pressed a kiss to his throat. "I love you."

He clasped her tightly. "I love you, too." He turned toward her and kissed her lightly. "And did I tell you how proud I am of you? How gratifying it is to see every other man in the room glare at me with envy?"

She smiled against his lips. "I know the feeling, though the women also bare their teeth."

He laughed. "How ferocious." He kissed a trail along her jaw to her ear.

"I was surprised you didn't want to visit the Black Horse this evening. I know you want to see Sevrin and the others."

He nibbled at her neck, just below her ear. "I thought I might go tomorrow, if you're amenable."

Olivia was fast losing interest in conversing. "Of course, they're your friends."

Jasper pulled back. "Have I told you how lucky I am, how happy you make me, how I couldn't possibly deserve you?"

She tugged him closer again, directing his lips back to her neck. "Yes, yes, and don't be ridiculous."

He licked a path to the underside of her chin. "You say that, but before I met you my heart was cold, ruined, utterly wicked."

She placed her hand on his chest over the heart that beat sure and strong—for her. "Your heart isn't cold, nor is it ruined. But I hope you won't mind if I prefer you remain the tiniest bit wicked."

He grinned as he lowered his lips to hers. "Anything for you."

THE END

Thank You!

Thank you so much for reading *His Wicked Heart*! I hope you enjoyed it! Would you like to know when my next book is available? You can sign up for my new release email list at http://www.darcyburke.com/newsletter/, follow me on Twitter at @darcyburke, or like my Facebook page at http://www.facebook.com/DarcyBurkeFans.

Reviews help others find a book that's right for them. I appreciate all reviews, whether positive or negative, and hope you'll leave one at your vendor or reading community website of choice.

Read on for an excerpt from the next book in the Secrets and Scandals Series:

A lady on the brink of disaster

Quintessential debutante Lady Philippa Latham is determined to avoid scandal at all costs so that she may marry well. When her mother's outrageous behavior threatens their family's reputation, Philippa unwittingly follows her to a party no unmarried Society girl would risk attending. As if that wasn't bad enough, Philippa is "rescued" from disaster by England's most notorious scoundrel, which sets them both on a path to public and personal ruin.

A scoundrel in need of seduction

Lord Ambrose Sevrin is infamous for ruining his brother's fiancé and refusing to marry her. Content to remain among the fringe of the upper ten thousand, he is an intriguing enigma to London's elite. Philippa thinks she's met the true Ambrose—a gentleman who would fight to defend her and help her secure a husband before it's too late. But he can't be that husband, even for her. He won't tolerate redemption—or love—for his crimes are far worse than anyone can imagine.

Chapter One

London, April 1818

FROM THE COMFORT of the Herrick coach, Lady Philippa Latham watched her mother alight from Mr. Booth-Barrows' carriage in front of a massive neo-classical house on Saville Street. Booth-Barrows tucked Mother's hand over his arm and they climbed the steps of the townhouse, their heads bent close together. *Like lovers*. Philippa seethed. Loveless marriage or no, how dare Mother openly cuckold Father? And only days after she'd informed Philippa she must marry this season. How was she to accomplish that while her mother was cavorting about town with a man who wasn't her husband?

Philippa clasped her fingers tightly around the door handle, and before she knew her own mind, she was stepping from the coach. The footman leaped to help her.

With murmured appreciation and a directive to wait until she returned, she dashed across the moonlit street. Nervous energy propelled her along her mother's path. Philippa had never done anything so rash before, but she was intent on convincing Mother to come home immediately.

A black and silver liveried footman opened the front door, and Philippa stepped into a cavernous marble entry. But instead of her mother, other guests, or some sort of receiving line, she found emptiness punctuated by the gentle swell of conversation and muted laughter coming from a chamber on the opposite side of the foyer.

"Would you care for a cloak?"

Philippa turned toward a second footman who held up a voluminous black cloak, complete with a large hood. She frowned. Why on earth would she want to wear a cloak inside? "No, thank you." Puzzled, she turned from the footman and squared her shoulders.

Head high, she strode across the gleaming marble and did her best to appear as if she belonged, though she'd no idea whose house she'd invaded. Not that she cared, so long as she found her mother and took her home. While it was true some women had liaisons outside of their marriage, her mother shouldn't be one of them. Not after twenty-two years of insisting upon propriety and respectability above all else. Philippa's outrage bubbled anew.

She paused at the threshold to the large, dimly lit room beyond the foyer. It was crowded with people. *Masked people*. Faint tendrils of trepidation curled in her chest.

She stepped into the room, seeking her mother's peacock blue gown. In the center, a woman stood on a table in nothing but her chemise and garters. Philippa gaped, completely unprepared for such a shocking display.

She spun about, clenching her teeth. *Curse her impulsivity*, which she rarely indulged. How fitting that on her first foray she'd stumbled into precisely the impropriety her mother had warned against. And how ironic that she'd done so in pursuit of Mother.

A man clasped her elbow. "Lady Philippa." The whisper came next to her ear and sent a shiver down her neck.

Philippa jumped. She turned her head to look at the man, but a dark mask covered the upper half of his face. Panic rooted in her belly. "How do you know who I am?"

He dragged her to the side of the room, deeper into the shadows, and pressed her against the wall. The edge of the wainscoting dug into her lower back. Then he stepped close. Too close. He put his hands up behind his head. "Quickly, take my mask." He worked another moment then muttered, "Bloody hell, the tie is knotted."

She didn't know what sort of event she'd stumbled into, but clearly it was wicked, and the only thing standing between her and certain ruin was—literally—this bold stranger. Right now, she'd take this man's audacity over discovery.

"Let me." She stood on her toes, for he was quite tall, and found the knot at the back of his head. He smelled of rosemary and sandalwood, very pleasant.

"Where'd she go?" a male voice behind her rescuer asked. "I saw the loveliest creature, dark hair, pale gown—no mask, if you can imagine. She was just here."

Her rescuer leaned his head down so that their mouths were a breath apart. If she nudged up the slightest bit, their lips would touch… Her fingers fumbled as she tried to work the knot free.

"Eh, there she is, against the wall."

Philippa gave up her struggle with the mask and moved her hands to her rescuer's lapels. She pulled him closer so that her bodice grazed the front of his coat. "Don't you dare move."

"I wouldn't dream of it," he murmured, his warm breath caressing her mouth.

More shivers. This time dancing down her arms.

He clasped her waist and she would've jumped back if the wall behind her had allowed any such movement. "I ought to convince the men behind me you are engaged, ah, with me. Pardon my familiarity, but I do believe kissing you is necessary. You might take the opportunity to continue working at the ties of my mask."

Before she had time to make sense of anything he'd just told her, his lips met hers.

The pressure of his mouth was warm and soft. She'd been kissed before—a swift brushing of lips that had left her curious—but pressed against a stranger in a dark corner, this was something quite different. Somehow more than just a kiss. A moment later his advice sunk into her befuddled thoughts. *The mask.*

She lifted her arms, which only served to bring her body up against him rather snugly. His chest pressed against hers in a terribly intimate fashion, while he moved his lips slowly, sensuously over hers. Her sensibilities were scandalized, but her body didn't care. Her flesh heated, and little whorls of excitement replaced the panic in her belly.

A dissatisfied grunt came from behind her rescuer, followed by, "Someone else got to her first." Two sets of footsteps trailed away.

She plucked at the ties of the mask, and at last it came loose. He broke the kiss and caught the mask before it fell. Then he turned it around and covered the upper two-thirds of her face. He quickly tied the thin strands around the back of her head. The mask was too large for her, but that only meant it covered more and she wouldn't complain about *that*. Not when there were plenty of other things to worry about.

Such as how disappointed she felt that their kiss was over. Ludicrous! She needed to concentrate on getting out of there without being identified. "You recognized me immediately. I suppose it's too much to hope no one else did." She tested the knot at the back of her head and was satisfied it wouldn't come loose even as she feared it didn't matter. Though the other men hadn't referred to her by name, her heretofore pristine reputation would be ruined if any of them had discerned her identity.

"You aren't sure if anyone saw you?" The dark timbre of his voice wrapped around her.

The mask tunneled her vision, and even squinting she couldn't make out his features in the shadowed corner they inhabited. "Just the footmen. One of them offered me a cloak. Oh dear, was that to shield my identity? How was I to know?"

"What were you expecting to find at Lockwood House?" His tone carried a hint of sarcasm.

"*Lockwood House?*" Dear Lord, she'd marched through the gates of Hell and straight into Lucifer's bedchamber. "Is this one of those...parties?" She wasn't even sure what those 'parties' were— proper girls like her never would—but she'd heard enough to know that being caught attending one would mean the death of her reputation.

She reined in her shock to indulge her rising panic. "I have to get out of here. Now."

"I agree." He took her elbow and turned her toward the door.

They took two steps and then stopped short as a group of people stepped inside. He drew her around and guided her along the perimeter of the room. "Sorry, I'd rather not go out that way, particularly since I'm now without a mask."

"I'm sorry to have taken yours. It was very kind of you to offer it, Mr...?"

"Sevrin."

She stumbled as the full reality of her situation permeated her panicked brain. "*Lord Sevrin.*" She sounded breathless, but the implications to her reputation were disastrous. And perhaps irreversible.

He clasped her waist to steady her. "As usual, I see my reputation has preceded me."

It most certainly had. Lord Sevrin was nearly as notorious as Lockwood's parties. He'd famously ruined a girl and refused to marry her, but Philippa recalled there might have been even more to the story.

She took a deep breath to calm her raging nerves. "Why are you helping me?"

He kept his hand at the small of her back, but guided her forward. "You seem in need of assistance. Do correct me if I'm mistaken."

"You are not. I appreciate your help even if I am bewildered by it." His touch and his instant recognition gave her an odd sense of familiarity, as if he had been completely aware of her for some time and she'd been oblivious to him. Though she doubted she would ever feel that way again. "How did you even know who I am? We've never been introduced."

"You have a remarkable face, Lady Philippa. I'd wager most men know who you are." The way he delivered the words—as a matter of fact without an excess of pretty words—sparked another smattering of shivers along her flesh.

Sevrin led her to a door tucked neatly into the corner. He opened it for her, and they entered a small sitting room. Also scarcely lit, it was currently occupied by not one, but two couples. Philippa's heart beat faster. She began to fully understand the nature of the party she'd unwittingly intruded upon.

Sevrin took her hand and pulled her toward a door on the opposite side of the room. "Pardon us," he murmured.

Though the well-bred miss in her urged her to avert her gaze, she couldn't help but stare at one of the couples as they passed. The woman was sprawled upon a chaise with her head cast back. A man lay over her, his mouth at her exposed breast. Philippa jerked her gaze away and stared at Sevrin's back.

The next room was better lit, but it was full of people playing cards. Without masks. Philippa recognized a handful of faces before Sevrin dragged her out onto the balcony. For once, she was glad to be wearing an indistinct, colorless gown reserved for young unwedded misses like herself. She could be one of any of London's young ladies. Although—and this made her heart hammer even faster—her pale yellow dress could lead anyone to assume she was an unmarried miss. Even that seemingly innocuous bit of information about her identity made her feel anxious.

Once outside, she plastered herself against the cool stone of the house's exterior. She breathed deeply, hoping her pulse would slow.

"Good Lord. I'd no idea of the...depravity of Lockwood's parties."

He stood a few feet away. "And you shouldn't."

She gestured toward the house in a thoroughly unladylike fashion. "But my mother is here!"

Sevrin's gaze flicked toward the door they'd just exited. "She is?"

Philippa adjusted the mask, which had drooped over her mouth in her excited exclamation. "I had no idea this was Lockwood House. I followed her."

His brow creased. "Is there an emergency?"

"I wanted to... that is... No, there's no emergency." *Except the danger to her reputation.*

She looked up at him. A sconce on the terrace cast flickering light over the angular planes of his face. Long, dark lashes fringed deep brown eyes. The line of his nose was imperfect, a tad crooked, but it somehow looked right on him. A slightly dimpled chin supported sensuous lips she too-clearly recalled kissing her.

He took her arm, and his touch was oddly comforting, considering he was a scoundrel. "Then let's get you back to your carriage."

Despite his seemingly genuine assistance, she cautioned herself to be wary. She'd spent a lifetime avoiding scandal, and just because she was standing in the dead center of one didn't mean she ought to throw all discretion aside. "You're being very gallant. I'd heard you possessed no such consideration."

He tipped his head toward the light, which brought his good looks into greater focus. "I would tell you not to believe the salacious rumors you've been told about me, but, alas, they're entirely true. Come, let's get you home."

She peered up at him through the mask. "I can't go back through there."

"Of course not. We'll skirt the house." He took her hand again. A pleasant, reassuring warmth stole through her glove and imbued her with a sense of security. He led her along the terrace and down a short flight of steps into the garden.

After a moment he asked, "If there was no emergency, why did you follow your mother?"

"She left Lady Kilmartin's with a gentleman. They appeared," she searched for the right word, "intimate." She looked at the ground where her slippers squashed the damp earth. "I wanted to bring her home before she caused a scandal."

"You think her leaving a ball with someone other than her husband will cause a scandal?"

Philippa paused and looked at him. "I've been raised—by *her*—to think so. You disagree?"

He rolled a shoulder. "It's not as if married women don't have affairs."

Was he defending her mother or merely stating the obvious? "But how can she behave in such a manner while requiring me to comport myself above reproach?"

His lips twisted into a faint smile. "Because life is full of double standards, especially for unmarried women."

"You're right, of course." She continued walking with him through the dark garden. Illumination from the torches on the distant terrace was feeble, but the path was easy enough to follow with a bit of help from a nearly full moon. "Mother's timing, however, is quite poor. I'm supposed to be finding a husband. Her scandalous behavior could drive potential suitors away."

"Perhaps you needn't worry. I'd heard your father had gone abroad to find you a husband. Surely none of them will be aware of your mother's activities."

She cast him a quick glance, but he was eyeing the path. "It appears I am not the only one listening to rumors."

He laughed softly. "Touché."

"The rumors are not, however, completely false. While my father is abroad conducting business, he did threaten to bring a bridegroom home if I didn't select one soon. He was disappointed when I didn't marry the Earl of Saxton last fall."

Sevrin slowed his pace. "And why didn't you? Marry him, I mean. Or anyone else, for that matter."

She bristled. He might as well have asked her outright if she was settling herself comfortably on the shelf. In this, her fifth season, she'd heard more than one matron musing about her marital prospects. Though she was still young enough, handsome enough, wealthy enough, her failure to accept a marriage proposal—and there had been several—was beginning to erode her standing as one of Society's most sought-after misses. Which was why she'd hoped her courtship with Saxton last fall would have led somewhere. He'd been the first gentleman who'd sought to court her without falling at her feet with flowery platitudes or overwrought declarations of devotion. The first gentleman to whom she might've said yes.

Now, recalling her aborted suit with Saxton, she quashed a niggling sense of disappointment. "He never actually asked me." *The Times* had misprinted news of their engagement, and to protect her reputation—at Saxton's insistence—she and Saxton had put it out that she'd refused his proposal.

"I know."

She stopped abruptly. Only she and Saxton had known the truth. Or so she'd thought. "How?"

His mouth curved up in a reassuring smile as his thumb stroked her knuckles. "Saxton and I are friends. Don't worry he told anyone else—he didn't. And the secret is quite safe with me."

She had to believe he was sincere. If not, he surely would have spread the gossip ages ago. "Thank you."

He tugged lightly on her hand, and they moved along the path. "Were you disappointed?"

"That we didn't suit? Yes, but I had the sense his heart was engaged elsewhere. Why aren't *you* married?" She cringed. In her haste to direct the conversation at him, she'd come dangerously close to the root of his notoriety.

"I'd make a terrible husband."

And then, because as long as he knew one of her secrets she ought to be privy to one of his, she went ahead and asked, "Is that why you didn't marry that girl?"

If he was offended by her question, he didn't show it. "Would you believe me if I told you she didn't want to marry me?"

Philippa thought for a moment. For a sinful rogue, he was charmingly honest and solicitous. "I don't see a reason not to."

He barked out a laugh. "You'd be the first."

She smiled, enjoying their conversation far more than she ought. He was, after all, an utter reprobate. "The first who believed you, or the first you told?"

Sevrin stopped at a five-foot tall stone wall that edged the yard. He let go of her hand and gave her a half-smile. "You're cheekier than I might've imagined."

She couldn't argue with his assessment. Tonight she'd strayed far outside her normal boundaries. If anyone saw her now, she'd be quite thoroughly and incontrovertibly ruined. And while the thought made her a trifle queasy, the sensation was surprisingly overridden by the excitement of Sevrin's company.

She suffered a moment of alarm—why was this exciting? Because it was forbidden? Because it was *Sevrin*? This escapade shouldn't be exciting at all, but with no one here to witness her inappropriate reaction, perhaps she could finally relax her guard. Why not? Her mother certainly had.

The mask drooped again, and she pulled it off, dislodging a lock of hair. The curl grazed her shoulder and sent a tickle along her arm. She brushed at the sensation and then offered him back the mask. "I don't think I need this anymore."

"Keep it," he said. "You never know. An alley runs between Lockwood House and the building next door. We'll take it through to the street. I'm going to lift you up to sit on the wall then I'll climb over and help you down the other side. Are you ready?"

She nodded. Although she expected his touch, she still jumped when his hands came around her waist. "I'm a bit ticklish."

"Lovely," he murmured. The sound, dark and rich, permeated every inch of her. She willed her body to remain unaffected the next time he touched her. Warm hands spanned her waist then lifted her. She held her arms up to grab the top of the wall and bit back a gasp as Sevrin's hands scooped her bottom and raised her higher. She pulled herself atop the stone and watched as Sevrin vaulted the wall with ease.

He reached up and clasped the tops of her hips. She burned where he touched her. When she was on the ground, his hands were gone far too quickly.

"This way." He led her into the dark alley stretching between Lockwood House and the building next door.

They were halfway to the street when two men stepped from the shadows.

The shorter of the two spread his lips in a malevolent grin. "Here's our lad."

Sevrin shoved her behind him and then her scandalous, yet shockingly pleasant evening went completely to the devil.

Acknowledgements

Other authors say the second book is the hardest, and I must concur. I have to thank my critique partners, Erica Ridley, Emma Locke, and Janice Goodfellow for reading a ridiculous number of drafts of the opening of this book. Who knew Regency Fight Club would be so daunting? Thank you also to Amy Atwell, Kris Kennedy, Jackie Barbosa, Rachel Grant, and Elyssa Papa for reading drafts and providing valuable insight.

I never would've made it to the next step in my career with this book if not for the staunch support of the Pixie Chicks and so many writer friends including Courtney Milan, Kristina McMorris, Leigh LaValle, and Kendra Elliot. I also want to thank my dear non-writer friends who've given me so much and encouraged me in ways I deeply appreciate: Jenni Duhl, Bonnie Anderson, Shelly Leritz, and Dominique Dobson. And thank you Leanne Karella for giving me a job when I needed it, which allowed me to refill my creative well.

I'm sincerely grateful to my agent, Jim McCarthy, for loving this book as much as I do and for championing its success.

About the Author

Darcy Burke is the USA Today Bestselling Author of hot, action-packed historical and sexy, emotional contemporary romance. Darcy wrote her first book at age 11, a happily ever after about a swan addicted to magic and the female swan who loved him, with exceedingly poor illustrations.

A native Oregonian, Darcy lives on the edge of wine country with her guitar-strumming husband, their two hilarious kids who seem to have inherited the writing gene, and two Bengal cats. In her "spare" time Darcy is a serial volunteer enrolled in a 12-step program where one learns to say "no," but she keeps having to start over. She's also a fair-weather runner, and her happy places are Disneyland and Labor Day weekend at the Gorge. Visit Darcy online at http://www.darcyburke.com and sign up for her new releases newsletter, follow her on Twitter at http://twitter.com/darcyburke, or like her Facebook page, http://www.facebook.com/DarcyBurkeFans.

Made in the USA
San Bernardino, CA
05 November 2017